The White Road Chronicles
Book 1

# Illuminated

Jackie Castle

Castle Library Publishers
Texas

Illuminated

Castle Library Publishing
Bedford Texas
Illuminated

This book is a work of fiction. Names, characters, places and incidents are either products of the author's imagination or used fictitiously. Any similarity to actual people, organizations, and/or events is purely coincidental.

Cover art by Elena Dudina – www.elenadudina.com
Edited by Lena Nelson Dooley- www.lenanelsondooley.com

# Dedication:

First, to the One who's been with me every step of the way as father, friend, and teacher. This book is for you, because of you, and belongs to you.

To Angela and Christian... May your own journeys be full of light and take you to amazing places.

To Bob who's made our life together a most amazing adventure!

# Acknowledgements

To all the messengers, warriors, generals, planters, healers and others who have helped and encouraged me along my own journey. Thank you.

A special thanks to the members of Communities of Grace church, my base-camp where I've learned, found healing, and the courage to live out my purpose. To my fellow scribes at ACFW and DFW Ready Writers, who've listened, pushed, and helped brainstorm my stories. And to those special friends who've allowed me to journey with them for a time. I couldn't have done this without your friendship and support.

Last, a huge thank you to my generous husband and kids for allowing me to run after my dream, even when the trail was full of twist and turns and uncertain of where it would go next. I adore you all.

Dear Reader, I hope you'll find encouragement to travel your own path as you read Alyra's story.

# Chapter 1

Winter's grip on the mountain realm crept along the stony dungeon floor and seeped through the girl's thin slippers. A biting chill encircled her legs, as gooseflesh spread up her back and down to her chapped hands. Shivering, she wished spring would hurry and show itself.

She pitched fresh hay into what were once stalls for horses and other livestock. Now King Darnel, ruler over the city of Racah, used the area to hold new slaves captured from the neighboring towns his forces had overtaken.

Her hand slipped over the weathered handle. A sharp jab sent tears welling in her eyes. She dropped the pitch fork, sucking at her splintered palm, covered in scrapes and scabs from previous injuries. To think, she'd traded a life of fine warm clothes and leisurely work for this. She picked the sliver from her hand. Every last injury was completely worth it.

"Hey, Princess."

She spun toward the voice. Tarek stood in the doorway. Four pheasants hung by their legs from a strip of leather tied around Tarek's belt. He wore the customary gray trousers and black shirt of the kitchen help. A spiteful grin crinkled the edges of his green eyes as he took in her work. Long, wheat-colored hair fell in his face and over the collar of his tunic.

At nineteen, he towered over her by nearly a foot in height and possibly two years in age. She had no memories of her past, including when and where she was actually born, or even more disturbing, her real name. From what little she did remember, she placed her own age somewhere around seventeen summers.

Darnel, who'd somehow managed to steal her memories, had ordered everyone to call her Princess, and they did so with much snickering and laughter. His little joke, she was sure.

Tarek pushed open the sliding door. A wave of cold air swirled in, stirring up dust and flecks of hay. "Ben wants you to bring a bucket of water out to the new arrivals. Right now."

She replaced the tool on its peg, then grabbed her thin cloak before heading outside.

Tarek blocked the exit, leaning against the frame with arms crossed over his strong chest. While she spent most of her time cleaning, taking care of Ben, her overseer, or searching the various tunnels worming beneath the mountain fortress, he hunted outdoors or chopped wood. Her pale white skin stood in complete contrast to his darkened sun-kissed color. Oh, what she'd do to trade places with him. Yet she'd not complain. Her job in the dungeon was much more preferable to the one she previously held.

"Looks like this group came a long way. What a wasted bunch of bones. Though something about them must be important, if you ask me."

Wanting to get away from him, she darted around and hurried toward the pump. The charcoal-gray castle towered hundreds of feet above, the stone walls blending into the cliffs. Below, nestled amongst the crags and plateaus lay Racah, consisting of stonework buildings and forlorn homes surrounded by high ramparts and steep peaks that circled the city.

Tarek trailed her like a lost puppy. "That Baykok Captain, the creepy one they call Bezoar? He brought them in himself."

She froze, her gut twisted. She had no desire to meet the inhuman creature-man today. Grabbing the pail, she set it under the spout. Her splintered hand burned when she grasped the lever and pumped.

Tarek leaned closer until his tanned face was inches from hers. "And," a taunt hid just below the surface of his words. "You'll be happy to know your father is out there to greet our new guests, as well." He bit his upper lip, keeping the mocking grin in check.

She gave the pump two more good pulls. "Aren't you suppose to help cook for tonight's banquet? Wonder what Darnel would say if he found out you were shirking your own responsibilities to play messenger boy?"

His annoying grin grew slack. Brows furrowed, he spat, "*King* Darnel. And I work hard. Even his majesty has bragged on my hunting skills. Unlike you, I appreciate *my* position and only want to serve *my* King to the best of *my* ability."

"Such a good little lap dog you are. Why don't you go fetch a bone or dig a hole and leave me to my own work?" She took up the pail handle and made her way toward the front of the prison where Ben would be waiting.

The weight of the bucket lightened as Tarek held the handle from the opposite side. She glared at him, despite being somewhat grateful for his help. He said nothing more as they walked. When the group came into view, nearly fifty people dressed in dreary, ragged clothing, she stopped a moment to gather her wits and steady her panicked thoughts. Just as Tarek said, Bezoar and Master both attended this group's arrival.

*Why?*

"He's not my father."

Tarek's brow arched.

"I wasn't born to him." She met his narrow-eyed gaze. "I wasn't. I came from another place, like them. And like you. This isn't my true home."

His chest rose with a deep intake of breath which he slowly blew out. "Perhaps, Princess, we are better off here in Racah. I am. My family now has work, food to eat, decent shelter. Where we came from, nothing grew. Everyone was starving." He brushed away the blond bangs from his face with his free hand. "Look at them. Their clothes are torn, ragged. Bet they will be glad, as well, once they see the King means them no harm."

Princess shook her head. Tarek had no idea the evil Darnel was capable of. She hoped he'd never find out.

When Tarek left her, she paused needing to completely clear her mind. Humming a silent tune, she headed for the gathering.

Bezoar sat upon his huge black steed. He resembled a living skeleton with grayish skin that clung to his thin body like a grubby, wet sheet. His long, boney fingers hooked around a leather whip hanging from the saddle horn. Deep-set, yellowed eyes peered from beneath the hood of his black cloak.

"Sire," the Baykok hissed, pointing to a man thrown over the back of a packhorse. "The messenger was a bonus. He's been spreading his propaganda amongst the towns. I ordered his life spared for the time being. You did request I bring such filth to you when we found them."

Lord Darnel chuckled with satisfaction. "Yes, that is a bonus, my good captain. Anytime we can stop such liars is indeed fortunate."

Keeping the silent melody playing, Princess moved toward the group, making sure the dungeon master Ben was between herself and Master Darnel. Ben wore his colorful robes, the purple, red, and yellow striped fabric billowing in the breeze. As she approached, she noticed his hand gripping his cane so tight his chestnut-colored skin paled. Though Ben was known to have a terrible temper, age and arthritis had tamed his angry outbursts. Since she'd taken over many of his responsibilities, he generally treated her decently. More importantly, he ignored her long disappearances while she searched new tunnels for a means of escape.

Ben nodded toward the chained group, then ordered in his deep, throaty voice, "Give 'em something to drink, girl."

Behind the messenger's horse stood a long line of men, women, and children, all thin and haggard. Their condition most likely resulted from their trek across the barren land that surrounded the mountain. The castle itself, built into the heart of the cliffs, was nearly impenetrable, as well as inescapable. Climbing the only road leading into the city was difficult on horseback... and even more-so on foot. No telling how long they'd gone without food or rest. Bezoar didn't concern himself with such human needs.

The prisoners clustered around her, eager to quench their dry mouths. They grasped the ladle greedily in their scraped, bloody hands. Princess avoided the scared expressions on the children's dirty faces as they gulped the cool water. Yet one dark-haired girl, about the age of five, reminded her of the first time she'd entered this forsaken city. Had the same look of terror been in her own brown eyes?

Princess dared a glance toward the man strapped on the horse. He raised his bruised head. A long cut tore down the side of his cheek. With his one good eye, he stared at his surroundings in defiance. A gold medallion hung from his neck.

Her breath caught when her heart lodged into her throat. Forgetting the prisoners, Princess stepped closer. Water sloshed over the rim and onto her feet. She steadied the bucket, then handed it to the eldest man in the group to hold. She had to see that pendant.

The messenger's face softened when he caught sight of her staring at him. She quickly turned, not wanting him to know she'd noticed him.

She chanced a glance at Master Darnel, surprised he wore his finest attire to greet a bunch of shoddy prisoners. He stood tall, a smile plastered on his smooth, handsome face. His deep purple button-down coat was trimmed in silver thread. Upon his head sat a silver crown, inlaid with rubies and emeralds, which had been collected while digging the tunnels throughout his mountain lands. His polished black boots stopped just below his knees.

Several large, brutish men flanked Darnel. She'd heard the newly appointed governors, who would run the new towns, were being presented at tonight's banquet.

She shuddered when one of them grinned at her and elbowed a trollish-looking man, who stood beside him. They whispered something, then broke into chuckles, all the while never taking their eyes off her. Princess's gut twisted, wondering what they found so humorous. She took the bucket from the elder and stood to the side, searching Ben's face to see if he'd give her the go-ahead to take them inside.

Ben remained a statue.

Darnel motioned to his men. "Release the messenger so he may stand with our other *guests*." His mocking smile widened.

Two soldiers untied the messenger's hands and feet and shoved him off the beast headfirst. He crashed to the ground with a loud groan. One man grabbed the pail from her and tossed the remaining water in the man's face. He staggered to his feet.

His nicely tailored clothes were bloodied and torn. Dirt caked his beard. The medallion hung outside his shirt, the symbol of a horn glinted in the morning sun.

The disk was different, yet similar. What could that mean?

Darnel stepped closer, scanning the group. She felt his stare and despite all attempts not to look, her eyes finally met his cold blues. His hateful laughter sounded inside her head. *Think. Fill your mind to keep him out!*

"How fortunate-" Darnel addressed the crowd, "-for all of you to be brought here at this exciting time in the history of my empire. We are, this very day, in the process of establishing new cities and villages in the western frontier. And you, most fortunate ones, are to be the first to inhabit them."

Now she understood why Bezoar and the governors were there. This group would be forced to build those cities. Maybe that was the reason behind his increased attacks on the border lands. He needed more slaves to send out west where he hoped to increase his kingdom. She gazed toward the rising sun, knowing something hindered his progress in that direction. Something that plagued her dreams and pulled at her heartstrings.

"My territory is expanding. My governors and I-" Darnel waved to the beast-men standing behind him, "-are discussing how best to achieve this. We petition you, good people of Racah, to listen to our ideas and consider joining the quest to revive these lands under my rule."

Princess shook her head and muttered, "Working as slave laborers."

With a gasp, she snapped her mouth closed. Those standing around her whispered to each other. They'd heard her! An outburst like that might result in more lashings. She chewed her lip, daring a glance at Ben whose brown eyes narrowed on her in silent warning.

The messenger's voice boomed over Darnel's speech. "*Lies*! Do not fall for this imposter's deception."

The closest soldier shoved the butt of his spear into the man's gut. "Shut up, fool!"

The man fell to his knees wheezing.

Princess gaped at him. He'd be the dragon's supper if he didn't quit.

The messenger took in a winded breath and continued, "Resist him! For the army of the true King is at hand! Do not give in to this evil traitor and his ways! Stand firm while time remains." He leaped to his feet and darted out of the soldier's reach. His steel-gray eyes scanned the frightened prisoners.

*Don't listen to the ranting of a fool, daughter!* Darnel's voice rasped in her head. She flinched, and tried once again to control her thoughts. The man continued talking, but she couldn't separate his words from Master's.

"The time of this evil one's reign…."

*Foolish girl, have you not learned your lesson yet?* Darnel stood still as a statue, an amused look on his calm face. His cruel eyes flicked in her direction. *I would be prepared to forgive your insolence and restore you to your rightful position.*

Her head pounded from trying to block his thoughts.

"…his army approaches as I speak."

The snap of Bezoar's whip cracked the air as it tore into the messenger's back. He flicked again, and another streak ripped open his shirt and skin. The man bowed over, going down on his knees in the mud.

"Enough," hissed Bezoar, drawing his sword from the sheath. "I'll take care of this, Sire."

Heart racing, Princess stepped between the dark hooded creature and the crouched man. "The dragon hasn't been fed in awhile, Master." She met Darnel's arctic glare.

Her mouth went dry at her own audacity. She'd have been better off staying out of the way and as quiet as possible. But she couldn't let them kill the messenger. Not yet.

"The dragon doesn't care if he's crazy or not. She'll eat him all the same."

The people standing around her gasped.

The eldest prisoner spoke up. "Perhaps we should listen to the Messenger." He pointed a dirty finger at Darnel. "That tyrant ordered our towns to be burnt to the ground, then says he wants us to help rebuild? Shoulda left us alone in the first place if you ask me."

Darnel closed the distance between himself and the old man. His hand clamped around the prisoner's neck. "I did you a favor. You're homes were crumbling, you had nothing to eat—"

"That's 'cause you've stripped this land of all that's good. I remember what it was like. I remember when we followed King Shay—"

With one quick movement, a dagger appeared in Darnel's hand and swept across the man's neck, splattering the bystanders in blood. The old man crumpled at Master's feet, red puddling into the ground. Darnel, ignoring the screams coming from the on-lookers, turned to Ben, his blue eyes flashing with rage.

"I'll expect you to convince them to accept my offer. If there are

11

others who wish to join the messenger at my dragon's dinner, don't hesitate to comply."

Ben nodded, then motioned for a couple of soldiers to escort the remaining group inside. Bezoar ordered the body to be dumped in the pit and the messenger to be taken to the holding cell until the dragon's feeding time.

Princess moved to follow Ben when a strong hand clamp down on her arm. Darnel yanked her around so she was face to face with him.

"It's your fault that man died."

She started to protest that he had the dagger not her, but he cut off her words.

"Stupid child. When will you learn that I mean to sever anything or anyone who denies my authority? If you refuse to serve me, I will find other means of curbing your disloyalty."

From behind her, the messenger yelled, "Don't give in, freedom is at hand!"

She watched as the soldiers dragged him to the dungeon.

Darnel gripped her chin, his fingers still wet with the man's blood. He turned her face back to his. "You are running out of time, daughter. My patience with you wanes."

"Will you also feed me to the dragon, Master?" she asked, emboldened by the messenger's chants of *Freedom!* filling her heart.

"I'll not give you such an easy way out, my dear." He shoved her away, then strolled toward the castle with his governors following. The troll-man kept looking back over his shoulder at her, smirking.

Princess reached into the inner pocket she'd sewn into all her skirts and pulled out a small golden disk which fit perfectly inside the palm of her hand. A tree had been engraved on one side. The other side had a fire flame surrounded by what might be a burst of light. Her medallion was similar to the messenger's yet different.

"For *freedom!*" He continued to chant. Suddenly, the sound of a loud smack brought complete silence from within.

There wasn't much time. She needed to hurry.

# Chapter 2

"Princess!" Ben's deep voice echoed off the stone walls. "Where is that ungrateful brat?"

She hurried inside, wiping the blood from her face while she tucked the medallion back into the hidden pocket.

Ben's wide eyes glared in stark contrast to his ebony skin. Thin lines criss-crossed his umber cheeks and forehead, giving his narrow face a wizened look. He paced in the guard room, cane rapping loud on the floor.

"How am I supposed to persuade them?" Ben whacked the stick against an oak table. "He kills their Sage right before their eyes. And now I'm to sweet-talk them into going along with his grand plans? I can only do so much." He smacked the table a few times more. He spun to her, pointing the dirty tip in her face. "This is your fault. You impertinent child!"

"I'm sorry. I know. I..." She cringed, waiting for the blow most likely to come.

He moved toward her, grabbing her long, brown braid in his hand. "No excuses. You help make this right or I'll surely flog you myself this time." He shoved her away. She stumbled, landing on her back. Air whooshed from her lungs. He towered above her, digging the cane's tip into her chest. "If this goes ill, I'll do worse than a flogging, you understand? The messenger can be that blasted dragon's dinner. I don't care. But if I lose one more person because of your big mouth, so help me—"

"Tell me what to do, Ben. I'm...." She stopped herself from apologizing again.

The cane smacked the side of her head. Lights flashed. She rolled over, leaping back to her feet and darting out of reach.

"Get to the kitchen. Find something excellent to serve. Once they are fed and comfortable, then perhaps I can reason with them."

He turned to the cells, stroking the thin beard growing down the sides of his full lips. "They will need clothes and blankets as well. I'll send for those. You take care of the grub." He kicked at her, but missed. "Get. Now!"

Princess ran from the room to the narrow-winding staircase leading to the cookery. A dark passage opened on the left, reeking of the rotten stench of decay and dampness. The tunnel led to the place for keeping those destined to meet the dragon. The rich, deep voice of the messenger echoed from the darkness. She paused to listen. A song? He was about to die ... and he sang?

They couldn't feed the dragon until nightfall. Her mind raced to form a plan to get to him before then. First she had to appease Ben. Rushing up the stairs, she burst into the cookery, a hub of activity with banging pots and loud voices.

"Hey there," she called to the kitchen chef. "I need good food for the new detainees."

The head cook, a bristly man covered in red sauces and white powder growled back, "Don't ya see I'm busy? We're preparing for the banquet tonight. Don't bother me wit your filthy prisoners."

Her jaw clenched, time slipping away. "Don't make me call Ben. He's not in a good mood."

At one time, such a threat would provoke people into action, but lately, its effects were wearing as thin as her boss.

The cook grunted. "Take the porridge left from breakfast. There's bread behind you. Now leave me be!"

*Porridge?* Princess groaned. Porridge wouldn't go far in getting her out of trouble.

She spotted a bag full of apples, oranges, and pears. Fresh from someplace called Denovo. Anything good here was shipped in from outside which explained Darnel's incessant greed for obtaining new towns and slaves... *or people*, she corrected herself.

She slung the burlap sack over her shoulder. Using the hem of her skirt to grab the pot handle, she then turned to get the loaves of bread. Tarek stood there holding them for her.

"Um, thanks." She wasn't sure how she'd carry it all anyway.

He also gathered a couple bottles of ale and headed out of the kitchen and down the winding stairs back to the dungeon. She followed close behind wondering what he wanted now. Shafts of light poured in through the rectangular windows along the circular wall, falling across the steps. Through the narrow openings, the sun nearly reached the noon sky.

"What's this new group like?" Tarek slowed until she caught up with him. "Anyone interesting?"

The heavy pot burned when the heated metal bumped her leg with each downward step. She cringed, realizing he sought information. He'd never believe her. Tarek believed Darnel was too good of a king to kill a Sage in cold blood, or send a messenger to a slow agonizing death.

He grinned. "Wait till they get a look at all this food. I bet they're thrilled to be here."

"Right."

His expression darkened as he pressed his lips together. "Not everyone is stubborn like you, Princess." He shook his head. "You had everything a person could want, and you snub your nose at it. I'll never understand."

"Nobody expects you to. I don't." She stopped and switched the pot to her other hand. "Not everyone is given cushy jobs like your family, Tarek. And not everyone came from a bad place. Some might have come from homes they loved and … just want to find a way back."

He stopped on the stair below her, brows furrowed. "Had much luck finding an escape route through any of those tunnels, Princess?"

Her breath caught. He'd tracked her? Heated anger burned her cheeks. Why would he follow her around? He certainly didn't like her. He made fun of her name and constantly told her how stupid she was for leaving the job she'd had as Darnel's apprentice.

"King Darnel would be angry if he knew about your free-time activities. Wouldn't he?"

Princess almost dropped the pot. "You'd be the one to tell him, wouldn't you? Is that how you plan to advance your position? By being Darnel's snitch?" She pushed past him. "What a miserable little bug you are."

They'd reached the landing. She set the porridge on the table. Ben would serve the prisoners himself, using the opportunity to calm them with his comforting words. Despite his temper, he had a gift of persuasion and winning people over to his way of thinking.

Tarek placed the bread and bottles beside the kettle. "I'd never—"

"Just leave me alone! Stay away from me and mind your own affairs." She shoved him.

He muttered a string of curses before retreating back to the kitchen. She didn't care. Why was he following her around if not to rat on her? She shuddered over the thought of Master finding out she'd been exploring those tunnels. He'd not only make her life miserable, but what would he do to Ben?

Maybe she shouldn't have been so hateful to Tarek. She started for the stairs wanting to reason with him.

"About time." Ben rounded the corner, his arms full of blankets. "I'll pass out the-" He lifted the lid and cringed, "-porridge? That's the best you could do?"

"They were really busy. I did get fresh fruit." She held up a bottle. "And mead! This should help calm their nerves, you think?"

He snatched the ale from her and pulled out the cork his yellowed teeth. The bottled tipped straight up as he gulped down several long swigs. Wiping his mouth with the back of his sleeve, Ben sighed. "Works for me. They can have water." He recapped the bottle. "Let's get to work."

If it kept her out of trouble, she couldn't care less what he did with the drink.

\* \* \* \*

After everyone had been served and given a few comforts, Princess returned to the leftover food and took an apple for herself. Ben sat in a chair rubbing his swollen knees and finished the ale.

"Any porridge left?"

She lifted the lid and nodded. "Enough for a bowl or two. You want it?"

He wrinkled his nose. "I should take some to that messenger fellow. Perhaps—"

"You'll never change his views, Ben. I don't know where people like him come from, but what craziness, huh?" A beam of an idea lit in her mind. "But there's no sense in wasting. I can take him some."

Ben's brows crinkled.

She'd better try harder than that. Ben might turn a blind eye to

16

her exploring the tunnels, but he wouldn't be too easily swayed about letting her get around an unruly prisoner.

Setting a kettle of water on the fire pit, she waited for the bubbles to form along the edges. Once wisps of steam rose from the surface, she dumped in a few rags. On the shelf above the hearth sat a jar of ointment one of the healers had prepared for Ben's sore knees. She scooped a glob of the smelly gel and ordered Ben into bed. He uncovered his legs and allowed her to rub the cream onto his swollen joints.

"Are you going to the ball tonight?" She took her time, knowing that between the mead and her massage, he'd soon be asleep.

He moaned a disgruntled affirmation.

"Well, it's been a long day already. You'll need to rest while you can. There's still a lot to do with the pris... uh, guests."

Ben groaned and took another swig of drink.

With a pair of tongs, she pulled the hot rags from the steamy water. Her hands stung from wringing out the excess moisture. "You rest and let this ointment do its work while I take care of everything else."

Once Ben drifted to sleep, she set off. Water rivulets ran down the passage walls, and the damp air nearly suffocated her. With the bowl in one hand and the last apple in the other, she stepped carefully along the wet, slimy floor. Luckily, a few of the torches still burned. She soon entered an enclosure of six cells. All of the thick wooden doors stood ajar, except for one in which a lively song was being sung.

The shuffling of her feet must have caught his attention because the top of his face peeked through the narrow barred window.

"Well, well," he chuckled. His voice sounded strained, like he'd swallowed gravel. "The little rebel, I presume?"

She stiffened. How'd he make that assumption? Breathing deep, she proceeded with caution. This prisoner was not one of the scared rabbits like the villagers, but rather a sly fox looking for a means to overcome his predicament.

Chin jutting out, she cleared her throat and announced, "I've brought you food. Please be kind enough to step ba—"

"Ah, no thank you. If I must end my journey this night, then I'll do so with a clear mind. I'll not allow that imposter's poison to fog my thoughts in these last moments." His nose rested on the window frame. Purple bruises covered his swollen eye. "What is your name child?"

"My name is of no importance to you." Not that she had a name to give him anyway. She'd certainly not tell him the name people really called her.

Why wasn't he more frightened? And what did he mean by *imposter's poison*? Perhaps he really was mentally unstable.

"You have questions in your eyes, my little sister. Speak."

She scowled. "I'm not related to you, sir. I better go."

Oh, he was definitely crazy. She bit her lip, part of her bubbled with questions and the other, more reasonable side, warned her to flee before it was too late. If anyone beside Ben found out she'd come down here to speak to him…. She shuddered.

As she turned to leave, the messenger said, "I saw how displeased your master is with you, child. Yet, you are even more displeased. This land holds no pleasure for you, does it?"

She froze. How could he know? On second thought, their conflict was probably obvious.

"You find your life here drudgery." His words grew more pressing. "Despite how hard you try to live his way, you fight every step. All the wonderful possessions this land offers still leave you empty and yearning for something more. And deep down, you know there is more."

Her heart raced so fast, her vision swam. She closed her eyes to steady her spinning head.

"Your master's attempts to break that yearning inside of you have been unsuccessful. He fails because once one has tasted truth, they can never fully swallow the lies he has to offer."

Sweat filled her palms, the bowl slipping from her grasp. She faced him again. Her throat felt full of old cloth.

"What else is there besides this?" she croaked.

"A white road, dear daughter. It will take you to his very throne."

"Whose throne?"

"King Shaydon, the true King. Ruler of all, including this evil imposter."

She drew in a shuddering breath, having heard that name before.

"He's only a fable. A bedtime story to put children to sleep."

"Is he? Are these the lies *your master* has fed you? Spit them out now! They are poison. King Shaydon is real. Aloblase is the beautiful city where he dwells. That apple you hold in your hand is a rock compared to the bounty which grows in his land. What I speak is all very real indeed, child. I have walked along the streets of Aloblase many times."

A trembling started in her knees and traveled up to her damp hands. She no longer saw the dark dungeon, but rather the city from her dreams. "Are there beautiful beings that seem to glow? I always see them standing next to a gate or archway of some sort."

The messenger's face pressed against the rusted bars as his voice grew excited, and his bloodshot eyes sparkled. "You have been there! When child? How did you end up in this wretched land?"

The bowl clattered across the dirt, the apple rolling into the shadows. Princess shook her head. They were only dreams. Reason warned her to go back now before Master found out she'd been disobedient. Again.

"Do you have a medallion?" He thrust his golden pendant through the window. "It looks similar to this."

Everything froze. Her words, her breath, even her legs refused to respond. Slowly, she reached into her skirt pocket and pulled out her medallion. She stared at the round disk resting in her sweaty palm. Torchlight reflected off the flame-emblem embossed on the surface.

"The Illuminate's mark," he whispered, his dark eyes widening. "Only those who've stood in King Shaydon's presence have one."

Her fingers closed around the pendant as she backed farther away. They were dreams, weren't they? Dare she hope? How could she be sure? A crazy idea tumbled into her head.

"If you have, child, run back home!" he yelled after her. "A medallion signifies that you are a citizen of Aloblase and under the king's protection! Return home to where you truly belong!"

His words pursued her along the dark, slippery tunnel, nipping her heels and driving her to consider attempting the most insane plan. Dare she? If she got caught... no, she'd not think about the consequences.

# Chapter 3

Quiet as a breeze, Princess crept through the kitchen. Ben, passed out on mead, would sleep long enough for her to check out the messenger's claim.

Cook barked orders, shoving people aside as he marched between the oven and stoves. Pots clanged and glasses clinked. Tarek sat at the end of a table where his mother made pies. He stuffed a whole tart into his mouth and received a smack on the head with her wooden spoon.

Princess, slipped into the dark pantry. Hands extended, she followed the shelf until bumping into several brooms propped next to the far wall. Pushing them aside, she ran her fingers over the smooth, wooden surface finding the knob. A quick twist and the hidden exit creaked open. She eased through. When she closed the door, some of the brooms tumbled into the opposite shelves. The cacophony of bangs exploded in her ears.

"Oh no, no!" Hopefully the cooks were too busy to hear the racket.

Not waiting to find out, she raced up the narrow staircase, dimly lit by several small square openings in the turret walls. Webs clung to her hair and clothes. Something scuttled over her shoulder. She swiped it away.

Six years ago, she'd stumbled on the hidden route while hiding from her tutor. The secret passage proved useful for looting snacks from the kitchen and moving between floors quickly when avoiding Master and other bothersome people.

Once she reached the forth door along the stairs, she stopped and pressed her ear to the dusty wood. With everyone preparing for the ball this afternoon, she'd need to be extra careful to keep from bumping into any floor servants. Or worse, Darnel.

Convinced all was clear, she pushed against the flap and ducked inside. Shelves of blankets and linen lined the walls on each side of the four-by-four room. Feather dusters hung beside the door. She took one of the towels and brushed the dirt and cobwebs from her worn, dingy dress and hair before daring a peek into the expansive hall. Statues and armor stood guard between the four rooms on this wing. Darnel's suites and study took up the entire east hall.

Her room, the second entry on the right, remained closed. A portion of gold glinted above her doorframe. *Great! The key's still right where I hid it.* She considered stopping to change into a cleaner dress, but decided to wait. First she had to break into Master's study. If he didn't find out and kill her, then she'd get new clothes.

The hall was empty, so she darted for the statue of Master. Ignoring the shudder knocking her knees, she listened a moment, before running to the hiding spot behind a troll suit.

"I knew it," said a voice from behind her.

Two terrible things happened at once. Princess first spun around to find Tarek standing next to the closet door, hands on hips and a satisfied smile on his arrogant face. In the opposite direction, clomping footsteps topped the grand stairs.

Princess grabbed Tarek's tunic and shoved him behind the troll armor. When he tried to protest, he clamped her hand over his mouth.

She peered around the floor-to-shoulder-sized shield, as one of the beastly governors stopped on the landing. A ginger colored cat wove between his thick, elephant-like legs. "Come now, my precious," He snapped his fingers. "King Darnel wishes to speak privately. Perhaps his-high-and-mightiness sees the real value in Sir Brollus, yes?" He patted his massive chest. "Perhaps he gives us biggest town."

The cat purred, but stopped and turned its yellow eyes in their direction. She pressed Tarek tighter against the wall. He grinned roguishly.

The governor sighed, "Amazing, eh, Milly? Strange how he keeps this armor in his halls, but will not welcome the wearers even into his city. Ahh, if he knew…yes, my sweet? If he knew our little secret?" The giant man's laugh sounded like grating rocks.

She was right! He had to be part troll. She'd never actually seen any of the fair folks before, except for the rare occasions she'd gotten hold of Master's private books. All creatures lived on the far outskirts of Racan land.

"Come, let us go see why his mightiness desires to speak to us." He headed in the direction of Darnel's meeting room.

Princess released a long breath, resting her forehead on Tarek's chest. His heart beat unusually fast against her brows.

"You know," Tarek whispered. "Even covered in dirt and sweat, you smell lovely. Like-" He pressed his face into her hair and drew in a whiff, "-apples? Maybe honey. I like it." An impish grin tugged his lips, causing his cheek to dimple.

She shoved away. "What are you doing here, Tarek? You almost got us both killed!"

Tarek rolled his green eyes. "Came to ask you the same thing."

She hated the way he smirked at her.

"You think this is a game? You think Darnel will invite us to tea if he catches us up here sneaking around?"

"King Darnel." He corrected. "And I'm not sneaking. I'm following." He stepped out from behind the armor with a low whistle. "I've never been allowed past the main floor. This place is ahh-mazing!" He turned back to face her. "You left this for the dungeons? You're more deranged than that lunatic rebel they brought in today."

He knew about the messenger? Did he also know about Darnel killing the old man, too?

"Go back to the kitchen, Tarek. This isn't your business."

"Making it my business." He brushed past her. "Let's hurry before someone else comes."

Not wanting to waste time arguing with him, she ran toward Darnel's suites, but turned at a narrow opening that led up to his watch tower. He stayed right at her side.

Breathless, she paused on the landing for her heart to quiet, before gasping, "You call me crazy. What are you hoping to gain by coming?"

"Sat...tis...faction." He spoke between breaths. "And bragging rights."

"You'll never be able to tell anyone. If word gets back to Darnel, you'll be severely punished."

"King Darnel." He corrected again pushing on the large

mahogany door. A crescent moon, surrounded by stars, was carved into the dark wood. Intricate snake-like patterns wove along the arches. Absently, she rubbed her right shoulder where a similar mark had been set, and caught Tarek doing the same. She followed him inside.

"So tell me, Princess, why are you here?" He stood in the center of the room, gaping at the massive shelves lined with various books and Master's strange magical instruments.

She ignored his question and headed straight for the balcony where a tubular shaped instrument sat besides the railing. Master called the contraption an *Imagiscope*. Intricate designs and a script she didn't understand was etched into the gold casing. Somehow Master used the device to see places and things. And people. Once he'd insisted she watch the dragon feast on a prisoner. She'd never wanted anything more to do with it since. Until today.

Tarek, still captivated by the vast bookcases along each wall, inched closer to a metal sphere. He reached out and touched the mechanism, which began to spin and whirl. With a yell, he jumped back and tumbled over one of the couches in the sitting area.

"Maybe we should leave," he whispered. "Before you get in even more trouble."

"Soon as I take a peek. I think I can figure out how this works."

"Why? What are you *looking for*?"

She hesitated. "I want... I mean, the messenger talked about how there's another king living in a place called Aloblase and—"

"You mean we're here because of something that cracked-nut said?"

Tarek rushed over to the balcony and stood beside her. A tinge of heat crept along the back of her neck.

"Listen, nobody's asking you to believe anything. This is my business, not yours."

Tarek's brows creased over his emerald eyes. "No, you listen to me. People who believe in that fairy tale king are simpletons. Mom told those stories when I was little to put me to sleep. *But it's not real! Don't you understand? It's not real!* There is no wonderful city where everyone lives in harmony." He waved his hands around while mocking in a sing-song voice, "blah, blah, blah. Just fairy tales."

Doubt crept into her resolve. "Tarek, if it's not real, then why is that messenger, and other 'simpletons' as you call them, willing to be put to death rather than serve Darnel? Give me a good reason, and I'll not argue with you anymore."

He took a step back as if she'd slapped his face, but didn't answer.

"Besides," she peered into the eyepiece, "we're already here." She turned the knobs, wishing she'd paid better attention before.

"How's it work?" He wrapped his hands around the tube and pushed her aside.

"Hey, don't do that. Break it and we'll both end up dead."

From behind them Lord Darnel's deep, cold voice said, "The mere fact that you have broken into my private chamber will indeed cost you dearly, child."

Princess' heart lodged in her throat. Tarek's tan face paled. Neither of them moved.

Master slipped off his purple coat as he glided across the room and laid it on one of the couches. Turning to them, he stared down his long, graceful nose. "You've brought a friend, I see."

She met his penetrating glare, keeping her back straight and chin high as she stepped off the balcony. Her hand caught Tarek's and pulled him along.

"He didn't know, Master. He tried to stop me from coming. Please let him return to the kitchens."

Tarek's thumb gently rubbed over the back of her hand. "I knew, sire. I'd heard rumors about all the magical things you keep up here." He cleared his throat before adding, "She did tell me to go back, but I didn't listen."

Surprise at his words, pricked her chest.

Master's flawless face, appeared amused on the outside. Yet the fury building behind the twitch in his cold, blue eyes and tightly compressed lips was obvious to her. In his stare, her heart quaked and she fought as long as possible before that usual fear overtook her resolve to stand firm. She turned away.

"I'm quite upset at you, daughter, for sneaking up here uninvited. I should have you and Tarek both flogged." His gaze bore into Tarek for a long, excruciating moment.

Was he probing the boy's mind, too? He knew his name. *What*

24

*else did Master know?*

Tarek's eyes widened. His fingers constricted around hers. But he said nothing, either out of fright or good sense.

Darnell finally let out a hearty chuckle, laying a slender hand on each of their shoulders. "Well now, daughter, you have made yourself a devoted friend, I see. How wonderful." His laugh sounded sarcastic. *Fake*.

He strolled over to a cord hanging against the bookshelves and gave a pull. Beside the cord, a metal tube poked from the wall. He spoke into the opening, ordering a tray of tea and cakes from the kitchen.

Tarek's brows arched. She shook her head, completely bewildered. Why wasn't Master calling for his soldiers to put them both in prison? Instead, he really was inviting them to a cup of tea. She rolled her eyes, knowing Tarek would never let her live this down.

Master sat on one of the couches and motioned for them to join him. "Thanks to you, daughter, the dragon will be rewarded with a special treat tonight. I noticed you were trying out my Imagiscope. Perhaps you two would be interested in using it to watch?" His voice became genial and even a little playful. She shuddered.

Tarek's face went from white to a slight tinge of green. "Um, I'll be working the ball tonight, sir."

The door opened as a kitchen servant entered. The errand boy's eyes widened when he saw Tarek sitting beside her, yet he said nothing. He set the tray on the circular table between them.

"Thank you, Roderick," Darnel removed the cover off the white frosted cakes. "Please remain outside the door. I may need your services again shortly."

The servant's gaze darted from Darnel to Tarek before he bowed. "Yes, sire."

When he left, Master stirred the tea pot, his other hand moved in a circle over the sweets. "You seem to be a fine young man, Tarek."

This brought the color back to the boy's face.

Darnel's voice lowered into a conspiratorial whisper. "You wear bravery well, my lad. I need more courageous subjects like you." He offered Tarek a cake.

His chest puffed as he took a hearty bite. She had no chance to warn him before he swallowed the tainted confection.

When the plate came her way, she refused, hoping Tarek would catch the hint and not take another bite.

"I have tried teaching such qualities to my daughter, here, but she lacks the mental capabilities, I suspect." He poured an amber liquid, slightly darker than normal tea, into three cups and offered one to each of them. "Despite all the wonderful things she is missing, she finds more joy in traipsing through dark tunnels which lead to nowhere."

Princess's head snapped up toward Lord Darnel. Tarek chuckled, taking another huge bite of pastry.

In her mind Master stated, *"Of course I knew! Who did you take me for?"*

She stared out the tall windows trying hard to focus on the brilliant blue sky. She took in every detail about the clouds and any other thought she could muster to keep away his intrusive voice. Her legs trembled from the effort.

Tarek snickered. His words came out slightly slurred. "Told you he would know. She never listens, your majesty."

Darnel smiled and offered him another square. He accepted, but didn't eat any

more. An odd glaze filled his eyes.

"I'm glad she has you as a friend, Tarek."

He set the platter down and then took a sip of his drink. "This is the best tea in all the land. Imported from a newly acquired mountain city in the east. I insist you try some."

Princess left her cup on the table. Tarek peered over the rim, eyebrow cocked. He took a small sip. A smile lit up his face and he gulped the rest down.

Darnel sat back on his pillows. "So tell me, my children, what did you wish to see? It must have been important for you to come here *at such great risk*."

Before she could form a plausible lie, Tarek blurted, his voice slurred and loud, "Princess here believes in that fairy tale king. She's obviously been talking to that crazy messenger, can you believe that?" He chuckled again for a moment, then grew somber. "I tried to tell—"

Darnel's eyes flashed as they settled on her. A pain shot from her head to the pit of her stomach and she gave out a small cry.

*"What were you thinking?"* demanded Master. *"Look at me!"*

She bit her lip, fighting back tears. Allowing them to flow would only make matters worse. *I'm sorry, I didn't mean for him to come. I'm sorry.*

"I really like these cakes," Tarek stated, and for a moment, the pain in her head ceased. "You sure are stupid, Princess, for leaving this place. It's nice here."

*"Yes, very much so. Then you dare to come back! What were you thinking, stupid girl? Now look at me!"*

"No!"

Master leapt to his feet. Tarek froze, the cake poised before his open mouth. Darnel waved his hand over him. "Sleep boy." Tarek's eyes slowly rolled shut and he slumped over on his side. The pastry tumbled onto the carpet.

Princess tried to see if his chest still moved with breaths. Master's hand clamped on the back of her neck as he dragged her over to the balcony.

"Look for yourself and see if there's any other king. Go ahead. Look!"

She jerked free of his grasp. "You and I both know the scope will only show me what you allow."

"There is no other king but me!" He roared. "Accept it!"

"No! I am not your daughter and I don't belong here."

"How do you know? Your head is so damaged you can't even remember your own name." His hands clenched into fist. From the rage burning in his eyes, she knew that he'd love to wrap them around her neck. "Lucky for you I've taken pity on your condition and provided food and shelter."

"I'm not damaged!"

He shook with rage, but she didn't care. The messenger was right. Despite the grandeur of this palace, she could no longer stand the yearning, and the dreaming of that other place.

Gritting her teeth, she spoke in a surprisingly steady and calm voice. "I will never be part of your kingdom. I'd rather you go ahead and kill me. Let the dragon have me!"

His hand swung across her face so hard, the impact knocked her to the floor. Blinding pain rattled through her head.

"You…stubborn, ungrateful…." He walked onto the balcony, facing the east. His long fingers dug into the banister as his shoulders rose and fell with deep breaths. To nobody in particular he yelled, "You'll never get her back. She's mine!"

Then he quieted, smoothing the long sleeves of his white shirt, slowly regaining his composure.

"You're much more use to me alive, than dead. At this point…" his words trailed off and he turned to look at Tarek, before his gaze fell back on Princess. "Yes, this settles my decision." He swooped down on her, grabbing a fist full of hair at the nape of her neck.

He stormed to the door and yanked it open. "Rod—" He began, but the boy stood right outside, waiting, as ordered. "Roderick, find Sir Brollus. Tell him I have made up my mind. If he'll indulge me in one more meeting here in my study, we will complete our plans for tonight's announcement."

"Yes, sire." He bowed and darted away.

Master dragged her down the stairs and toward the west wing where she and Tarek had entered. He stopped at her bedroom suite.

"Tonight, I'll require your attendance at the ball. The five new governors will be introduced to the public during a special ceremony."

He opened the door and shoved her inside.

"I will also announce my blessing on your marriage to Sir Brollus. He's establishing a new city in the far west. *Very far west.* You, dear daughter, will never find your way back from that pit."

# Chapter 4

Her room appeared untouched since she'd left months ago, except for the few necessary items she'd taken to the dungeons. Earthen hues of red, gold, and orange hung from the iron bedpost and curtains. A carved, mahogany desk sat beside the wide windows. On the opposite corner, tall glass doors opened to a balcony. The room spoke beauty and comfort. She missed the beauty and comfort. She didn't miss the reason she'd been able to enjoy the beauty and comfort.

Darnel rummaged through the gowns hanging in her wardrobe. He handed her a cream-colored, crushed-velvet dress trimmed in gold.

"This should do well."

She shook her head. *This. Was. Not. Happening.* Feed her to the dragon, but not…this. A shudder ran down her back. Not this. She hugged the dress to her chest, staring toward the balcony, wondering if she jumped…. No, he'd stop her before she reached the banister.

"Master, please, I can't marr—"

"Put it on. Now." He shoved her behind the dressing screen. "I'll send someone up later to fix your hair and face. You'll need to appear more mature."

Slowly, she pulled off her ratty dress and slipped on the clean one. The stiff fabric rubbed against her skin. Wrong. All of this felt completely wrong. She wiped the dampness from her cheeks before coming out from behind the screen.

"Ahhh, much better. There's a resemblance of my daughter."

She winced.

Darnel grasped her arm so she had to face him. "I know this will be for the best."

His voice grew gentle. She stiffened, bracing herself for the darkness. His finger stroked her cheek where he'd struck her, and a sleepy heaviness clouded her mind. She barely realized he'd led her to the canopy bed.

"You will come of age within the next two summers. Until then, you'll help build our new city." He touched her temple and her eyes grew heavy.

*No, no, no.* She sank into the silk pillows.

"Rest now, child, so you'll be fresh tonight. I want you at your best."

Her vision dimmed as a sense of falling, spinning, and blackness swallowed her. *No, no...go away...no, I won't let you....*

They came, the shadow creatures. Sharp claws reached scratching, pulling downward into pitch black. She struggled against Master's will to form another image. The scene changed to a white city sparkling in the morning sun. Tall, angular, and stern-faced being, glowing like lanterns, stood before a gate. She'd never seen anyone so beautiful except for Master, but he didn't shine with light as these creatures. The images faded, and she was back on the bed. She kept her eyes closed and listened.

Roderick had returned and stood beside Master at the door. The page let out a low whistle. "How does she do that? What's it mean, sire?"

"It means, my dear boy, that we must keep her abnormality a secret. Imagine what people will think? Already they believe she is a freak and not of sound mind. You can see why I must send her away. For her own good and for everyone's safety."

"She's frightening, my Lord, for sure."

"Indeed." He let out a long breath. "Now, boy, did you do as I asked?"

"Yes, sire. Sir Bollus is waiting in your study."

"Very good. Now, go inform the jailor I'm depriving him of his assistant. A new one will be provided by tomorrow. Then find the boy's parents. Have them escorted to a dungeon cell for not keeping better control of their son. I'll insist on an extra two years of servitude to make up for his transgression. The boy will serve his remaining time working in the dungeon."

Roderick bowed. "Yes, sire. Anything else?"

"Call for one of the staff to come here before the ball and prepare the Princess. Both children should sleep for a couple of

30

hours at least. When the boy awakens, have him taken down to the dungeons and shackled. Tomorrow, he can start his new duties."

The door closed with a click of the lock.

Bolting up, Princess gripped her stomach as the sensation of free-falling into a bottomless pit remained. Her mind whirled. Master was sending her away with that beast-man. She jumped to her feet. No, she had to find a way out this mess.

At least Tarek was still alive, otherwise Darnel wouldn't plan on giving him her job. He might be a rat, but she hated to see him come to harm, too. She wondered if he'd take care of the old dungeon keeper as she had? Hard to tell which side of the fence Tarek walked on any given day.

She went to the door and tried the knob. Locked, of course. The key was outside above the frame. Her forehead rested against the smooth wood. If only she had grabbed it earlier. How much time before the ball? She might try escaping during the festivities. Find a way to the messenger. Then what? Possibly hide in one of the tunnels.

Not for long. Master had too many ways of finding people when he wanted to.

Flopping back on the bed, Princess' thoughts raced until her head ached. Even if she did escape, then what? Where would she go? Perhaps she should give in. Or give up. Perhaps she needed to end it all herself?

She closed her eyes and took a deep breath. No, she didn't want to die. She wanted to be free.

The dress rustled like paper as she gathered her old clothes from behind the screen. From the hidden pocket, she took out the medallion. Her finger traced the vine surrounding the tree. Squeezing the disk tight she wished for a way to get her out of this mess. Yet nobody could help her now.

"You're on your own," she said to her reflection in the mirror.

Dismay drooped her shoulders as she stared at the gaunt girl in the mirror. Working in the prison may have provided some freedom , but not without cost. Dark circles sank under her gold-brown eyes. Her reddish-brown hair hung limp around her oval-shaped face. Taking a brush from the vanity table, she worked out the tangles, allowing the tresses to fall over her narrow shoulders. The rough dress itched her pale skin. How would she endure this night? From the tall windows, the sun now arched toward the west.

Something thumped outside her room.

Princess dropped the brush. Had they already come for her? She shoved the medallion into her bodice and leapt to the bed, pretending to sleep.

"Psst, you there?" whispered a familiar male voice.

"Tarek?" She sat up and hurried over. "How? Is it really you?"

"Yeah." His voice sounded groggy and hoarse. "Can you let me in?"

"No, Master set the lock. But listen…" A loud thump hit the door. "What's that?"

"Huh? I'm so tired." He whined. "Can I come in and take a nap with you?"

He was still drowsy from the food. "Tarek, listen! We don't have much time. Grab the key above the door frame."

Silence. Maybe he was looking. She pressed her ear to the wood and heard snoring. "*Tarek*!"

"Key? Up there?" he muttered. Something metal clattered onto the floor. "Ouch, my head!"

The knob rattled, turned, and she yanked open the door as he stumbled inside. Grabbing the key, she quickly secured the lock.

"How did you manage to wake up?"

Tarek collapsed on the bed. When his eyes closed, he jerked himself awake. "Monsters chasing me. Scary. Long nails." He arched his fingers mimicking the dream spirits. "I woke up, like my dad told me to. Said if you're having bad dreams wake yourself."

She snorted, shaking her head.

His lids began to close again. He shook his head, fighting against the potion.

"Works for me, so there." He chuckled. Then getting back to his feet, he grew serious. "We are in so much trouble. King Darnel plans to marry you off. To that troll goon we saw in the hall. He's disgusting and stinks."

He stood unsteadily over her, eyes glazed and bloodshot. "No matter how annoying you've been, nobody deserves that."

Why did her heart have to race so fast when he got close?

His warm breath smelled like the sweet cakes and tea. "Wow,

you look…incredible."

Her cheeks began to burn. She shoved him back.

"We have to get you out of here, Princess."

"Come with me. Please? We can both escape his punishment."

A smile dimpled his cheek. "I've had a feeling you cared about me, too. You know, it was obvious the way you were always calling me names and all."

"Tarek." She grabbed his shoulders.

He talked craziness. Most likely from the potion. When he came out of the stupor, he'd regret saying all this.

"You are so cute when you're irritated." He snickered, smiling wickedly. "I'd hide you in my pocket. But I can't. It's not big enough."

"Tarek! Stop." She shook him harder. His arms went around her. She groaned, trying to push him away. "Snap out of this! We have to get out of here. Now. Any ideas?"

He rubbed his face, slapping his cheeks.

"You need shoes." He went to the closet. A pair of traveling boots flew out across the room. "Put those on," his muffled voice came from within. "I don't see… ugh, there's only dresses."

He stumbled backward, grasping the door frame for support. He sounded more in control of his speech when he said in a commanding tone, "You get back down into the dungeon, but keep out of sight. Don't let anyone, and I mean nobody catch you. Got it?"

She retrieved the boots and slipped them on.

"Go find the loon, or the messenger. He's probably crazy enough to try getting past the dragon."

"But, I've looked and—"

He held up a hand to silence her. "Listen, there are no tunnels out of the mountain, but one will take you to the river. Right beside the dragon's feeding post is a narrow passage. Bushes hide the entrance. From there, follow the river. You'll find a trail leading down the cliffs beside the falls."

"I've never heard—"

"'Course not. Not a secret if everyone knows," he whispered, placing a finger over his mouth. "I won't lie. It's really dangerous, but possible. That's why he keeps the dragon in that area. And why nobody cared about you wasting your time exploring."

He rubbed at his face, pressing the balls of his hands against his eyes. "Help the messenger escape, and I bet he'll help you. People have gotten out before."

"Tarek…" She couldn't believe he knew of more tunnels than she did. "Come with me. He's going to make you work in the dungeon."

He headed to the door. "No, I can't. I probably should, but I can't leave my family. And I … just don't… I'm not sure about all *that*…." He peeked out before adding, "Besides, if I behave and show I'm willing to work hard, King Darnel might be willing to forgive." He smirked again. "You'll be back anyway. You'll find out all those dreams you have are just that. Dumb dreams."

She glared at him, hating how smug and self-assured he seemed. "Then why did you… come?"

The door clicked shut as Tarek turned to face her. His emerald eyes appeared clearer. In one quick motion, he crossed the space between them, grabbed her in his arms and pressed his lips to hers. She stiffened at first. Her racing heart slowed as she melted into his embrace. For a solitary moment, in the swirl of tumbling emotions, she forgot everything except for the sweetness of his kiss that tasted like the berry tea. Remembering the drug, she pulled away.

Before releasing her, he whispered against her ear, "That's why."

Next thing she knew, he was slipping out with a last warning, "Stay safe, okay? And hurry."

Her mind whirled with a desire to go after and make him leave with her. But what if his affections were brought on by the tainted food and not his real feelings? No, she had to hurry before she missed her best chance for escape. Not daring to look back at her room, or Tarek, she rushed out into the hall and into the closet which led her to the secret stairs. She didn't slow until reaching the kitchen. No one seemed to notice as she hurried on to the dungeons, Tarek's kiss still burning her lips.

# Chapter 5

Boots slipped across the damp floor as Princess entered the silent chamber. She stopped to listen.

*Why so dark and quiet?*

She felt along the cold, stone wall of the first cell, moving slowly to keep from tripping. Ben had probably come to visit him despite his tiredness. When unsuccessful with a prisoner, he usually turned off the lanterns and let them sit in the quiet darkness with their last thoughts.

That is, unless they'd already come for him.

Dread seeped through her heart. The grand ball started in less than two hours. If she turned back now, Master might never know she left. She pulled out the medallion, her fingers squeezing the round disk. For some reason, the feel of it in her hand always gave her courage.

"How will I get down the mountain alone?" Despair weighed so heavily, she sank onto the dirt floor in a miserable heap. She couldn't go back. *Wouldn't.* Tarek said there was a way. Her knees quaked. Fear tightened a harsh fist around her gut.

Then a whispered voice came to her in the darkness, barely audible. A solemn song. He still lived!

She leaped to her feet and ran to the narrow window on his cell door. A dark shadow crouched in the corner.

"Well, well," the man chuckled. "You're back."

Relief coursed through her tired body. "I need help getting out of here. I think there's a way. A trail leading down the mountain. Would you be willing to...?" The question faltered. What if he didn't want to help her? Why should he?

"You never told me your name, child. You must have returned at great risk."

If only she had a real name to give. No way would she tell him what everyone really called her. Cheeks burning, she dug her toe into the dirt, keeping her gaze on the ground. "Master Darnel has taken my memories. I don't know my name. I only know—"

"That you don't belong here." He stood and met her at the window. "I am Dean, messenger of the great king, Shaydon. I am at your service, dear sister. We will learn the truth soon enough when we reach Aloblase." His rough hand rested on her fingers through the bars.

She blinked back tears. He was willing to help.

"Is it far to—?"

Harsh voices came from the corridor. She gasped, searching for somewhere to hide.

"Get in the next cell," he whispered. "Do not take any chances to help me. While the dragon is busy..." he cleared his throat, "find the trail down the mountain. Head east until you come upon a town with the same emblem as that on your medallion. They will lead you to the King's Highway."

Princess ducked into the next cell moments before three soldiers entered the small, circular room. Boots scraped over the rock floor. The chamber filled with flickering light. Keys rattled. The heavy oak door wailed as they yanked it open.

"I don' see nobody else," one of the black clad guards said. "She ain't gonna come dis nasty place. Not for some ol' loon liken this one."

Princess peered through a crack between the door and frame. Four guards pulled Dean into the center and tied his arms behind his back.

The captain asked, "I don't suppose you've seen the Princess girl, have you?"

"A Princess? Here?" He chuckled, shaking his bruised head.

She hunkered behind the oak door, making herself as small as possible. The cell door swung open wider, hitting her leg. Light flooded the square room sending several rats scurrying in different directions. Her teeth clamped on her bottom lip to suppress the scream rising up her throat.

Two more guards appeared. "Ain't no sign of her. She's hiding somewhere up in the castle, I tell ya."

Master knew she'd escaped! Oh no, no, no! Had Tarek been

caught returning to the tower?

Bringing her fisted hands to her mouth, she pleaded silent words against the medallion that he'd not be killed for helping her. Please, let him be okay.

One of the rats darted toward her hiding spot, coming too close. She pulled her skirt tight around her trembling legs.

"Well, not our problem then," replied the captain. "Let's get this done. We can enjoy our evening more with him out of the way."

The soldiers grabbed Dean by each arm and led him into the tunnel to the dragon's feed post.

She held her breath, not daring to move until their footsteps were a mere echo down the walkway. Her boot sent the rat flying into the shadows with a loud squeak.

Keeping their torches in view, she removed her clomping shoes before following at a safe distance. Shadowy things moved across the rocks. The tunnel sloped gradually upward and soon a rush of coolness blew her brown tendrils. Her pace slowed, ears fixed on all sounds—the dripping of water, crickets chirping, the thump of booted feet on dirt, and wind whistling down the tunnel. A shaft of sunlight reflected off the chiseled surface.

Outside, she heard their struggling grunts as Dean fought his bindings. Pausing to form a plan, she peeked out and spotted a clump of bushes next to the exit. That might work. Hopefully, the dragon wouldn't be interested in dinner before the moon rose, though it had been a long while since the last meal.

She eased to the opening, until she had a clear view of the soldiers and Dean. Fresh blood ran from his nose. His bruised eyes caught sight of her, and he struggled harder, giving her the chance she needed to duck behind the foliage.

"There," said one of the guards. "Let's see you get out of that." He spat at Dean then turned to the other two. "I'm ready for some ale and food. How about you?"

A mumbled agreement spread through the group. The youngest one hesitated. "We ain't gonna wait 'til the dragon shows up?"

The other men laughed and shook their heads.

"No, thank you," replied the captain. "We'll give a ring." He pointed to a large bell attached to the cliff wall next to the opening. "And head out of here. Not sure she'll come out before dusk, but maybe. Don't care to take the chance of getting roasted myself."

With that, they all disappeared down the hole. The last one in yanked the cord a couple of times, sending out a loud jangling melody. Princess counted to ten, allowing them to get well into the tunnel, then bolted from her hiding place.

"We need something to untie you." She yanked on the thick ropes.

"My pack." He jerked his head toward the bag on his back. "There's a dagger to cut the cords."

She reached inside and brought out a knife much larger than the bag itself. No time to question the logistics now. She sliced through the binding.

He pulled a long leather sling from his pants pocket and took the dagger in his other hand. Quickly, she slipped back into her boots. They both looked around for a minute, taking in the open valley below the cliff. Only death lay in that direction. The land was burnt, charred, and parched. Princess searched for the adjacent cave Tarek described. A narrow crevice opened behind some dried brush.

The ground shook as a terrible, earsplitting roar filled the valley and bounced off the cliffs.

"Through here!" She tugged at his arm.

Dean pushed her toward the opening. The earth shook again as the dragon bellowed after them. Dirt and pebbles poured onto their heads. They raced into the darkness.

"I wish I had a light." she stumbled into several sharp edged rocks. "Should have grabbed a lantern."

The tunnel filled with a dim brightness, and she could now maneuver the twists and turns ahead. Dean gasped. Princess figured he must have found some kind of torch. The floor dipped, and she ran faster hoping the dragon was unaware of the passageway. They burst from the tunnel into a thick patch of pines. Off to the south was the sound of rushing water.

Dean stared at her, his mouth agape. "You really are…. You're a—" Her grabbed her shoulders. "Oh, we must get you home."

He slid off the backpack and handed it to her. "Keep this. If anything happens to me, you'll find many necessities for traveling inside." He then lifted the medallion from around his neck and slipped it over her head. "Hold this for me too, please. King Shaydon will be sure—"

The dragon's screech cut him off. Grasping her wrist, Dean dragged her toward the shoreline. Her side ached from running full speed. A warm wind caressed her body. Thunderous wings beat above the oak canopy. A black shadow blocked out the orange sky. Billowing fire blasted the tree tops, engulfing the dried branches.

He shoved her ahead. "Run, girl, run fast! Do not stop despite what happens. Flee to the river!"

"But—"

He waved her to go.

She watched over her shoulder as he fitted a large rock into his slingshot. Before she could stop him, he darted into the clearing.

Flames crackled above. Princess sprinted on, but edged toward the tree-break instead of keeping to the shore. The beast's wings beat like the smack of a whip, and its ear-splitting cry caused her to fall on her face.

Dean the Messenger yelled in a loud, rolling voice, "FOR FREEEEEDOM!"

He swung the sling in a wide arch as the monster swooped down on him. The rock smacked the dragon's left temple. It faltered and fell hard on the ground.

"For my King!" Dean shot several more rocks from the sling. The stones bounced off the beast's tough hide.

"What are you doing? Run!" Princess leaped to her feet. He didn't listen.

The dragon shook its head and rose into the sky. Shafts of fire and smoke discharged from its nostrils, its roar loud and fierce.

Dean charged at Princess and yelled, "Run, now!"

Princess sprinted, pushing every muscle past the normal limit. Her leg muscles screamed in agony. From behind, Dean the Messenger shouted, "For My King. For Free—"

The night grew quiet.

She halted beside the rushing waters, heart threatening to burst from her chest.

*No, no, no!*

The seconds passed with her panting breaths.

He'd come racing toward her any second now. She searched the woods, the shore, straining her ears to listen. No running feet. No bellows from the dragon. No beating of wings from above, only the white-capped river.

"No!" She fell to her knees.

The medallion burned against her chest, reminding her that his sacrifice had bought her precious time to escape. She raced for the water as the messenger's challenge echoed though her whole being, giving her a renewed vigor and energy. *For freedom! I want freedom! I want to be free!*

Princess sprinted along the shoreline, repeating this to herself. The water foamed a brilliant white. Then another sound filled the air. Crashing limbs. Pounding feet. A terrible bellow, followed by a toasty burst of flames.

The dragon now came for her.

The beast plowed through the trees, perhaps too full to fly. Could she be so lucky that it might be too full to eat her as well?

Heat seared her back. She dove into the river. Icy coldness prickled her body like a thousand sharp spikes. The stench of filth and decay filled her nostrils and throat. She clamped her mouth shut to keep from swallowing the putrid water. The shoreline flashed past, a blur as she spun in circles, left to the mercy of the crashing current.

A mountainous splash knocked Princess into a mighty swell. She coughed, catching sight of blue wings and a spiked tail disappearing below the surface. Another wave pushed her forward, then the watercourse dropped out from beneath her. Princess tumbled into nothingness, completely airborne.

# Chapter 6

The dragon tumbled over the waterfall right behind Princess. In desperation, she grabbed onto the downy mane growing along the beast's back. Billowing wings flapped in the rushing wind like sails on a warship, at least slowing their decent a fraction.

They plunged several feet into the swirling mist. Water filled her nose and screaming mouth. As the beast swam for the surface, she sought for a better grip. A golden cord tied like a leash around its neck provided the perfect hold as she rode the dragon down the rapids.

"Get off," gasped dragon over the roaring waves. "Get off me!"

Shocked to hear the beast speak, Princess almost released the rope. It bucked like a wild horse. She held tighter, too frightened to let go.

"You chokes me, pleeeaaase!" It not only spoke, but spoke in a child-like girl's voice.

"No!" Princess' knuckles whitened. "You'll eat me!"

Coughing smoke and sparks, the dragon dragged itself up onto the shore.

"The rope-" The beast's eyes bulged as her long, claws clutched at the binding. "-hurts me… when you touch…."

"How do I know you won't hurt me?" The river had tumbled down into a mountain lake, surrounded by sharp, spiraling crags. *How will I ever get down from here without being caught?*

"I swear! Please." The young dragon started to cry.

The childish whimpering tore at her heart. "All right! All right! But I'm staying right here where you can't get me! Understand?" She hooked her legs beneath the wings, and grasped the mane below the cord. The pang of pity which tinged her conscious was cautionary all the same.

"Don't try anything, dragon, or I'll pull until you stop

breathing."

The drake's body expanded as it sucked in a deep, ragged breath.

Princess touched the creature's shimmering, glass-like scales. *Beautiful.* Fine, flaxen tresses grew along her back. White, silken wings were almost transparent. At the end of the tail were small spikes, resembling a goat's horn.

"What's up with the cord, dragon? I wasn't pulling that hard."

"He makes strong magic. I chokes every time I get too near the edge of the mountains. And if I even just touch." The dragon took another deep, gulping breath, and settled on the rocky shore. Smoke puffed from her nostrils in a steady stream as she groaned, "I should have never left my home! I should have listened to Gran-Maton."

"You're captive, too? What happened?"

"Well, I was just a baby and not big enough to have a good fire yet. A soldier caught me. Played a trick on me, the cheater. Then brought me here as a present to the dark king." Another snivel caused a shower of sparks and steam. "He even tied a red ribbon around me." Choking sobs shook the beast's body. "I. Was. Humiliated."

Princess tightened her legs to keep from getting bucked off. Her hands accidentally fell back onto the rope, yet the dragon didn't seem to notice this time.

They might have made it half-way down the cliffs Princess reasoned. The castle towered high upon the mountain's crest. From the distress the dragon seemed to be in, she'd probably reached her limit. Any farther and the cord would most likely cut off her breath.

A rank smell from the lake still burned Princess's nose and roiled her stomach. She had to get out of this putrid land. *Had to.* Would she be able climb down the rest of the way before Darnel realized she was gone and sent soldiers to bring her back?

The dragon huffed another smoky sigh and rested her head on a rock. Princess felt sorry for the poor beast. *Although the poor beast had just eaten a grown man.*

Her pity remained cautionary. They seemed to have a lot in common. Perhaps the dragon wanted to escape, too.

Princess fidgeted with the knot. The cord loosened slightly.

"I've also been a prisoner." Princess broke the silence. "My

chance to finally escape had come. Until you…took my one hope."
She shuddered, trying not to think of Dean's death for the moment.
Somehow she had to convince the dragon to let her go. "Now I don't
know what I'm going to do." She continued tugging the rope's knot.

"But…you're not supposed to escape. That's bad." Dragon
shook her large head, and then added with awe, "Your friend was so
brave, though. Yelling 'For freedom!' and all.

"Oh, I wish *I* could be free of this hateful, rotten, stinking place!
I know how you feel, girl. But if I don't obey, he hurts me." The
dragon settled into the sand, her voice growing wistful. "My land
was so beautiful, too. Tall evergreen trees, pristine waters and falls.
There were so many fat cows and sheep to eat. We are guardians of
King Shaydon's treasure. He provides everything we need and
more."

"King Shaydon?" exclaimed Princess. "That's who I'm going to
see. The messenger was to show me the way to the White Road. He
said it would take me to Aloblase."

The dragon's head twisted around to face her. "You want to…"
Her eyes widened. "What are you doing?"

"Nothing." She jerked her hands away, despite seeing the knot
had loosened.

The dragon's brilliant blues narrowed suspiciously. "You will
have to go back. Go now, while I'm still full, and I'll pretend I never
ever saw you. Our little secret."

"I'm not going back!"

"Don't make me eat you, please. People really don't taste that
good, if you want to know. I can't let you escape. He'll find out and
that would be very bad. I don't want to be punished again." A shiver
tore through her body, ruffling her brilliant scales.

Sweat beaded upon Princess' forehead. The moon peeked over
the horizon. Master already searched for her. Her back tingled.
Would he use the looking scope to find her? She could pull the cord
with all her might and kill the dragon instead. Her stomach twisted,
as she realized she didn't have the ruthlessness in her to harm the
poor beast. In her nervousness, she continued to poke the knot until
the loop moved again. Another idea, a slim possibility came to her
mind.

"Dragon, if I can get this off your neck, would you help me get to Aloblase?"

"It's impossible! Bad king made it magic. I'm trapped."

"What if I can?"

The dragon stopped crying a moment, and turned to look at her. "Could you really? Will it hurt? Please don't hurt me."

Biting her lower lip, Princess studied the knot, then she looked to the dragon. "What's your name?"

"Back home, I was called Crystal. I would have guarded those stones. We are named for the treasures we safeguard. My Maton protected the emeralds and my Gran-Maton, she watched over the King's ruby mines. Very important she was." Her blue eyes misted. "I really, really, really want to go home."

"Me too. They've called me Princess here, but I hate that name. I'd rather be called anything else."

Crystal wiped the wetness from her eyes with a long claw and said, "How about friend?" She smiled, showing two rows of razor sharp teeth.

Princess gave a nervous laugh, no longer fearing the dragon, but instead, growing fond of her. "Friend is better than you calling me dessert." She slid off the dragon's back and now stood face to snout. "Do we have a deal?"

Crystal's wings trembled. "The White City is too far. Too dangerous. Dragons seldom fly far from their treasure. We'd stick out, you see?" She shook her head sadly. "But if you free me, I will take you to a safe place. Mountains are hard to get down. I'll find you a nice town away from here. We both escape then. I hurry home. You hurry to Aloblase. Hurry real fast so the dark one can't catch us again."

Her offer seemed fair enough. Princess had little hope of actually getting down the mountains safely by herself, anyway.

Shifting the backpack, Princess studied the knot for a moment. Too bad she no longer had messenger's dagger. Yet…magic worked according to one's will, not force or weapon. If she focused her own will into making the cord come loose….

She grasped the twine, thought hard on untying, and began to work the loops.

Crystal gasped and choked. Princess let go. Her heart pounded so hard inside her chest, her ears vibrated. No matter what, Crystal couldn't be harmed. She concentrated harder.

The dragon cried for her to stop. "It's useless. His magic is too strong."

"Listen, I've loosened a bit." She wiped her sweaty hands on her damp skirt. "Can you take the choking for a minute more?"

Crystal whimpered, but nodded. Princess tried not move the rope too much. It slipped a little. Crystal gasped for air. Princess tugged harder. Crystal fought to breathe, eyes popping.

Frustrated, Princess yelled, "Let loose you stupid thing!"

The gold cord fluttered to the ground.

Both of them stared in shocked disbelief. Crystal took a step back, rubbing her claws over her bare neck.

"Get on. Oh, hurry," she pleaded. "He's going to know. He'll send out his bully soldiers to catch us!"

Princess leaped upon Crystal's back, right in the crook of her wings where she fit comfortably and secure. She grabbed a handful of silvery mane.

"You're going to love this!" Crystal's wings beat loudly, sending up a cloud of dust.

Indeed, as they rose into the velvety sky, Princess's heart shot up into her throat. The dragon flew with such ease and care, Princess actually opened her eyes to the sparkling stars above. She held up her hands, wanting to touch them. Cool wind whipped through her tangled hair, drying the wetness and sending a pleasant chill down her spine. Laughter rose from within, and she whooped and hollered until Crystal gently reminded her to not make too much of a ruckus.

In the east, a silvery band outlined a mountain range. "Is that Aloblase?" Princess leaned closer to the dragon's head.

"No, that's only half way. The white city is somewhere past those mountains. I was very small when I visited, Aloblase, but I remember."

Princess's joy waned. Such a long journey. Yet a good king really lived in a beautiful city. He wasn't a mere fable. She was now on her way to meet the king who'd given her the medallion. Exhilaration coursed through her body like a lightning bolt.

As they flew past the last mountain range, Crystal let out a loud whoop and cried, "I'm free! I'm really free! You did it! I'm free!"

She shot higher amongst the stars. Both yelled with joy and

laughter as the dragon twirled and spun through the purple sky. Princess was so excited, she forgot to be scared of the dragon's acrobatics hundreds of feet in the air. The wind on her face and the expanse of land spreading out in the valley below settled the realization that *she was finally free!*

Laughter eventually ceasing, Crystal pointed her nose in an easterly course. Desert spread below, occupied by a few sparse hamlets. Soon, the dead land became spotted with trees and meadows and farmland.

Feeling like she was being pulled out of a mud pit, she took in the new land beyond her place of enslavement. A few towns appeared below, but Crystal didn't slow in her easterly flight.

The moon hung overhead when they came upon a valley where nearly a hundred pale tents reflected the moonlight. Dragon circled, rising higher. A short distance to the north, they both saw the twinkling lights of a village.

Crystal flew in a zigzagging pattern, searching out the land.

They set down in a small clearing next to a dirt road, which disappeared into dense woods. Princess slid off her scaly back onto damp grass.

"If I get any closer, they might shoot me. Follow this road to that town." Crystal instructed. "They should help you."

"What are all those tents?"

"Might be Aloblase warriors. In this dark, I'm not sure. They looked colorful which means they don't belong to the bad king. That's good. But who knows if the Racan army isn't around somewhere? That would be bad. Do be very careful."

Princess's legs wobbled from the ride, and she stepped from one to the other to get blood flowing again. The flight had been fun, but she was glad to be back on the ground.

"Hurry real fast and stay on the road so you don't get lost, friend."

Princess stepped in front of the dragon and smiled. Who would have dreamed the terrible beast contained such a tender heart. Who, like herself, only wanted to go home?

"Thank you, Crystal. That was…amazing."

The dragon brushed her warm nose against Princess' neck. Sulfuric heat washed over her chilled body.

"I'm sorry about.... I...I...wish I could undo everything," Crystal paused. "Well, almost everything. I will always be your friend, and you mine."

Princess's throat tightened, but her words faltered. She threw her arms around the dragon's neck and hugged her tight. She'd had few real friends in her lifetime. Quickly she let go and headed toward the road.

"Stay hidden," Crystal called after her, "until you get to the village. Stay away from beasties."

Princess stopped, "What are beasties?"

Wings flapped, sending dust and the dragon up into the sky. "For Freedom!"

"For Freedom!" Princess waved goodbye. Fighting down the growing apprehension about beasties, she entered the shadowy woodland.

# Chapter 7

*Beasties, huh?*

The dark woodlands swallowed the narrow dirt lane barely wide enough for a horse cart to maneuver.

Even if she met one, how would she know? Wouldn't a dragon be considered a beastie? That ugly troll-man was certainly beastly. *And* he smelled of rotten eggs.

Her stomach rumbled. She started for the tree-lined road, legs wobbling like thin reeds. A loud grumble came from her gut, a mixture of fear and hunger. Did the messenger have any food in his pack? After her trip down the waterfall, everything inside was most likely wet.

If only the black tree limbs didn't loom over her head like jagged teeth. She imagined the road turning into a giant tongue and threatening to gobble her up. Her feet stumbled. *Oh, what silliness!* There'd be many woods on the way to Aloblase. *Now is no time to lose courage.*

A piercing screech echoed through the forest. She peered back to where the dragon left her. In the hazy distance the mountain city of Racah shone like twinkling dots. Crystal had spared her a few days of traveling, yet she was still too close.

The full moon crested in the star-sparkled sky. There might be four or five hours before daylight. Master would come after her. She needed to keep going, no matter how long the journey took. *Don't think of the distance, just focus on getting to the little town. That's all you need to do.*

Weariness hung on her like a heavy woolen blanket. She shifted the backpack. No sense carrying a bag full of wet, ruined items. Finding a flat rock a short distance off the road, she collapsed, letting the pack slide from her aching back. Now that she'd finally stopped, her body protested its recent treatment. The creamy velvet dress hung around her scraped legs in stained tatters. Hopefully once she reached the town, she'd be able to find a place to take a hot bath.

She unlatched the buckskin flap, and pulled out a water-bag, nearly full of water. To her astonishment, everything was dry!

"How?"

Next she removed a tinderbox with fire-starting supplies, and a wooden box containing string and hooks. A cloth bag held several coins. She found a small pan to cook in and a tightly rolled blanket. *Amazing!*

The cover warmed her shoulders, warding off the night chill. At the very bottom was a leather-bound book along with some jerky and bread wrapped in cloth. She shoved a chunk of meat into her mouth.

"This is the best pack ever. How'd he get all this stuff in there?" She examined the inside and outside thoroughly but couldn't figure it out. The water went down her parched throat like soothing honey. She took one chunk of bread and another bit of jerky. Maybe in the town, she'd use the coins to buy traveling supplies and clothes.

Glancing down the shadowy path, she decided to rest beside the rock. Once dawn broke, she'd move on. At least, thanks to the dragon, she had a good lead on any soldiers Darnel would send. Of course, also thanks to the dragon, she had to travel alone.

She clutched Dean's medallion as she rolled up in his blanket like a cocoon on the leafy ground. Why did he fight Crystal? She'd never met anyone who purposefully risked their life to save someone else.

*Just don't get caught or what he did will be wasted.*

\* \* \* \*

As the sun rose, golden rays of light filtered through openings in the forest canopy. A brilliant ray shone down on a springy patch of fern, wet with dew. A petulant blue jay fluttered from tree to tree, chirping a warning of her presence in their world. Soon, robins and finches replied to his calls, and the whole forest was filled with a joyful song.

Princess stopped in a shaft of light and spun around, arms outstretched, enjoying the bright sun on her face. Ah, freedom from Master's awful, hate-filled laugh. Freedom from his vicious words. Freedom to be herself. She sighed, *whoever that may be.*

She hurried along the road, her pace swift and her heart full of excitement.

By time the sun had climbed directly overhead, her feet dragged over the rutted ground and again, her stomach begged for something to eat. She considered stopping for a short rest, when a scent drifting on the breeze caused her mouth to start watering. *Cookies?* She sucked in a long whiff through her nose. *Was that apple pie?*

Her pace hastened along after the delectable aroma. The road took a sharp turn, before coming upon the back of a rundown old shack. Yellow paint flecked the wood walls. Chickens pecked the dirt in amongst broken wagons, crates, and some kind of rusted cage on wheels. Maybe she'd offer to clean up in exchange for a pie.

A rooster crowed. From inside a crackly voice called out, "Keep yer feathers on, I'm a comin'!"

The back door flew open with a smack against the house. A hunched old woman, holding a bag of feed, stepped out onto the rickety wooden porch. Long, gray hair hung in her face and her threadbare blue dress was covered in dirt smudges. She hurled seed out across the yard.

Princess crept closer to get a better look at the lady. A startling realization hit her. She recognized the old woman's face! Then the memory rushed back upon her: *A long ride inside a stifling, dark carriage. Starving. The man refused to open the windows and let air in, or stop for food, saying they had to hurry before they lost her. Lost who?*

Rubbing her temples, she focused hard to recall the details. Why had she been with the man, and who was he? All she could remember was the smell of cookies. A kind old woman finally gave her food and then filled the man's hand with silver coins. Princess had fallen asleep only to wake up in another horse-drawn carriage heading up the mountain, this one with bars like an animal cage.

Now she clearly remembered meeting Lord Darnel for the first time. He'd seemed quite pleased with her. He'd called her one of the Illuminated, whatever that meant.

He'd filled the woman's gnarled hand with even more golden coins saying, "Well done, Witch. Soon enough I'll have her light snuffed out. It's so easy when they are young."

"Someone out t'ere?" screeched the old woman. Chicken feed

poured from her hand like sand. "Show yerself."

Princess dove behind an elderberry bush.

She remembered the old woman as sounding kind, and her house had been white stucco with thatched roofing. Yellow daisies and hollyhocks grew along a cobblestone walkway. Jasmine covered the porch banisters and roof. There had been a rosy-cheeked old lady, sitting in a rocker petting her fat, gray tabby. That house had not been rundown and littered like this.

The door slammed shut. Princess slowly rose and peered through the green branches, finding the backyard empty. Now was her chance. She scampered across the road, keeping hidden in the tall fern and brush. She didn't want to leave the path and get lost in the woods, but it passed directly in front of the house. When the porch came into view, she gasped. A fat, yellow cat sat on the balustrade amongst thick jasmine. The pretty cottage was a facade, an illusion.

The witch wobbled outside and took a seat in rocker. Her long, tangled gray hair was now sparkling white and put up in a neat bun. The tattered frock had become a ruffled peach-colored dress. She set a basket of knitting in her lap as her gaze searched the road. The tabby stared out across the yard, tail twitching. Feline yellow eyes seemed to glare right at her.

Princess ducked behind a thick elm.

"Someone's out t'ere, eh, my pet?"

The cat meowed.

"I's feel 'em too," said the witch. "But t'ey are coming from ta other direction. Strange, eh?"

Princess bolted into the woods, away from the enchanted house. Tree limbs swatted at her body like a whip. Up ahead, a fallen tree trunk blocked her path. Without slowing, she took a flying leap, feet leaving the ground. Nearly half way over, her skirt caught on a knobby branch. She tumbled forward, landing flat on her face, right in front of a fire pit. A campsite, tucked in a cluster of trees. She unhooked her dress from the log and searched for the occupant, but the area seemed deserted.

"Hello?" She called out not too loudly, hoping they might be near.

"How do you do?" replied a tree stump sitting across the fire from her.

She blinked and looked again. The speaking stump had a pair of sad looking eyes and a crooked grin. *No, that can't be.*

Standing on two short knobby-looking legs, the strange creature bowed low. Its nose nearly touched the ground. "DezPierre, at your service, miss…uh…miss…" He paused.

She stared, brows pinched while trying to fit this creature into the list of beings she'd seen before. Now that she realized the tree was actually a living being, she could make out the nose, eyebrows and mouth. What she'd thought was grassy moss was instead a beard, and what looked like a bird's nest made of straw and leaves was hair and a woven hat. His skinny arms were gnarled like limbs of a tree. She wanted to touch his face to check if he felt like a bark or skin.

He straightened. "This is where you would tell me your name, miss. If it pleases you to do so, that is." The creature was gracious, regardless.

"Oh … umm … I would … but…" she stammered. Besides, telling people she was called Princess might give her escape away. Who knew the extent of Master's reach in this part of the land? She stood and gave him a polite bow in return. "Miss will do."

He scratched at his mossy beard a moment. "Humm, interesting, indeed… Miss."

"Sir, I am sorry to stare. I've never seen anything— This is probably rude, too, but what are you?"

"I'm an Okbold, of course, Miss." He was about three feet high. His clothes consisted of a vest the color of oak bark and pants made of leaves. "I am of the Oakabole Tree Family. Perhaps you have heard of my clan?" When she shook her head, he concluded with a click of his tongue, "You must not be from around here, if I may presume."

"No, I'm not." She dusted the dirt from her dress, not that it did much good. "I was following the road over there…and…something frightened me. I'm sorry to burst in on you."

"Oh, no. It is I who must apologize. I didn't think to warn you." He bowed again. "I was a bit startled to see you running through the woods. I was frightful of what may be pursuing you, I admit and wondered if I shouldn't join you."

A laugh burst from Princess, the first she'd had in a long time. Her laughter caused the corners of the Okbold's mouth to turn up on his sorrowful face. Whatever the creature might be, he couldn't be one of the beasties Crystal warned her about. DezPierre was much too polite.

She shook her head. "There was nothing pursuing me. I just got…spooked I suppose. I'm trying to get to a town up the road."

"Ah, I see. Of course, traveling all alone, tuh-tuh—this shouldn't be. DezPierre will help you now."

"Are you heading that way, too?"

He nodded with a big grin. "We walk together, yes? Young miss should not be by her lonesome when another goes in the same direction."

Relief filled her, washing away the pent up fear. She plopped heavily on the log. "That would be wonderful."

He bowed again. "I was taking my morning meal, come join me. Then we will be off." A bowl of boiled eggs sat next to the fire. "I find these delicious treats at witch's cottage. She won't miss them, indeed." His eyes sparkled with mischief. "DezPierre also helped himself to this sweet bread on her windowsill. This she might miss but…" He took a long whiff of the loaf, "DezPierre could not resist."

Her stomach rumbled. "Umm," she hesitated, fearful of the witch's food. "Maybe I'll just have some eggs."

DezPierre's eyebrows rose. She hoped she hadn't said too much. This was not the time to get careless, despite how kind the Okbold seemed.

He grinned. "No need to worry, Miss. This is witch's personal batch. Not treats she saves for … er … passersby." He broke off a corner and put it into his mouth. "DezPierre isn't interested in taking long sleep. He has things to do. His nose tells him what is good to take, and…" he bent forward, "what is not. See?"

He offered her a piece. She watched him for a moment, and seeing he had no ill effects, greedily ate a large chunk. Buttery pumpkin filled her mouth and her stomach with pleasure. DezPierre handed her a couple of boiled eggs, a hint of a scowl on his bark face. She chastised herself for her rude manners and chewed slower.

"Ah, Miss feels better now, yes?"

"Yes, thank you."

The Okbold gathered his belongings into a woven bag which he slung over his shoulder. He stamped out the fire with his bare foot. "You come with DezPierre to Yarholm. I'm meeting some of my kin there. We will arrive by nightfall."

Glad to have someone to travel with, she followed her new friend deeper into the woods.

DezPierre asked where she came from, but she avoided telling him too much. Eventually, she needed to make up some kind of story about her past. She tried to work out a plausible explanation but her mind was a jumble of apprehension and fear.

Filling the awkward silence, he began talking about himself and his Okbold clan, describing all the wonderful things they did for Yarholm. They were good at planting seeds, milking cows, and collecting eggs from chickens. Some even did more domestic duties such as cleaning out homes and cooking meals.

"Now, our cousins, the Elmbole, they aren't nearly as sociable and tend to keep to themselves deep in the woods. But the Okabole Clan, we like the comforts of a quiet town. Yes, indeed. Does Miss have friends or family in yonder village?"

"No." She thought it safer telling him where she was going rather than where she came from. "I'm looking for a road called the King's Highway."

"Oh, poor brave Miss." DezPierre shook his head, his voice dripping with dismay. "Poor disillusioned Miss. You plan to go to that remote city in the White Mountains? Do you not know what a long, perilous journey that is? Few ever actually reach the borders. And you are all by yourself. I do not envy you, poor child."

Her heart sank at his words.

"DezPierre thinks you will like his Yarholm. Yes, it's very nice place. Nice people. Nice Miss can save herself such heartache and disappointment if you find a home to call your own. DezPierre come visit often. He likes his town very much, so does his kinfolk."

She remembered how far the half way point looked from Crystal's back.

"Yes, Miss would be free to do as she pleased there. Yes, indeed."

She grasped the medallion around her neck and then quickly let it go before he noticed. "I need to find my way home. I once lived there, I know it."

"Humph! Foolishness, says I. You left, Miss. That speaks volumes. There's thick forest to get through, rivers to cross, and tall mountains to climb. Ohhh," DezPierre gave an agonized cry. "Happiness is right—"

DezPierre grabbed her arm, breaking her despairing thoughts, and pulled her down behind a fallen log.

They had come upon a clearing that sloped down into a wide meadow with a lone tree growing in the middle. On one end sat the white tents she'd seen from the dragon's back. Their banners bore the tree crest matching her medallion. They were Alburnium soldiers! Would they be able to help her? Her eyes scanned the clearing, and on the opposite side was another camp partially hidden within the trees. To her dismay, they carried the Dark Lord's insignia, the crescent moon and stars. She shrank beside DezPierre. Was Bezoar down in the valley as well? Her breath lodged in her throat. DezPierre urgently tugged at her arm, motioning for her to follow him back into the woods.

He bounced from one twiggy leg to the other, wringing his hands. "We must go now. It would be bad for us to be caught here by them."

Princess, not wishing to face Bezoar hurried after him. "Do you think they spotted us?"

"I certainly hope not! I prefer to keep my head, thank you. Now we will hush and make haste. We must hurry to the town." His little brown feet scurried along past the tall pines, not slowing until they'd reached the road. Dez darted through small openings between the thick growths. Once she lost him, but his continued lamenting about *this being the worst thing ever to happen* helped her find him again.

He stopped every now and then along the path to listen with his long ears. "The woods tell me all is clear," he whispered. "They are not near yet. But soon, to be sure, yes indeed. They are terrible sneaks! Terrible soldiers. Fight. Fight. Fight. Why can't everyone just get along, eh? DezPierre thinks it all foolishness."

He ran on, not waiting for a response from Princess. She had a hundred questions, but figured she'd ask when they reached the town. Remaining in Yarholm was no longer an option, especially with Racan soldiers prowling around. She'd have to go on, one way or another.

DezPierre remained quiet for the rest of their trip, keeping up his quick pace and muttering to himself about the rotten troublemakers who spoil everything. Then he mumbled something about rallying together to fight them all off if they came anywhere near his home. He only hoped he'd get there in time to warn the others.

She spotted lights through the trees and her heart leaped. "Is that Yarholm?"

"Yes, yes, we've finally arrived," he heaved a deep sigh. "We go straight to Inn for dinner and to get you a room. I'll find my kin, indeed. They'll know what to do about this catastrophe."

# Chapter 8

The sky turned from pale blue mixed with orange to cobalt. Finally, the thick spruce parted revealing Yarholm. Princess followed DezPierre, the Okbold, into the heart of the township.

Gray clapboard buildings lined the dirt road running through the center of town. Mud splattered the warped, wooden walkways. Some of the shop windows were cracked or busted out. In the center of the village sat the skeleton of a two-story meeting hall, left unfinished long ago from the way vines and brush grew up between the framework. She wondered why they'd never bothered to finish what might have been a grand building.

If DezPierre considered this dilapidated hovel a *nice* town, he must have spent the majority of his life living in a cattle pen. Looking around, she wondered if Tarek had lived in such a place. Perhaps worse? She could see how he'd find Racah a paradise in comparison.

The Okbold walked a few strides in front of her, waving to the occasional passerby who never returned the greeting. He beamed an oblivious grin at her. "Nice, eh? Didn't I tell you?"

At the end of the street, they passed a dilapidated stable, housing several sorry-looking horses, before entering an inn. The faded wood sign over the entrance read simply, *Yarholm Inn and Bar.*

She waited just inside the door a moment for her eyes to adjust to the dark interior. The small tavern, in contrast to the ghost-town appearance outside, bustled with activity. Bodies crammed around the bar like puppies at a mother's teat.

DezPierre found a spot in a corner, near the front doors. Princess sat across from him, swiping away dirt and crumbs with the side of her hand. Faded lace curtains hung on the cracked windows and cobwebs swayed from the thick beams overhead.

Once sitting, exhaustion shrouded her unlike anything she'd

ever experienced before. Never had she walked so far in her life. *Better get used to long days of traveling if you hope to reach Aloblase. If such a hope was even possible.*

A blonde waitress arrived, a head-full of curls tumbling across her scowling face. DezPierre ordered them both roasted pork and hot tea.

"And my friend here," he gestured toward her, "will need a comfy room for the night. You give me the bill."

Princess started to protest, but he held up a gnarled hand. "Shush now, Miss. I insist." The few coins she did posses needed to go toward purchasing items for traveling anyway.

The waitress tucked a wayward lock behind her ear, giving Princess a curious look before nodding to the Okbold. When she left, DezPierre politely excused himself and hurried across the room to speak with his kin.

Princess glanced around the tavern, wondering why the other patrons kept gawking at her before turning back to their companions with a whisper. Yet, once the food arrived, she concentrated on eating instead of the people's rude stares.

The meat melted in her mouth. Her stomach rumbled appreciatively as she tore into a buttery biscuit. DezPierre, though, returned to his seat, set the crumpled napkin in his lap and daintily forked his herbed potatoes, chewing slowly as if savoring each bite. Her cheeks warmed with embarrassment over her bad manners. She had been taught better than to eat like a starved dog.

If DezPierre noticed, he didn't show it. Instead, he told her all about the villagers, what kind of houses they had and how most farmed or raised livestock for a living. "Lucky people, to have us around to help."

After a second cup of hot tea, she began to relax and enjoy the laughter, talk, and food before a group of Okbolds approached the table and asked to join them. DezPierre nodded, and Princess scooted over to make room. She felt awkward and large beside to the small creatures.

The one sitting next to her- slender like a willow with long, cascading hair-like tendrils growing from his head- was called Striphen. He leaned in toward DezPierre and whispered, "Our scout has left with our message for King Darnel's captain." His bulging eyes grew twice their normal size. "Let him know we're ready to fight, iffen it comes to such. If the pushy skunks try any tricks, we'll be ready."

Princess spewed a mouth full of tea across the table. The Okbolds stared at her in shocked surprise as she quickly apologized saying the drink was hotter than anticipated.

The phrase, *Darnel's captain* pounded in her ears. *Bezoar*! She'd fallen right into the enemy's hand! Did DezPierre realize where she'd come from? Was he keeping her close until he had the chance to turn her over to the Racan army for a reward?

Her stomach roiled, and she feared doing worse than spewing tea over everyone.

DezPierre patted her arm. "Miss, is you ill?" He explained to his friends. "The poor child was lost in the woods. Lucky DezPierre found her, yes? I help and bring her here." He leaned closer to Striphen and whispered rather loudly, "But she is sorely misguided about finding that White Road. We all know no such thing exist anymore."

Wanting to run, She leaped to her feet. The other Okbolds surrounding the table blocked her retreat. Even if she did bolt, they would certainly suspect her. She remained frozen her mind racing for a plausible excuse to get away from them.

DezPierre studied her for a second, before he opened his mouth to say something.

The doors to the inn burst open. A burly youth with an angry scowl stood in the entrance. He held a three-foot log in his upraised hand and a loaded slingshot that swayed like a pendulum in the other. His pale blue eyes scanned the now quiet room.

"I've had enough!" His voice rumbled like a snowy avalanche. "Enough of you blasted little pests planting weeds in my crops! Enough of you spoiling my milk and everything else I try to do! Heads will roll. I swear it!"

DezPierre hopped from his seat. "Oh dear, Jerin's on a rampage again. Stay here, Miss. I need to help smooth this out." He hurried off to face the irate youth.

The other creatures dove beneath the tables or behind the bar. Some even leaped through the nearest opened windows. Chairs scraped over the dirty floor. Five men surrounded the boy. Behind them, a handful of braver Okbolds stood in their shadows, DezPierre one of them.

Jerin glared at them all, his stubbly chin jutted out in contempt. He nearly matched the height of a grizzly, with sinewy arms and legs thick like pillars, though he looked no more than twenty summers.

The log swayed threateningly above his block-shaped head.

"Might as well back off," Jerin warned in a deadly tone. "This is between me and them."

A tall, lanky man rushed from the kitchens. In a soothing voice, he coaxed, "Now Jerin, you know this won't help a thing. Not one bit." Hands up with palms outward, he edged closer. "Be a good lad and go on home. Take it up with the town leaders tomorrow."

Princess spotted the blonde waitress standing behind the bar, biting her lip, brows pinched in apprehension.

Jerin shook his head. "Uh-uh. I'm not wasting my time with them anymore. They're as much afraid of these little pests as you are. Their mischief ends now!" A vein bulged along his forehead. "And it's not anybody's business, but mine. So stand back!"

One of the Okbolds, a bright green color, darted toward the door. Princess couldn't believe how fast the little creatures ran.

Jerin spotted him and quick as a blink, hurled a rock from the slingshot. The stone smacked the back of the its head, and with a screech, it tumbled over several times before landing next to a table where his kin huddled underneath. They whimpered and clung to each other in utter fright.

The wounded creature sat up, rubbing its obviously hard skull, eyes now red with anger. Crouching like a cat, it pounced toward Jerin. His stick connected at mid-jump and sent the stumpy little beast flying into the wall where it moved no more.

"That's one." Jerin turned to the men. "Now move."

Princess eased away from the table but first had to disengage two Okbolds from her skirt. They'd been clinging to the hem, trying to hide. She wove through the crowd to a place next to the bar where she had a clearer view. This was her chance to get away from DezPierre, but she had nowhere to go now that darkness had settled. Hopefully Jerin would manage to drive them all out. From the corner of her eye, she caught the blonde waitress staring at her. Princess moved away, feeling uncomfortable.

Another man on Jerin's right said, "Please listen to Rog. You don't want to go busting up his tavern, do you? Just put the stick down."

None of the men made an effort to get any closer. They seemed to fear him as much as the creatures did.

"I don't plan to bust up the tavern, Rog. Just their heads, that's all. They've got to go, and they've got to go now."

DezPierre spoke up. "Oh, come now, boy. Why all this anger? Come and have a sit with Ol' Dez, yes? We work this out. We learn to live together and get along, yes?"

"No!" Jerin brought the stick down over his head. The club hit the ground so hard, it splintered into pieces. DezPierre darted under a table and continued his peace talks from there.

"Foolish boy! Is this necessary? I tries to be reasonable. All this-" He waved his twig like arms around, "-is big mistake, yes? Perhaps you not clear all weeds from your fields before planting, eh? Is this not possible? And perhaps you set milk too close to stove and it sours, no?"

Jerin paused a moment as if considering. "No. I planted a whole field of corn and instead, produced blasted dandelions. The milk came out of the cow soured and somehow curdled into moldy cheese in a matter of a day. So, no, the mistake wasn't mine."

DezPierre glanced at the others, and with an innocent laugh, said, "Oh… well then… I thinks everyone had better… *run!*"

The room exploded in scraping chairs and upturned tables. Okbolds scattered like bugs when a light suddenly came on. Jerin swung right and left with his busted club. The men surrounding him grabbed chairs to beat the creatures with. Even the bartender found a mace from behind the bar and clobbered a few as well. Once the room cleared, the men filed back in and tried to set the place in order.

The bartender, Rog, chuckled, "Worth a bit of broken furniture to have a night's peace from the little beasts."

Princess gaped. These people actually hated the Okbolds. She let out a long breath' glad to be rid of Dez for the time being. She considered leaving right then and there, but the darkening sky stayed her. In the morning, she'd have to depart early before he found her again.

Jerin sat on a stool among the other men. The waitress, still scowling, served them each a mug. He gulped his down in one swallow. He wiped the foam from his lips. "If we band together, we can get them out of here for good. It's been done before. We can do it again, just like tonight."

The waitress spoke up, fury tainted her voice. "You think you accomplished anything? What a bunch of knuckleheads you are. All you've done is angered them. They'll be back." She shook her head while filling more mugs. "You wouldn't have so many problems if you and your Pa would just give them what they want."

Everyone around him nodded and muttered hopelessly. Princess waited at the edge of the bar, wondering if she should speak up about the Okbold's plan. She feared drawing attention to herself. What she heard next, froze her in place.

"Lydia's right, you know." A burly man in mud-caked coveralls said, "Ain't nobody around here that knows how to fight them and make them leave. An' Lydia's right about them getting us back later. All you done, you dimwit, is make more trouble for everyone."

Jerin's head sagged. "Remember the trolls? They nearly destroyed this town. Took near everything we owned. King Shaydon's warriors came and cleared them out. If only..." he sighed. "I'm tired of working and working and them ruining everything I try to do. Pa and me aren't ever going to get anywhere with them around. We have debts. We'll lose our land if we can't produce a good crop."

Lydia waved her hand. "So? You go down to the apothecary and see if he'll buy the dandelions. I hear he uses the flowers in some special kind of tea."

Jerin frowned at her.

"All we can do," she sighed, "is try to make the best of every situation."

Jerin slammed his big fist on the counter and exclaimed, "That's your solution, then? You all are going to just sit and take it? Make the best of it?"

Another man pulled a stool up beside Jerin. "Maybe so. They're not leaving their comfy little town. I heard them whispering together tonight about some meeting before you came in. Something's up with them, no doubt."

Princess blurted. "They're planning to side with Lord Darnel's army. They're camped not too far from here."

Every eye up and down the bar bore into her.

She shifted uncomfortably, figuring she'd already opened her big mouth, again. Still, he should know. "There's also a unit camped nearby with a tree emblem on their banners."

The noise level ceased until all she heard were crickets chirping outside and Jerin shifting on his stool. Perhaps she'd made a mistake. Perhaps she should have kept that information to herself. She took a step backward, clutching the key to her room. Perhaps now would be a good time to go off to bed.

The waitress called Lydia blurted. "She came in with one of their leaders, that one named DezPierre. Don't listen to her. She's probably on their side and trying to set a trap for us. Probably going to go tell them all we said."

"I am not!" Princess retorted hotly. How could the blonde woman accuse her without even knowing her? This wasn't a *nice* town in the least. "He just helped me find this place. He's not like a real friend or anything."

Chin out and back straight, she met Jerin's firm stare, despite the trembling in her knees. "I'm searching for the road to Aloblase."

She knew from his narrow-eyed expression, he was trying to measure her, see if he should listen or not. Finally he shook his head and faced his friends again.

Anger boiled up sending heat all the way up past her ears. "I don't care what any of you think. I only came here in the first place because the dragon said you'd be willing to help me."

"Dragon?" repeated Rog.

Jerin stood, towering over her. "There are no dragons around here... unless... you're referring to the one belonging to the Dark King? The one that guards his lands?" He shook his head, waving his hands. "Can't be. Nobody's ever seen that blasted monster and lived to tell about it."

"I didn't mean..." Princess stammered. "I meant ..."

Lydia eased up behind her. Princess felt a tug on her singed hair. She spun to find the woman had a strange look of wide-eyed shock.

Regaining her composure, Lydia smirked with a forced laugh. "Girl, you can fool some of these people, but I've seen and heard everything. I think you should go on and save your fairy tales for the fireside, eh?"

Gritting her teeth, she fought the urge to tell the whole lot of them off. Better to not draw any more attention to herself.

*Fine, then.*

Off from the main room hung a sign reading Guest Rooms and pointed toward a hallway. She turned and stormed away from the group, heading down the long corridor searching the door numbers for the match to the number on her key. Hysterical laughter echoed after her.

# Chapter 9

Princess dumped the backpack's contents onto the narrow straw bed, reviewing her provisions. She marveled at everything the light-weight pack held, but was there enough to get her to Aloblase? She counted ten gold coins all with the tree emblem. Racan money had Darnel's face on both sides. Which did they take in Yarholm?

She sighed, realizing how ignorant she'd appear going around asking stupid questions normal people should know. If only Dean hadn't sacrificed himself. She closed her eyes, not wanting to think about him anymore. Nor Tarek's refusal to escape with her. Though he expected her to come crawling back. A pang twisted her gut as she realized she might never see him again, because she'd never return. No matter what. Better to push both of them out of her mind and focus on what was ahead, not behind.

A wobbly table, topped with a washbasin and mirror, sat in the corner. A bath would feel wonderful. Such niceties had to wait until she found a more hospitable place. Her torn dress needed to suffice as well.

She splashed water on her face, then peered into the mirror. A gasp escaped at the sight staring back with tangled brown hair, dark circles beneath honey-brown eyes, and scrapes across the cheeks. Must have happened when she'd run away from the witch's house. She shuddered, not wanting to think about that right now either. Too bad the amazing pack didn't contain a brush. Dragging her fingers through her locks, she hoped for the best, but finally gave up. Who cared anyway?

Returning to the bed, she picked up the small leather book. Inside the cover she read: *Sir Dean, the King's Messenger.* A lump formed in her throat. She held up his medallion and pulled hers from inside her bodice. Slipping the chain through hers, she let them rest together around her neck. Every time she sought comfort from hers, she'd be reminded of what he'd done for her and reminded to never stop until she reached her destination. No more thinking about settling down. Somehow, she'd get to Aloblase.

A knock sounded at the door. She froze, her thumb pressed on the silver edges of Dean's book. *Please don't be DezPierre.* She wanted no more to do with that blasted creature.

Princess answered to find Lydia, Rog, and Jerin. Lydia introduced herself, and the two men both looking uncomfortably sheepish. To her surprise, they all filed in uninvited.

"We need to talk to you." Lydia ordered, arms crossed over her chest.

Rog took a chair and placed it next to the window. Jerin sat on the edge of the bed, clasping his big hands in front of his knees.

Princess quickly scooped her belongings into the pack. "Look, I don't know what all this is about, but I don't want any trouble. I'll be out of here in the morning."

"Trouble is what you got, dearie," Lydia answered. "Whether you want it or not. There were unfriendly ears out there that heard your remarks about the dragon." Her hands went to her hips as she placed herself directly in front of Princess. "If you've been tangled up with the Racan King's beast, and from your scorched hair and clothes, I'd say you were. Then there may be a price on your head."

Princess's mouth dropped. She sank onto the bed, heart pounding. They were going to turn her in. Glancing at the door, she considered running. The woman must have read her expression because she sidestepped to block the exit.

Jerin stood with an awkward bow. "Please excuse Lydia, Miss. She's all business. Sounds like maybe you have an interesting story. We just need to be certain you're not on-" He lowered his voice to a whisper, "-King Darnel's side."

"Since you came in with one of his servants, we're a bit concerned. I'm sure you understand?" Rog finished.

Words clotted in her throat as she realized how close she'd come to being caught. And so soon. She hadn't even gotten out of the shadow of Master's castle yet.

"She don't look good," Rog wagged his head.

"Where you from, kid?" Jerin sounded interested. "And what is your name?"

Princess glared at him, wondering if she should trust anyone. Especially someone who called her kid. She might not know her age, but she knew she'd outgrown the "kid" status. Her mind raced to form some kind of story to pacify them. Anything to keep them from turning her in. She'd not go back.

Lydia moved to sit beside her on the bed. In a surprisingly gentle voice, she said, "We want to help you, honey. Did you escape from Racah? Or are you from another town in this area?"

Basically, she couldn't totally trust anyone. Yet, as she studied each person, she saw what she hoped was concern on their pinched faces.

"I lived in the Racah. I... I'm an orphan... and was working in the castle." She tweaked her story. "I wasn't happy there and wanted to leave. A friend-" Her throat constricted thinking of Tarek, "-told me how to get down the mountain. The dragon almost got me. But—" She shrugged her arms.

The three eyed each other with what looked like apprehension. Lydia gave a slight shudder, before turning back to her.

Jerin, leaning against a wall, rubbed at his ruffled blonde hair when he asked, "How'd you end up with that scamp, DezPierre?"

"I got lost in the woods. He seemed nice. Real polite. I had no idea Dez was one of the Darnel's servants or I would have run from him, too."

Lydia let out a low whistle. "Well, the Okbolds don't directly serve the king, but when there's a side to take, they all jump over to Racah's."

"Look," Princess said in her most authoritative voice. "I just want to find this white road. And find my way to the city called Aloblase. I might have family there. Maybe."

Finally Rog spoke up, "They'll be looking for her, Lydia. She set his dragon free. The Dark King will be furious. He'll scour every town in these woods."

"Perhaps." Lydia eyed Princess with her steel gaze. "What's your name, dear?"

Princess's mind reeled. She hated lying. The woman spoke kindly. So did the men. Then she remembered so had DezPierre. Was there anyone she could trust?

Jerin crouched in front of her as he met her gaze with the most amazing pale blue eyes she'd ever seen. "We want to help you. Honest. We're not going to turn you in. I swear." He placed a big, calloused hand over his heart. "You said earlier that the Alburnium army was near? The flags show a golden tree emblem. Is that what you saw?"

Princess nodded, wiping her damp eyes on her sleeve.

"Well, we're willing to trust you and offer help. Can't you trust us with your name?"

She ducked her head with a shrug. "I honestly don't know. Dez called me Miss. I'm fine with that."

Lydia looked her up and down. "We're you injured, dear? I've heard of people suffering from amnesia. They forget everything." She squeezed her hand. "They must have called you something where you lived."

She'd never tell another soul about that awful name.

With a loud sigh, Jerin pointed to Dean's book. "Is that a copy of *The King's Book of Letters?* I haven't seen one of them in... ages. May I?" He reached out, and she set it in his big hands.

"What is that, anyway?" she asked.

His brow cocked. "A...book of letters. From the king. Duh." He rolled his eyes.

Rog nudged the big guy, glaring at his sarcasm. "From King Shaydon. Letters he's written over time to his people." He leaned forward, looking on with interest as Jerin flipped through the pages.

Jerin's blue eyes shot from the cover where Dean's name was written, to her before he snapped the book closed. "Think you remember how to find their camp?"

She nodded taking her book back. Jerin had to suspect she wasn't being completely honest. Sweat beaded along the nape of her neck.

"Good. I'm going with you." He waved toward the couple. "Rog and Lydia are willing to offer us supplies. She even has a traveling outfit that will fit you." He studied her torn dress, forehead wrinkled in an unasked question. Blinking, he offered instead, "If you'll take me to the army's camp, I swear to get you to the highway. I need their help in fighting off these pests."

They weren't going to turn her in! Energy surged though her despite the heavy tiredness. She couldn't thank Jerin enough, and was eager to leave right away.

Lydia patted her shoulders soothingly. "You should get a good night's rest. I suggest starting out before dawn."

Jerin nodded. "I'll let Papa know where I'm going. He can handle things until I return." He faced Princess. "Stay here until I come for you. Okay?"

She promised, smiling wider than she remembered smiling in a long time.

Once they left her, she returned to her bag and carefully repacked each item. Lydia brought her a bar of soap and a brush. The extra items fit easily inside. Lydia also provided a black traveling cloak, a shirt and pants. The outfit was slightly too big, but much better than the torn dress.

Princess was so grateful, she wanted to hug the woman, but stopped herself. "I wish there was some way to repay you. This is more than—"

"Hush." Lydia waved her off. "Least I can do. One day I should make the trip myself." Wistfulness creased her brows. "I've heard that the White Road is hard to follow at times, but there are people who watch over it and are willing to help travelers. They say once you pass the Semitamon mountains, the road widens and the land is the most beautiful you'll ever see." She stared into an unseen distance. "It's like walking into a dream. Trees are bountiful with fruit and you can help yourself to as much as you like. It's as close to perfect as one could ever hope to get."

"Why haven't you already gone?"

"Well…" she looked at her husband, who'd just entered with her canteen filled. "We've had this tavern to run. Kids to bring up. We …"

"We never made the time," Rog finished. "And now here we are, helpless to protect our own town. Wouldn't be that way if we'd listened to the Alburnium warriors who came through a couple of years ago. They'd told us to send some of our people to go learn from the King's Academy. They promised we'd be taught how to keep the enemy away and how to make the land abundant. We were supposed to pick a few who would go learn and come back to teach us. But it never happened."

Lydia waved her hands, dismissing the subject despite the

glimmering dampness along her lower lashes.

"I'll leave the food pack by your door, honey. Best you get some rest before Jerin returns."

Princess nodded, but as Lydia and Rog left, she wondered if she'd find sleep tonight. Her mind spun with hope, fear, and excitement. She forced herself to move and not think about either what lay behind or in front of her.

She put on the new clothes, tied her auburn tresses into a braid. Once she lay down, sleep took her quickly.

In her dreams, a man stood before a mound of freshly turned brown earth. Princess felt like someone had ripped out her heart, her chest hurt so bad.

"Come, Alyra," the dream man held out his hand. "She's not here anymore."

"Noooo." Her child-self shook her head.

"Alyra...come. Now."

Princess bolted up and searched the darkened room. There, next to the door, sat a bag full of food.

That name. *Alyra*. Where had she heard it before?

Outside the window, harsh voices thundered through the silent township. She peeked through the lace curtains to find a group of Okbolds surrounding a large figure mounted on a black horse. Five other riders, bearing torches, sat upon shadowy mounts as well. Prickles went up her spine when she spotted Darnel's red insignia on their backs.

Bezoar! He'd come for her!

Where was Jerin? They'd never escape undetected now. Her mind raced as she shoved her feet into her boots. She threw the cloak on over the backpack. There were soldiers in town looking for her. With or without Jerin, she had to get away now.

Then another thought struck her. What if Jerin was also killed trying to help her? Like Dean? She snatched up the food bag and raced out toward the back of the hotel. No, she'd not be responsible for another person's death. If she found the camp on her own, she'd be sure to tell them about Yarholm.

Quietly, Princess slid into the predawn darkness, keeping to the shadows as much as possible. The woods surrounded the edge of the yard and she headed in that direction. Something caught hold her arm. A hand clamped down over her mouth, closing off her startled scream.

Her captor shoved her hard against a tree trunk, his dark face only inches from hers.

She cringed from his foul breath.

He whispered, "Obedience isn't one of your best qualities, is it?"

# Chapter 10

"Where have you been?" Princess shoved her hands into Jerin's boulder-like chest. Shock waves resonated up her arms. "Racan soldiers are here."

Jerin placed a thick finger over his mouth and motioned for her to follow him deeper into the trees. He turned to her with a low growl. "So happens, they are searching for a runaway. Yeah. And they say this 'runaway' is Lord Darnel's daughter."

She chewed on her upper lip, not liking where this was going. His voice dripped with sarcasm, his brows crinkling tightly over furious eyes.

"Oh, and they also said this princess *stole* his pet dragon." His eyes narrowed. "Is there something you're not telling me?"

"I'm not his daughter." Her heart skipped a few beats. She shook her head, regaining composure. "And I hate being called Princess, so don't even think about calling me that, mister!"

Jerin's mouth hung open as he stared at her. He peered over his shoulder at the sound of yelling in the street. "No time now. That little vermin you came with has told them everything. We need to hurry. Which way to the Alburnium camp?"

So Darnel definitely knew she had escaped. With the dragon. Did Master pursue Crystal, too? And what had happened to Tarek? She closed her eyes, fearing the blood rushing to her head might cause her to pass out.

Jerin's jerk on her arm brought her into focus. "Well?"

"To the south, I think."

He glared at her, tightening his grip until it hurt.

"For sure. I mean." He seemed to have the disposition of a grizzly bear freshly wakened from hibernation. She'd have to try not to anger him too much before they reached the warrior camp. Swallowing down a lump-full of doubt, she glanced past him toward the road. "The soldier's are blocking the only way I know that will get us there."

Brows scrunched in thought, Jerin studied the invaders. A slow smile spread across his block-shaped face.

"Keep hidden. I'll return in a minute." He started to leave then stopped. "This time stay put, kid." He poked her shoulder hard. Heading behind the buildings lining the main road, he added, "I mean it."

She scowled. He didn't have to treat her like a child.

Crouching behind a thick oak, she watched the street where several lanterns illuminated the riders' shadowed movements. Five watched on horseback, while nearly a dozen on foot searched the small cottage shops. Busted doors, breaking glass, and angry voices shattered the pre-dawn quiet. One rider lit a torch from the streetlight.

Bezoar's distinct voice roared, "The whole village will burn if I don't get the truth this instant."

"No," Princess gasped.

DezPierre ran from one of the buildings and stopped before Bezoar, hopping from one foot to the other. The captain reached down and grabbed the little fellow by the mossy hair on his head.

"How was I to know, sire?" DezPierre squealed. "I tells you everything, indeed. I swears it, sire, I swear! Don't hurt our nice town, sire, please!"

Bezoar hissed and hurled him into a clump of bushes.

No matter how much she disliked the Okbold, she cringed at Bezoar's cruel treatment. If not for Dez, she never would have found Yarholm. Fire burned in her chest. She'd not stand by and let him get hurt. Nor would she allow the Racan captain to set the town on fire, especially not after all Rog and Lydia's help.

Aside from giving herself up, though, what could she do? Most likely, he'd burn the place down anyway for helping her.

No! Nobody else could be harmed because of her. The guilt over Dean still hung about her neck like her pendant. She considered the main road that headed south. If she ran fast enough and led them away, then maybe, once Bezoar caught her, he'd forget about this place.

Slowly, she stood. Her legs trembled like blades of grass.

A loud bang echoed across the town, followed by several yells. She jumped at the sound.

"They've escaped with the horses!" someone hollered.

Bezoar took off toward the commotion at the stables. Most of the Okbolds and foot soldiers hurried after him.

The woods around Princess shook from splitting limbs and crunching earth. She spun, her heart leaping into her throat. A huge shadowed figure bound right for her.

Jerin reined his mount and reached for her hand. In one swift motion, she landed on the roan's back. He kicked the horse into a full gallop. Three of the Okbolds remained at the crossroad.

When DezPierre saw her, his bulbous eyes inflated. "Miss! No! Don't do this!"

Jerin pulled the club he'd used earlier from his belt loop and struck a hard blow at DezPierre. The creature flew off his feet and landed in a briar patch beside the road.

Oh, poor Dez.

Yet, she had to laugh as Jerin swung the stick around like a sword. "You'd make one heck of a warrior, Jerin."

He sat straighter in the saddle.

Her fingers dug onto Jerin's cloak as they galloped full speed into the dense trees. The pounding of hooves multiplied. Princess dared a backward glance. The black riders converged.

"They're following us. Better make this nag move."

His boots poked the horse's ribs, spurring it to run faster. "I'll have you know this fine horse is built for endurance. She's tilled miles of corn rows across the fields of Yarholm."

"Unless she's built for speed, we're done for."

The riders pursued, the distance between them closing.

"Just hang on, kid. And keep me informed on how close they get."

Jerin ducked low over the horse's mane, zigzagging through the woods in a southerly direction. The sky turned pink, making it easier to see Bezoar's troop. She didn't notice the leafy object fall from the trees until it landed on Jerin's shoulder. He yelled out as the Okbold dug sharp claws into his arm. She recognized the willowish Striphen and tried grasping a handful of the whip-like branches growing from his head. He snapped viciously at her hand.

Using the club, Jerin tried to beat him off. Striphen slid down until he hung to the hem of Jerin's cloak. Princess lifted her booted foot and stomped him in the face. With a loud wail, he fell away and was nearly trampled by the Racan soldiers.

"They're getting closer!"

"Where's the camp, kid?"

Apprehension wrapped around her throat like a tightly wound scarf. She recognized nothing. "Keep going south. There was a field. A tree grew in the middle." Dare she admit to being completely lost?

"I thought you knew where we were going?" He barked.

Nope, better not tell him. "Are we heading south? I said they were a few miles south."

He grunted, checking back at the riders closing in behind them. "I think I know of a field nearby. For your sake, better hope it's the right one."

Above, more Okbolds scampered along the tree-tops like squirrels.

"You wouldn't think such short, stumpy creatures could be so agile." She grasped his cloak tighter as their speed increased.

He passed the stick to her. "If they come too close, wallop them. Aim for their head."

She raised the bat as another Okbold attempted to hop onto Jerin. Something whizzed past her ear, lodging into the top of her weapon. The feathered end wobbled. She waved the imbedded arrow in front of Jerin's face.

"I hate to tell you this."

Jerin's head snapped around again. Princess watched as the horse raced straight for a large clump of brush. "Hey, watch out—"

Yanking the reins, he maneuvered past, then jerked back, leading the horse in a zigzagging run. Princess checked behind, her spine tingling. Another rider readied his bow. Bezoar knocked his horse into the archer. The archer's horse stumbled. She let out a long breath. Master must have demanded they return her alive. They'd have to catch her first. She laughed with satisfaction.

Their horse slid to a stop, rearing.

She tumbled off, landing hard on the leaf-covered ground. From the dense woods, another group of men dressed in earthen colored clothes burst out with arrows readied. Several shot toward Bezoar's oncoming soldiers. The black riders pulled away, splitting in different directions.

A warrior towered above, a sword pointed at her face. Another grasped the horse's reins, motioning Jerin to dismount. Two archers aimed bows at him.

He slid from the mare. "We seek refuge. I see by the emblems on your shirts you are Alburnium warriors. Please, we're being pursued."

"I see that," said the soldier guarding her. "The others are engaging that rabble filth. Now, identify yourselves."

"I am Jerin of Yarholm. Those dark soldiers attacked my town." He pointed at her. "They are seeking to capture the girl."

Princess caught the glint of a medallion peeking from the collar of one of the men's shirts. Were they like hers or Dean's? At least these men were not of Darnel's army.

The warrior poked the sword under Princess's chin. "She must be a spy of that black-hearted thief, no doubt. State your true business or be run through, traitor!"

"I'm no traitor." Princess tried to stand. The sharp point of his sword insisted she stay put.

Jerin held his hands up in surrender. "She has a fascinating story to tell. Please, we must see your highest commander first."

Shouts and the clanging of metal to metal rang through the woods around them.

The warrior standing over her motioned for the others to lower their weapons. Princess gasped when he removed his helmet, allowing long, dark braids to blow free. The soldier was a maiden!

"Whoa." Jerin's blue eyes turned into round pools.

"I am known as Carah." She pointed toward a clearing barely visible through the trees. "First we intend to rid that rabble filth from King Shaydon's lands."

Sheathing her sword, she offered Princess a hand. "When we are finished, then you may speak with General Marcel."

Carah gave a nod. The warriors closed in, grabbing their arms to bind ropes around their wrists.

"The General will then decide your fate."

* * * *

The troop dragged Princess and Jerin to the top of a rocky hill

76

overlooking an open meadow. Behind them spread nearly a hundred tents all waving flags with the Alburnium emblem, the tree with star-shaped leaves.

Carah, who held the lead of Princess's rope, pointed across the plush, green slope. Where the forest took possession of the land again, an assembly of beasts and men lined up amongst the stately spruce. Between the two opposing armies, a lone oak stood like a referee.

Princess grinned up at Jerin. "See? Told you there was a tree in the middle of the field."

He glared down at her.

"My problem, Princess, is not with what you have told me, but what you haven't." His last words rumbled into a growl.

"Don't call me Princess. Eeeerrr!" She glared back, growling her last word, too.

He cocked an eyebrow, his lip twitching at some joke only he found funny.

The cacophony of talk and clanking gear grew quiet. All eyes were focused on the opposing army. A tall, black-cloaked figure mounted upon a black steed emerged from the trees and paced before the troops. Bezoar.

Pulling on her bonds, Princess edged around behind Jerin, her heart faltering. He had her now.

Another rider, sitting on a dapple gray horse, appeared at the top of the hill, next to where they stood. The man was dressed in full military attire, his barrel chest covered with silver mail and his bronze helmet adorned with a silvery plume. His face held a calm, yet stern, expression as his piercing eyes narrowed on the dark rider below.

Bezoar spurred his stallion across the meadow, stopping at the tree. The mount danced and snorted, as if eager to charge.

"General Marcel," Bezoar called, his voice hissing like the blasting winds of a storm. "You have a traitor in your midst. She belongs to King Darnel. He wants no more than to have her back. Release her now, and we will withdraw from these lands."

Brows wrinkled over his steel tinted eyes, he momentarily turned her way. He then considered Jerin before asking Carah, "Are they whom he speaks of?"

She nodded in Princess's direction. "I believe she is, sir."

In a loud, composed voice, he responded, "None who seek help of us are turned away. You know that, Captain."

Bezoar closed the distance, stopping before the archers and spear-men, yet giving them as much interest as he would a pesky fly.

"General, I cannot imagine you wish to protect a thief. Even you will agree a criminal deserves to be held accountable of their crimes."

"You do speak of the girl child, am I correct?" Marcel leaned forward, the Baykok's repulsive smell didn't seem to faze the man in the least.

"Indeed. Do not let her small, rodent appearance fool you. She is a most insolent, trouble-maker. A thief of King Darnel's pet dragon. She stole the beast and who knows what's happened to the helpless creature now. She also released a dangerous prisoner. And these are infractions caused in just the last moon-cycle. Neither of us have the time to go over all the past misfortunes she's caused her father, the king."

"Really?" Marcel turned back to her. "Is this true, daughter?"

Jerin's face wrinkled as if he smelled something disgusting. Carah stared wide-eyed.

Indignation boiled, burning away Princess's fear. How dare he twist the truth around and make her out to be a deranged criminal?

"Unbind her. Bring her here, Carah."

The warrior maiden cut loose the rope. With a gentle nudge, Carah pushed her closer to the horsemen. Jerin followed, dragging his guard along with him.

The general asked in a grave voice, "Are the captain's accusations true?"

She met his gaze. "Most of them, sir."

From behind her, Jerin asked, "So, are you the dark one's daughter?"

Her eyes leveled on Bezoar. "No. And he knows it." She reached for the chain hanging around her neck and held up her medallion bearing the flame emblem.

Marcel blinked, shaking his head as if he couldn't believe what he saw. Carah gasped, looking from the pendant, to the general, then back to the pendant.

Bezoar's claw-like hands clenched. "She stole that, General. The messenger had one in his possession. She must have taken his."

"Dean the Messenger had this one." She held up his with the trumpet emblem. "I've had the other one since that old witch brought me to Darnel." When Bezoar sneered, she added, "Yes, I remembered when I passed her house."

Princess regarded Marcel. "Dean said anyone who possesses one of these is a citizen of Aloblase. I escaped because I want to go back home."

Several people burst out talking at the same time. She heard the word medallion, Illuminated, and prophecy before Marcel shouted for everyone to be silent.

"Well," he said, shifting on his gray horse. "This is an interesting turn of events. If she wishes to make the journey to Aloblase, she will not be deterred."

"Then you choose death." Bezoar growled, his voice sounding like steel grating against steel. "I assure you, General, the insolent girl is not worth the trouble you are bringing upon yourself."

"That is not for me to decide. King Shaydon decides such matters." He turned his horse to leave, but Bezoar whipped out his sword and sprang forward. The General already had his own sword ready. Metal clanged against metal, resounding across the valley.

Carah withdrew a bow from her quiver. In a flash, it was loaded and pointed at Bezoar along with half a dozen other arrows and spears all aimed at his shroud covered head. Jerin demanded to be cut loose. Perhaps his size worked in his behalf, for the young man guarding him brought out a dagger and sliced the rope. He even offered Jerin his weapon, but he waved it away, pulling a slingshot from his pocket instead.

Bezoar lowered his sword and pulled his horse away to a safer distance. "Return now, Princessss, and all will be forgiven. Your father is willing to forget past behaviors and start afresh." Bezoar grinned. "However, upon the King Darnel's honor, Princessss, if you do not return this very instant, I will hunt you every step of your pointless journey. You are just as much a part of Racah as I am. Our kind doesn't find acceptance in the White City. I assure you."

Her legs shook so hard, she feared they'd buckle under her weight.

Behind her, she heard Jerin's sharp intake of breath. The other warriors stared at Bezoar with pure hatred in their narrowed eyes. Even Carah muttered something under her breath that sounded like lying scum and possibly the name of a creature that lived in such places.

"Daughter." Marcel's voice was quiet and calming like rustling leaves. "You must make a choice. Do you wish to return to Racah, or undertake the journey to Aloblase?"

The words 'journey to Aloblase' rang in her ears. Perhaps if she did return peacefully, Master would keep his promise. She could even demand for Tarek's release from his punishment, too.

However, if she refused, if she ran for her dream, she might actually make it. But then what? What exactly did she hope to find? If only she remembered her life before Racah. She looked again at Jerin. He refused to meet her eyes. The warriors simply stared at their hated enemy, waiting. There would be no peace. Bezoar would constantly hunt for her. If he captured her…she shuddered, not wanting to let that thought form a mental picture. The hate dripping from his angry scowl told her he meant every word of his threat.

Then she caught sight of General Marcel sitting upon his horse, sword lowered but ready. A calm, somewhat amused smile played at his lips; a smile that seemed to say it would all work out. His steely eyes met hers and he gave her a quick wink.

All trembling stopped. Her breath returned to a normal rhythm. Dean had promised the warriors would keep her safe. Marcel's confident demeanor caused her to believe him.

Princess backed away from Bezoar. "I'm not going back to that land of living death. Tell Darnel this is what I think of his offer." She spat on the ground.

With a fierce yell, Bezoar raised his sword. The General bounded in between him and Princess. Jerin grabbed her by the cloak and yanked her out of the way.

Bezoar yanked his horse backward, forcing it to jump out of the General's reach.

Carah leaped onto a rocky overhang where she stood over everyone. "Mighty Warriors…" Her deep voice trumpeted from her small frame and rolled across the valley like thunder rolls across a stormy sky. "Mighty warriors of King Shaydon! Take up your weapons!"

The clang of swords banged in her ears.

The warriors surrounding them chimed, "Take up your weapons and fight!"

"FOR FREEEEDOM!" Carah's voice rang like gongs from a bell tower, pulsating right into Princess's heart. A group of soldiers, carrying drums and horns joined her, their voices matching her chanting rhythm.

Bezoar reared his steed, his face twisted in pain, and raced over the swaying grasses toward his troops.

With a mighty shout, the Alburnium troops surged forward, raining arrows across the valley into the enemy forces.

Marcel spurred his stallion after the captain. "Let's rid the King's land of this filth. To arms!" Swordsmen charged behind their leader, cutting down anything that stood in their way. Clanging metal and pained yells filled the valley.

Drums beat boom-boom, ba-boom-rum. The tempo grew faster and fiercer. Windpipes joined in, flowing across the meadow like a summer gale. Something inside Princess's chest stirred with excitement. Her fist clenched with the desire to fight.

The louder Carah's troop sang and played, the more disorganized the enemy soldiers became. Most ran for cover in the thick woods, the rest were taken down by Marcel and the warrior's mighty weapons. The Racan troops scrambled in confused circles, as the leaders tried to regain order and form a stable line.

Jerin stood gawking at the sight, his loaded sling hung limp in one hand as rocks dropped from the other, one by one.

Carah sang, "Victory is ours!" followed by the others resounding calls of "Victory is ours for our Mighty King!"

The Alburnium warriors cleared the field of what was left of the dark army.

Princess's mind reeled in fear, surprise, and disbelief. Realizing she'd escaped being captured by Bezoar once again, her legs gave out, and she crumpled onto the soft ground.

Victory was indeed sure and victory was quick. A loud pop sounded, followed by sparks and smoke that threw several fighters off their feet. Bezoar was there one moment and when the smoke cleared, he was gone. She knew that trick. Many of the heads of military kept the explosive powder handy for magical escapes like that. If only he would disappear for good.

Jerin remained beside her. "I've never ..."

Princess looked up at him, and chuckled at the stunned expression on his pale face.

"I've never seen a battle like this. Never." He gaped at Carah, his hand over his heart as he stared, open-mouthed, in complete adoration of the maiden warrior. "She. Is. So. Awesome."

Carah, turned and gave him a crooked, knowing smile. "What did you think of that, young warrior?"

"That..." he stammered, "That was *sooo* amazing."

"You bet'cha it was."

# Chapter 11

Sparks from bonfires shot high into the dusky sky. Lyres, flutes, and tom-toms played as dancers twirled and sang amidst much laughter. In the middle of the camp, Racan weapons and other gear lay in a pile.

The smell of roasted boar and deer filled the air.

Princess sat with a group of ten, her stomach full and her mind finally calmed from the fright of facing Bezoar. For the first time in a very long while, she was happy. If only the *What if's* and *What nows?* would stop pounding on the door of her consciousness. She wanted to enjoy this moment, and the euphoria of having slipped from Bezoar's claws. His threat to hunt her all the way across Alburnium still rang in her ears and churned her gut. She'd push that aside for now.

"It's true!"A boy, of around nine years, drew her attention when he jumped atop a flat boulder, his freckled face set in a defiant scowl. "I was lost in the woods and the centaur gave me a ride home. Didn't he, ma?"

Intrigued, Princess straightened. She'd heard that centaurs were used in Darnel's army, but she'd never seen one in person. She glanced around at the warriors surrounding the fire, wondering why no creatures fought with these men and women.

The boy's mother, an older woman wearing a red dress and tan smock, nodded. "I'd never been so frightened and surprised in all my life. He weren't like any of them other centaurs we've often fought against." A shuddered went through her as she stirred a pot of stew.

"They are pure vicious, them beast." She tasted a steamy spoonful of the meaty soup. Grabbing a handful of some kind of pungent plant, she crumpled the leaves over the pot. "Been pulled from their nursing mama's and trained to kill, they have. But this one, he weren't wild at all. Didn't seem so anyway. Then again, he didn't say nothing to me. Jus' dropped Jeremy off and disappeared back into the woods."

The group muttered a collective gasp, some shaking their heads, others nodding in understanding.

One man, whom Princess had seen with the archers on the battlefield, said, "We was lucky today. That captain was just leading a scouting troop." The man's gaze fell on Princess. "Will bring a full unit of nasty beasts with him when he comes back. I'd rather shoot the monsters afore they get me. Been face to face in battle with too many of 'em."

Tapping her large wooden spoon on the pot, the mother nodded, "Never would'a thought them creatures to bother helping us. They normally don't give heed to two-leggers, except to attack and pillage innocent towns."

"I agree!" Jerin joined the group. He held a greasy pork bone in his hand which he'd nearly completely cleared of meat. Grease and bits of fat clung to the downy hair growing over his chin. "They are savages and nothing more. The whole blasted lot of them, Okbolds, dwarves, all of them. Unnatural creations that should be avoided."

Princess gaped at him, nose wrinkled in disgust. Somebody needed to hand him a napkin.

Confused, she shook her head. Maybe Dez had been on the enemy's side, but he helped her and treated her with kindness. Despite the fact he turned her over to Bezoar. Crystal might also be lumped into the beast category. Where would Princess be today if the dragon hadn't flown her down the mountain? Even if Crystal did kill Dean, she'd done it out of fear, not malice. What about the others that served Darnel? Were they willing servants, or forced slaves?

Did motivation matter to those from Aloblase? If they found out how she had served Lord Darnel, would they consider her a beast or traitor as well?

Jeremy jumped down from his rock and stood before Jerin. The youth had to crane his head to meet his eyes. "I disagree, sir. I was lost and scared, and he helped me get back home. He could'a left me lost in the woods, you know." The boy looked around at the others sitting in the group. "Don't forget they have just as much right to be part of King Shaydon's family as the rest of us,.."

Jerin cocked an eyebrow at the lad, then snorted a reply.

Princess spotted General Marcel approaching. She cringed over having to meet with him soon. What should she tell him? Would he still be willing to help when learned the truth about her? She sighed, remembering all of Bezoar's accusations. Already they knew more than she cared for anyone to know.

Everyone greeted him warmly, offering him food and drink, but he refused graciously. He sat on a fallen log beside Princess. Firelight shone off his solemn gray eyes as he took in each person, finally stopping on the lad. A small grin puffed his beard.

"I find your conversation interesting." He picked up a stick and drew a large X in the dirt. "The simple truth is this: there is only one true heir to the Great King." Making a circle around the X, he added, "The rest of us are simply included in his realm by invitation. I can't help but feel saddened over the divisions in our kingdom. It hasn't always been this way.

"Unfortunately, lies and treachery have brought about much animosity between the different inhabitants for ages." The stick wove around and through the circle, distorting the firm lines.

The boy folded his skinny arms. "Maybe now's the time for change. They are wonderful creatures, the centaurs, dragons, and all. Those who are for the King anyway."

General Marcel chuckled and patted Jeremy's shoulder. "Indeed, bright son of Aloblase. Perhaps you will be given the opportunity to bring such changes about."

Jeremy beamed.

The General's gentle voice and confident air, even when face-to-face with a Baykok, had won her over. She'd never met anyone who set her troubled mind at peace like he did.

He stood and motioned for her and Jerin to follow him.

Princess started after them, but stopped next to the boy first. "You're right about dragons. I met one and she saved my life, like the centaur saved yours. They can't possibly be as bad as the others think."

He grinned, revealing a gap between his front teeth she found endearing.

As she caught up with Jerin, Marcel explained, "I've called a council meeting and wish for the two of you to attend. We'll discuss our next move and need your input."

Jerin's chest puffed. "Certainly, sir."

Princess remained quiet. A nagging worry pecked at her heart. Marcel said all were welcomed into the kingdom. Did the invitation extend to Racan filth? Bezoar had said there was no place for people like them in Aloblase. Dean told her Aloblase was her home. Said she'd met King Shaydon at some point, and he'd given her the medallion. If only she remembered....

Would King Shaydon even want her, a servant for the dark lord, to return?

They entered a large tent set in the center of camp. Several lamps flickered along the rectangular table, casting wavering shadows that danced against the linen walls. Jerin took a seat across from her, Carah sitting on a cushioned bench beside him. He fidgeted with his slingshot, his cheeks flushing a dark pink every time she tried to include him in the conversation with the other warriors.

Princess studied the group of men and women seated around her. Though they seemed friendly, their stern looks of determination and strength made her shiver. Then she remembered Dean the Messenger. He'd had that same expression.

General Marcel raised his hand, and the room instantly grew quiet. He gazed upon both Jerin and then her, and his mouth turned up in a kind smile before he cleared his throat and called the meeting to order.

"Warriors of Alburnium." He stretched out his arms. "Let's first take a moment to consider our gratefulness for a swift victory over our enemy today. Then we will discuss how to best help our two new friends."

Everyone stood and clasped their arms together as they all said in unison, "We are thankful to our King for this victory."

The general added, "We seek wisdom on what course to follow next and the courage to follow it through."

Their upturned faces puzzled her. Who were they talking to? Then an amazing thing happened; the walls of the tent began to sparkle with a glistening light which moved about like dust particles in a sunbeam.

Marcel finished with, "We thank you for the chance to give aid to your lost children. We thank you for the ability to re-take what was rightfully yours from the start."

She blinked her eyes tightly shut, wondering if lights weren't all in her head. Maybe she was coming down with something. Then a warm breezed caressed her cheek and ruffled her hair. Goosebumps flowed up her arms and down her back, yet she felt comforted, not frightened. Since nobody else seemed to notice the dancing lights, she kept it to herself.

Everyone returned to his or her seat. First item up for discussion was the actual battle. The warrior to Marcel's right stood and reported only a handful of warriors suffered minor injuries. One serious but stable and resting in the medic tent. The enemy soldiers that hadn't fled before the charge were engaged and killed. Bodies had been burned, and the plunder collected. They would disperse the items to the neighboring towns as needed.

Marcel nodded when the speaker took his seat.

"So, Jerin of Yarholm, if you'll please stand and tell us about the condition of your town?"

Jerin gave his report, ending with, "this is why I've asked to be trained here, with all of you. Then I can go back and clear away the pest." He sat heavily, nearly tumbling off his cushion, before quickly righting himself. Redness crept up his neck.

"You wish to attempt this on your own?"

"If that's what it takes, sir." Jerin shrugged, still keeping focused on the lantern in front of him, his square-shaped jaw set in a firm line.

Marcel's thick brows arched as his steely eyes bore intently on the large boy. Jerin seemed unwilling to meet the general's stare. Princess wondered why.

"Is this your calling, son? Do you possess the medallion of a warrior?"

Jerin shook his head. "No, sir. I've not journeyed to Aloblase, yet."

"Yet? Have you been asked to go before?" General Marcel rested his chin on the tips of his fingers.

"Yes." The flush tingeing his neck red began to flow up toward his temples.

"And the reason you did not?"

"A group from my town was planning to travel together. They could never agree on a time to leave." The large boy avoided the stares of the others gathered around the table.

Jerin squirmed on his cushion, twisting the slingshot between his hands. Her heart went out to him, being drilled like this. Sweat beaded along the back of her neck, wondering how they'd treat her when she spoke.

"So why not make the trip yourself?" Marcel dug, though his voice remained gentle. She didn't feel he was being overly harsh with Jerin. More than anything, she feared how she'd handle herself when her time came. Knowing her propensity for rash words and ill behavior, she slouched lower, wishing she could somehow disappear.

Jerin closed his eyes and lowered his head. "I guess...sir...to be honest, everything was going good. I didn't see the need to go."

A low murmuring went around the table, as some shook their heads.

Marcel leaned forward on his elbows and asked Jerin, "What say you now, son? How would you feel about receiving your training in Aloblase? That is where we all received our knowledge."

Jerin sighed, his fist tightening around his small weapon. "General, I truly desire to meet King Shaydon. My greatest dream has always been to go there. Someday. But right now, Yarholm needs me. I know I can fight. I'm good at it."

Princess had to nod in agreement after seeing how he handled the Okbolds.

"I see," replied Marcel. He took in a deep breath and sat quietly for a minute. Finally he said, "I will give my decision after all have had a chance to speak." He asked a few more questions concerning how many in Yarholm had made the trip to Aloblase, what was the state of the township, and if there had been other enemy presence.

"Aside from the trolls that invaded us some years back, there's been no other Racan disturbances until the Dark Lord's soldiers came looking for her."

His foot nudged her from beneath the table. Her gut lurched.

"We managed to escape," He added, his voice taking on that growl she'd started to grow accustomed to. "She had promised to lead me to you, and I promised to help her find the White Road. It is her desire to meet the King."

"I see." General Marcel's gaze now turned to Princess. Instead of the stern look he'd given Jerin, he actually smiled. "Tell me, child, how you came to meet up with young Jerin here. I've heard part, but I wish to hear your version of whole story."

Princess swallowed down a fist-sized lump of nervousness clogging her throat. Would they believe her? More importantly, would they still want to help if they did?

General's kind, gray eyes held the same calm confidence that had emboldened her to stand up to Bezoar.

Clearing the apprehension from her throat, she determined to be as honest as possible with the General and take her chances. "Darnel tried to convince me that I was his daughter. That I'd always been in Racah. Yet," she pulled out the chain with the two medallions linked together. Several sharp gasps sounded around the table. Carah leaned forward, eyes narrowed as she studied the disks more closely.

"I knew I came from somewhere else. I've always had these dreams, about a city. A beautiful city. Master tried to get me to accept his ways. But those dreams, I…" she shook her head, staring into the depths of one of the burning candles. She snorted a derisive laugh. "He thoughts sending me to work in the dungeons would finally break me. But I preferred cleaning cells and sleeping on a pile of hay. Finally, I didn't have to see Master every day. The cold and dirt was worth it."

Ben, despite his temper, treated her well enough as long as she did most of the chores for him. At first, he was ordered to lock her in the cell where they'd kept Dean. Then, seeing an opportunity to ease his burden, Ben talked Master into letting her work for him, promising to whip her into shape.

"I had bits of time to search the tunnels for a means of escape. I'm not sure there is such a tunnel, but I've heard some have actually made it down the mountainside."

She thought about Tarek again, worry poking her heart. Did Master know he helped her escape? Would he kill him if he did?

Carah's eyes widened. "You've traveled through the secret places of the dark lands?"

"Well, yeah. Tunnels run all throughout the mountains."

"Sir, did you—"

He held up his hands to stop her. "Yes, Carah, I'm sitting right here as you can see." This brought a round of chuckles.

"What I wish to know, daughter, is why you finally decided to escape?"

Princess twirled the medallions between her fingers. "Because of Dean the messenger. He knew... me." She grasped his medallion and held up. "He was captured and brought in with a group of prisoners. He called Darnel an imposter, a liar." The disk blurred. "Master was going to kill him, but I suggested the dragon." Her voice cracked. "We made a deal. I would help him escape, and he would take me to Aloblase."

She dared a look at Marcel to find tears pouring down his cheeks. Hers let loose as well.

"Please understand, General. The dragon *had* to keep us from escaping. Not because she was evil. Darnel would hurt her if anyone got past her. Dean... he went back to fight her, to give me a chance to escape."

Marcel nodded. "Dean traveled with us for awhile, then struck off on his own. He was to seek out towns in need of aid and send word for us to come. How did you obtain his medallion, child?"

Princess took in a ragged breath, her voice clogged on the emotions gathering in her chest. She stared at the gold disk, unable to take the General's pained expression. "Before... for some reason, he gave me his pack and asked me to make sure I returned his medallion to King Shaydon. I'm afraid, for some stupid reason, he made a decision to sacri—" She couldn't say the word, sacrifice. Shame glued her mouth. He had no idea she wasn't worth what he did.

Everyone remained silent for a long moment. Focusing past the medallions, Princess saw Jerin's face set in a scowl. Was it from her not telling him the whole truth? Perhaps he believed what Bezoar had said about her.

"General," Carah whispered. "Could she be the one? The light that will come out of dark?"

General Marcel cleared his throat and gave Carah a warning look. "Finish your story, daughter."

Princess described her escape with Crystal and how she ended up meeting Jerin in Yarholm. "Despite what he says about Dez, the creature helped me when I was lost."

"Then he went and ratted you out to the enemy soldiers," added Jerin with a smirk. "Some friend."

"I didn't say—"

General stood, wiping a sleeve across his face. "Very well." He interrupted. "Does anyone have anything to add?"

Carah's hand shot into the air. "What about her medallion? What about the prophecy? Her knowledge of Racah? It all seems to fit, doesn't it?"

"Does anyone have anything else to add, besides that?"

"General!" protested Carah.

Jerin sided with the maiden warrior. "I'm interested in this thing about her medallion, sir. Who's to say she didn't steal them?"

Princess glared at him.

"Or find...perhaps?" He added hastily.

"I'm not a thief!" Princess stood, banging the table with her fist. "I know little of my past. Not where I came from, or what my real name is. I do remember a witch taking me to Darnel and selling me for some coins. And I know," she clutched the medallion with the flame burst. "This has always been with me, and I've always felt the need to keep it hidden. And I did. All those years, I kept it a secret."

She turned to General Marcel. "I doubt there's any prophesy about someone like me. Bezoar's description of me is basically true. I cause trouble for everyone." *Tarek, Ben, Dean...* and no telling how many others. "I don't get what the fuss is about. I'm nothing but a Racan slave, sir. I just want to get away from Darnel, as far away as possible."

"Daughter," Marcel asked. "Do you know the meaning of the emblem on your medallion?"

"No sir." She grasped the chain and stared down at the flame.

He nodded. "Do you remember your age when you entered Racah?"

She shrugged. "Five, maybe six. I can't recall much except looking for something...or someone. I don't know, sir."

He leaned in closer to her and held out the pendant hanging around his own neck. Two swords crossed over a tree on his.

"Each of us carries a medallion according to our purpose, or what our natural talents incline us to do in this life. As you see,

Dean's has a trumpet on his signifying he had an ability to *trumpet the truth*, so to speak. He was a messenger, gifted with persuasive speech. He called people to listen to the truth, wherever he went. There are many types of messengers. Some of us, you may notice, have different kinds of weaponry, and some have weaponry with instruments or other objects. There are many types of warriors, too."

He gestured toward the maiden warrior. "Carah can frighten the enemy with her rebel call." Several people laughed, nodding in agreement. Carah clutched her own medallion, which Princess realized also had a trumpet loaded like an arrow in a bowstring.

Now he looked each warrior sitting around the table in the eye. "The important point, my friends, is that only King Shaydon can tell a person what his or her purpose in the kingdom is." To this, they also nodded their affirmation, each most likely having stood before the king at one time or another. Marcel's gaze paused on Jerin for a long moment, before he turned back to her.

"At some point in your life, daughter, you met King Shaydon and he's told you of your purpose. However, in an attempt to control you, Darnel blocked those memories from your mind. I have no doubt, my dear child, that as you get closer Aloblase, your memories will return and you'll remember what you are meant to do. It is not up to us, or up to any prophecy to dictate that to you.

"So I find it imperative we get you on the White Road, and you can begin your journey home."

Home? She liked the sound of that. Maybe she still had a real family somewhere and the King could help her find them.

"As for our young warrior friend, Jerin. I've decided that we will go to your town and assist the people in ridding themselves of these Okbolds."

Jerin sat up, face lit with excitement. "Oh, sir, I...it's more than I expected. How can I thank you?" He looked at Princess and grinned before adding, "I am in your debt, General. I'll work hard to learn from all of you."

The General let out a long breath. His gaze met Carah's and they seemed to have some sort of understanding. "Your training will not come from us, son. I believe the best course for you and your town will be for you to go on to Aloblase with the girl child."

His grin drooped as the color drained from his block-shaped

face. "But, sir...."

Everyone rose and followed the General from the tent as he issued orders for departure.

Only Princess heard Jerin's last whispered words.

"I can't possibly go with...her."

# Chapter 12

The carriage rolled along quietly beneath the midday sun. Princess shifted her achy legs, her body moving like stiff cloth. The effects of her escape and long walk had finally taken its toll. Strange how only three nights had passed since leaving Racah. She closed her eyes and gave in to the swaying of the transport, not wanting to think about the distance remaining.

Jerin slumped next to her, quiet and sullen. Across from them sat Carah, who continually watched the dense forest outside the curtained window, her slender fingers running over the string on her bow.

Beside the maiden warrior, General Marcel attempted to make notes in a journal, despite the bumps and jolts. He tapped the graphite rod on the page twice before closing the cover. For a moment, Princess swore the letters actually lit up. He slipped the book in his shoulder bag, giving her a wink.

Marcel turned to Jerin. "I will get word to your father of your decision to journey to Aloblase. Do not worry, son. He will be well taken care of in your absence. I swear upon my honor."

Jerin shifted in his seat and despite any misgivings said, "I'm grateful for your word, sir."

Carah turned to him with a warm smile. "You will learn from the best, Jerin." She leaned in closer and rested her hand on his arm which caused his cheeks to turn crimson. "I trained at the academy, too, and plan to return next season. I know you'll love it. I'll be eager to hear the stories of your travels when I get back."

The bright flush crept over his forehead and ears. Princess realized he'd grown very fond of the maiden warrior. Perhaps that was part of the reason he didn't want to leave.

Marcel interjected, "Traveling to Aloblase is the wisest course of action for you, Jerin. Even though you desire to be a warrior, it may not be the King's desire for you."

"But sir…" Jerin protested.

"Besides, the girl-child will need someone along to help her."

"No I don't." Princess retorted. "I've done fine on my own."

Jerin snorted a laugh. "Like when you picked DezPierre to be your guide."

"I didn't pick—!"

"The decision has been made." General Marcel held up both hands to stop their bickering. The carriage jolted to a halt. "You two can settle your differences on the road." He opened the door on his side and stepped out.

Carah gave his arm a gentle squeeze. "Of course, you have the choice to completely reject the General's suggestion and do whatever you want." She opened the opposite door and climbed down. "Though I've never seen such choices turn out well. Still it's yours to make."

Princess waited a moment, watching Jerin, who remained slouched in his seat with a look of utter bewilderment. She shook her head and left him to work out his thoughts. Though it would be nice to have a traveling companion, she didn't need a babysitter. And she didn't need anyone along who didn't want to be there in the first place.

Several warriors surrounded the carriage. Upon the General's orders, they dispersed and faded into the woods to scout the area.

The troop had stopped at a wide-lane crossroad. She wondered which of the four roads led to Aloblase.

Jerin handed down the packs from the top of the transport.

Carah helped her with the backpack. "We've stocked you with jerky and wafers. Should last about a week. As you travel, gather food growing along the highway. You can refill your canteens from the springs you will pass. Be careful which you fill from though. Be sure the steams run from the east."

Then Carah cupped Princess's face in her hands. "May you stay safe on your journey and may you find allies during your travels. Take care and remain on the path. Help will be found when you need it, for such is the way." She gave her a quick hug. "Until we meet again."

"I hope we do." Princess wished she had more time with Carah.

Would they have been friends? She seemed goodhearted and level-headed. Why couldn't she come along on the journey with her instead of that obstinate warrior-wanna-be?

Jerin joined them, shoulders slouched and his mouth turned down in unhappy resolve. Carah handed him the food pack and whispered something that caused him to smile before she went to stand by the general.

Princess studied the three byways. The carriage was parked on the one leading westward. Off to her left the road wove in a northeasterly direction across an open field before disappearing over a hill. The center one, lined with tall oaks, pointed straight east. The one to the right headed due south. "I guess we'll be taking the middle lane?"

Jerin shook his head. "None of these are the King's Highway."

"But I thought—"

General Marcel held up a hand to quiet her. "The way is narrow. Few find it and even fewer take it." He pointed at the ground and said, "Look down here, child. Do you see the white glistening rocks?"

Both Jerin and Princess looked, trying to discern the white rocks from the others.

"Behold, the White Road also called the King's Highway." General's hand swept across the white rocks sparkling discretely beneath the dust and leaves. They formed a path that led between the east and south road, right into the heart of the woods.

"You have to be kidding me!" Princess said. "That's nothing more than a foot trail. It's hardly wide enough for us to walk side by side."

Carah stepped forward and began to sing in a sweetest voice Princess had ever heard.

"Listen my children, hear what I say,
And may the tread of your feet be wary."
Those standing around her joined her in the chorus.
*"Follow me, follow me, follow me home.*
Let me guide you by night and by day,
Through forest, mountain, and prairie.
*Follow me, follow me, follow me home.*
Turn not from this path or be led astray.

Follow me, as I provide the safest way.
*Follow me, follow me, follow me…home."*

Princess stood to the edge of the woods, staring down at the glistening rocks, as she considered the song. The melody and words tugged at her racing heart as her feet wriggled with the desire to start moving. Every muscle and nerve tingled with anticipation. *Home.* Was there such a place she could call by that name?

"What do I do if it branches like these roads do?"

"It won't," said Carah. "Many other roads will join in as you go along, but they all head in the same direction. If you do get off the path, continue east until you come upon it again. No matter what, always face the rising sun."

Princess turned to Jerin, wondering what he would choose. All other eyes seemed to be on him as well.

General Marcel cleared his throat, getting everyone's attention. "Jerin, have you made your decision?"

Jerin nodded his assent.

"Very good." Marcel scanned the group, stopping on them. "So you head for the same destination, though for different purposes. You will find harmony in accepting both the sameness and differences between you. Where one lacks, the other may have abundance. Look to each other's strengths and be humble in weakness."

The general gave a quick whistle for everyone to gather closer. "We leave you now to travel to Yarholm. Our hope is to be there by nightfall. Stay on the white path, and you will remain safe."

He bowed. Jerin and Princess returned the gesture.

Before Marcel entered the carriage, Princess ran after him, and made one final request. "Sir, if I may please ask?"

He faced her expectantly.

"If by chance you do catch the Okbold called DezPierre, please don't kill him." She glanced over to Jerin who rolled his eyes in annoyance. So what. "I know he's a servant of Lord Darnel, but he helped me. He even paid for my dinner and a room. I would have been lost in those woods if not for him. I just ask…." She hesitated, unsure, then she finished, "Not all in the dark lands are evil. They are stuck like I was. You know?"

General Marcel nodded reassuringly. "I'm touched by your request and will remember it if we do meet this Okbold." His foot met the step before he stopped and added, "You are right. Many are merely a choice away from freedom, child. Never forget that."

He entered the carriage, and they headed toward the west, the one place Princess never wanted to return. So she turned her face toward the east, looked longingly at the wide road, and then followed Jerin along the narrow path leading into the dense forest.

*  *  *  *

They walked for the rest of the day in near silence, Princess in front with Jerin right on her heels and snapping at her to walk faster. The path of white rocks wound through woods so dense they could barely push through. Finally, exasperated at their slow pace, Jerin took the lead hacking away the undergrowth with a sword the warriors had given him. Carah had provided her with a dagger, similar to Dean's. The weapon fit nicely in her backpack.

Jerin remained sullen and constantly nagged her to walk faster. She found him to be terrible company and tended to keep to her own thoughts in hopes he would eventually lighten up.

The first two days were uneventful. They walked from sunrise until high noon when he'd allow them to break for a small meal. Then they'd be off again until the sun turned pink in the western sky. Jerin would search for a covered spot in a cluster of trees or brush growing beside the trail for them to rest. At first, every inch of her body hurt and each step was agony. As the miles passed, her muscles grew accustomed to the pace. By the third day, she finally kept up with Jerin who eased on calling her a castle brat.

The nights were most difficult for Princess. Between the strange forest noises and the vivid visions plaguing her sleep, she often woke still tired and irritable. The dream-man, who called her Alyra, visited her nightly. Could that possibly be her real name?

Since entering the white road, a new character now visited her night visions. A glowing woman who stood with arms outstretched. Yet, when her dream-self tried to get closer, the woman always vanished.

"Hey, look." Jerin broke into her reverie. He pointed to a spot on the ground near the path. "That millipede is passing us, I swear it." His blue eyes narrowed on her.

98

She scowled back, but upped her pace. General Marcel had promised they would come across several towns and homesteads along the way where they could stop to restock and rest. And bathe. Oh what she'd do for a hot bath.

Any place that might offer her a short break from the sullen troll-head would be paradise to her.

Eventually, the woods thinned, allowing a breath of fresh air and late afternoon sunlight. Jerin found a bush of wild raspberries growing beside the path, and they both gathered a handful. Not nearly enough to make a meal.

"Let's stop by this steam for the night. You collect wood, I'll see about rounding up some dinner." He dropped his pack on the shore. "Maybe we can catch a couple of fish."

"Catch fish?" Princess collapsed on the mossy bank.

After checking to make sure the water flowed from the right direction, she took a long drink from her cupped hands. Amazingly, it always had a hint of fruity sweetness. She let her tired feet soak in the coolness for awhile. Wouldn't all steams flow from the east? She had no idea. Nor did she have any idea on how to go about catching a fish.

"Yes, little miss castle brat, we will need to hunt and find food along the way." He shook his head while digging out a small tinder box from his bag which stored hooks, string, and fire-starters. "Go make yourself useful and gather some wood." Jerin fashioned two fishing poles from his kit.

Princess bit back the evil retort pounding on her lips to get out. Finding broken limbs along the white path was easy enough. She'd tripped over several during her walk when her mind wandered. By time she returned, Jerin had two sticks propped over the stream and secured by large rocks.

"You watch our poles and I'll start a fire. Just so you know, you gut what you catch." He chuckled, obviously noticing her angry expression. "Kid, you'll have to get over your prissy girl attitude if you hope to make it on this road."

Her fingers dug into the squishy mud, filling her palm with sludge.

"You're not living in royalty out here, Princ—"

The mud ball she hurled smacked the side of his stunned face and dripped off like brown frosting. He sat dumbfounded a moment before wiping the dirt globs from his tunic. "That wasn't right."

"It's not right for you to make fun of me like you do. If you don't want to travel with me, then don't. I told you I could take care of myself!"

"I never—"

"I'm doing the best I can. Yes, I've been sheltered. But I'm not prissy, and I'm not a brat, either."

He rolled his eyes.

Tears burned. She was so fed up, so tired, and so sore from walking. She grabbed her pack and stormed off, not wanting him to see her cry. No need to give him more to taunt her with. Traveling with him was no different from living in the dark lands. People always mocked her for her weaknesses. Hated her. Even Tarek. At least, he sometimes acted like he hated her. If it weren't for the tainted food, Tarek probably would have left her to marry Troll-man. Certainly wouldn't have kissed... she shook her head to get rid of that thought.

"Come back, Pri... I mean, Miss. Whatever," Jerin called after her. "I'm only teasing."

She ignored him, heading on down the path a good distance away. Just for a while. Just long enough to get control of herself. She knew her reaction was wrong. Knew she needed to go back and apologize. But she hated people making her feel dumb, incapable. Master had told her over and over she was damaged. Her shoulders drooped. Maybe he was telling the truth.

Through the trees, she still heard him calling her. "I'm sorry, kid. I have a bad habit of teasing people. The guys on the farm think it's funny."

She continued walking but slowed her pace, knowing deep down he truly wasn't the brightest stone in the river. Maybe she did need to lighten up. Jerin wasn't cruel like Master or the others in Racah.

"Hey, a fish. We caught one."

A loud splash echoed through the elms.

"What a monster. Enough for both of us. Come on back, I won't make you gut it. Promise. Long as you wash up the dishes after." He added in a lower voice, that she could still hear

Her lips twitched in a small grin. What an oaf. Taking a deep breath, she turned to head back when she spotted a patch of pretty white flowers growing along a clearing in the woods. She recognized the flowers from the cook's garden. Strawberries! Hundreds of the bright red fruit grew several yards from the path.

Her mouth watered at the thought of eating her fill of the fat balls of goodness. They'd be a wonderful addition to dinner. But she'd have to leave the white rocks. Her stomach rumbled, as if urging her to chance the short distance. Scanning the woods, she decided to take the risk.

Sweet juices ran down her chin as she popped a strawberry into her mouth. She filled both pants pockets, and stuffed as many as possible into her backpack. Then cupping her shirt into a make-shift basket, she collected more. They tasted delicious!

Princess stood, arms circling her bounty, as she realized she'd wandered farther than intended from the road. She looked around, listening for Jerin's voice, or even the sound of the stream. Everything grew quiet… darker. Sure the path lay directly behind her, she turned and headed in what she hoped was the right direction.

A black shadow streaked between two trees off to her left. She froze, heart pounding like a woodpecker against tree bark. Leaves rustled behind her. She spun in time to catch another blurred movement, followed by a low growl.

"Hey, Jerin?" Her voice cracked, no higher than a mosquito's buzz.

She cleared her throat and forced her feet to move toward the path.

A black wolf leaped from the woods, blocking the way. The canine's eyes glowed orange and its body seemed slightly twisted and disfigured. A ridge of spiky hair ran down its arched back.

She screamed. The strawberries fell from her shirt and tumbled around her boots. Another fierce growl sounded from right behind her. Red eyes flashed in the dim light, and she was locked in its stare. Princess froze, not wanting to move, not caring what happened. She tried hard to call out for Jerin, but she could do no more than whimper. One of the black canines slowly edged closer, white teeth flashing, snapping. She stepped away, deeper into the woods.

# Chapter 13

The wolves edged closer, driving Princess deeper into the trees. She grabbed a broken limb and swung with all her strength. The beast ducked out of the way. The stick hit a tree and burst into pieces.

*So much for that idea.*

She braced herself for the ravenous carnivores to leap in for the kill, but instead they only advanced, pushing her toward a steep ridge. Their orange eyes burned into her, causing her mind to lose focus. The scent of campfire smoke drifted in the dank air. Her heart sank fearing soldiers were waiting over the rise.

"Jerin!"

The lead wolf growled, black lips drawn over long teeth. It lunged. Princess ducked, tumbled over a rock, and landed flat on her back. Massive paws hit her chest.

A small object whizzed through the trees and smacked the dog's rump. With a yelp, it spun in the direction of the new attack. Jerin stood beside the strawberry patch. He reloaded his sling and released another stone.

Princess took the opportunity to crawl out of the way.

The second rock sank into the canine's forehead, directly between its fiery eyes. The glow dimmed as it crumpled to the ground. The other two howled charging for Jerin.

"Watch out!" Princess screamed.

"Get back to the path!" He reloaded his weapon and knocked out another one.

She ran, not even sure which direction to go anymore. How had she managed to get so far from the road?

Three now surrounded Jerin.

He tucked the slingshot into his pocket and unsheathed his sword. As the wolf leapt, Jerin's blade swooped in a wide arc. The blade sliced through the beast's flank. With an agonizing yelp, it tumbled over, lifeless. Two more appeared at the top of the ridge.

"Come on you blasted curs!" He stood his ground, feet planted firmly apart, the sword gripped in his large hand.

Two blocked Princess from reaching Jerin. She grabbed another, longer stick and swung, hitting the side of one's head. The second jumped, knocking her to the ground. Foul breath brushed against her cheek. She kicked her foot, landing a blow in the beast's gut.

"Get your dagger," ordered Jerin. "Kill them."

She reached over her shoulder but couldn't grasp the knife tucked inside her backpack. The air left her lungs when another wolf pounced on her back. Snapping teeth kept her hand from grasping the bag's flap.

Pained yelps echoed through the trees as Jerin killed another. She struggled to get away from the canine pinning her down. Jerin loaded another rock. When the stone flew, she covered the back of her head with her arms. His shot was sure. The wolf tumbled off.

Her boots gripping the soft earth, she ran full out. Jerin followed close behind.

"Which way?" She'd lost all sense of direction.

"Just run, I hear more coming. Hurry!"

With Jerin on her heels, and the two remaining demon hounds on his, they raced around trees, constantly searching for the white rocks in the dimming light.

"I can't see, Jerin."

"Keep going. Whatever you do, don't stop."

The pounding of his boots grew faint, then stopped. Remembering Dean's sacrifice, she stopped and found Jerin battling another oncoming wolf. The blade sliced through its throat, spraying blood. The last one plowed into Jerin, teeth bared and snapping.

"No!" She searched for something, anything, to scare off the beast. At her feet, several gray rocks peeked through the forest debris. She grasped one in each hand. Both began glowing with a dim light. Surprised, she nearly dropped them.

The wolf's angry bark and Jerin's yell snapped her back into action. Hurling the fist-sized rock, she gasped at the speed the projectile flew. The glowing stone hit the monster's skull. A blinding flash burst the wolf into a powdery dust.

Jerin scooted away, grabbing his sword. The last hound received a deathly stab directly to the heart.

Shouts came from deep in the woods as several torch lights appeared through the shadowed trees.

"You never listen, do you?" Jerin shoved her forward. Blood drenched his shirt and arms. She wondered if any of it was his. "Go, go, go!"

Her feet met rocks again, but in the darkness she couldn't tell if they'd found the path.

"Keep going. They're getting closer." Jerin pushed her on.

Pain stabbed her side. Daring a glance behind, she spotted bobbing lights following, but no sound of barking wolves in pursuit. Hopefully they'd killed them all.

"Look out," Jerin warned moments before she plowed into a tree.

Her forehead smacked against the rough bark. Lights flashed behind her eyes. Hands grabbed her pack and dragged her beneath a prickly bush. Jerin collapsed over her, covering them both in his black cloak.

"Shhh, quiet." His whisper faint and his breath puffed in her ear. "Don't move."

Feet thundered around them. Shouts and lights flashed across the blurred dirt. She blinked away something wet and sticky flowing into her eye. Her mind reeled with fear and pain as everything faded into a foggy haze.

\* \* \* \*

Bright sunlight woke Princess from a fitful sleep where orange-eyed monsters chased her and sharp teeth tore at her flesh. She sat up, her cheek numb from resting on the, smooth, round rocks. The White Road! They'd left it. Or she had. Blinking, she gingerly touched a stinging spot on her forehead. Her fingers drew back a smudge of blood.

"Ewww, is that mine?"

Jerin sat across from her, his knees drawn up to his chest and a furious scowl on his face.

"Rule number one... You're not supposed to get off the blasted white rocks!"

She blanched, his roaring voice thundered inside her achy head.

Her boots were covered in mud and red stains caked her pants. She dug sticky, gooey strawberry pulp from inside her pockets.

"I wanted... strawberries." She found her canteen and drank several long gulps to quench her parched throat. "Now I need more water."

"That was all you had?" His roar grew ferocious. She scooted farther beneath the covering of the bushes, fearing he'd turn into one of those evil beasts any moment.

"We'll get some more. The stream isn't very—"

He stood, towering over her. "You left the path! We were lost in the woods. Luckily, we somehow came upon another fork of the White Road. I wouldn't have known if you hadn't picked up those... rocks..." His eyes widened in what she thought was either fear or confusion.

"You made them glow." He shook his head, walking away a few paces. "I've heard tales of the Light People, but never... I've never seen anything like that."

"What are you talking about?" Princess stood. Instantly, her head swam, and she almost fell.

Jerin caught her arm and steadied her. "Your medallion says you're an Illuminate. One of the Light People. When you grabbed the white stones, they glowed."

She shook her swimming head. He talked craziness.

He handed her a stone. "Try. See if it doesn't glow."

The morning light glistened off the sparkling white surface.

"Humm, nothing." She considered throwing the rock at him but let it drop instead. Maybe he'd banged his head, too. She couldn't make rocks.... A vague memory hit her. Glowing balls of light. Knocking a wolf off Jerin. The beast exploded.... No, impossible.

"Are the soldiers still around?" She patted her shoulder for her pack strap, relieved to find it still there. Thank goodness she'd taken it with her before storming off. Then she noticed Jerin only had his sword.

"Let's not stay to find out." He looked around nervously. "Can you keep up, or do I need to hold your hand?"

"I'll keep up!" Princess tried to scoop the remaining squished strawberries from her pockets, hating how her pants stuck to her legs. How would she ever wash out the stains? "This is just great!

Try to do something nice and see what I get?"

"Save me the favors, kid. All right?" He stomped down the path, ordering her to hurry up.

For a long while, they walked in silence. Thirst burned her throat. She shook her canteen, finding only a swallow or two remained.

"Think we'll find the stream again? Or another?"

"No idea. When I backtracked for my stuff, I realized we were on a completely new road."

"You left your pack behind? Why?"

He spun to face her. "Well, let's see.... First you disappear. Then you're screaming. Humm." He scratched at his head while glaring at her. "Sorry I didn't stop a moment to repack everything before I came to your rescue." His voice increased in volume with each word, his sarcasm not lost on her.

Princess cringed against the ache in her head. Her shoulders slumped. "I'm sorry. Really, Jerin. I was about to come back and apologize for losing my temper. Honest." She shifted her feet, staring at the glistening rocks. "Then I saw the strawberries and thought they'd be great with the fish. I wanted to make it up to you. Being a burden and throwing that temper tantrum."

Now he ducked his head, looking as sheepish as she felt. "You're so blasted quiet, kid. I'm used to loud, boisterous people. Thought teasing you would lighten you up some. I hoped you'd start to trust me. Like you trusted the General."

They continued walking shoulder to shoulder now.

"In Racah, you're a fool to trust anyone. I don't know why I trusted Marcel. Maybe he reminded me some of Dean." She shrugged her arms, exasperated. "I'm so stupid about everything out here."

Jerin started to protest, but she held up a hand to stop him.

"Serious. I have been sheltered. Master wouldn't let me leave the castle unless I was with him. I thought I had more freedom when he sent me to the dungeons, but even there, he knew everything I did. I'm sure he's still watching me."

"How?"

"He has magical...things, that help him see whatever he wants."

Jerin shook his head, as if he didn't believe her.

106

"You have no idea of his power, Jerin."

He grinned. "You have no idea of the White Road's power, Missy. I'd wager my plow horse and slingshot that as long as you stay on the King's Highway, he can't see you. There's a reason they told us to avoid straying off the white rocks."

Princess hoped he was right. Her heart raced, wondering how far Master's power reached across this land. She knew those deranged wolves belonged to him. She'd seen how he turned normal creatures into monsters. Still, she and Jerin did manage to escape from the soldiers once they reached the rocky path again. Maybe he spoke the truth.

"I'll share all my supplies with you. I have some coins we can use for you to restock when we reach a town."

He patted her shoulder, his smile widening. "Uh yeah! You so owe me big time." He laughed, and she knew he'd never be able to stop teasing her. Such was his way and she decided then and there to accept him, as Marcel told them to do before they parted ways.

They traveled nonstop until the sun went down. Princess remembered the strawberries she'd stashed in her pack and shared them. They ate a light meal of bread and jerky. Without water, the dry meal went down like sand in their throats.

"Ah, delicious. Sweet and perfectly ripe." Jerin popped another fat, bright red berry into his mouth. "Nexed dime you doop dis, let me know." He finished chewing and swallowed.

Princess didn't intend on there being a next time. She scooted the remaining strawberries toward him. "Why?"

"One of us can scout the area first." He winked, gulping the last ones with many slurping and smacking noises.

"I hope we find a stream soon." Princess wrapped the messenger's blanket around her, settling comfortably on a bed of pine needles. "My pants are all crusty with dry strawberries. Disgusting."

Jerin chuckled and muttered something about her getting what she deserved for not listening.

She turned her back to him and went right off to sleep while he took the first watch. The next thing she knew, her world shook. She grabbed hold of something to steady herself and awoke clutching Jerin's shirt front.

"Your time to guard." He said gruffly. "My sword is propped against the tree in case anything happens."

Princess stood and stretched. "I was sleeping so well, too. I had this dream of a beautiful city. There were all kinds of wonderful, bright plants, and fruit growing wild along the road. I was just about to bite into a big juicy peach when you woke me up."

"Good for you. G'nite." Jerin growled from beneath the cover she loaned him, "You stay awake this time, hear me?"

Princess stuck her tongue out at him.

"Loud and clear, Capt'n, sir!" She sat beside a stout oak, ignoring the sword. If something did happen, she wouldn't know how to use it anyway.

The remainder of the night went so uneventful Princess remembered nothing more until Jerin shook her awake. His glowering face was tomato red.

She quickly packed her bag and forced down a bite of bread as they walked, keeping silent and a good distance behind him. Her raw throat burned and her head throbbed, but she didn't complain.

They found no sign of water before stopping for their midday rest. Jerin perched on a flat boulder overlooking a wide field. Off in the distance stood a small cluster of trees and brush growing up like an island in the ocean of yellow grasses. Princess lay exhausted beside the path, her head propped on her backpack as she watched a bumblebee dance around a black-eyed-Susan. She didn't remember seeing much wildlife in the barren mountain city. Somehow, Tarek always brought home game. She wondered where he managed to find a place to hunt.

*Stop thinking about Tarek. He's in your past. Focus on what's ahead!*

"I'll bet there's water over by those trees" Jerin pointed to a cluster of greenery. He refused to eat anything, complaining food made him thirstier.

She sat up. The trail wove across the meadow, toward the stand of trees, but then veered off to the north before disappearing. "You sure, Jerin? We'll have to leave the path to check."

He shrugged. "Something is helping those trees to grow." He studied the open meadow for awhile.

Where had the enemy gone? They seemed to have vanished.

Jerin insisted they keep their guard up all the same. The plush trees growing in the cluster would at least offer some shade, but still, they'd be leaving the path. Out here in the open, if there were enemy around, surely they'd be able to see some sign of their presence.

"This time, we do it right." Jerin stood. "I'll keep my slingshot and sword ready while I go check. You'll be in charge of filling the canteen as soon as I give the okay. We'll get a drink and then hurry back to the path."

Princess put her pack on.

They jogged toward the trees, stopping at the point where the road turned northward. Jerin pulled his sword form the scabbard and collected a few rocks which he slipped into his pocket. "We'll be quick. No playing around, hear?"

She saluted when he wasn't looking.

"Okay," he whispered. "When I whistle, come on."

Princess held her breath, ready to run in either direction depending on how things went. Her ears tuned for any sound. All was quiet, not even a bug chirped. Finally, a shrill whistle sounded. She raced toward the trees.

A natural spring formed a deep pool and fed the small oasis. Oh, what she'd give to jump in and wash off the grime. Instead, she settled for dipping her canteen into the water. A strange smell, familiar in a way, hung around the pond.

Jerin dunked his face into the water, splashing his neck before taking a slurping drink from his cupped hands.

Princess had already taken a long gulp from her canteen. The taste matched the smell. *Bitterness.* But she was so thirsty she'd swallowed a whole mouthful before realization hit and she spit the tainted liquid out.

"That water comes from the dark lands." The deep voice came from behind them.

They spun around. Water streamed down Jerin's face, drenching his shirt.

"I wouldn't drink from there, if I were you." A tall man, dressed in linen traveling clothes, and leather boots stepped off the white path and came toward them. He took the canteen from Princess and poured out all the water.

"Hey, what do you think you're doing?"

He walked away, calling over his shoulder, "Come along."

Jerin scowled, but trailed after the man who'd returned to the white path and soon disappeared around a bend in the road.

"Do something, you troll brain!" Anger raged inside her at the nerve of the stranger. What did that big oaf, Jerin, think he was doing following along like a hungry dog?

"You do something," Jerin yelled back. "You're always expecting me to get you out of trouble!"

"Do not! I told you I could take care of myself. You're the one who's always bossing me around. And I never asked you to come along."

"No, but good thing I did. You can't stay on the path, and you fall asleep during your guard. You'd probably still be snoozing if I hadn't been a light sleeper and woke you up."

"Are you saying I'm lazy?"

Jerin stopped and looked down at her with a sneer. "I'm guessing they had their reasons for calling you *Princess*!"

*Oh, that was it!* She charged after him. He held out his giant hand and caught her by the forehead, holding her out at arm's length. She swung and kicked, her fist sweeping a few inches short of making contact.

"Enough!" hollered the stranger.

Jerin let his arm drop. Princess tumbled forward and sprawled on the ground.

"Here-" The stranger held out the canteen, "-drink some. Both of you. Let's sit and talk awhile."

Jerin shook his head. "I'm not thirsty now."

The man helped Princess stand. She jerked loose as soon as she was up and grabbed her water container. Fury, resentment, and frustration boiled over and bubbled out. "I've had it!" She stomped over to Jerin and pointed her finger up in his face. "I've had enough of you nagging at me and bossing me around." Then she turned to the man adding, "And I don't care to sit with you, whoever you are."

"Well," said the stranger with a kind smile. "There are many names I go by. Around here, I'm called Guardian. However, in the towns, I'm often referred to as Teacher, sometimes even..."

"Teacher?"

He looked like nothing more than a dirt-covered traveler like herself.

"Why don't you go find yourself a schoolroom full of pupils and leave me alone?" She turned to Jerin. "And as for you, I'm done. I don't need you either."

"Fine with me." He stormed off into the woods.

"Jerin," called the stranger. "You're going the wrong way." But he was already gone.

Princess marched over a stone bridge crossing a river, then along the white path in the opposite direction.

The man followed her. "Where are you going?"

"To Aloblase. I need to find King Shaydon. Thank you and good day!" She hoped he'd take the hint and leave her alone.

His footsteps sounded behind her. Wonderful, he didn't get it.

"I can help. Come and eat the fish I've caught. We'll bring Jerin back here and talk awhile."

She stopped and spun around. "What part of 'No, thank you' do you not understand?" Taking in a deep breath, she tried again. "Listen teacher-man, I can take care of myself just fine! I don't care what that oversized ogre says. If you had any idea of what I've been through so far…"

The man moved closer until he stood practically nose to nose with her. "I do know, Alyra." His brown eyes held a warm light and his voice sounded kind, yet stern. "You're brave, none can deny. You've escaped from the dark one. You've freed the dragon named Crystal. You've traveled far and I've been waiting here for you."

Her heart lunged in her throat. Backing away, she recoiled from his powerful stare. His intense eyes probed right through her very being, like Master's often did.

And that name…from her dreams. *Alyra.*

Her mind spun in confusion. She wasn't sure whom to trust anymore. This stranger couldn't possibly know her. And if he did, then he must come from the dark lands. She broke free of his gaze and ran blindly down the path and into the forest.

# Chapter 14

Low hanging branches scratched Princess's tear-streaked face. Anger, seasoned with bitterness and hurt, boiled so hot she saw nothing but a green haze. *What a nut!* She glanced behind to make sure the so-called teacher-man wasn't following. Only pines and brush. *Good.*

How could he have known the ordeals she'd been through since leaving Racah? Despite the heat, chills ran up her spine. He must be from the dark lands. Her steps quickened, fear drove her deeper into the woods like fire on her heels.

Sweat trickled down her face and neck, lungs aching from her hard and fast breathing. Good riddance to Jerin, as well. No more of his nagging and pushing to go faster.

*Never should have left in the first place,* hissed a familiar sounding voice in her mind. *You had everything you wanted. A nice, comfortable castle to live in. Servants at your command. All the delicious delicacies you might desire.*

Her stomach rumbled. She'd skipped lunch because of her dry throat. *If* anyone could consider the tough, dried meat in her pack food.

*You gave up so much for a journey into nowhere. You have no idea where you are going or where it will end.*

Princess slowed, her head spinning like the other times Master invaded her thoughts. She glanced around expecting him or his henchmen to leap from behind one of the tall pines. The only sound in her ears came from her racing heart.

Opening the water pouch, she took several gulps, hoping to wash away the dryness and bad taste. Instantly, the angry emotions churning inside her gut subsided. She thought harder about the stranger, his linen shirt and brown pants, his strong hands clasping the walking staff. His face and build were similar to Master's, but there was a calm gentleness to the traveler she had never sensed with Darnel. The difference between them was like a campfire on a cool night compared to being caught out in a blizzard.

The stranger had called her--*Alyra*.

Memories of riding upon a man's shoulder flooded her mind. White, sparkling towers rose against a brilliant blue sky.

"That's where you'll be trained, Alyra," The man craned back his head. His eyes were the same gold-brown as hers. He was a slightly younger version of the man she dreamed of standing beside the grave. "Your mother and I both had our training there. You'll be taught how to use your special talent."

*Special talent? Your mother and I?*

She plopped down on a flat rock, rubbing her aching head to settle the rampant, tumbling thoughts.

Had she dreamed of her father all those years? Was the sparkling city where King Shaydon lived? Maybe she really did come from Aloblase. If so, how did she end up in Lord Darnel's castle? She took another drink of the sweet, honey tasting liquid. Was her real name *Alyra*? Not Princess, but Alyra.

"Ah-lear-ah," She liked how the sound rolled off her tongue.

*Where was Jerin?* She bolted up and spun around, searching. *Where was she?*

The narrow path, weaving through the deep woods, was covered in pine needles and dead leaves. She brushed the debris aside with her foot to find rich, brown dirt.

*Oh no, the white rocks were gone!*

"Don't panic. You just need to backtrack to the White Road." She took several deep breaths to calm the rising sense of dread. Maybe if she returned to the stream, the teacher, or guardian-man... whoever he was, would still be there. She'd apologize for being rude and ask him to help her find Jerin.

Leaves crunched beneath her boots. The trail wound through such deep forest she lost all sense of east or west. The thick canopy of trees made seeing the sun's position impossible. Remorse at her carelessness overtook her, and she threw down the pack in utter misery, falling in a heap on the damp ground. She'd spoken horribly to Jerin. He was probably glad to be rid of her. Tears filled her eyes. She deserved to be caught and taken back to the Master.

A movement in the bush rustled the dried leaves. A dark figure, hidden behind the foliage, slowly circled. *Enemy or animal?* She searched for some kind of weapon and found a thick limb within arm's reach. She might deserve to be caught, but she'd not go without a fight. Pretending to sob, she watched from between her dirty fingers, hoping to find nothing more than a hapless animal. Through the undergrowth, she made out four spindly horse-like legs. Her gaze traveled up, catching a glimpse of a rider. He darted off, swift as a deer, behind a bushy pine.

Decision time. Either fight and hopefully scare them off, or run like crazy. She didn't know where to run though and feared becoming more lost. If an enemy solider had found her, she'd at least try to inflict some pain, then run.

Breathing in as deep of a breath of bravery as she could muster, she gripped her make-shift weapon and stood, coming face-to-face with a Wildman. His dark brown hair and beard hung below his neck and was tangled with leaves and twigs. He wore no shirt and his tanned arms rippled with muscles.

Her hands went sweaty around the rough stick. To her dismay, he clutched an even bigger and wider stick.

Alyra stammered, "Who a-a-are you? I-I don't wa-want any trouble."

"Trouble is yours only if you cause it. Lay aside your weapon." The man must have been riding a mule.

"Put yours down first." She backed away a few steps, grabbed her backpack, and prepared to run.

The man entered the clearing. He wasn't riding a mule; *he was the mule.* She blinked, not believing her eyes.

"What the... who... I mean...." The trees kept her from retreating any farther. Then she remembered the boy who'd told the story about riding such a beast as the one standing before her.

"Are you one of those centaurs?" *Please be friendly like the one the boy met.*

"One of those, indeed." He trotted around her, sniffing. "Explain yourself, servant of the Dark Lord. Do it quickly." He raised his club, the length and thickness of her thigh.

Stomping her foot, she yelled, "I am not his servant! How dare you call...?"

He sniffed her hair and clothing. She swung her useless twig of a stick at his head. He darted out of the way, his movements as graceful as a gazelle.

"I smell the stench of the dark lands on you." He circled again, but kept out of her reach. "And this is curious—the breath of a dragon has been at your back." He snatched her weapon and hurled it into the woods before coming to stand in front of her. His gray eyes reminded her of storm clouds and his features of a man in his late twenties. His horse body was much smaller than a regular horse. She had to tilt back her head, which reached his chest, to see his stern face.

He tucked his club under a leather strap tied around his waist. "How have you encountered a dragon's fire and yet stand here today?"

"That's none of your business." She took a whiff of her shirt and hair. Could he really smell Crystal's breath on her back? She cringed, realizing she hadn't washed since before leaving Racah. "I probably need a bath, don't I?"

This caused the creatures mouth to flicker into a half-smile. "Indeed." He examined her so intently she became uncomfortable. "You must be the one I am looking for. What is your name, girl-child?"

"I... uh... well?" she shifted her feet, unsure what name to give. "I was called... never mind about that. I'm not sure... but...the man at the river called me another name. And I remember being called that a long time ago. I think." She sank back onto the ground, cradling her forehead in her hands. "I honestly don't know."

The centaur snorted. "I search for the human named Alyra. The Guardian told me to bring her back to the White Road. I've been following you, hoping you were the one. But you've been talking such foolishness. Have you drunk from the polluted pool?"

She nodded. "The man... that's what he called me." Alyra must really be her name. "Who are you?"

"I am Lotari. This is my home. We are caretakers of the woods."

"Who was the man that sent you after me? *Guardian*?"

"He also goes by Issah. He is the caretaker of the White Road. He aids travelers heading to the King's city."

"He helps travelers?" She shook her head. "He told me he was a teacher."

"Indeed, he teaches people about King Shaydon and Alburnium ways."

She dug the balls of her hands into her tired eyes. "This makes no sense! I need to go back and find Jerin. No wait, he went in the opposite way...I think. Oh, I'm so confused."

"Then you are the one I'm looking for. Come now, I'll take you to the river. You can...er...bathe and rest. Then maybe I can help you not be confused." He pulled at her pack until she stood.

She began to follow, but he moved quickly and disappeared into the trees. Tiredness and hunger dragged her steps. She reached into her backpack, pulled out some jerky to chew as she walked.

The centaur soon returned. "Are you not coming?"

"Yes, I'm coming."

"Okay," he disappeared again.

She moved as fast as her exhausted legs would carry her. Lotari needed to go slower. Running to keep up was out of the question. In a matter of a few minutes, he returned yet again, frustration etched on his tanned face.

"You traveled much faster when you were mumbling craziness to yourself."

"I'm tired. I'm hungry, too. This is the best I can do."

His gray eyes searched the surrounding trees. He pulled his goatee as if considering something. The woods seemed devoid of life. Hardly a beetle buzzed. Had she made so much noise they'd fled the area? She sighed, wondering how she'd avoided getting caught with all her carelessness.

Finally he said, "Very well, I will allow you to climb on my back."

"Uhh... you mean like a horse?"

That was obviously the wrong thing to say. His gaze darkened, and he turned to face her, stomping his front hooves. "I am no pack animal! Are you so simple-minded you cannot tell the difference?"

"No! I'm not stupid! It's..."

"You're rudeness will result in you being left in these woods."

She ducked her head, feeling bad over insulting the centaur. He was trying to help after all. Maybe Master was right. She certainly had a way of chasing off every last friend she came across.

"I'm sorry. I didn't mean it like that. I've… just… I've never ridden… oh, I'm just sorry." Alyra stomped her foot, feeling terrible. Obviously he was a dignified and proud being. She was a big-mouthed oaf.

"Fortunate for you, Issah is the one who asked this favor of me." He turned and ordered, "Get on and say no more, foolish human."

She did as he said. Her hands fluttered awkwardly, unsure what to grasp to keep her balance.

"All you must do is sit still," he explained. "I am sure-footed and will not allow you to fall off. Understand?"

"Okay." She held her breath as he trotted along a sun-dappled trail winding between brush and fern.

Lotari moved at a swift pace, unlike the swooping, wild ride on the dragon. The trees flew by in a blur, yet she was never jarred or bounced like when riding a horse.

They'd traveled a good distance when Lotari came to a sudden stop, his long, deer-like ears twitching. His hand circled around the hilt of the club.

"What's the matter," Alyra feared they'd met up with enemy soldiers.

"Hush!"

She was about to protest his harshness when the foliage parted. Another centaur, umber colored like an oak tree, burst onto the narrow foot trail. He towered over Lotari, his black brows furrowed and his teeth bared. Lotari took a couple of quick steps backward.

"Get off," he whispered. "Get off quick and go stand behind those trees."

Did the dark beast want to fight? Was he one of Darnel's servants? She obeyed this time without a word.

The larger one's gray-streaked beard flowed nearly to his stomach. Deep lines etched across his forehead. His eyes were black and piercing like a hawk.

The elder centaur's voice boomed, "You know better than this! We have work to do. Here I find you acting as…one of *their* pack animals. *Again*! There are seekers roaming our woods freely."

"Wyndham, I'm only—"

The elder smacked Lotari hard against his head, sending him stumbling into a clump of fern. "Foolish youth! When are you going to learn?"

He didn't deserve that! Alyra stepped out of her hiding place and shouted, "Leave him alone! He was just helping me get back to the river. He offered me a ride because I was too tired to keep up and we needed to travel fast. I didn't order, he offered!"

Lotari scrambled to his hooves and stood between her and Wyndham. The older centaur glared hatefully at her. "What is this insolence?"

"Wyndham," Lotari spoke in a calming voice. "Hear my words, please. The Guardian, Issah, asked me to find this child and take her back to the white path. We needed to make haste. I am aware of the seekers. She is the one they are in pursuit of. She escaped from the Dark One. Would you rather I ignored our Guardian and allowed this one to be caught by the very ones we are fighting against?"

Wyndham's brows tightened over his scrutinizing glare, as he considered Lotari's words with several grunts and humphs. He pushed the younger centaur aside and bent closer, his nostrils flaring as he took in a deep whiff. "Yes, it does have the scent of that foul land. And ... something curious."

Alyra took a step back. "I'm going to take a bath." If Wyndham called her *it* one more time....

Lotari covered a grin with his hand. "She escaped the dark one's dragon, I suspect."

"Not escaped from. We helped each other get away, okay? It's a really long story. I'd rather not get into it now." Quickly she added, "If you don't mind."

"You mean to tell me the dragon also ...?"

Alyra nodded. "I got the magic rope off, and she flew me down the mountain. That's it."

Wyndham's fierceness receded as he straightened. Even Lotari stared at her with wide-eyed wonder.

"Very well. Because this is the Guardian's request, you may take it to the river. That will lead back to the path. You are not to take it all the way. You know we can't risk being seen by *them*. I expect you back with the clan before the sun rises. Understand?" He stared hard at Lotari.

Alyra's hands balled into tight fists as she glared back at the man-mule.

"Yes, Wyndham." Lotari bowed, pushing her aside as he stood between them. "As you say."

The older centaur gave a snort as if he questioned Lotari's sincerity. He disappeared as fast as he had appeared. Lotari let out a deep breath.

"I don't like him." Alyra turned to Lotari who rubbed his cheek. "He hit you hard. Master used to hit me when I messed up. It would hurt so much."

A bright red splotch appeared on the side of his face. Lotari shook his head, avoiding her eyes. "Not so hard. It doesn't hurt. Wyndham is not like the dark one. He is our leader and my teacher. He is very wise and only wants me to learn to be careful. He does not believe we should have anything to do with humans. It's understandable. Most hate us." He motioned for her to climb on.

She stepped back, thinking she might better walk and try harder to keep up. "I heard a story about a boy who'd been saved in the woods by a centaur. Some of the people there didn't have nice things to say about your kind, but he defended you. Told everyone they were wrong and should change their views."

A smile played across Lotari's face, as his tail began swaying. "I don't necessarily agree with Wyndham's view on humans."

Alyra's heart warmed toward this creature. "Thank you for helping me, Lot. I'm so grateful."

His cheeks flushed, when she'd shortened his name. Yet the nickname seemed to please him.

"Climb on, Alyra, and let's get going."

"How far are we from the river? Maybe I'll walk from here. I'm not as tired now."

"We have a ways to go yet. I may not be able to take you all the way to the white path, but I can get you close. You will not be truly safe again until you are back on the King's Highway."

She did as he said, but something had changed between them. Lotari spoke more casually now as they traveled, without the formal mannerisms he used before. He wanted to hear all about her travels, especially how she and the dragon escaped. He often laughed, especially when she described how Jerin had tricked Bezoar when they fled Yarholm.

"Do you think my friend will be okay? We got into such a fight after drinking that bitter water. What I do remember, I really regret."

The centaur stopped next to a raspberry bush. "I'm sure he will be fine. The Guardian will care for him, as he's done for you. It's hard when one leaves the path though. You are fortunate that I was nearby."

He then went on to tell her how to know the good berries from the poisonous ones while Alyra filled her shirt with the plump dark fruit.

"It's important to learn what you can and cannot eat while traveling." His hooves clomped softly over the leafy ground.

By time the sun sank into the west, they came upon the sound of a rushing stream. He sat Alyra beside the shore and told her to wait until he scouted the area. Finishing off the berries, she removed her boots and let her feet dangle in the cool water.

"All is clear," he said upon returning. "They will not come near the white path. It is repugnant to them." He set down a few logs he'd gathered and began making a fire. "You should bathe now, before the moon shows her face. I will stay here and prepare the evening meal."

She took her backpack and walked a short distance away until she found a private area where the river formed a shallow pool. She scrubbed her clothes first, dismayed over not being able to wash out the strawberry stains. Laying them on a bush to dry, she dove in relishing the perfect temperature that soothed her tired muscles. The soap Lydia had provided washed off the dark land's filth, except for her servant mark, a crescent moon and stars, which would never disappear no matter how hard she rubbed.

The bruise on her temple was still tender to the touch, but the small cut had scabbed over. She cleansed that area carefully.

Once her fingers began to wrinkle, she forced herself to climb out and dress in her damp, stained clothes. At least they were no longer crusty with crushed strawberries. Perhaps the stains would keep her reminded to stay on the white road.

Feeling completely refreshed and even a bit invigorated, she brushed the tangles from her long hair, grateful to Lydia for giving her these small necessities. Lotari soon called her to eat.

To her surprise, when she returned to the campfire, Lotari had prepared a meal from a fish he'd managed to catch, and made a salad from some wild greens, roots, and onions. He'd fashioned plates out of wide pieces of bark. Beside the fish, he'd set three strawberries for each of them. "You managed all of this while I was in the river? You're amazing!"

"Yes, I am. But you were in the river long enough for me to make two meals. Did you manage to get yourself clean, Alyra?"

She grinned, loving the sound of her real name. "It felt good. I've been so scared, I didn't even think about stopping to wash."

"You are safe now." His voice held comfort. "The clan is watching out for you. The intruders will be tracked down and driven out of our woods. We despise them and do not welcome them in our land."

"Your clan owns all this land?" She stuffed crispy fish into her mouth. She was so hungry.

"Own? What do you mean?"

"You know, do they belong to you? These woods?"

He chuckled, folding his spindly legs as he rested against a tree. His tail swished back and forth. "Such silly talk you make, child. We are simply caretakers. How can you own something that has been here long before you came and will remain long after you leave?"

Alyra bit into a wild radish, thinking about the logic of what he said. "I see your point. It is crazy. But people fight over land all the time. Where I came from anyway."

Lotari scowled. "You mean that filthy black thief? Greedy beast. He lies and causes trouble between the races. I despise him!"

"Yeah, me too." Alyra sighed, plucking the last bit of flaky meat from her fish.

He took her empty plate and tossed it into the fire along with his. "In the morning, you only need to follow the river a short distance to the path."

"Do you think the Guardian will be there? Or Jerin? I hope he waits for me, though I can't blame him if he doesn't." Jerin was right, if she didn't get over her prissy, castle-brat attitude, she'd never see this journey to the end. The thought of continuing alone pierced her heart like a thorn.

"If he has not, do not wait or go looking for him. You must continue on until you reach the town of Many Rivers. Once he finds the white road again, you will eventually be reunited." Lotari stood and went to the river to wash his knife. "I see much good in you. The dark one might have taken your memories, but he wasn't able to break your heart, and that is saying much. Not many make it this far from the dark lands, Alyra, not many at all."

Alyra smiled, encouraged by his words. She wanted to believe she wasn't such a terrible person. "I had to find a way to escape or die trying."

"He said you were brave." Lotari sighed. "And determined."

"Who?"

"Issah. When he warned me to be careful about how I approached you."

# Chapter 15

Alyra woke to the sun shining bright in her face. Lotari had left, just as he'd said, but next to the dying fire sat a bark plate piled with some flat biscuits and about a handful of raspberries. Extra cakes were wrapped in broad leaves and secured with vine. She assumed they were to take with her. She smiled, despite the overwhelming sense of loneliness clouding the beautiful, clear morning.

The grainy bread tasted sweet with bits of fruit and nuts which made them filling. Lotari promised to sneak away when possible and visit her along the trail. She already liked the goodhearted centaur and wondered if she might be able to talk him into going to Aloblase with her.

She gathered her belongs, her eyes scanning the surrounding woods. He also promised his clan would be watching the area for enemy soldiers, or seekers, as he called them. Still, she'd breathe easier once her feet were back on the White Road. Kicking dirt on the fire, she followed the river in a northerly direction. In no time, the stones sparkled beneath her boots again. Her heart sank to find neither Jerin nor the Guardian at the bridge. She topped off her canteen and sat beside the bridge, nibbling on another biscuit. Then remembering Lotari's warning to not wait for them, she continued on alone.

*Please let Jerin be okay.*

She chuckled, knowing he was far more capable of taking care of himself then she was. She'd been a complete nuisance. Her shoulders sagged. Most likely, he was glad to be rid of her. Tears stung her eyes as she determined to change and try harder. She didn't want to chase off her new friend, Lotari, as well. She'd prove she was capable of making this journey without getting into any more trouble.

Her gaze followed the sparkling white path as it wove into the deep woods.

"Don't you leave these rocks again," she ordered herself as she walked.

The silence got on her nerves. She tried humming along with the birds chirping song, but her throat grew dry and she needed to reserve her water. She missed Jerin nagging at her to hurry up. Without her holding him back, perhaps he'd reach Aloblase before her. She walked faster, intent on not letting that happen.

However, the private game caused a stitch in her side, and she reverted to her slow, casual pace. Last night Lotari said they were both heading in the same direction and eventually their paths would cross again.

She'd asked Lotari if he'd ever traveled the White Road to Aloblase.

He shook his head but didn't look at her. "We are commissioned to guard the woods from the dark enemy. This is my home. We are part of the woods, and the woods are part of us." Then he'd paused, adding kindling to the fire. "Besides, we are not received well in your world. , "But I've read all about King Shaydon. His book of letters is like sitting down and talking to him face to face.""

Alyra remembered the talk back in the soldier's camp. The old woman had said that centaurs were wild and better off being left alone. Jerin called them *unnatural creations.*

"Why, Lot? Why do some people seem to … to think…?"

"We are abnormal? That we don't belong and should be avoided at all costs?"

Alyra turned away, nodding.

"Yes," he sighed, "there has been much discontent between humans and centaurs. I might add, between humans and most creatures." He chuckled while stirring the embers. The firelight shone on his stern, yet tenderly kind face. "The dark one's fault, I believe. It wasn't always like this."

"What do you mean, Lot?"

"It's a long story, my little friend. You must be growing tired and need to rest. You are still two days away from the next town."

"Please? I want to hear about King Shaydon. The truth. I want to know the real story about him."

The sun climbed higher into the sky. Alyra stopped when a doe appeared on the pathway. A fawn ambled from the brush and paused beside its mother. The mother's ears twitched, as she chewed a mouthful of grasses. For a long while, they all simply stared at each other. She'd never seen wild animals wandering freely in Racan lands. Another sign she was getting farther away from Master's grasp.

The deer must have grown bored with her and moved on into the woods. She wanted to follow but knew she couldn't leave the path again.

The feeling of isolation pecked at her heart. If only she hadn't angered Jerin so much that he'd stormed away. If only they'd both listened and stayed on the White Road. They'd been so close to a river, too. What an evil trick to place a spring in a spot where travelers went so far between being able to replenish their water. Alyra knew the trap was set intentionally by Darnel.

What other traps of his might she come across?

She continued along without hindrances for the remainder of the day. That night she started a small fire all by herself. From her backpack, she took out an oval-shaped pot. It resembled more of a bowl, but was deep enough for her to cook a simple stew with the jerky and a few herbs she'd seen Jerin use when he cooked. She used the hem of her cloak to hold the edge and protect her fingers from burning. The stew was blander than Jerin's, but good enough for her first try.

From the bottom of her pack, she withdrew Dean's little book and flipped through the pages. The night before, Lotari had brought out a similar book and read by light of the campfire.

"Even though I've never made the trip to Aloblase, I have read all I can about King Shaydon."

"I have a book like that. The Book of King's Letters, right?"

"Indeed." Lotari's goatee puffed as he grinned. "Then if you wish to learn to truth about King Shaydon, read it. Within these pages will you find all you need to know about him and his kingdom."

Alyra scooted closer to her small, crackling fire and opened the book to a random page. Her eyes fell across a passage that raised gooseflesh over her arms.

*I have established your path, even before your first step. I am he*

125

*who walks by your side on your journey home. Come to me, my beloved. Here you will find peace from your struggles. Here you will find respite from your troubles.*

*Beloved?* Her vision blurred and she quickly closed the book. Did a caring ruler really exist? Tarek said people who believed in such nonsense were simpletons. Dean didn't seem like a simpleton. He was brave, determined, and firm in where he stood.

Oh, she wanted to believe. However, she traveled alone. Where was this great ruler who's supposed to walk by her side? She shoved the book back inside her pack.

The fire's heat warmed her feet. Restless and unable to sleep, she dug out the book again and started at the beginning. The story told of how the Peoples were charged with being the land's caretakers, in partnership with the King. But something happened. Another ruler rose up, spreading lies and deceiving the people. They broke their accord with Shaydon and went their own way.

The sad story raised a lump in her throat and reminded her of what Lotari had said the night before.

"The dark one had so twisted the people's thinking, they caused destruction upon themselves. A few survived. Shaydon gathered them to him once again and they began to rebuild. He delighted in their stories, and brought fourth creatures such as my kind into the world to help bring harmony and variety." Sadness flickered in his eyes. "Unfortunately, not all chose to follow the King. Again. Some went their own way and from this group, that evil thief rose to power. He spreads lies, dividing Shaydon's children. So much animosity has grown between the different races, most keep to themselves. Like our clan. Wyndham says we are only answerable to King Shaydon and nobody else."

A star shot across the expanse. The moon shown against a few wispy clouds and she marveled at the beauty. Alyra shook her head. Did Darnel realize what her purpose was? Was that why he kept her sheltered? Why hadn't he gone ahead and killed her while he had the chance?

She'd shown the centaur her medallion, and he'd said only Shaydon had the answers she sought. But he had the same strange look that Carah and Marcel had when they'd seen flame-burst emblem.

Then later during the night, after settling down to sleep, she'd noticed him searching though his book. "Interesting," he whispered while reading a particular passages. "I wonder."

She too wondered what the big deal was. Even more, she wondered why no one would tell her.

The next morning, Alyra woke with a crick from where a tree root jabbed her back. The small fire still burned, which seemed strange. The flames should have died out long ago. She sat up and found a blackened fish waiting on a spit, along with another days worth of Lotari's grain bread. She bolted up and searched for him, but she was alone. The fact he'd been there and was watching made her feel wonderful. With chagrin, she bemoaned the fact that she'd carelessly slept through his visit. What if enemy soldiers had come upon her while she slept like the dead?

She ate the breakfast and stored the remaining bread into her pack. Even her canteen had been refilled. After putting out the fire, she took a thin stick and drew a face in the dirt then added long wild hair and a tongue sticking out. Next to the sketch, she wrote, *Thanks,* just in case he came back to this spot.

Sometime later, Alyra stopped at a wide clearing and searched far to the left, then the right. She spotted no spirals of smoke or any other disturbance that might mean an enemy camp nearby. A hawk circled above, swooped in her direction then soared east until it disappeared in the glaring sun. Lotari had told her what to look for-such as the birds growing quiet or flying away quickly, animals acting nervously, or smoke rising into the sky.

By time she crossed the meadow, pink and orange swiped across the western sky. The path ran right beside a grove of birch trees. She stopped for a quick rest in the shade wondering how much farther to the settlement where she could restock her supplies and purchase a new outfit. She glanced at her stained pants, another jabbing reminder of her stupidity.

Her spirits sank as she worried over how she'd make it to Aloblase on her own. She knew nothing about hunting, cooking, knowing who to trust and who to avoid. What if she came upon another unfriendly town? The biscuit she munched on felt like dust in her mouth. The centaur had been kind to provide for her so far, but once she left his woods, she'd be alone again. She depended on

Jerin to help her travel, even if they didn't get along well. Washing down the biscuit with a small sip of water, she determined not to become dependent on anyone else. She had to figure out how to take care of herself. Most of all, to not sleep through someone coming into her camp and preparing a meal for her!

She shook her head, resting against a birch trunk. *Nope, time to grow up, Alyra. You have a real name now. You're not the rebellious princess anymore.*

The cool breeze and flickering shade relaxed her worries and tiredness. Closing her eyes for a moment, she drifted into a dream of a beautiful land. Fruit trees grew wild and people picked as much as they wanted without fear of retribution. The roads were wide and sparkling white. A small child ran along the street beside a shaggy, brown dog, past yellow and pink roses, up a narrow walkway to a two-story house built around a sprawling tree. The girl raced up a spiral staircase ascending into the branches. Standing upon a balcony was a tall woman, her hair flowing down her back in golden red ringlets. She looked familiar, *a looking in the mirror kind of familiar*. The woman turned and stretched her arms wide. "You're home!"

Alyra bolted awake, breathing heavy. A high-pitched scream sent her leaping to her feet. A flock of birds swarmed into the air. The screech pierced the sky again. Up above, a hawk, looking like the one she'd seen earlier circled. An alarm went off inside Alyra. She snatched her pack and jogged along the path, feeling the urge to hurry. At least she was now hidden by the forest again. She tuned in her ears for any sounds or sign of danger. Except for the bird flying about nervously, she saw nothing. And except for her pounding heart and heavy breaths, she heard nothing. The hawk continued to circle overhead, quiet now.

Perhaps the birds had been startled by a predator like a wolf. She didn't want to be caught by wolves either. She kept up her pace until her side ached and everything grew peaceful. The path began to slope upwards. Near the crest, two elm trees grew on each side of the path, their splaying branches weaving together overhead. She decided to stop for the night. Just in case soldiers did lurk around, she'd forgo a fire and eat dinner cold.

Alyra slept fitfully up in an elm's branches, hidden in the leaves.

The next morning more food had been prepared for her along with a small fire. In the dirt, next to a squirrel on a spit, was a bearded face with its eyes crossed. Beside the drawing was written, "Welcome. Don't dawdle."

She wondered at his words, wishing desperately he'd come while she was awake. More importantly, she hated how soundly she slept during his visits.

After walking all day, she was much too tired to sit up at night keeping watch. Even now exhaustion dragged down every part of her aching body.

When she finished eating the food Lotari left, she drew another face and wrote, "Missed talking to you."

As she stood to go, she looked east and west along the path, wondering if anyone else ever traveled this way. Was Jerin ahead or behind her? He moved fast, so if he were behind, he'd catch up eventually. How much farther did she have to go? Why didn't Dean pack a map? She fought hard to not become disheartened over the endless path, the loneliness, and uncertainty about what she'd meet next.

"The only way to get there is to keep walking, no matter how far," she told herself. DezPierre and General Marcel had both warned her it was a long, hard journey. Hefting her pack onto her shoulder, she forced one foot to move in front of the other.

By midday, sweat covered most of her body. She wanted a breeze so bad she could hardly stand it. Up above, the tree limbs moved slightly. She also wished for a river to cool off in. Anything that brought some relief would do.

*You could have stayed where you belonged and not had to go through all this.*

She squeezed her eyes shut and forced the thought from her mind.

*All this trouble and pain for nothing.*

Don't listen to his lies! Think of the book. "I want to go meet the author of that book!" She determined to win over Master's voice. She tried to concentrate on other things, the road, Lotari's kindness, and even the strange dreams she'd been having. The dreams seemed to come from a fairytale story about a wonderful paradise where people were happy and the land was pristine and bountiful.

*Not in this world. It's only a dream.*

She didn't care. Going back to Racah would be a hundred times worse. Her feet dragged over the stones. Tiredness hung on her like a yoke.

A shiny object next to the path caught her attention. She stopped and leaned closer toward the silver-colored rock. There, drawn in the ground, she spotted Lotari's silly bearded face. Next to it was written, "Many Rivers" with an arrow pointing the way. "Don't lose heart, my friend."

Tears sprang to her eyes. She wasn't alone. Collapsing next to his drawing, she took in several deep breaths. The town was close. She should hurry. Her stomach rumbled. The sooner she got to the village, the better. They might even have real food, though she enjoyed the breads the centaur made. When she tried to stand, her legs began to shake. No, she needed a short rest, something to eat, and then she'd go on. Nibbling the last biscuit, she rested back against a tree, and closed her eyes for only a second....

"Wake up you foolish child!"

Alyra snapped awake to find Lotari standing over her and nudging her with his hoof.

"Why are you still here? Get up!" He grabbed her cloak at the shoulder and yanked her to her feet.

"Hey!" she shouted, shocked not only at being awakened in such a startling way, but at his rough manners as well. "What's wrong with you?"

Lotari swooped up her pack and handed it to her as he shoved her down the trial. "Those dirty, rabble filth have trespassed into the forest. They have no care for anything living. You must hurry now and get to Many Waters. They will keep you safe."

"Whoa! Hang on, Lot. Are you telling me enemy soldiers are somewhere near?"

"Yes, yes. Now go." He shooed her with his hands, giving her another shove.

"But... is Bezoar with them? He's tall and wears a black cloak with a hood. He's..."

"I haven't seen them. There are many, too many for us to engage. Wyndham will not allow us to get too close until help arrives."

She backed along the path a few steps. "What if I meet them? I only have a small dagger and I don't even know how to use it. Please, can you come with me?"

He shook his head. "Wyndham is not aware I am here. We must keep it that way. You will be safe in Many Waters. Now go. Hurry and do not, no matter what, get off the white path."

Alyra began to run, hoping to reach the town in time. Hoping they would be able to help her and keep Darnel's army from taking her prisoner again.

# Chapter 16

A sharp pain stabbed Alyra's side as she jogged over the white rocks, weaving through the thick woods. Her feet slowed when the trees opened upon a newly built settlement. She stopped on a bridge that crossed a swift river flowing past the western township.

"Beautiful." She paused to catch her breath and massage the ache below her ribs. Filling her lungs with the scent of pine and smoke puffing from tall, stone chimneys, her racing heart slowed a little. She'd finally reached safety.

The town, resting along the edge of a precipice, overlooked the green-swept valley. Below, a patchwork of farms and groves reminded her of a quilt pieced together with mismatched shapes. Misty waterfalls tumbled from the surrounding cliffs and streamed into a large, pristine lake at the end of the basin.

She followed the white path to a road circling the township. Many Rivers was larger than Yarholm. In contrast, these buildings were made of fresh timber and stone with and sparkling windows. People dressed in colorful attire headed toward a sprawling, two-story, white-stone building that stood in the center of town. Several elders, holding small children by the hands, hurried inside. A group of adults- wielding pitchforks, scythes and other deadly looking tools- gathered in the town's center.

When Alyra reached the steps, she realized the walls were the same stones as those lining the King's Highway.

"That's the meeting hall." A boy, dressed in green overalls, stood on the top step with a hawk perched on his gloved hand. "You must be Alyra. We've been expecting you."

Her mouth dropped. "How?"

He held the bird higher. "Rohond tole me. So the elders tole me to keep an eye out for you."

"Row...hond?"

The hawk fluttered its wings and then spoke in a distinct female voice, "I have been watching your progress. It was I who told the centaur you had fallen asleep. *Again*. The enemy was closing in and I knew you needed to make haste."

Alyra could only manage, "Whaa...huh?"

She squeezed her eyes shut and opened them to find the boy staring at her with wrinkled brows and the hawk with tilted head. *What kind of craziness was all this?*

He came down the stone steps with an impatient snort. "I know it's a lot to take in. Look, my name is Beave, and Rohond here is a messenger and scout for Issah. She comes from Aloblase where this kind of stuff is common." Beave spoke to the bird. "Thanks for showing her to me."

Rohond took flight, her speckled wings flapping until an air current swooped her over the treetops.

Alyra continued to stare at him, dumbfounded.

He grabbed her sleeve and gave it a tug. "You'll see. But we need to get in the Meeting Hall and wait until all this passes."

"What passes?" She allowed him to pull her toward the building.

"We're under attack." Beave pulled harder. "Now come on. We'll watch from the roof." He moved forward.

So Issah, also known as The Guardian, was from Aloblase? Her shoulders sank with her heart. He'd probably been put off by her rudeness. She hadn't seen any more of him since her split from Jerin.

"Are you hungry? I'll get you something to eat." Beave glanced over his shoulder to make sure she followed.

"Yeah ... No!" She dragged her feet. "Wait, wait! Attack? I need to get out of here! They're probably after me."

How could he be so calm about this? Just like Marcel's warriors and Dean. Didn't anything faze these people?

They stopped before two heavy, wooden doors with carved intricate vines, intermingled with various animals, human, and beast. Each door had a tree with star shaped leaves engraved into the surface, like the one on her medallion.

Beave pushed one of the doors opened and yanked her inside after him. "You'll be safe with us."

They came into an open hall where people darted in all

directions. A dwarf, wearing a helmet and breastplate, stood on a chair yelling orders to those who rushed past.

"We'll make do with what is on hand!'" He bellowed in a growling voice. "These tools will break the earth, and they can break the enemy as well." His dark eyes caught sight of Beave. "Is this the one we've been told to expect?"

The boy gave a quick nod. "Yes, Elder Wain. This is Alyra."

The dwarf bowed low, his long grizzled beard swept the ground. "Welcome, daughter" His voice now gentler. "You are safe here. Follow young Beave's instructions, and you will be well cared for." Then he turned back to the gathering crowd surrounding his chair. "Take your places along both forks of the river. They'll dare not pass the King's waters without regret!"

A cheer filled the hall as the throng flowed out the wide doors like a mighty ocean wave.

Beams of sunlight filtered through the open ceiling onto a circular atrium. A young tree grew in the middle, its limbs, white and smooth, reminding her of a dove's body. The same star-shaped leaves, as those on the doors, covered the branches along with small, plum-sized, blood-red fruit. This had to be the tree from her medallion.

She reached out to touch one of the hard fruits, but the boy swatted her hand away "Don't pick them. They're only to be taken when needed."

"When would they be needed?"

He shrugged. "I'm not sure. What I do know is if someone takes one they don't need, the fruit spoils right after it's picked. The smell is horrible, and your skin will be stained red for nearly a month." He wiped his hands on his coveralls. She wondered if this information didn't come from experience.

"Let's go." Beave's bare feet slapped over the smooth stone floor as he led her toward one of the side wings. He appeared to be around eight or nine years old.

These people must be crazy, the whole lot of them. They acted as if facing Darnel's army was no more than a game. Didn't they realize how dangerous he was? She followed the boy, but her insides quaked with fear and she scanned the rooms to check for possible escape routes. If the army came across the river, she'd run, no matter what these people said.

The eastern wing reminded her of a market center she'd once seen in Racah, one of the few times Master had let her go into the city with him. Fruit carts, vegetable and meat stands lined one side. Stalls of shoes and brightly colored garments filled the other. She glanced down at her worn, stained clothes. Maybe there was enough money in Dean's pack for her to purchase another outfit. She'd also like a bath. Her heart sank when she realized she'd most likely be back on the run if the enemy penetrated the town's defenses.

The boy grabbed a loaf of bread, a chunk of cheese, and two brown bottles before motioning for her to follow him.

"Shouldn't you pay for that?"

"Pay?" His nose crinkled as if the word were foreign to him.

"Yeah, you can't just take people's goods. That's stealing."

"Not stealing. Sharing. Now come on."

Confused, Alyra followed up a set of spiral stairs. What did he mean by *sharing*? Normal people didn't appreciate others helping themselves to their possessions. With a shrug, she planned to blame the boy if anyone mentioned the missing food. As they passed the second floor, she paused to watch a group of children playing a game of tag. Several older adults tended to the infants. An elderly man sat near the balcony with children around his feet as he told a story.

She caught a few words as she passed. "Just when everything looked the bleakest, something spectacular was happening, though none knew what. You see, Shaydon promised to take care of his—"

The trump of a horn blew from outside.

"Hurry!" Beave urged. The bottles clanked in his arms as they rushed to the very top landing. Once on the roof, they picked one of the tables on the wood deck where they had a good view of the town and valley. Below, she spotted another glistening path weaving through the fields, orchards, and pastures like a stitched seam.

"Hey, is that the White Road, too?"

Beave set down his loot. "Yep, there are three branches that meet the main one that you were on." He broke off a chunk of bread and handed it to her, then took out a pocketknife and sliced a piece of pungent smelling cheese. "Alburnium towns are built along converging paths to help travelers like yourself." He glanced at her outfit, wrinkling his nose. "Your clothes need to be replaced. Our tailor will provide you some."

Alyra couldn't believe her ears. Glancing down at her stained pants, her cheeks burned because of her appearance. "I have a few coins. Maybe I can work on the farms, too."

"We're here to help you along on your journey. We'll give you whatever you need."

"Why?"

"I know what you are thinking. This is a real shock to outsiders. We share what we have. Then nobody is without." He popped the corks off the bottles and handed her one. "Apple cider. My family runs the orchard. The best you'll have ever tasted."

Sipping the tangy-sweet juice to wash down the bread, she thought about the practicality of the way of life here. How did anyone get ahead in a place where they simply gave away their stuff?

In the valley, Alyra spotted another white road, different from the one she'd traveled. "I don't suppose you've seen a young man named Jerin, have you? He's tall and big, like a bear. He's a friend of mine, but we got separated."

Beave shook his head, then gulped down the bottle's contents. "You're the first visitor we've had since seed time." He sat up and leaned over the railing at the front of the building, shielding his wide eyes with his free hand.

"Look!" Beave pointed toward the opposite side of the river where a group of trolls gathered. "There's at least ten."

Their guttural challenges echoed across the town and hit her like a fist. The cheese sandwich slipped from her grasp.

"Trolls aren't very smart, are they?" Her voice squeaked with fear.

"Naw. I heard they're mainly used as brute force." Beave answered with complete indifference. "They can tear down a tree and throw it like a javelin. But if they touch the white rocks, or the rivers, whoo-wee, they'll regret it."

Alyra backed away and started for the stairs. "I have to leave."

Beave grabbed her arm. "You can't go."

"Don't you see? They're here because of me! If I go, then they'll leave you alone."

"No they won't. We're not going to let them take you."

A shout rose up from below. Beave turned back to the battle brewing at the river. The trolls bellowed at the farmers wielding their pitchforks, mattocks and scythes. The townsfolk were not warriors like Marcel's army. What hope did they have against trolls? If Bezoar was behind the giant beast, this town was done for.

"Wow, would you look at all them?" He grinned.

A flash caught Alyra's attention. She peered harder, trying to see into the shady woods. Smaller creatures, maybe dwarfs or something similar gathered around several trees. She heard pounding, then cracking moments before a tall pine tumbled over. One of the trolls caught the tree and tossed it over the river's banks. As more came down, the large beast began forming a makeshift bridge over the water.

A unit of soldiers used the tree-bridges to cross into the town. Horsemen followed, taking a bit more care, but breaching the obstacle in a short amount of time.

Alyra couldn't move. She searched around wildly, wondering if she could just leap over the edge and run. The fall would probably break too many bones. She'd not stay in the building and be captured. No, she had to get away and hide. If the people won, then she'd come back out. If not, she'd have to keep going east until she outdistanced the enemy soldiers.

While Beave's attention was riveted on the advancing army, Alyra slipped away and raced down the stairs. When she reached the landing, an elderly woman stood in her path with hands held up to stop her. "Stay here, honey. Help will come soon."

We're they crazy? "They've crossed the rivers. Nothing can save your town now."

The old woman grinned. "We'll be all right. Don't fear, child."

There wasn't time for this madness. Alyra darted around her.

"Come back," Beave yelled from above.

Ignoring the boy's pleas for her to stay, she ran toward the nearest exit. Once outside, she had no idea which direction to take. Fear crowded her mind and shoved reason out, causing her to run without consideration. Away from the attack was the only reasoning her consciousness grasped.

Head turned to watch over her shoulder, she plowed into

something. Rough hands grabbed her, clamping down on her mouth. She was dragged behind one of the buildings where a sign hung that said, *Leather Crafts.*

She kicked at her captor, hoping to connect with a leg.

"Stop." He shoved her against the wall. "It's me, Princess. Please, stop fighting."

Alyra gasped and turned. "Tarek!"

He closed his eyes a moment, breathing deep. "I was so afraid I wouldn't be the first one to find you." He peered around the building before pulling her farther behind where they were sheltered from the battle.

"That's not my name." She never wanted to hear Princess again. "I know now who I am. My name, Tarek, I know my real name now."

He slowly shook his head.

"Alyra. My name is Alyra."

He only stared at her, disbelieving.

"What are you doing here?" she asked. "I've been so worried about you. Does Darnel know you helped me escape? Were you..."

Tarek held up his hands to stop her. "Yes, he knows. *King* Darnel said if I brought you back, if you return willingly, all would be forgiven." He took in a deep breath. "Please, come home. I've been worried about you as well. I can't imagine what you've been through."

"It's... I'm alright. I ... I'm not going back there, Tarek. Ever." She tightened her fist, determined to stand her ground. Would he force her? Her body tensed. Not without a fight, he wouldn't.

He leaned against the building, as he groaned. "I was afraid you'd say that."

The harshness in his voice, the familiar tone when he'd mocked her, returned. He stared down at his feet, causing his golden hair to cover his face so she couldn't read his eyes. He was dressed like one of the Racan soldiers. His hand rested on a sword tied at his waist.

She didn't want to fight him. No, she'd have to run. She took a step backward.

His chin jutted out stubbornly. "Haven't had enough, huh? Still think you'll make it there? On your own? Look at you in those horrid clothes. You're a mess, Princ—"

"Alyra."

For a moment, his hardened face relaxed and shoulders sagged. A small smile played across his lips as he finally met her with his softening green eyes. "I like Alyra. It's a beautiful name."

"Come with me, Tarek. Then I won't have to travel alone. Actually, I've not really been alone. People, or ... well, I've had help. I'm okay."

He stepped closer her, and she noticed a band of dark blotches covered his cheek.

A loud screech sounded overhead. Alyra spun toward the sound. The hawk swooped low. "Come, Alyra. Flee, the Baykok comes for you."

Tarek gasped, peering over her shoulder.

"Bezoar?"

He nodded and pushed her further behind the building.

"Hide. He's looking for me. Sent me ahead to find you. Stay hidden. I'll go deter him."

She grabbed his arm before he ran off. "No. Come with me. You can't possibly want to be with them. You have to see what they are."

His face hardened. "I don't have a choice. If I disappear, he will kill my family." He shoved her away. "I won't force you to return. I won't. So go on. Hide. Run. Just don't let Bezoar catch you. He's out of patience, and I'm afraid he'll not take you alive if you put up a fight."

Giving her shoulders a quick squeeze, he ran to the center of town. A black steed charged toward him, Bezoar upon its saddle, sword in one hand, the whip in the other.

Alyra hid in the shelter of the building, unable to leave him. She couldn't see the fighting from her position, but she heard the screams, yells, and clanging of sword against pitchfork.

"I haven't found her," Tarek lied.

He really was covering for her? Tarek always had been close to his mother, father, and a younger sister. All worked in the kitchen, Tarek learning to hunt from his father who also worked the gardens while his mother and sister prepared pastries and desserts. Alyra always envied him having a family.

Bezoar snapped his whip. "If we lose her, when we are this close, you'll pay, so help me. Find her. Bring her to me, dead or alive, I care not anymore. I've tired of this pointless hunt. It ends today!"

The whip slashed across Tarek's chest. He hugged himself, falling to his knees.

A dwarf wearing Racah armor ran past carrying two torches. Bezoar ordered Tarek to help set the fires while he searched for her. The bearded creature tossed a fire stick to him. He missed, and it landed in a pile of straw, beside the livery, instantly igniting.

"Run," Rohand ordered, landing on the roof where Alyra hid. "Follow me. I'll take you to safety. Come child." Her massive wings spread as she flew into the woods toward the eastern river.

Alyra hesitated for only a moment, until Bezoar turned his horse in her direction. Ducking out of sight, she raced into the woods as smoke and flames billowed up from behind. More than from Tarek's miss-catch. The soldiers must have purposefully set the town and surrounding forest on fire. *To draw her out?*

Their plan was working. Alyra ran blindly through the rolling haze, hoping she headed east. She used the edge of her cloak to cover her nose and mouth but her lungs still filled with searing smoke. Flames leaped from branch to branch, engulfing the dried, summer trees. She followed the deer and squirrels, figuring they'd know instinctively which way to get out of this inferno. The thickening haze caused her to lose sight of the hawk.

Spotting a group of people running in the same direction, she tried to keep close to them. A loud crack sounded overhead. She covered her head with her arms. A flaming tree crashed directly into her path. She jumped aside, but not quick enough to escape the hot embers landing on her arm. Screaming, she swatted at the flames, tearing away the fabric of her sleeve.

The group disappeared in the black haze. She stumbled on, hoping she ran from the fire and not deeper into it. The heat cooked her throat. Her stomach heaved, and she lost what little bit of sandwich she'd eaten on the rooftop.

She stopped, trying to catch her breath. Her eyes watered from the stinging. She had to find that other river. Water had saved her before, perhaps she'd be able to use the stream again.

From above came a screech. A shadow passed overhead. Rohond!

The hawk swooped low. "This way. Don't stop."

Hoof beats pounded over the roaring flames, but she saw nothing.

Alyra forced herself back to her feet, stumbling and half crawling through the burning timbers. Rohond perched on a fence beside a wheat field. A band of sparkling blue wove across the golden grasses. The clang of swords told her the fighting continued nearby. She turned away and began heading to the river when several Racan soldiers burst from the smoky woods a few yards ahead. She ducked, caught in the middle, with nothing more than the tall grasses to hide her.

Shouts rose up from the Racan forces. She'd been seen! With a burst of speed, she ran with everything she had. Arrows shot past. Thundering hooves pounded in her ears. Once she reached the shore, she dove in and was instantly carried away by the strong current. The hawk swooped over the churning waves, her calls barely audible over the rushing water. Alyra kicked her aching legs, trying to swim to the other side.

The cold river soothed her burning body. Something whizzed past her head. She stopped paddling. *Hiss, hiss, hiss*, from the right shore was followed by a *plunk, plunk, plunk*. Sharp pain tore across her thigh. Water swamped her mouth when she cried out. When she came up again, the Racan soldiers disappeared as the river careened around a bend and swept her past the smoky forest. Blackness threatened to overtake her.

Her body connected with something hard. A rock? Mind reeling, she struggled to stay conscious. She coughed, trying to replace the liquid in her lungs with air.

"Kick your feet, Alyra."

Was that Tarek's voice?

"Come on, kick. Help me. Swim across."

Her aching legs moved. Tarek's arm circled her waist, keeping her head above water. She kicked harder, feeling them make better progress as she relaxed and allowed him to guide her across to a low hanging limb. She grasped on. He ducked under, but hung on to the other side, clasping her hands in his.

"Don't let go." He gasped between deep intakes of breaths. Tendrils of drenched curls fell in his eyes. The bruises on his face stood out clearer against the pale whiteness of his wet skin. "Soon as you can, let's start edging toward the shore."

Her heart raced. He'd saved her again, but at what cost?

"Come," she gasped, "with me."

He didn't answer. Keeping his hands over hers, he moved them along the trunk a few inches at a time. Her feet finally touched the bottom, but her leg was too weak to support her weight.

One of the enemy's arrows plunged into the water inches from Alyra. She cringed, almost losing her hold on the branch.

From their side of the river, another group of soldiers burst from the woods and covered the shoreline. Archers, dressed in gold armor, sent hundreds of arrows across, driving back the enemy.

"Who are they?" Tarek asked, mouth hanging open.

One glance and Alyra knew by the tree on their breastplates. "Alburnium warriors." But they were different than Marcel's troop. These human-like beings seemed to glow.

"Alyra," called a familiar voice. She found the Guardian, Issah, standing on the shore. He was dressed like the warriors, instead of in the brown traveling clothes he'd worn before. Or, maybe it was someone else who looked like him.

"Come," He reached out his hand, the same hand that had beckoned her before. She'd spurned him then, but not this time.

Using the last bit of her strength, she flung out her arm. His fingers clasped around her wrist and pulled her to safety. She flung out her free arm for Tarek.

He was gone.

# Chapter 17

"Nooo!" Alyra cried, trying to dive back in, but something restrained her. "You have to save my friend."

Her vision blurred, and everything went blank as she collapsed. The next thing she knew she was on dry land. Rohond perched right above her head. "Is she hurt?"

Alyra opened her eyes. The Guardian they'd also called Issah, crouched beside her. He checked her arms and legs. Next to him stood two of the most beautiful warriors she'd even seen, with pale skin and flowing hair. Their gear sparkled with newness. Behind them, a group of centaurs stood partially hidden in the bushes.

"Nothing too serious." Issah lifted her in his arms. "She's going to be fine." Alyra gaped at the white-clad warriors, the centaurs, and then Issah's kind face and wondered if she'd fallen into an even stranger dream than Lord Darnel could conjure.

"Tarek?"

"He made a different choice," Issah whispered, his voice sorrowful.

Why hadn't he held on? They would have saved him, too.

Issah carried her to the stern-faced centaurs. Lotari stood beside Wyndham.

"We must get her to safety." His gaze locked on Lotari. "Will you take her to the next stream that crosses the Highway?"

Lotari turned so she could be placed on his back. Wyndham scowled, but said nothing.

The hawk flew down and landed on the man's shoulder. "Rohond," Issah pointed. "Lead the way for them. I'll see what I can do to calm this situation. Go, make haste."

Lotari took off without a second glance. Alyra wrapped her arms around his waist as the trees turned into a blur. The hawk stayed a few feet ahead. Head swimming, she feared passing out.

The centaur's hand grasped both of hers and held them tightly against his chest. "Hang on, little one. We'll soon be safe."

She nodded, burying her face in the thick fur running down his back. She shut her eyes against the motion, hoping to quell the churning in her stomach. When his galloping hooves eventually slowed, she opened one eye. The familiar white stones flash by and she began to breathe easily again.

Lotari didn't stop until the river reached his flank. Alyra slid off his back and let the cold water wash over her, soothing the pain in her leg and arm. Unfortunately it didn't sooth the searing pain inside her chest.

*Tarek....* Disappearing in the blink of an eye. Everyone she had contact with ended up in trouble or dead. Dean killed for helping her. Jerin angry and now lost. Her mind whirled with fear and concern that Many River's misfortune was her fault. Those soldiers were looking for her. And Tarek... prisoner and forced to hunt her down for fear of what might happen to his family.

Yet he let her go. Would he suffer for that as well? Her stomach twisted. She crawled to the edge of the stream, fearing she was going to get sick again. She swallowed down the burning bile, blinked away the tears, and held back the sobs threatening to escape.

Rohond landed on the shore and fluttered her feathers. Boiling clouds obscured the sun completely. Thunder rumbled, followed by heavy sheets of rain, pushed on by a stiff wind. Lotari hurried out of the water and stood beneath a sprawling willow.

Alyra tilted up her face, allowing the tears to flow now and mingle with the rain pouring down her cheeks.

"Come under the shelter, silly girl," Lotari chided.

She ignored him. The damp air soothed her charred lungs. The pain in her chest didn't ease, but at least she could breathe again.

Hands grasped her shoulders, pulling her to her feet. His hooves clomped over the rocky ground as he led her beneath the willow. He pressed his water bag to her lip, urging her to drink. She obeyed. The liquid eased her tender throat. Rough thumbs wiped the wetness from her face. For a moment, his concerned eyes came into focus.

"I have some berries I collected this morning. Are you hungry?"

She shook her head, knowing her stomach would reject anything she tried to put into it. He helped her settle down in a crevice formed by the tree's thick roots. He checked her wounds, wrapping her leg with the torn edge of her charred cloak to slow the bleeding. He then pulled a small wooden instrument from his bag and began playing a calming tune on his pipes. His horse legs folded as he sat beside her.

Resting against the rough bark, she let the music still her racing heart and anxious thoughts. The downpour lasted for nearly an hour before slowing to a softer shower. The boughs of the tree hung heavy with raindrops.

Water dripped on her, but she ignored the irritation. She couldn't feel any more miserable anyway. Her leg hurt from the gash, her arm from the burns, and her heart broke for the people of that beautiful town. Lotari seemed unconcerned over the whole ordeal. A smile played across his usually stern face as he picked a couple of burrs off of his horse legs.

Finally, as the heavy rain subsided, he asked, "I don't suppose any of the bread I made you remains?"

Taken aback at his callousness, she glared at him. He'd seemed kind and caring when she was traveling alone. Did he not care for the townspeople anymore than his clan did? Alyra pulled off her pack and threw it at him.

He caught it, brows knit in confusion for a moment before his face relaxed. "Alyra , they will be fine. Why did you not stay in the meeting hall like the others?"

"I didn't want to get burned up! Why wouldn't they flee?" Hot tears stung her eyes. "All those children..."

"Foolish child, have you not listened to anything? The white path is safe. The white buildings are safe as well."

She shook her head, unable to believe his words.

He nodded in affirmation. "This is the reason I told you to make haste. The kingdom town offered a protection against the enemy. The only damage was to a couple of buildings and the surrounding woods. We centaurs will help the trees re-establish themselves."

Fresh tears pooled in her eyes as she wondered how much more damage she would leave in her wake as she made this journey. Perhaps going back would at least save others from suffering because of her foolishness. She took a deep shuddering breath, sealing her turmoil and confusion inside. At the moment, trying to sort everything out was more than she was able to handle.

"Such a beautiful place. What a waste."

He shrugged. "Never a waste. Before they established Many Rivers, we fought all sorts of evil pests polluting the woods. Those bred in the evil lands. We spent most of our days keeping them out. But once the kingdom people moved in with their white roads and safe houses, the mutated beast retreated." He opened her pack. His brows shot up in surprise as he dug through the contents.

"They will rebuild. We are a marvel at tending the forest and helping them re-grow. This bag must be Logorian made. Nothing is damaged or wet." He took one of the cakes for himself, and tossed the hawk a chunk. "What do you think, Rohond?"

She pecked away the treat. "Most rebuild. Some may give up and return to the safety of Aloblase. Usually, they are the ones who weren't ready to go out in the first place." She grew quiet for a moment, her head bobbing and tilting as if listening. "I must go now. I'm needed at this time. Good bye for now." Spreading her massive wings, she took flight, heading back toward the town.

Lotari sighed. "Nothing in here will help with your burns." He searched through the surrounding plants and trees. "Perhaps I can find something…"

"I didn't hear anything, did you? Why'd she leave?"

His shaggy brows knit in consternation. "I am not her keeper. How am I supposed to know? Rohond serves as a messenger and scout for the Guardian, though she'll help anyone who asks."

Alyra wondered if she had seen Jerin anywhere.

The rain stopped, the clouds evaporating as rapidly as they formed. Lotari stepped from under the willow into the warm sunshine under a bright blue sky. Alyra could only stare in wonderment. The centaur turned back toward her with a wide grin. They both burst into laughter.

Lotari lifted his arms and shouted, "Praises to King Shaydon, protector and provider of all his people."

Another person's laughter joined his. "And many thanks to the Great King for hearing the request of his beloved children."

On the bridge, stood the man who'd saved her from the water. He no longer looked like the warrior she'd seen next to the river, but rather like the simple traveler she'd met the day Jerin and her split.

Lotari walked into the water and looked up at him. "You're not even drenched from that downpour?"

The man shrugged with a mischievous smile.

Lotari's eyes narrowed as a crooked grin crossed his bearded face. He gave the water a kick, sending spray up onto the bridge and wetting the man's feet.

Issah looked down at the spots on his brown pants. "Really now?" With that, he leaped down about four feet into the river. The splash fight began.

Alyra crept back beneath the willow to watch in safety as the man and beast battled with much laughter and shouting. The man had the centaur in a headlock and attempted to wrestle him down into the water. The centaur spread his four legs apart, wrapped his arms around the man's waist and both tumbled over together.

She couldn't help but laugh at their play. They seemed like good friends. Part of her wished to jump in and join them. Yet the larger part held a cautionary fear of lowering her guard. Then she noticed blood had soaked through the bandage around her aching leg. How would she continue like this?

"That looks painful." The man wiped wet hair back from his face.

Lotari came over, shaking the water from his horse body. "I had no supplies to repair the gash, so I wrapped it as tightly as possible."

He knelt beside her as Lotari added, "I considered pine sap for the burn, but it'll take me a while to prepare a concoction."

"You've done well taking care of her, my friend. I may have something that will help." His brown eyes looked intently at her. "Will you trust me to tend to your wounds?"

Did he know she was frightened of him? She put on a brave face and shrugged, "Sure, if you think you can." Show no fear, she reminded herself. It only makes things worse if they know you are afraid.

He removed the bandage then tore back the cloth of her pants. They were singed anyway. "This water will help a great deal'" He filled his cupped hands and washed off the blood. Alyra cringed and turned away. She'd be left with a terrible scar once it finally healed. From a bag slung over his shoulder, he pulled out a small wooden cup, which he filled with water. "Drink this. You'll get the best from within and without."

She looked from the man to Lotari who nodded for her to accept. When she sipped, though, she tasted not water, but a rich, thick liquid that went down her throat like warm oil. She spat the potion out quickly and handed him back the cup.

His brow furrowed. "Alyra, the drink will help ease the pain."

She shook her head. "I'm fine." Darnel had often treated her to drinks that brought on unwanted sleep and frightening nightmares. She'd not be gullible now.

Lotari muttered, "Stubborn child."

What did he know anyway?

"Should I find something to tie her leg with?" Lotari asked. "Seems like the only way we'll get the bleeding to stop."

"No, not the only way." He pinched the skin together, brows knit tight in complete concentration as he whispered, "Renew."

A warm sensation flowed through her thigh that joined the warmth emanating from her belly.

Tearing strips of linen from the bottom of his shirt, he tied one around her leg. He took the other, dipped it into the water and covered the burns on her arm. His touch was gentle and words soothing. "It'll be as good as new very soon, precious, you'll see."

Alyra watched him intently, shamed over her behavior toward him. She wanted to apologize, but couldn't make the words form in her mouth.

"You have nothing to be sorry about." He tied the wrap into a small knot.

She gasped. Could he read her thoughts like Darnel?

"I know your heart, Alyra."

Now she found her tongue. "Have we met before? Is that how you know my name?"

"Yes."

"Who are you, really? Lotari says you're the guardian of the white road. But you called yourself teacher. You look like a simple traveler to me. But then, in town, I heard someone call you...Issah?"

"Yes. That's one of the many names I've had over time. I would like it very much if you simply called me friend."

"Friend? That's it? Just friend."

He nodded with a playful smile. "Yes, exactly. And my friends call me Issah. You can too, if you'll call me friend."

She wasn't sure how to respond. If he saw into her heart so well, then he'd know she feared him. How could someone you fear be a friend? Yet deep down the desire to trust him was there. Covering that desire was a suspicion that he was so like Master in his abilities, he might be in actions as well. Plenty of people who followed Lord Darnel thought he was wonderful. Just because people followed someone didn't make them good.

His penetrating gaze bore into her as he nodded silently.

Almost proving her suspicions, he said, "Trust isn't to be given carelessly. Sometimes it comes with time and with a sound relationship."

He stepped out of the water and Lotari helped her to her feet. The stinging pain now felt more like a dull throb, especially when she put too much weight on her leg. At least blood no longer seeped through the bandage. Issah offered his arm for her to use as support but she limped past on her own.

"Sir, the man I was traveling with… Jerin... do you know what happened to him?"

A shadow crossed Issah's face. "Jerin has not returned to the path and has not responded to those sent to redirect him. Hope remains though."

She considered asking about Tarek, then decided against it.

When she gazed at Issah, his mouth turned up in a crooked grin. "Don't give up hope on your friend, either. Like you, fear drives his choices."

Lotari's brows knit in confusion. She didn't want to tell anyone about Tarek, yet Issah seemed to know of her worry for him. Were her choices really driven by fear? Maybe he was right about that, too. She was so scared of not only what pursued her, but what lay ahead.

As she hobbled a few steps along the rocky path, she realized this would slow her progress even more. Biting her lip against the ache, she determined to make it on her own. He said nothing, but stayed close anyway.

Lotari disappeared into the woods and returned shortly with a stick. "Use this. If it gets too painful, I'll let you ride."

She took the stick and used it as a cane. "No, this will work."

"Good." Issah's voice sounded sad, yet he smiled anyway.

"That should get you to our destination. I will go with you to the healer's house. You can stay there until you've mended enough to continue your journey."

Lotari's legs pranced like a young colt. "You're going to go see Marya? Wonderful!"

Issah laughed at his excitement. "Yes, my friend, and you as well. Though Marya is a talented healer, I know she will appreciate your help."

He stopped bouncing for joy and the smile on his face faltered. "Oh, yeah I'd love to help. If they'll let me."

# Chapter 18

Nearly an hour passed as Lotari talked nonstop about Marya the Healer. Three summers ago, he'd broken his back leg and had been taken to her to have it set. Aside from Issah, she was the only human Wyndham would allow them to socialize with. During his recuperation, she taught him the healing arts. Plant lore came naturally as he'd grown up in the woods, but she showed him how to set broken bones, stitch cuts, and even how to deliver babies.

"Not that many humans will allow one of my kind to aid in delivery." He stared ahead at the road, his voice deadpan. "They fear we might bring a curse on the infant. But I have aided the births of many animals and my clan mothers, as well. Quite exciting." His tail swooshed as he smiled with a joyfulness she'd never seen from him.

Alyra piped up, "So when will we get to this healer's house?" Her stomach growled, leg hurt- even with the support of the cane, and her feet were weary. Surprisingly, the burns on her arm no longer stung as much. "If it's going to be awhile, can we stop for a quick rest and something to eat? I still might have a few of Lot's grain cakes left. "

"Something to eat?" Issah, had remained quiet the whole time Lotari talked. "That will be wonderful. But after the day we've had, I think we can do better than grain cakes. No offense my friend."

"None taken." Lotari grinned, as if he and Issah were in on some private joke.

"I could eat a whole baked hen." Issah closed his eyes and took in a deep breath. "Do you smell potatoes with thyme?"

Lotari sniffed deeply. "With roasted lamb?"

Alyra took in a deep breath of nothing but damp earth and pine trees.

"Yes." A wide smile spread across Issah's face. "And music, my friends. I do love the melody of violins, you know."

Alyra closed her eyes and listened but heard only crickets. The sun had set and the cobalt sky had a sprinkling of stars across its surface.

"Oh, I have my pipes!" Lotari's hooves clattered as he began stepping and clapping to a tune that obviously wasn't there. He broke into a canter and disappeared amongst the trees.

"All right, enough!" Alyra banged the cane against the rocks. "What kind of joke is this? If you don't want to stop, say so. Just quit trying to make a fool of me."

Issah stared at her with pity in his gaze. "Come on, let's get something to eat. They've prepared a wonderful meal for us." He extended his hand.

Standing firm, her feet planted slightly apart, she determined to have nothing to do with this madness. The moment she lowered her guard and started to believe Issah might be different from Lord Darnel, that he spoke the truth about trusting, then he plays mind games with her. And Lotari followed his game like a pet dog. Some friend.

Issah's hand never lowered, nor did the concern leave his eyes. "Just because you don't see, doesn't make it not true."

She turned away. Her fingers dug into the bark of the cane. Why were they teasing her like this?

"Alyra." His tone grew stern. "You'll have to trust me on this. I won't leave you here."

She glanced at his outstretched hand. Somewhere deep inside she heard a voice, *You can do this. It's not at all what you think. Just trust me, and you'll see.*

Sweat dripped down her forehead and neck, sapping all moisture from her mouth. She spun around, searching for Lord Darnel. "Master?"

Oh, she hoped not. Not here. Not now.

"Alyra, don't be afraid. I'm the only one here." His piercing gaze leveled at her. "Is *he* still your master?"

Her eyes burned. The names she'd been called, the words said about her came onto her like a colossal avalanche. Pain stabbed at her gut, and she desperately fought the torrent of tears threatening to explode.

"No! I hate him. I'll not be controlled again!" She turned to face

Issah straight on. "I'm not damaged, or stupid. I'm not! And I'm not a freak!"

"Hush, daughter." He stepped closer and reached to touch her shoulder. She jerked away. "I know exactly who you are. Alyra, child of Alburnium. Daughter to Stephen of Belluvita. Born to those of the light. *The Illuminate*."

Her quaking stopped and she gaped, wondering at his words.

"I do not wish to control, but to guide. I desire a true friendship. You'll need my help to reach Aloblase. You have nothing to fear, dear one." He stepped closer again, hand still extended. "Will you turn away from what was and walk with me now?"

Haltingly, she stretched her fingers toward his, only to quickly draw back. She wanted to believe she was doing fine on her own, but in reality, if not for all the people who'd helped her, who'd ended up suffering because of her, she wouldn't have survived this far.

"Follow me." His fingers beckoned her. "If you'll take my hand, child, so much will become clear to you."

The way he spoke caused stirring warmth in her heart, as if she'd been offered a tantalizing challenge. Trembling, she warily laid her hand in his.

A bright light burst about them, and all her senses came alive. Music filled the night air. The most beautiful beings she'd ever seen appeared, some playing flutes and stringed instruments, while others sang along. At first their song sounded like a waterfall but soon the words became recognizable and somewhat familiar. They were dressed in bright, festive clothing, both male and female. Every fear, every worry she'd had only moments before dissipated.

In the center of the gathering sat linen-covered tables heaped with roasted meat, fruits, and glossy loaves of bread.

Lotari stood with a large chicken leg sticking from his mouth.

Laughter and talk rang in her ears. She clutched Issah's hand tighter, afraid if she released him the wonderful vision would disappear.

His free arm circled her shoulder, pulling her close as he whispered in her ear, "Come, my precious child. Join me for a banquet?"

She shook her head, unable to move. "Issah, this is too much. What kind of trick have you conjured? Even Mast—, I mean, Darnel couldn't pull this off."

"Not a conjured trick, Alyra. The Logorians love to host fine festivities. I'm so pleased to have you heading back home. You've been sorely missed, dear one. In all the troubles you've endured, I simply wished to treat you to this little celebration. A mere shadow of the one that will greet you when you finally reach Aloblase." He turned her so they faced each other. He cupped her chin in his hands. "Please allow me share a bit of extravagance with you just for this one night."

Alyra blinked back tears. "Everything looks so... good. So beautiful. Thank you, Issah."

Still clutching her hand, he led her to one of the tables. "What are you hungry for?" He reached for the roasted bird. She hadn't eaten fresh meat since she'd left Marcel's camp. *Was wanting a taste of everything too much?*

One of the beautiful beings offered her a plate heaped with foods cooked to perfection. Crisp, steamy vegetables and soft, warm bread. She relished each tantalizing bite.

"Issah, who are the Logorians?"

"Many serve as King Shaydon's warriors. Some are instructors and messengers of a special order."

"Lotari said the Logorians made my back pack. I can't believe all it holds and nothing ever gets wet."

One of the servers smiled at her with a wink. "We are also astonishing craftsmen. I'm quite gifted with a needle and thread, among my many other useful talents." He rested his hand on the long hilt of his sword. "If I say so myself."

Issah laughed. "They are not well gifted with modesty, I might add."

When she could eat no more, one of the female Logorians came and led her away. A gold band inlaid with red and green jewels circled delicately around her flowing yellow hair.

"I am Gwynedd." She headed deeper into the trees. Small lights flickered within the leaves, illuminating the way. On closer inspection, Alyra realized the balls of light were actually tiny fairies. Amazing!

They came to a small pool fed by a hot spring. Candles burned along the rocky crevices. Misty steam swirled along the surface like a natural bathtub.

"We thought you might enjoy a warm bath." Gwynedd pointed to another woman. This one had wavy red hair and sat upon a mossy stone, sewing a bright yellow cloth. "Meghan has been working on new outfits for you. Since this one is practically ruined with stains and scorch marks."

The redheaded woman lifted the shirt, and Alyra marveled at the intricate ivy she'd embroidered around the neckline. "What do you think, dear?"

Alyra gasped with pleasure. "So beautiful. Thank you." Carefully, she touched the sleeve finding the fabric soft like silky cotton, yet thick enough to endure traveling. She couldn't remember ever being able to wear something so bright and pretty.

They left her to bathe. Alyra sat on the edge of the natural basin and unwrapped the bandage. The blistered burns were now reduced to pink splotches. On her leg, the gash was simply a long cut, no longer bleeding or open. Her heart skipped a beat as she realized that even Darnel never did anything this amazing. Matter-of-fact, most of Darnel's feats were only tricks, usually meant to harm, not help. But Issah had really made the blisters go away and her skin to fuse back together. If only he'd make the emblem on her shoulder disappear as well.

After the bath as Gwynedd braided her hair, Alyra looked at her. "You know, I used to dream of people like you, when I lived in Racah. I'd hear singing, like tonight."

"Perhaps Alyra," replied the red-headed Meghan, "it's a memory and not merely a dream. For in Aloblase many of our people dwell near the King. Do you remember anything else?"

Alyra thought hard. The lavender scented soap she'd bathed with gave her a vision of a flowered meadow on a warm spring day. "I have memories of running with a group of children."

Then she saw herself sitting in a woodland clearing. A woman with red hair sat on a log, reading from an open book. The children recited what she said, word for word. "I remember someone who looked like you teaching us poetry!"

Meghan clapped. "Wonderful. We heard the Dark One had taken most of your memories. I knew they'd return. I just knew."

Gwynedd added, "We asked to come along, hoping if you saw

us again, you'd begin to remember some of what he'd stolen."

"So you taught me when I was small?" Alyra turned to the golden haired Logorian and remembered her as well now. "Do you know what happened to me? How I ended up in Racah?"

Gwynedd shook her head. "I'm sure all will come back to you in due time."

They soon rejoined the main group where the music had turned lively. Lotari, looking like he'd had a good brush down, danced with arms outstretched as his hooves pounded the ground in rhythm to the drumbeat. He wore a circle of oak leaves around his head and a necklace of daisies.

He stopped when he noticed her and gave with a hearty laugh. "You do clean up well, don't you?"

She looked him over with a smirk. "Is that the new fashion in crowns, your furriness?"

"Funny, very funny." He bowed in a most gentlemanly manner. "Do me the honor?"

Alyra took his hand and they swung around the brightly lit clearing. Her leg hardly ached at all now. Laughter rang out at the sight of her trying to keep up with the four-legged centaur that kept bumping into other dancers. Others tried to join in but had to keep dodging out of the way of his hindquarters. His tail whipped about, smacking people who got too close. Yet nobody seemed to get upset at the beast, but rather laughed louder until he was purposefully bumping everyone.

Alyra finally managed to break away and took a seat at one of the tables. The meats and vegetables had been replaced with desserts and fruit.

Issah sat beside her, deep chuckles shaking his broad shoulders as Lotari found two new partners. Despite the enjoyment of this strange gathering, Alyra couldn't help but wonder about the villagers. The music grew quiet.

"Will the people of Many Rivers be all right?"

"Yes. They have what is most important to them, and that is their lives and each other. Buildings can be rebuilt. You will see some of them tomorrow at the healer's house. I think you're going to enjoy meeting Marya.

"For now, let's enjoy the good company and laughter. Are your wounds better?"

"Yes." She pulled back her sleeve to show him that all remained was a light pink mark. "Hardly even looks like I've been burnt. How did you do that?"

He leaned closer. "With love, dear one." Then he stood. "Would you indulge me? We'll show that silly centaur how dancing is supposed to be done."

She agreed, uncomfortable at first, but as they swung around the clearing, the stars lighting the sky above and the earth soft beneath her feet, she experienced something new. She didn't really understand the word *love* but wondered if it described what she felt at that moment.

Late into the night, they all danced and sang lively songs. She grew tired and found a soft-pillowed cushion to lie upon as the music lulled her into a peaceful sleep. Visions of a magnificent mountain city filled her dreams. The white road leading up to the gates glimmered in the sun. Children ran through the streets, giggling loudly as they pursued someone. She never saw the person, as every time he came into view, he darted around a corner or tree and disappeared again. They raced up a hillside until reaching several tall columns the color of jade. They skipped through an archway and stopped as the man stood still in the open room. His back remained turned to her. She tried to move through the group of children to see his face but was blinded by a brilliant radiance.

Alyra blinked and covered her eyes from the morning light shining in through the window. She sat up and looked around the small room. A fire burned in the stone hearth, where a steaming pot bubbled with what smelled like vegetable soup. Herbs hung on the walls, along with a few paintings of landscapes and waterfalls. She lay upon a plush couch covered with a knitted afghan. Two matching chairs sat opposite her. The front door stood open. She got up wondering if the night before had been a mere dream. But the new shirt she wore told her the feast had been quite real. Her backpack sat on one of the chairs, along with a spare set of clothing the color of a yellow daisy.

Outside the door, voices chattered.

# Chapter 19

Alyra limped outside, still using the cane to keep her weight off the sore leg. She blinked against the bright sunlight, pausing on the door-stoop until her eyes adjusted. Ivy and purple Morning Glories covered the cottage's stone walls and draped the square glass windows. The front yard burst with a variety of colorful flowers and herbs. Along one side of the house grew a neatly arranged vegetable garden. Voices drifted from the back so she headed in that direction.

The woods circled around a delightful open area behind the cottage. A bubbling creek flowed along the edge of the yard, and the White Road ran past the front. Across the crowded backyard sat a small barn. Several villagers went in and out of the double doors, some with arms laden full of blankets, or buckets of water drawn from the well. Others huddled in small groups beneath sprawling shade trees. Most of them wore bandages, or splints, but didn't seem in any great stress or pain. As a matter of fact, the atmosphere was not nearly as solemn, as she expected. The group's lively discussion was seasoned with boisterous laughter.

In the center of the yard spread a long table covered with plates of rolls, fruits and vegetables. Nothing compared to last night's feast, but tempting to her rumbling stomach, all the same. A large black caldron cooked some kind of stew over an open fire. More people were seated at the table, eating soup from carved wooden bowls. Chickens pecked around the yard, gobbling up the bread crust people tossed them.

A slender woman streamed across the backyard. Her narrow, sharp face beamed into a smile when she spotted Alyra. Gray streaks flowed through her wavy black hair. She wore a brown smock over a simple green dress.

"So, you are finally awake, I see. I am Marya. How do you feel, sugar?" To Alyra's surprise, she embraced her in a motherly hug, and then planted a kiss on each cheek. "Are you hungry, sweetheart? Issah said that he's already tended to your injuries."

Pulling back her sleeve, Alyra checked the burns, now no more than pink spots. Though the skin remained tender, it was no longer painful. She hadn't seen her thigh since last night, but knew Issah had somehow caused the gaping cut to fuse back together. Yesterday hadn't been a dream after all.

"Much better now." She looked around, not seeing Issah or the Logorians. "Is he still here?"

"No, they all left after carrying you in." Marya took in a deep breath, scanning the people crowded in her yard. Her narrow shoulders sagged, as if in weariness. Had she been working by herself on the wounded?

"If you are hungry," she said, "Help yourself to some soup."

Alyra's appetite was pushed aside by an acute sense of guilt. "Is there anything I can do? This is all my faul—."

"Don't you even entertain such thoughts!" Marya held up her hands, palms out. "This is the work of the enemy. They've caused havoc on all the Kingdom towns for some time." Sadness deepened the wrinkles over her brows. "Only lately, they've become more vicious about it."

Three children ran by giggling as they pounced on one of the dwarf men. He hollered out for help, pretending they were overpowering him, which caused the children to shriek even louder. Alyra recognized him as the same dwarf directing the people in the Meeting Hall.

"Elder Wain," Marya chided. "Don't you irritate that head wound. Lotari did an excellent job stitching you up, we don't want you messing up his work and creating an ugly scar."

The dwarf stood, knocking the children off his back. "My lady, we both know scars are a mark of valor. And a nice way to catch a lady dwarf's attention, if I might say."

Marya shook her head, laughing. She turned back to Alyra. "Yes, there is something you can do. Lotari is in the barn tending to some of the critical patients. He's such a help to me. We could use more bandages. If you go on in, he'll tell you what to do. I need to check on how my herbs are stewing inside. Can you do that, dear?"

Alyra nodded and headed toward the barn, now converted into a small hospital. Several beds lined the walls, and most were full. Lotari, also wearing a blood-splattered apron, stood inside a curtained area where two severely burned people lay on tall tables.

"Marya said I could help." She waited in the doorway, wringing her hands nervously. What good would she be here? Like with everything else in her life, she felt completely useless and stupid.

"Maybe make bandages?" She offered, figuring that couldn't be too hard.

His focus remained on a frightened young girl who had an ugly gash running down her arm. Her left leg was covered with a wet cloth, and Alyra assumed she'd also suffered burns. The curly blonde child looked to be around ten summers. She bit down on her lip as he washed the blood from the wound.

"Are you squeamish?" he asked.

"Huh?"

"I could use assistance right here, if you think you can stomach the blood. I don't want you passing out on me while I clean and suture her arm." He wiped a clean cloth across the girl's sweaty face and said soothingly, "You are being so brave, precious."

Alyra didn't know if she was squeamish or not, but said she wasn't. Tears streaked down the girls cheeks. Alyra really did want to help.

Lotari directed Alyra to hold her still while he closed the cut. The sight of deep gash made her stomach churn, but she grasped the girl's hand, laying her arm across the child's chest to keep her from jerking.

Taking the damp cloth, she continued to gently stroke her red, sweaty face.

"Do you live in Many Rivers?" Alyra kept her voice calm despite the bile rising in her throat when Lotari threaded the needle.

She nodded, her blue eyes darting to where the centaur worked.

"Look at me. What's your name?"

"Ah-Alyssa." Her voice squeaked with fear.

"That's a beautiful name. Mine's Alyra. Our names sound alike, don't you think?"

Alyssa's eyes, still wide, eventually focused on her. Alyra held the rag in such a way to block the child's view of her arm.

"I just got to Many Rivers. Can you tell me about your town? I met Beave and he says his family runs the apple orchard."

"I know Beave. He put a worm in my lunch one day." She gasped, closing her eyes for a moment as she bit down on her bottom lip.

"Well, that wasn't nice." Alyra dared not look at what the centaur was doing.

Alyssa slowly exhaled as she focused again on Alyra's face. "My family owns a cattle farm. Wanna know what I put in his lunch bag to get him back?"

Alyra suppressed a grin. Lotari snorted a laugh, but said nothing.

"I think I'm afraid to ask. Does it have anything to do with those cows?"

Her pink lips turned up in a mischievous grin as she nodded.

"That's it," Lotari whipped out a roll of bandages. "I'm done. Told you I'd be quick."

Alyssa yawned, "And you was right, Lottie. Didn't hurt much at all, either. But I'm getting sleepy."

"Good, you little imp. Go to sleep and when you wake up, I bet you'll feel all better."

Alyra found a blanket to cover the child with. Lotari lifted her in his furry arms. His hooves clomped softly over the wood floor as he carried her to the next vacant bed and gently set her down on the feathered mattress.

"Wow, you're a real master at sewing, Lottie." Alyra said, giggling when he threw a pillow at her.

"Helped that Marya gave her something to ease the pain. I think the anticipation of being sewed up like one of her rag dolls frightened her more than the actual procedure. She was caught in the woods when they set the trees on fire. Luckily, she only has a minor burn on her leg, and the gash from falling while she ran for the meeting hall."

He went to a basin and washed his hands. "You have the knack." Lotari smiled proudly as he removed his smock. "Perhaps there's a healer hidden inside of you."

"What do you mean? I wouldn't have known how to sew a cut." She went to a table piled with linen and began tearing strips into bandages. "Besides, all I did was talk to her."

"Exactly, but you were able to soothe her. That's the sign of a true healer. Marya or I can teach you how to heal physical injuries. That's the easy part. Not many are truly gifted at helping soothe the fears on the inside."

Alyra shook her head, thinking he talked silliness. She had so many fears inside of her own, how could she help others with theirs? She did feel good having helped the little girl. Maybe while her own injuries healed, she could learn a few things from them. Maybe then she'd actually start being useful for a change instead of always causing everyone more trouble.

\* \* \* \*

Alyra pounded her fist into the squishy dough, then formed small balls as Marya had shown her. In Racah, she'd seen Tarek's mother form mounds of bread many times, but enjoyed the sensation of floured softness between her fingers. She wondered if his parents had found a way to escape. Without Crystal the dragon there to guard the border getting out of Racah had to be possible now.

For the millionth time, she also wondered about Tarek. She slammed her fist into the dough, angry that she'd let herself fall so easily into thinking about him. He'd chosen to leave her. Again. She didn't understand his actions. He wanted her to go back to Racah, but wouldn't make her. Risked his life to help her get free, only to abandon her to trek this journey alone.

"Sweetheart," Marya broke her dark thoughts. "I said, knead, not beat it to a pulp."

Alyra noticed the dough had several fist sized indentions. "Sorry. I wasn't paying attention."

"Yes, I see that. Your heart weighs heavy. I can see it in your glowering eyes. Would you care to let some of those thoughts out so your mind doesn't feel so cluttered? People say I'm a wonderful listener."

Shaking her head, Alyra plopped the bread dough onto the pan. "This is the first time I've been allowed to do anything normal. It feels good. You've been kind to me. I hope you don't end up regretting it."

"Why would you think that, dear?"

"Seems I bring trouble everywhere I go. Those Racan soldiers were after me, Marya. If I hadn't stopped here … I don't know."

"It would have been the same, either way. Racan soldiers have been causing trouble for a long time. It's one of the risks people take settling this land."

"Have you ever been harmed by them?" She was especially worried about soldiers attacking Marya and destroying her beautiful little cottage and all the good work she did here for others. Never had she met anyone with such a generous heart.

Telling her she could stay as long as she wanted, Marya had made her a bed up in the loft. She'd looked Alyra directly in the eyes when she said, "My home is your home, Alyra. Whatever I have is yours to use while you're here." *Who did such things?*

Marya set the loaves on the counter to rise. White flour covered her hands and speckled her dark hair. Outside the large kitchen window, stars sparkled in the black sky.

"No, dear, the king has given me a safe place here to do my work. As you may have noticed, the White Road runs in front of my house and the river flows behind. I'm un-plottable, and unreachable, except for those who know I'm here. No matter what kind of trickery they might use to search the land." Her gaze leveled on Alyra. "Whenever you find a healer's house, you have found a safe place to stay. Remember that." She poured them both a cup of steamy herbal tea.

Did that mean Darnel couldn't use his Seeing Scope to find her? She let out a long breath. Dare she hope?

"He really can't see me on the path, Marya? Really?"

She nodded. "Really. That's why you've been told numerous times to stay on the white rocks. They will indeed keep you safe. Believe it or not."

"But the path didn't stop Bezoar from getting across and burning down the town." Alyra took a whiff of the tea and felt a sense of calmness settle in her tight muscles. She wondered if this was some concoction to help her sleep. Tonight, Alyra would gladly welcome a good night's rest. The warm liquid went down like a soothing balm.

"Tomorrow, you'll see for yourself the damage isn't as bad as you think. We'll be transporting the remaining patients back to town in the morning. Elder Wain has invited us to their celebration picnic."

*What could they possibly have to celebrate?*

Marya cleared the table of bread ingredients. "I'll need your help convincing our centaur friend to come along. He's a little shy around towns, you may have noticed."

Alyra gathered the bowls and washed them in the sink. Peering out the window, she spotted Lotari resting beneath one of the trees. Moonlight illuminated him in a silvery halo as he played from his pipes. She remembered how he'd finally lulled her to sleep by playing a soothing tune the first night she'd met him. His music had a way of chasing away worries and he probably played now to lull his patents inside the barn to sleep.

She understood his reservations. How would the townspeople feel about her bringing those soldiers down on them? No matter what Marya said, she knew their hardship was all her fault. And she had no doubt that anywhere else she dared to run to would be in danger of the same.

Once the dishes were washed, Alyra climbed up to her sleeping area and soon fell into a dreamless sleep.

Bright and early the next morning, Marya filled several baskets with her breads, jars of herbal medicines, and what vegetables they'd picked from her garden the day before. Lotari set Alyssa in the back of the wagon beside two other burn patients who'd also been trapped in the forest fire.

"Honey," Marya called to Lotari after he had the girl settled. "Can you help us with these? I have no idea how I'll manage all this stuff on my own today."

His brows crinkled as if perplexed as he gathered the baskets and set them beneath the bench seat. "I'm sure you'll have plenty of help when you get there."

"Well, I sure would appreciate *your* help, all the same, dear. You're such a jewel to me. Won't you reconsider coming along?"

Alyra leaned on her cane, watching her centaur friend squirm uncomfortably as Marya poured the syrup on his ego. Even though the townspeople had been gracious and appreciative of his assistance, he remained wary of actually entering the township. Wyndham forbade the clan from visiting the settlements. And though the injured accepted his healing aid in their dire need, that didn't mean the rest of the group would welcome him in the same manner.

Lotari began to shake his head, when Alyssa sat up and said with a huff. "This hurts my arm. And my leg. Lottie, can I please, please ride on you and not in this bumpy ol' wagon?" She clasped her hands under her chin, her cherub cheeks red from the morning heat. "Please?"

Alyra knew Lotari was a goner.

His shoulders sagged as he moved closer to the rail so Alyra could help the child climb onto his back. "You human women are going to be the end of me, I swear it."

Biting back a laugh, Alyra took a seat beside Marya who smiled with satisfaction as she flicked the horse's reins.

\* \* \* \*

Many Rivers bustled with activity as they pulled the cart into town. Lotari assured Alyra the enemy had moved on. Once the Logorian warriors had arrived, they'd scattered the remaining enemy soldiers, including the Baykok captain, who'd called for a retreat the moment they appeared.

People surrounded the wagon unloading Marya's supplies and helping the patients she'd brought along find a comfortable place at one of the many tables. Alyra limped after the healer. Lotari stayed at Alyra's side, his hand on her arm offering her support, and she wondered if for his own comfort. He looked as nervous as she felt.

Alyssa's parents came to retrieve their daughter who was reluctant to leave her new friend. The father shook Lotari's hand and the mother pulled his face down so she could plant a kiss on each cheek as she thanked him over and over for taking care of their Alyssa.

He blushed. "My pleasure. She's a brave young lady."

As they left, Alyra grinned up at him. "Looks like you're a hit, Lottie."

He pointed a warning finger at her but laughed instead of scolding her. The thick muscles in his arms relaxed. Marya took hold of his hand and pulled him over to one of the tables.

"Marya," he protested, "I helped you get everyone here. Now I really should go before Wyndham loses the last of his patience with me."

"After you've had something to eat. Wait just a bit longer, dear.

Then if you still want to leave, you can go and I'll not say a word."

Alyra stared at the healer wonderingly. Why did she want Lotari to stay? Obviously from the satisfied smirk on her thin, angular face, something was up.

While waiting to fill the basket Marya had brought for them, Alyra realized hardly any of the buildings were damaged. Some were smudged with smoke. The leather shop and livery were burnt. And the surrounding woods were charred and still smoldered. Come next year, she doubted anyone would be able to tell the land had been touched by fire.

Lotari stared down her with an *I-told-you-so* expression on his bearded face.

Once everyone was served, Mayor Tember, a gray-haired, distinguished looking gentleman stood on a platform in the center of the gathering. He raised his hands to quiet the crowd.

"First, let us take a moment to offer our gratefulness for minimal damage and victory over our assailants." His flowing voice, reminded Alyra of General Marcel.

Like rumbling thunder, voices joined in giving thanks. Many thanking King Shaydon, though Alyra didn't understand what the King had to do with what happened here. He lived far, far away in Aloblase. Yet, hadn't Issah said that the King hears the request of his beloved children? *But how?*

Even Marya blew kisses into the air, her eyes closed as she muttered thanks for protection and prosperity of the land as it heals itself.

Alyra shook her head, wondering if she'd ever understand these strange people.

The mayor waited for the voices to die down, before he turned toward Marya and held high his glass of cider. "Healer Marya, we owe much to your services once again. Many lives were spared at your skillful hands.

Marya bowed to him.

"We are also grateful for the care given by the centaur, Lotari. Please, sir, we hope you'll accept a token of our appreciation." He motioned toward the crowd. "Elder Wain, would you do the honors?"

The dwarf hurried forward carrying a leather quiver full of

slender white feathered arrows along with a beautifully crafted bow made from white wood.

Lotari blinked, his shaggy brows wrinkled in bewilderment. Slowly, he began to shake his head, taking a step back.

Marya grabbed his arm. "Do not discredit their appreciation, sugar. Go, be gracious and accept their gift."

He looked at Alyra who nodded, even giving his flank a gentle shove to get him moving.

Head ducked, he clomped toward the platform. Elder Wain waited at the edge, quiver in hand. He lifted the strap over Lotari's head and set it across his shoulders. The centaur tenderly ran his fingers over the supple leather.

Holding up the bow, Wain said in a loud voice for all to hear, "This was crafted from a limb of the white tree. When they fall, we gather them and our craftsmen create tools and weapons of extraordinary quality. This bow will shoot with the finest precision, sure to meet any mark."

Lotari's mouth hung open as he took the bow. "I ... I don't know what to say. This is more than...." He swallowed, then gave Elder Wain and Mayor Tember a low bow, his hand placed over his heart. "I'm honored to receive such a fine gift. I thank you."

Cheers went up from the crowd. People gathered around Lotari, shaking his hand, patting his back. and thanking him over and over for helping their people.

When Mayor Tember called everyone to order again, Lotari made his way back to Alyra and Marya, the bow clutched to his chest. His brown eyes glistened with unshed tears. He tried several times to speak, but couldn't form the words.

Marya patted his shoulder. "You can go now. If you want. Or stay and enjoy the celebration. Your choice." She shrugged and turned toward the mayor.

Lotari shook his head, causing Alyra to laugh. She felt happy for her friend, glad he'd found acceptance and appreciation here. He deserved it.

"We will not be hindered!" Mayor Tember was saying.

Elder Wain's dark eyes scanned his fellow townsmen. "You know, the Meeting Hall is much too cluttered and noisy. I say we expand! Build a new market area that can be opened up on nice days and yet be closed in during the winter. Then we have more space to teach the children."

Another one of the leaders nodded agreement. "Absolutely! Then there will also be more room for people to seek safety if necessary."

From the crowd, someone yelled, "And we'll rebuild those buildings that burned. We'll fortify them with the white stones like all the others. Then if this happens again, we'll stand even stronger!"

"That's right," roared the dwarf in a mighty voice, shaking his fist in the air. "'Tis rightfully the King's land, and we will reclaim it!"

"Or die trying," several cheered.

The assembly broke up as men gathered together discussing how to rebuild and add to the grand meeting hall. They waved Lotari over for his input and soon he was talking animatedly about possibilities for growth.

"You're good for him." Marya nudged her arm.

"How does any of this have anything to do with me?" Alyra helped her gather the leftover food. Marya distributed most of it to the families at their table.

Afternoon sun peeked through the leafy trees, dappling the grass with yellow light. Marya sat beneath a sprawling oak and stretched her bare feet over the tickling blades. "You're acceptance of him has lured him from his woods. If not for you, he never would have stayed so long helping me. Matter of fact, he's never stayed before to help me with human patients. Only creatures."

Alyra watched the horseman for a moment. "He's the first real friend I've ever had, Marya."

The healer looked over at her with sad eyes. She grasped Alyra's hand and gave it a squeeze. "You'll never lack for friends ever again, I assure you. You not only have a devoted friend in Lotari but me as well."

"I'll need to leave soon. I can't intrude on you..."

"Hush, you welcomed to stay until you're ready to leave. Allow your leg to heal. Maybe your heart as well."

# Chapter 20

An orange butterfly danced around the spiked yellow flowers. The slight wind caused by its wings fanned Alyra's fingers. She squeezed the plump tomato to check for ripeness, then gave a quick twist from the limb. As Marya strolled down the row of beans, she dropped the tomatoes collected into her basket.

"These will make for a nice trade," Marya examined the bounty with satisfaction.

Three weeks had passed since Alyra came to stay with the healer. Every day felt like a dream. One of those sweet, blissful dreams she sometimes had in Racah, of a place bright and happy.

Marya took Alyra with her on her rounds where she would teach her about tending the sick, answering every last question with the utmost patience. If they were near the town, she'd drop Alyra off to help Lotari repair damaged buildings. The centaur offered her a ride home when dusk settled. Whenever they were together, he instructed her on the name and healing properties of every plant they passed. He'd even lent her his personal botanical journal.

His knowledge of plant lore and artistic renditions of vegetation amazed her. She kept the book in her pack which she wore wherever she went, mostly as a precaution in case she had to suddenly run again.

Marya handed her the basket, asking her to prepare the beans for soaking. "We'll add some to the stew for dinner, Sweetpea."

Alyra sat on the front stoop, trimming the pods and sorting which they'd take to town. The sun glistened off the white road running past the healer's house. She followed its course with her eyes until it disappeared around a bend, and from there, who knew? Soon, she'd need to find out.

Issah's words from the night he brought her there often repeated themselves in her quiet moments. "I know exactly who you are.

Alyra, child of Alburnium. Daughter to Stephen of Belluvita. Born to those of the light. The Illuminate."

*Daughter of Stephen.* Her father? Why couldn't she remember any of her other family members? She suspected the glowing lady from her dreams might be her mother. Still, she had no idea what happened to her. Were they waiting for her? Had they given up hope that one day she'd return? Would they even welcome her back?

Alyra sighed, breaking the tops off four velvety green pods.

*Born to those of the light. The Illuminate.* Jerin said that's why she made the white rocks glow. Because of what her medallion said she was. Why couldn't she make things light up when she wanted to? And what would it mean if she could?

Taking the basket inside, Alyra stopped before Marya's bookshelf, mostly consisting of plant lore and healing remedies. She found a couple of books about a place called the Halls of Knowledge, and Great Philosophers, but nothing to help answer her many questions.

"You should see the libraries in Aloblase, dear." Marya took the vegetables from her and headed toward the kitchen area. "Books beyond your most imaginative beliefs."

The cottage was open and airy. Alyra hoped one day to be able to settle in such a quaint little home.

"Have you been there, Marya?"

"Oh, yes." The healer's face lit up with the memory. "So, so beautiful. That's where I learned my life skills. At the Academy."

The word, *academy*, struck Alyra as familiar. Someone was going there. Was she? A memory of a young boy, about Beave's age, with wavy brown hair and dazzling green eyes. Who was he?

"Hello, Marya to Alyra, are you there, dear?" The woman chuckled when Alyra blinked back into the present. "Oh, there you are. Thought you took a mental vacation on me for a moment. Was hoping you'd write."

Alyra laughed at her teasing. "I keep having these dreams of people and places. The Logorians told me my lost memories would start to come back. I just wish there were some books, or maps, or something...."

"The meeting hall, dear. They have a splendid library. Not as elaborate as Aloblase, or what the Halls of Knowledge once had, but you might find something useful."

"Does everyone go to Academy, Marya?"

"Those who wish to learn about their gifting. I'm sure you would have gone to learn about being a light bearer when you came of age. Usually, children in their tenth year begin attending. We all have the opportunity to learn the skills needed to do our life's work, dear. It's not too late. When you return, you'll be given the chance to go, as well."

She clutched the two medallions, feeling a sense of relief over still having a chance to find out what hers meant. How to make the Illuminate talent work.

"You could take this basket with you, dear. Ride Gabby," Marya gestured toward the horse paddock beside the barn. "I'm sure she'll love the exercise."

An hour later, Alyra trotted the mare into Many Rivers. Fresh paint covered many of the smoke damaged buildings, and new ones were going up to replace those burnt in the attack. Even the Meeting Hall was having a new wing built on, just as Elder Wain suggested. A special market area. She spotted Lotari helping to set the wall. He'd brought some of his clansmen with him, a small group of younger centaurs. She couldn't help but smile at how much he seemed to enjoy working with the townspeople. At first, he'd shown up with fresh bruises, but eventually, Wyndham must have relented, especially as the people continued to share provisions for the clan and send countless invitations to ask for anything they needed.

Alyra located the man who traded produce and gave him the basket. He placed several pouches of herbs that Marya would use in her tonics in a bag. After their transaction, she asked where she might find the library, and he pointed to the east wing.

"Yer welcomed to any books you fancy. Jus' let Ol' Angus know. He keeps tally o' where tha books get off to."

She nodded and found the grand study. For a long moment, she stood in the archway staring at the two-story gilded walls in utter amazement. Marble statues of various creatures and people she didn't know stood guard over the shelves. A couple of people sat at the polished wood tables, piles of books surrounding their bent heads.

A hunched, elder gentleman approached her. "What can I do

you for, young scholar?"

"Oh... uh... I was wondering if you have any maps. Like of Alburnium, or Aloblase? Or just places?"

He peered at her through a pair of thick spectacles. Waving a long, twisted hand at her, he led her to an area in the back. He reached up to the third shelf and pulled down a leather book, nearly the size of a serving tray. Setting the book upon a podium, he opened to the table of contents.

"Within these pages are maps of nearly every established town in the Kingdom realm. You can look up the towns in the table of contents." Then he flipped to the very back. "Here is an overall map of Alburnium." He pointed at the upper left corner. "That's where Racah would be." His arthritic finger traced along a golden line and stopped near the crease in the book. "This is Many Rivers. Since we are relatively new, there is no page of our town. But I've taken the liberty to mark it on the overview map. We do like to know where we stand in the big scheme of things, don't we?"

Alyra smiled at his joke. "Yes sir, that's for sure."

"Now, this book is much too large, and too old to be taken from the library. But I'll leave it out if you think you'll want to explore the maps again at a later time. For now, feel free to spend as much time as you wish looking. The books near the front are available to take home, though we expect you to bring them back. Hear?"

"Yes sir. Thank you."

Angus gave her a bow, then left her to return to shelving his stack of books.

She studied the large map first, finding the spot he'd marked Many Rivers. Her eyes scanned the area between there and where Racah would be. Eventually, she found a small dark spot labeled Yarholm. The kingdom towns were marked with a gold dot. More gold dots clustered on the right side of the map, and spread out over the left side. There wasn't even a line connecting Yarholm to any of the other towns. The White Road went nowhere near the small settlement.

That explained a lot.

Several gold dots covered the upper part of the map. Near the bottom, she found a sketch of a mountain range labeled, *Drakensburg*. Wasn't Crystal from such a place? There was no gold line heading in that direction either. She pinpointed the White Road leading from Many Rivers and found Aloblase at the right side of the map.

To her dismay, there lay a large mountain range she'd have to cross. The town at the foot of the mountains read Denovo. Another smaller town laid further south.

"Denovo?" She'd heard of that name before, too, and searched her shattered memory for when. An image of Tarek holding two bottles of ale flashed in her mind. "Of course! The bag of apples. But...." She leaned in closer, for a better look, then decided to flip through the thick pages until she found the city. Indeed, the path went beside the borders and there was a Meeting Hall inside the city. How did Darnel get goods from there if they served King Shaydon?

She shook her head, then returned to the large map and searched through the cluster of gold dots, wondering if she'd locate Belluvita.

A shadow blocked her source of light. Alyra jumped back with a gasp to find Lotari standing beside her.

"You scared me, Lot. Don't sneak up on me like that."

"My, my, but you're a little tense, aren't you? What's up with my favorite human?"

He leaned his sweaty arm on the edge of the podium.

Argus bellowed across the vast quietness. "Boy, you better wash up before you touch my books!"

Lotari jumped. "Yes sir." He handed her a small book. "Hold that for me. I'll be right back." His hooves clattered over the wood floor as he darted out.

Alyra glanced at his book. Kingdom Peoples, the title read. She turned to the table of contents.

*Arcadian, Artisan, Craftsman, Curian, Draconian, Drake keeper, Healer, Illuminate, Instructor, Mason, Messenger, Musician...*

*Illuminate?*

Her gaze shot back to the word that defined the emblem on her medallion. She turned to the page, but found little more than a standard definition. *The class of peoples with abilities to cast or channel light.* Below the description was a list of names of people who were Illuminate and had done something important.

"I was disappointed in the information as well." Lotari said, now freshly cleaned of dirt and sweat yet still smelling of earth, and damp animal.

"Were you looking up information about my medallion?"

He shrugged. "Some. And other peoples. I was simply curious." He set the book on Argus' return shelf. "Elder Wain said that in Aloblase, even creatures are given medallions. I had no idea."

"Creatures?"

"My kind. Non-human. Fauns, centaurs, dwarfs and such."

She smiled, thinking she'd never think of him as something different from her, even if he was. She didn't care.

"You could come with me. When I go to Aloblase."

He let out a long breath, looking down at the map laid out before her. "Wyndham forbids it. I'm pushing his limits as it is. He's so angry he's taken to completely ignoring me." He flipped through a few pages. "Besides, my Matron and siblings would be without a hunter."

"Matron?"

"Mother in your tongue."

"Lot, you have a mommy?" She grinned when his cheeks blushed. "I didn't even know there were female centaurs."

"Of course there are. They stay close to the warren though. Few are willing to leave the safety of their homes."

"Would you take me to meet them someday?"

He shook his head. "I'm afraid not. Humans so close to the warren are terribly upsetting to them. Besides, we're far from the white path. I'd fear for your safety on many levels."

"I've noticed your leg is better now. Have you considered when you'll continue on your journey?"

Alyra rubbed her arms where all that remained was a white scar from the burns. Her leg also had an ugly line where the arrow had struck. At this rate, by time she actually reached Aloblase, she'd look like a patchwork ragdoll.

"Soon. I'm still learning from you and Marya."

His brown eyes narrowed. "You'll receive the best training from the Academy."

"I know." She reached into her backpack and pulled out his journal. "Here's your plant book. You're amazing, Lot. The illustrations are beautiful."

He flipped to a page, holding up a picture of an orange flower, its petals resembling a head of rumpled hair. His thumb covered the plant's name. "What's this one?"

"A marigold." Alyra said rolling her eyes. "Won't you even think about going to Aloblase?"

He sighed. "No. Now tell me the marigold's uses."

She relented when his face looked pained. Maybe he wished he could go, but really couldn't. Like Tarek, there were things holding him back, responsibilities, people he cared about.

She recited his words. "The flower petals can be made into an infusion or lotion to help with chapped hands."

"What else is the marigold beneficial for?"

Alyra rubbed her forehead. She'd read all this, but wasn't in the mood for a test right now. "Sprains? Or no—"

"Yes, sprains." Then he finished, "Marigold can also be used as a cold compress on inflamed areas and are wonderful for open wounds. The petals can be squeezed for their juice and used for toothaches as well."

Alyra shrugged, staring at her map. "Oh yeah, and all that. So how far away is Aloblase from here?"

He snapped the plant journal shut and handed it back. "I don't know. Ask Marya, she's been there. This is my home and it's all I know. Keep the book awhile longer. You need to study more."

A gonging bell sounded from outside. Argus and Lotari hurried to the tall windows.

Alyra followed. "Are we under attack again?"

Lotari pulled the bow from his quiver and loaded an arrow. "You stay here, Alyra. Understand? Wait until I come back for you. If there is danger, you'll be safe inside. Remember what Issah told you?"

She nodded, her heart thudding against her chest.

In the courtyard, Elder Wain stood on one of the picnic tables, giving orders. She watched the centaurs gather and talk together. Lotari looked concerned, but put his bow and arrow away. Alyra let out a long breath, maybe they weren't under attack after all.

The dwarf called Lotari over and they talked a moment, the centaur nodding and motioning toward the meeting hall.

Thunder sounded over the commotion as a group of horsemen galloped into town. The riders weren't clad in black, but white and gold. At the head was Issah.

With a cry of relief, Alyra ran outside, knowing if he were there, everything was safe. The Logorian warriors followed the horsemen, hefting litters laden with bloodied bodies.

"What's happened?" She raced to Lotari's side.

The fury on his bearded face alerted her to his impending scolding. Yet he bit back his irritation. "They're bringing in wounded. Marya's on her way. I can use your help until she gets here."

She nodded and followed him into the white building where they were setting up a medical room for the wounded. He asked Alyra to help separate the seriously injured from those who could wait awhile. According to one of the Logorian warriors, there were only twenty men left from a unit of fifty.

Once Marya arrived, she immediately issued orders to everyone standing. Those with open wounds and broken bones were sent to Lotari. Marya joined him.

Alyra took care of the less severe men, bandaging small cuts and binding sprains with ice. She prepared a calming tea to help with the pain and to soothe nerves. Each man was made as comfortable as possible on the makeshift beds.

Outside, several people were always working on preparing food to feed them all.

Issah and his warriors helped as well. Two of the Logorians took over cooking and before she knew it, the table was laden with breads and meats and fruits. She saw the scene with her own eyes, but couldn't figure out for the life of her how they accomplished such a feat.

Once the soldiers outside were taken care of, Alyra went to see if she could do anything in the hall where the worst of the injured waited for treatment. Lotari was occupied stitching a head wound.

Marya tended to a young man, no more than fifteen summers. She called Issah over who sat with the boy and whispered something in his ear. He gave a nod, slowly closing his eyes.

Issah pulled the blanket over his head.

Marya wiped at her face and moved on to the next one

struggling to breathe.

Issah came to their side and laid a hand on the man's head and chest. "In and out," he whispered. "In and out and in and out." After a couple of minutes, he breathed normally again. Marya took over from there and tended to his wounds. Many of the injuries were beyond Alyra's abilities, so she cleaned up bloodied linen and tried to offer encouragement to those who were waiting.

Lotari called her over to one particular patient who kept thrashing around in his bed. The man kicked his good leg and yelled, "Get away from me you savage!" The other leg lay twisted grotesquely. His face was so bloodied he probably couldn't see in his state of shock.

"You're going to be crippled if you don't let me set that leg!" Lotari yelled back.

"Don't touch me!"

Alyra got between the man and the centaur. "Hold on a minute. Let's all calm down." She took a wet cloth and began washing the man's face. "Here, let me clean off this blood so you can see what's going on. We only want to help."

"I...I'm sorry." He gasped.

"No, you're fine. Just calm down. Okay?" As she cleared the dirt and blood away, she gasped. "Jerin?"

He squinted and slowly opened his dazzling blue eyes. A slow grin broke across his pale face. "Princess!"

From behind her Lotari repeated, "*Princess*? He must have swelling on his brain."

"Long story. This is the one I was traveling with. Remember me telling you about him? We split up right before I met you?"

He stepped closer and peered over her shoulder at the giant boy. "You don't say?"

Jerin started fighting again, fear filling his eyes. "Get him away from me!"

Alyra continued to wash down his arms and checked for other wounds. His pale blonde hair had grown considerably and his beard now completely covered his chin.

"Jerin, try to keep still. You're safe, okay? Everything's going to be fine. Lotari is just going to set your leg, I'll stay right here with you."

The boy glared hatefully at Lotari and growled through clenched teeth, "Over my dead body. He better not lay one grubby paw on me if he knows what's good for him." With that, he passed out.

"Paw?" Lotari said with indignation. "Did he just say I had *PAWS*?"

# Chapter 21

"I had such a strange dream." Jerin rested in one of ten beds lining the temporary medic room in the Meeting Hall. Alyra sat beside him on the edge of the straw mattress, a bowl of Marya's herbal soup, made from the fruit of the white tree, heating her hands.

She tipped a spoonful to his bruised lips, urging him to drink down the healing concoction.

He swallowed. "That's really good. Did the healer make this soup?"

His eyes darted nervously toward Lotari who busied himself with helping Marya make more bandages. Jerin's splinted leg hung from a sling post attached to the foot of his bed. He'd also suffered a cracked rib and numerous bruises. The leg was broken when some kind of trollish beast, as he described, stepped on him. Issah and Marya worked together to set the broken bone.

"Yep, she's a great cook." Alyra held up another spoonful for him. "What was your dream?"

"I was walking around a dark cave and kept hearing someone call my name. The voice sounded like the Prince's. If not for him coming to our aid, we all would have been dead." His eyes took on that distant, lost appearance she'd seen several times since he'd returned.

She hadn't seen any Prince, and wondered if he'd hit his head harder than they thought. What she did remember was how worried she'd been when Issah and Marya worked so diligently on him after he'd passed out. Issah remained at his bedside, quietly calling to him and whispering in his ear until the fever broke and the danger passed. Before Jerin regained full consciousness Issah left, needing to take care of other things, Marya explained.

His pale brows knit over his blue eyes. "I'm sorry, Pr—, I mean, Alyra. For all the stuff I said. And did."

179

Her words clogged into a large, painful lump in her chest, so she offered more soup instead.

After several attempts to clear her throat, she managed, "So what happened? Where'd you go?"

"Well...." He scooted higher in the bed, wincing.

Alyra adjusted his pillows and when she tried to give him another spoonful, he took the bowl and began feeding himself.

Between sips, he continued, "I didn't realize I'd even gotten off the path until I drank of the good water from the stream I was following. Then everything seemed to snap in place and I realized you weren't with me." He shrugged. "Probably just as well. You might not be speaking to me now if you'd heard all the stuff spewing out of my deranged mouth. Again, I apologize."

"Can't be much worse than... well, never mind. In the past, right?"

"Right." He gave a nod, grinning. "Carah told me that if I got off the path, to remain heading east until I found it again. But then I came to a small town and found out that I could reach the White Road within a half-day's journey." He went on to explain that a group of men were traveling in the same direction, so he joined them.

"The problem was we all got so engrossed in talking about our hometowns and adventures we'd had, or hoped to have, that I completely missed the White Road. You know, you really have to keep your eyes open."

Marya came to his bedside with a cup of steamy tea. "This will help with your pain, sweet boy."

His cheeks flushed as he handed Alyra his empty bowl. Marya took a seat on the other side of his bed, a basket of bandages resting in her lap.

"Anyway, I didn't even realize I'd missed the path until we reached the next town."

"Was this one of the Kingdom towns?" Marya asked.

Jerin shrugged. "I don't know. Reminded me of my own hometown. You know, the people were hard workers who just wanted to live in peace without intruders. But huge! Simply amazing, with all kinds of people and homes made of brick and clay. Some of the houses were stacked up on each other, unlike I've ever seen before. So several families could live in the same spot but have their own dwelling."

"I've seen that before," Alyra remembered the stacked houses in Racah.

Marya looked pointedly at her. "You know a Kingdom town when you see it."

She nodded, knowing exactly what Marya meant. The people of Many Waters had a different perspective on how to get along and what mattered. Work was important, but not the main importance. She also noticed how hard they tried to show kindness to outsiders, including Lotari's centaur clan.

"So tell us what happened then."

He drained the cup, then set it on the bedside table. His brick-shape faced became animated as he started the rest of his story.

"Well, I was going to backtrack the next morning and find the Highway again. I stayed at an inn with the other men. Then word came to us at dawn that the city was enlisting soldiers. Evidently a band of trolls were plaguing the out-lying villages. Since I'd told them about my desire to be a warrior, they thought I might be interested. My friends signed up for what sounded like a *grand adventure*." He waved his hands for emphasis. "I didn't need any special training. Just a willingness to fight. "So I signed on."

He sighed and shook his head dismally. "Big, big mistake … in the end, anyway."

"Is that how you were wounded?" Alyra took his dishes and set them aside.

Lotari's hooves clomped across the room as he headed outside onto the front porch. He became antsy when indoors for too long.

Jerin's narrowed blue eyes followed his retreat, and once the centaur was gone, he let out a long breath. "No, we won that battle. But the next thing I knew, we were sent off to stop a raid of dwarves and ghouls. We put an end to those little monsters, as well." His voice grew dismal. "If only I had stopped there. I'd actually found the White Road again. I should have turned off then and made my way east, but…well, I was…I was so enjoying being a soldier. You know?"

Marya nodded with an understanding smile. "Sometimes, dear boy, the easy and quick way to your dream isn't always the best way. Though you were in the battle, you found yourself ill-equipped for real warfare, didn't you?"

Jerin let out such a long breath his shoulders slumped. "I did all right until we went up against Lord Darnel's soldiers. They were the most evil, brutish men and-" He hesitated a moment, glancing at Alyra, "-beasts, I've ever seen in my life." His eyes misted and he stared out the window, his face etched with a lingering pain. "We were no competition. I wasn't ready to deal with them or their war tactics." He rubbed his bandaged forehead and said more to himself, "Seemed so easy when I watched General Marcel's warriors. I can't..."

Marya laid a comforting hand on his splinted leg. "That is why training is imperative. You must be well equipped before facing such a fierce enemy. You must be under the King's protective cover, fighting not for your own glory, but for his greater good. Not all battles are meant to be fought, dear. When you are Shaydon's warrior, instead of being just another soldier, you will know the difference."

His brows wrinkled in confusion. "Isn't a warrior and soldier the same thing?"

"No, they are not." She stated with finality. "Someday, you will see exactly what I mean, sweet boy."

He shook his head, clearly confused by her words. "Most perished. Our captain. All the men I had traveled with were dead." His brows wrinkled as he stared at his large, calloused hands. "If not for the Alburnium warriors arriving when they did, we would have all been slain. The Prince's forces conquered the enemy in no time. Just like General Marcel's unit did, you remember?"

Alyra leaned forward, giving his hand a gentle squeeze. "The real Prince? You're lucky. I'll probably have to wait until I get to Aloblase before I get to meet him."

Marya rocked in her chair, a smile crinkling the lines around her mouth. Alyra was about to ask what she found humorous when Jerin interrupted, "Now you tell me your story. How did you end up here? I figured you would have been long gone by now."

Before she had a chance to respond, Beave burst into the room, his small chest heaving as he tried to catch his breath. "There's a lone soldier. Out in the woods. He's hurt bad. Everyone's arguing about if they should... help." He sucked in a couple more breaths as he went to Marya's chair. Lotari returned, watching the boy with interest.

Lotari asked, "Is he one of the vagabond militia these belonged to?"

Beave shook his head. "He has the dark lands emblem. I think the Mayor wants him captured and you know, but—"

Marya leapt to her feet. "No, they can't. Not if he's defenseless."

"Thought you'd say that." Beave wiped his long bangs from his eyes.

"Marya," Lotari placed a hand on her shoulder. "What if it's a trap?"

She seemed to consider this a moment. "Will you ask your clan to circle the woods where he's at while I gather some supplies? If it's a trap, they can send back warning. Otherwise, I'm going to try to help him." She darted around the room, filling her medic bag with bandages and other items.

Alyra stood and went to her. "Why would you want to help an enemy? What if...."

"You stay here, sweetheart. Understand? You're safe here. I'll be fine. Life is a risk, dear. Shaydon will keep me safe, I believe that."

She kissed Alyra's cheek, then hurried out. Lotari insisted on going with her.

Why would Marya help an enemy soldier? He deserved to ... she stopped herself. What? Die? He deserved to die? For doing what he was ordered? She closed her eyes. *Please let Marya be all right.* She should have offered to go help.

Beave stood at the tall front windows. "I'm going upstairs to watch what's going on. You coming?" He turned to Alyra.

"That won't technically be leaving the safety of the Meeting Hall, right?" she asked.

Jerin growled, "You were told to stay here."

She glared at him. The roof would still be safe.

He rolled his eyes, settling back on his pillows. "Never mind. Look who I'm talking to. Miss Never-Listens. Just make sure you come right back and tell me what happened."

"Deal." She ran after the boy who was already halfway up the stairs. From the roof, Alyra could see the township and the farms spread over the valley down in the canyon.

"There." Beave pointed toward the burnt woods. "I see them. It's a dwarf that's injured."

She hurried over to see Marya slowly approaching the small man-creature. He crawled away, dragging his leg. Perhaps his leg was broken like Jerin's. The Healer's words must have eventually calmed him because he stopped and allowed her to move in closer. Lotari stood guard over her, hand on his club, but made no move to draw his bow and arrow. Alyra hoped his clansmen also had him covered.

Beave sat on the stone wall, his skinny legs hanging over the side. "Knew she'd want to go help. We don't take much to harming others, but with all the recent attacks, everyone's on edge. We still gotta be careful."

Below, in the clearing, Lotari cut down a limb to fashion into a crutch while Marya splinted the dwarf's leg. They seemed safe, so her eyes began to wander around the town and down the cliffs into the surrounding valley. Along an outcropping halfway down, she spotted several mounds of fresh dirt. "What's that place over there?"

Beave narrowed his eyes, following her pointing finger. "Burial grounds."

"You said nobody died in that last battle."

"We didn't, but the enemy suffered. We lay them to rest as well. See that stone arch? That marks the area of where we bury fallen outsiders."

Alyra's breath caught. *Tarek!*

Tearing downstairs, Alyra ran to the edge of town with Beave on her heels.

"You was told to stay in the Hall. Please don't do this again, Aly. Please come back. I'll get in trouble this time if I let you get away again."

She stopped, spinning to face him. "Take me down to the burial grounds."

"But...."

"I have to see something." She continued toward the cliffs, intending to climb down the side if necessary.

184

She was pulled up short when the boy grasped her hand. "Okay, but this way. You'll walk right off the rim if you're not careful." He tugged her toward a narrow white path, leading into dense woods. Soon, they came upon a walkway cut into the side of the rocks. Alyra tried not to look down into the depths, misted from the many waterfalls cascading over the edge. If Tarek went over in the river, he'd never have survived the drop. Had someone found his broken body on the shore of one of the rivers? Her head swam and she had to press herself to the rock face for a moment to steady herself.

"Best not to look down. Just keep going. We're almost to the bridge. Gets better from there." He jogged along as if walking upon solid ground and not a narrow ridge. Eventually, as Beave said, the path moved away from the cliff and turned into a mossy stone bridge. To one side poured a waterfall. The other looked out over the farms below. What a breathtaking view. Her clothes, dampened by the mist, clung to her body. She walked carefully over the slick stones. Beave was already across and waiting at the edge of the cemetery.

"This is where we bury those who've crossed the curtain."

She didn't understand what he was talking about.

He pointed toward the green splattered archway. "That's where we put the fallen soldiers. Outsiders. I don't get what the big deal is, Aly. I don't even know why we bother, 'cept Mayor says they still deserve respect for fighting for what they believed in." He rolled his eyes.

From the valley below a gong sounded.

"That's my call to go home." He wrung his hands. "I hate to leave you here. Why don't you go on back to the Hall before they realize you've gone? There's nothing here to really see."

Alyra nodded, her eyes focused on the arch. "Sure, you go on, Beave. I'll be fine. I'm on the white path, right? I'm safe then. I'll head back in a bit."

He hesitated, his eyes darting to his home below then to her.

"I won't stay long."

His shoulders rose with his deep breath. In resolution, he nodded, then scampered along the path that would lead him on down into the valley. Sometime before she left, she wanted to explore the farms spread across the basin. Maybe Lotari would take her soon.

With slow steps, she headed toward the soldier's burial site. Passing beneath the arch, she read the engraved words, *"Pugnaverunt, fortiterque pugnantes."*

Her tutor in Racah had taught her some of the ancient languages. She knew the words roughly meant, "They fought a good fight."

The patch of turned soil was several yards long and about two yards wide. A mass grave, she supposed because of the number of beings that lost their lives that day. Her heart banged inside her chest. She'd seen many soldiers in the castle. Some standing guard, others there for meetings or certain celebrations. A few treated her kindly. Like Tarek sometimes did. When he wasn't mocking her for her attitude. Yet, as she considered his actions, more often than not, he helped her clean the dungeons, brought her fresh bread or a special pastry his mother had made. She'd hated her life and everyone there so much, she missed the few acts of kindness people did extend her. Even Ben gave her freedoms she knew he wasn't supposed to give. She'd been too wrapped up in her own problems to see what others also had to go through.

Her legs wobbled as the weight on her heart grew too heavy for her to bear. Collapsing on the damp, mossy ground, she hid her face beneath the hood of her cloak as uncontrolled sobs shook her whole body.

"I'm sorry I didn't pay more attention. I am a selfish castle brat. I am. I never paid any heed to what others were going through." The tears poured out like an unstopped spout, first sputtering out the clogging dirt, then flowing freely, washing away the clustered debris until the water flowed freely.

"I'm so sorry, Tarek. You weren't my enemy. You were just trying to help me. Always trying to help me." And in that moment, she realized her greatest pain was from the possibility of him being below the pile of dirt. Of her not having the chance to thank him for rescuing her. Twice. Of not telling him she … cared for him, too.

Rustling grass sounded behind her. Too paralyzed by her sorrow, she couldn't make herself look up. Hands grasped her shoulders, lifting her to her feet.

"What are you doing here, silly girl?" Lotari eyes widened when he saw her tear covered face, then softened as he brushed his rough thumbs across her cheeks.

"Again you cry. And there's no rain to cover your sorrow today. Tell your friend Lotari what's troubling your heart."

She allowed him to pull her over to a stone wall where she could sit. His back end sat as he settled beside her, one arm around her shoulder as he removed his water-bag with his free hand and offered her a drink.

The cool, healing waters quenched the emotional fire burning her throat. After several deep breaths, she found her voice again. "It's a long story, Lot. I'm afraid you'll see what a wretched person I am if I tell you."

He chuckled. "Doubt that." He tightened his hug on her shoulder. "Tell me what happened. Talking about your life there will be a step forward in the healing process. Trust me."

If she trusted anyone, it was the centaur. And Marya.

"I had a friend in Racah. His name is… was…. Tarek. His family had been taken as slaves when his town was destroyed. He always thought they were better off in Racah. He said they were starving in the town. Working as a slave in the kitchens was paradise to him. I never understood him, and he never understood me. He thought I was crazy to turn up my nose at the finery I was living in."

Lot nodded. "If I put my hooves in his shoes, despite not being a good fit, I think I'd understand the allure of the grand castle. Especially when one has lived with starvation and need."

Alyra told the centaur how irritated she'd get with Tarek and how irritated he'd get with her. "Yet, he helped me escape from Racah. He knew Master, uh, I mean, Darnel was going to marry me off to one of his governors. A half-troll."

"Ew." Lot's nose wrinkled. "The smell."

"Exactly." She left out the part where Tarek kissed her, but told everything else about how he found her in Many Rivers and released her, then saved her from drowning in the river.

"A gold-headed lad, correct?" Lotari's brows scrunched in thought. "I was about to shoot him with my bow fearing his uniform and what he'd do if he caught you. But Issah stopped me. I lost track of you both as you went around the bend. Issah told me to meet him downstream where my clan was gathered."

Alyra stared at the brown mound. "Lot, I'm afraid…."

"Oh, sweetheart. You can't know for sure."

"I'm more worried what might have happened to him if he did live. Bezoar has to know he let me escape. What if—"

"Stop, you can't speculate."

Yet, speculation was all she had to go on. What was worse, she was sure her feelings for him matched what he said he felt for her.

# Chapter 22

Alyra scrubbed at the iron pot, trying to break loose the crust of whatever concoction Marya cooked the night before. The potion might be for anything from getting rid of warts to making hair grow longer and fuller. Though, the few people she knew who had taken *that* tonic now grew thicker hair over their arms and feet, too.

Even Marya admitted she was still a student in her own way, constantly learning.

Jerin sat at the table surrounded by books from Many Rivers and maps he'd started constructing during his convalescence. Marya had given him a room in the barn, though several people in town offered to let him stay with them. For some reason, Marya insisted he still needed her healing touch, despite his ability to get around fine with a crutch. When Alyra questioned this, the healer said not all wounds were visible.

In a way, Alyra was glad to have Jerin back. Since their talk in the hospital, they'd gotten along better, and she was as fond of the big oaf as she was of Marya and Lotari. Too bad Lot and Jerin couldn't see each other in the same way.

She glanced out the window, expecting Lot to show up any moment now for their daily lesson. Golden brown leaves mixed with the green summer foliage, as the days grew increasingly shorter. Just as her time in Many Rivers. Soon, she'd need to move on. Alyra scrubbed harder, determined to not give up on the crusty pot, loving the calming effect of mundane activity.

The wind kicked up a cluster of leaves and sent them dancing and somersaulting across the back yard. Still no Lotari.

A slender hand rested on her shoulder. "Are you thinking about your forest friend, dear heart? I see you staring out of my window." Her arm slid around her waist as the older woman pressed her cheek against Alyra's.

Would having a mother feel like this? Or at least, having someone who actually loved you? The familiar pang returned to her chest.

"I've been thinking, my dearest, that the biggest obstacle to continuing on your way is leaving behind those you've grown fond of. Am I right?"

Alyra scrubbed with more vigor. "Yes, I'm going to miss everyone. Especially you and Lot." She let out a long breath. "I know this is his home, but his clan doesn't seem very nice to him sometimes. Though, I'm glad he hasn't had any bruises lately. I'd ask him to come. Except it might be worse for him out there. I've seen that people don't think very highly of his kind."

She shot an angry glance over her shoulder at Jerin.

He looked up from his stacks of books. "What?"

"Nothing," Alyra snapped. "Are you going to eat everything on the table or are you finished?"

The oak chair scraped against the floor as he scooted away from the table, collecting his dishes.

Marya turned to him with her big, motherly smile. "We were just discussing how hard it will be for Alyra to say good-bye to her friend the centaur."

Jerin rolled his eyes, but said nothing.

He still avoided Lotari, along with the other creatures that lived in Many Rivers. Even Elder Wain, though the dwarf didn't seem to take offense. When patients showed up needing medical treatment, Jerin assisted Marya, so long as they were human, or even animal. But he gave a wide berth to the creatures.

Marya had tried reasoning with him. Alyra told him all her experiences with Lotari and Crystal. He'd simply reply, "If you saw what those monsters could do to a town, then you'd understand. They aren't natural. And who can tell which ones are nice and which are not by looking at them? Better to just leave the whole lot alone."

"You can't tell about people either, until you get to know them." Alyra had shot back angrily.

"After your encounter with the Okbold, one would think you'd show more sense about who you trusted."

"You're never going to let that go, are you?" she stormed. "Even bad can turn to good, Jerin."

190

"I have my reasons!" He was relentless, so eventually, they both let the subject go.

"Sometimes," Marya told Alyra, "we must learn from experience, not from what we are told."

Marya let his aversion to creatures drop. She no longer tried to convince him to change his mind but instead accepted his views as a part of who he was. Alyra lacked the healer's patience. Jerin's attitude toward creatures irritated her beyond reason.

Gathering his dishes, Marya kept her gaze on the large youth. "Good friends are hard to find and should be cherished. One can never have too many friends."

"I suppose you are right as usual, Marya." He planted a kiss on the top of her head. "I'm going out to water the garden. You want me to bring in the ripe vegetables?"

"Yes, you big lump of sugar." As usual, her pet names brought deep shade of red to his pale cheeks.

There was nothing Jerin wouldn't do for her though. Alyra knew the big oaf also adored the healer and her mothering ways.

"I was thinking he was a lump for sure," Alyra smirked. "But I wouldn't call it sugar."

Marya popped the dishtowel at her.

\* \* \* \*

Lotari's hooves clomped over the white cobblestone road that wove into the valley below Many Rivers. He insisted Alyra ride, and kept his bow in his hand as they traveled. She wondered at the way his muscles along his back and arm remained tensed, as if ready to spring into action. His long ears twitched with every sound.

"Where are we going today, Lot?"

He breathed in deeply, answering as he exhaled. "The apple orchard. The boy, Beave," he stopped again, sniffing the air, before he continued. "His family invited me to stop by. I know you've wanted to visit the valley, too. We can't explore today. I must get back to my clan before nightfall."

"What's going on?"

They made the last turn on the narrow, winding path, and entered the plush, green basin. Everything smelled earthy, damp, and sweet with the fresh-cut sent of hay. Harvest was underway. The land spread wide with golden wheat, red-topped corn and trees filled with apples, pears and nuts, all in the process of being gathered into the storehouses.

"Nothing. Wyndham wants everyone in before nightfall. That's all."

She knew from his tone of voice that he kept something from her, but didn't press. Not yet anyway.

As they neared the orchard, the scent of apples stewing over a large fire set her stomach growling. The family was already preparing their famous cider.

Beave ran out to meet them first, dragging both of them by the hand toward the storage barns.

"Mom's made tarts, pies, applesauce... I'm all appled out."

Alyra laughed. The moment they entered the back yard, the whole family swarmed around them. The men took Lotari off into the orchard to help collect apples. Alyra stayed with the children and women, helping them core, peel and cook. The time there went by like a sweet dream. Her heart ached to find a place like this to settle down in.

*I could be happy here. I could. I'm safe here. Everyone says so. Why go on?* Yet the medallions felt cold against her chest. Issah said she had a family of her own, in Belluvita. Would they be farmers or builders? Would they be good-hearted and happy like those here in Many Rivers? Would she someday sit with her father, and brother and … mother? Cook, laugh, and work together?

By the time they left, Lot's back was weighed down with large sacks of apples. Alyra also had a bag filled with tarts and jars of sauces, along with a couple of bottles of cider.

He followed a different path that led through dense woods, then up a steep incline beneath one of the many waterfalls. She had to walk now because of his burden, but the kindness the family wished to extend to the centaur clan was worth her sore feet. Lotari walked in silence with a small smile fluffing his beard.

"What are you thinking about?" she asked.

For a moment he didn't answer, then finally shrugged. "I'm thinking how the little ones will love these apples. The elders will refuse them, of course. They are so set in their ways. But the colts, they'll go crazy when they see what I've brought. The wild apples we collect aren't as sweet or large."

"I love everyone here, Lot. They're so... good. Almost too good."

He laughed. "Well, you've not been in town near enough, or you'd realize they are just as prone to mischief as anyone else. Mr. Tom, the market manager, is known for keeping the best ciders and ales stored in the Hall's cellar. For 'special occasions' he said one day when I caught him leaving the storage room.

"Mayor Tember talks too much when he's found the ale stash and helped himself to a few bottles. Elder Wain has a special key, dwarf made of course, that opens all the secret places, so he is the one who helps the mayor break into the secret cellar. Miss Waddlesore, the innkeeper, is the worst gossip. Oh, and she has a terrible crush on Elder Wain."

Alyra laughed so hard she snorted, which caused the centaur to laugh until he neighed. Both were near convulsion when Lotari stopped short, his long ears perked. His hand went over Alyra's mouth.

"Hush."

She froze, trying hard to hear what his keen hearing picked up. Eventually, the pounding of hooves came to her, though far in the distance. Lotari was sniffing the air again.

"Tell me that's your clan running through the woods," she whispered.

His ears jerked. "No, riders. Not sure who though. They are too far away to catch their scent." He grasped her hand in his and started walking again, his pace quicker. "Let's return to Marya's where you'll be safe."

"I'm safe here, aren't I? We're on a path."

His brows pinched over his worried eyes, as if he wasn't sure how much to tell her.

"Lot, you've always been honest with me. Am I in danger?"

"There is still a war going on, child. The dark ruler still seeks to destroy any good that prospers. Many Rivers has survived because they are protected. You saw the Logorian warriors. Not all settlements enjoy such privileges. Those townships fall, the people enslaved, the buildings and homes destroyed." His gaze grew distant and his voice sad. "We had noticed an increase in black soldiers even before you showed up. Burning and stealing. Wyndham says the humans can take care of their towns but we are responsible for the woods. And our clan. You know the Dark Lord uses centaurs in his army. I'm sure your friend Jerin has seen firsthand how ruthlessly we can fight when prodded."

A nervous lump grew in Alyra's throat. "Is that why he doesn't like you?"

Lotari's face broke into a sly smile. "I don't take his attitude personally, child. I'm sure we are just one of many on his hate-list."

Alyra shook her head. "I've tried reasoning with him. So has Marya."

"Don't worry. By time he gets to Aloblase, he'll have to come to terms with his issues one way or another."

The path widened and the woods thinned. In the west, the sky had turned a peach and lavender color. Lotari let out a long breath. "To answer your original question, yes, you are safe to a degree. The enemy can return and probably will. Those who come into this land, build here, they know this. Yet, they are willing to take the risk."

Alyra shifted the burlap bag to her other shoulder. "Lot, you once told me about a prophesy. Even some of General Marcel's warriors mentioned it. Something about a light coming out of the darkness?"

His voice grew low, and he focused his gaze far in the distance. "I remember."

She placed her hand on his arm, but he still wouldn't meet her eyes. "Repeat it to me. Please?"

Lotari's tanned chest rose with the deep breath he took before saying,

"A light will come out of the dark,
When the lion frolics with the lamb.
A Kingdom will find its mark
When a child leads them by the hand."

Alyra considered the words for a while, but could make no sense of them. *A light comes out of the dark*? What did that mean? "A child? I don't understand. What do you think, Lotari?"

He shrugged and stared down at his hooves. "I think something is happening. I hear it in the trees and in the air. The night sky cries out that change is here. I'm not sure what, or how, or even who. I just feel that it is."

"Wow, Lot … that's … really … confusing. What are you talking about?"

He chuckled, throwing his arm around her shoulder. "Never mind. You're so human sometimes."

To her surprise, they entered Marya's yard from the back. Good thing Lotari guided her, or she'd never find her own way around those clustered woods.

The wagon was parked beside the barn. Jerin must have returned from his trip to town.

Lotari froze. Alyra followed his line of sight to where a dwarf dressed in black armor stood on the other side of the White Road running in front of the cottage. She thought they couldn't stand being near the glittering rocks. Yet this soldier seemed unharmed, though reluctant to cross.

In a flash, Lotari whipped off his bow and had an arrow aimed directly at the creature's heart.

"Get Marya. Be quick. Tell her Talen is back."

Alyra ran toward the house, finding Marya and Jerin outside next to the large oven. He helped her put a platter of buns in to bake.

"Marya, there's an enemy dwarf beside the road."

Jerin laughed, shaking his head. "Impossible, kid. Has to be one of them from town."

"Lot called him Talon."

Marya rushed past, running full force for the front of the house. Alyra followed, but kept behind Jerin. Lotari remained in his same position, bow still poised.

"Put that down," Marya ordered.

"Soon as he disarms himself." Lot spoke loud enough for the dwarf to hear.

With a curt nod, Talon unlatched the belt holding a wicked looking ax. He untied the breast plate covering his heart. The helmet slid off next, landing at his feet.

Marya stepped onto the White Road and spoke quietly to him for some time. She pointed in the direction of Many Rivers, then toward Aloblase.

For a long moment, the dwarf stared up at her, eyes wide with anxiety. Slowly, they closed as his foot inched over the white rocks. When nothing happened, his bearded face lit up into a wide grin. He took another step, then another until he stood right beside her.

Marya clapped, throwing her head back in laughter which was joined by the dwarf's deep, rumbling chuckles that shook his small body.

Tears welled in Alyra's eyes. She remembered the feeling of taking the first step to freedom. The elated feeling of leaving a life of slavery behind.

He jumped into the air with a loud whoop. Leaving all his belongings behind, he began jogging down the road, not toward the safety of town, but toward the hope that lay in the direction of Aloblase. Alyra felt as though he'd cast hooks into her chest and was pulling her heart along after him.

Nobody moved until he disappeared around the bend. Marya gathered his gear in her arms. Jerin ran out to meet her. When she turned to him, tears streamed down the woman's face.

"This is why I do it. Do you all understand? This-" She held the armor up higher, "-is why the risk is worth it."

Pushing past the big man, she took the items back to the barn and put them into a storage closet where other wicked looking weapons and armor were kept. Nobody dared to move until Marya locked the door and went back to her garden.

Jerin returned to the house.

Alyra stared at the rocks glistening in the afternoon sunlight. Lotari returned the arrow, then hung the bow back over the quiver. His hand on her shoulder brought her out of her deep thoughts.

Though her blurred vision, she looked up into the kind face of the friend she'd grown to love dearly.

"It's time, Lot. I'm ready to go home."

\* \* \* \*

The next morning as the three of them ate breakfast in Marya's kitchen, Alyra announced, "I'm going to leave with you, Jerin." When they sat there in silence, staring wide-eyed at her, she quickly added, "If that's okay with you."

Grins spread across both their faces as they looked at each other with relief.

"Yes!" Jerin pumped his fist. "I was hoping you'd decide to come."

Her breath returned. "I was worried you'd rather go without

me."

He slapped the table with a loud chuckle. "I thought the same, especially when you didn't say you'd go, too. Oh this is great! We have so much to do." He jumped from his chair and began pacing as he spoke. "The shoemaker in the village has promised to make me new shoes and a new traveling outfit. They were so kind. I never knew a town could be…well…I just didn't know." His hands waved about excitedly. "I think he would have given me the shoes off his feet except they weren't big enough."

Marya gave him a motherly hug. "Such is the way of Shaydon's Kingdom, you'll see." She began gathering up dishes. "Yes, we have much to do. I think we'll make a trip to the village tomorrow so Jerin can get his things. They will provide traveling food there. Think about what you'll need Alyra, and we'll get that too. I can trade my preserves for supplies."

# Chapter 23

Moonlight shone through the small, open window. Alyra dangled the chain with the two medallions in a shaft of silvery light. They spun first one way, then the other. The messenger emblem. The fiery emblem. Messenger, fire, messenger, fire. *Illuminate*.

Since arriving in Many Rivers, her life had fallen into a series of mundane days, each one passing with nothing significant or frightening happening. Including no lighting rocks or other things up. Tomorrow, she'd leave the mundane behind. Her heart flip-flopped between relief and disquiet.

She sighed, letting the chain slip from between her fingers. The disk hit her chest with a muffled thump. Not that she didn't cherish the reprieve Many Rivers had provided her. Still, since she'd made her decision to continue, an eagerness to seek the answers to her many questions escalated. She wanted to find her real home, her family, and the truth about who she really was.

First she had to get past telling Lotari good-bye. He'd promised to meet her when the moon crested the spruce. She peered out into the velvety indigo sky splattered with thousands of sparkling stars. The crescent's tip barely peeked above the forest line. She stood, deciding to head down early. Marya had a cauldron of the healing fruit stewing. A fresh batch, she'd said, for them to take along on their journey.

Downstairs, Jerin still sat at the kitchen table, his map spread out as he made notes in a small book.

He looked up from his work, brows knit as he gazed out the darkened window. "Kind of late to be heading out. Off to meet with your pet?"

She scowled. "Why are you so hateful toward him? Is this how you are with everybody who's not just like you?" She headed for the back door. "And don't you ever call him my pet again! Understand?"

His eyes widened, as if realizing he'd gone too far. "I'm sorry."
She ignored his apology.

"Aly." He'd taken to using Beave's nickname for her. "Really, I
am sorry. You're right. I shouldn't speak of your friend in such a
way. Please come back here a moment." He stood, his big hands
motioning for her to take a seat. "I want to show you this. Before
you go."

He seemed sincere, so she took the chair next to his.

"Be quick. I don't want to keep him waiting. And I need to stir
the cauldron."

He nodded, moving the candle closer to the parchment. "I've
managed to recreate this map of the whole land. I've charted where
all the known Kingdom roads are and which towns we'll encounter
along the way. Marya said some of the settlements have probably
changed. New ones get built and, as we know, many get destroyed.
But look here." He pointed to a spot in the middle. "This is Many
Rivers. See how all these rivers converge in the farm basin? See this
line?" His finger traced a gold-inked line that ran from one corner of
the paper down to the other where Aloblase lay. "This is the King's
Highway. What I found amazing was how it goes all the way to
Racah. Did you know that?"

Alyra followed the gold line to the east. The gold line on the
map practically went right up to the Dark Lord's doorstep. How
could that be? Perhaps they'd covered the white stones?

"I never saw anything white there." Even the snow was always
gray and dirty. "So this is how you've spent your time on all those
trips to town."

He shrugged. "Most. I've also helped people with stuff, like
farming. Worked off a few things I wanted, like a shield and new
sword. They are happy to give me supplies, a new pack, and clothes.
But I worked for the extra items."

She was impressed. He'd not wasted his time here at all. She, on
the other hand, had taken little thought to where or how she'd travel.
Dean's pack always seemed to provide what she needed. She stared
at Jerin's map. He'd drawn in rivers, towns, and the regular roads
running across the land. They would know exactly where to find
good water. He'd even written little X's on places they needed to
avoid.

199

"This is amazing."

He sat up straighter, a satisfied smile tugging his thin lips. "The White Road will take us to the Semitamon Mountains. There is a town at the foot of them, where we can get supplies for the climb. I sure hope they aren't too blasted steep. You know, this road leading south seems shorter and we wouldn't have to climb over those peaks."

The line he pointed at wasn't drawn in gold. "Is that the White Road?"

Biting his bottom lip, he shook his head.

"We're not supposed to get off the highway, Jerin."

"But it looks quicker."

"Maybe, but haven't we had enough experiences to know better?"

Jerin's face clouded as he stared at the flickering candle flame. He rubbed at his forehead, and his brows relaxed, as if he'd managed to rub the troubling thoughts away. "You're right. We'll do our best to stay on the path."

"You've been in a big hurry ever since we started. You really that eager to start warrior training?"

"Yeah, well...."

"What?" Alyra rested her elbows on the table, propping her chin in her palms.

Red crept up over his cheeks, starting from his neck and traveling up to his forehead. "I just... I... uh... well, I admire General Marcel. I'd like to be part of his unit. But he said he wouldn't take anyone who hasn't seen King Shaydon first."

From his stammering and his flushed face, she had a strong suspicion there was more he wasn't willing to say. Then she remembered the warrior maiden he'd been so taken with. The one who'd stood up on the rock and encouraged the fighters on with her song.

"Wait. Carah belongs to that unit, right?"

Beads of sweat formed along his temples. He shrugged with a heavy sigh. "Umm, I think so. But... well, I... maybe she is." He balked at her impish smile. "Stop looking at me like that." He tapped his fingers on the map. "Thing is, we are halfway there. Even if we do stay on the white path—"

"Which we will."

"Of course we will. I think without any major mishaps we should be there by the next full moon."

"You really think so?" Alyra's heart soared.

She hoped beyond all hope his figures were true. Aloblase sat right on the other side of the mountains. Her heart raced. Hopefully, the King wouldn't cast her out. Tarek even said there was no place for people like them there. She sighed wishing the knife-like pain in her chest would ease whenever she thought about him.

"It's not perfect." Jerin broke her discouraging thoughts. "But at least we'll have some idea of our progress. I've already wasted so much time."

She smiled, glad to be traveling with him. Sure they had their disagreements, but he had a good heart, as Marya said, and foresight to plan ahead.

Jerin extended his hand. "Let's make a promise. From now on we work as a team. If we both don't agree on a decision, then we find another way. Okay?"

His big hand nearly swallowed hers as they shook.

"Agreed."

\* \* \* \*

The bubbling cauldron sent off a warm heat against the chilled night. Alyra added more wood to the fire and peeked inside. The thick liquid had the color of river rocks and smelled like dirty feet. She crinkled her nose and set the lid back on top.

The air was heavy with moisture, which meant rain might fall before morning. She sat close to the warm flames and poked at the bright red coals. Had something deterred Lotari?

The grinning moon hung high in the sky, surrounded by dark clouds gilded with faint silver. Crickets chirped. Leaning back against an old oak, she closed her eyes and listened to the peaceful sounds. A slight wind bent the top branches and caused the other trees to do a slow swaying dance. The rain would do the vegetables a world of good. She'd miss tending the garden. If the chance to settle down ever came, she'd plant her own. Her eyes grew heavy and she allowed them to close for a bit, yet she found it harder and harder to fight off the sleep that kept creeping over her tired body and mind. Not wanting to wake up drenched in a downpour, she slowly forced herself to stand.

Maybe Wyndham had caught Lot trying to sneak out. Her heart sank. Hopefully, he'd visit before they left in the morning. Feet dragging, she headed toward the house.

A voice echoed from the woods. She stopped. Had soldiers finally found her? She quickly dismissed the idea, knowing the path and river kept them far away from the Healer's cottage. Turning, she walked down to the water's shore. Through the trees, she spotted two shadowy figures, and one of them sounded distressed. Lotari! Was he arguing with Wyndham again?

Anger boiled in her stomach. She hated the way the elder centaur treated him. Wyndham had no tolerance for *differing opinions*.

They were next to the river. If Wyndham was giving him a hard time, she'd tell him off. She stormed down the footpath leading to the shoreline, fist clenched and jaw set on a thorough tongue-lashing. As the white-foamy water came into view, her steps faltered as the size of the hulking centaur filled her mind. The path opened into a sandy clearing. To her relief, Lotari argued, not with Wyndham, but instead with... Issah?

Moonlight broke through the thick boughs and shone down on both of them. The moving water sparkled in the soft light. Lotari paced along the shore as the man stood with arms across his chest and feet slightly apart. His intensely familiar gaze, the one that felt as if he saw right down into your very core, calmly followed the centaur.

"They need your skills, my friend." Issah's voice sounded deep and stern as the night when he'd helped her see the banquet table. "Darnel realizes she will not turn back so easily. Once they begin their journey, the danger increases."

Alyra crouched behind a tree and peered through the tall ferns.

"He's a soldier." Lotari cried. "Let him fight for her." He turned to face Issah "How will he react if I go? You saw how he treated me when he was injured. I've not seen any indication of him changing his opinion. He despises me, and anything like me." Then he added in a quieter tone, "As do most others."

Issah continued to stare silently at him.

Lotari went on, desperation growing in his voice. "There must be someone more qualified to go, Sire. They could be turned away from help because of me."

Issah remained still as a marble carving.

"Please, this makes no sense!" Lotari's voice cracked. He stomped his hooves like he often did when agitated.

Finally Issah repeated, "They need you to go along. She needs you. I need you, as well, my friend."

Lotari spun away, wiping his face. He shook his head in response. "Why didn't I listen to Wyndham? He told me not to get caught up in affairs too great for me. *Oh why didn't I heed his words?*"

"And why didn't you, Lotari? What possessed you to disobey your elder? What drove you to endure his threats and beatings just so you could help a human girl, of all beings?"

Lotari shrugged not answering for a long while. He stared down at the foaming water rushing past, before he finally turned to Issah. "Not once has she ever looked at me with disgust." His voice was gravelly, yet dead serious. "That first day, when I followed her, listening to her ranting, she sounded so frightened, so angry and so alone." His hooves stomped the ground. "And she... she... made me feel... like maybe I really did have something to offer...." He shook his head. "I've never felt like that before, except with Marya. But Marya loves everyone, even the enemy soldiers, for goodness sake."

Issah chuckled. "So she does. She is one of a very few who actually understand." He laid a hand on the centaur's shoulder. "You do have a lot to offer, my friend, and you have more to teach Alyra. You have already endured much for this friendship, have you not?"

Alyra's eyes filled with tears. Her fingers dug into the rough tree bark. She wanted so much to run over and hug Lotari tight but didn't dare to move from her hiding place. Eavesdroppers got severely punished. She'd been whipped once because Darnel thought she was listening in to his private business.

"Sire, my clan...they will never allow me to leave.... They—"

"If I send you, Wyndham will not stand in the way."

Lotari looked at him long and hard as the dim moonlight illuminated his distraught expression. His bare chest rose and fell with deep breaths. Issah returned his stare with a calm, expectant gaze.

"This is madness!" Lotari finally exclaimed. "Wyndham is right, I've been such a fool."

Issah began to laugh. "That is what your elder says, my friend. Tell me what your heart is says."

"I … I'll lose everything. He will banish me from the clan."

Issah moved closer until they stood face to face. His hands rested on the centaur's shoulders. "You have read King Shaydon's book many times. You know those who cling to their lives will lose it. But for those who are willing to give everything up—"

"They will save it," finished Lotari. "And they gain even more."

"Indeed they do, my friend."

Alyra held her breath wondering if this meant he'd come with them. Oh, she hoped so. But how would Jerin take the news?

Then Lotari spoke again, but in such a whisper she had to strain to hear. "Sire, about her medallion. I've pondered about her account in the Dark Lands. And I've wondered … is she perhaps the one— the light child?"

Issah held up his hand, index finger extended as if to silence the centaur's question. His penetrating gaze aimed in her direction, right at her hiding spot. Alyra hunkered into the sand. There's no way he could have spotted her behind the fern and tree. *Could he?*

"It's for the King to decree each one's purpose. It's also up to that person to choose to accept their purpose. I believe that is all that needs to be said concerning this matter."

Scooting away on hands and knees, Alyra moved far enough into the woods to stand and run back to the cottage. She hurried, not wanting to be caught eavesdropping. Yet, a happy relief flooded her. Even if Lotari didn't go, which she had a feeling that he very well might, she knew the centaur was a true friend who really cared about her. She'd never had that before. Before opening the door, she decided to keep this information to herself.

Inside the cottage, Jerin was asleep on the couch with a book open on his chest.

How would he respond to Lotari joining them? She'd promised they'd do nothing unless both agreed first. Yet, if Issah insisted, he'd have to go along. *Wouldn't he?*

# Chapter 24

Alyra checked over her supplies one more time. Marya had made the white tree fruit into a healing cream for use in treating minor injuries. The healer had also provided several packets of herbal teas to help with aches and pains.

"You're medallion might not say you're a Healer," Marya helped Alyra pack. "But knowing other skills helps you to be well-rounded and knowledgeable, sweet-pea. From Jerin, you can learn to fight, and you can teach him what you know about healing herbs. Iron sharpens iron, as they say."

The people of Many Waters provided her with a new dark brown cloak, along with another new pair of shoes, since the others had worn through. Carah's dagger was strapped to her waist, something Jerin insisted on. She looked around the homey cottage, her chest aching over leaving the comfort and security she'd enjoyed there. Yet Marya insisted they would meet each other again, sometime in the future.

"I want you to know you'll always have a place here whenever you're in need. Always." She kissed her cheek. "Always." She kissed her other cheek. "Always!" She ended with a peck on her nose.

Alyra slid her arms into the straps of the backpack, then secured her cloak, fearing her heart would shatter if she didn't leave soon. Taking a deep breath, she headed outside. The morning sun glistened off the wet ivy covering the porch railings. The flowers growing along the walkway sparkled as though they were made of glass. The tall, green grasses wept tears she fought hard to hold back.

Jerin waited beside the road. His new shield, adorned with the emblem of the white tree hung over his shoulder covering his backpack. A chainmail vest peeked out from beneath his pale blue shirt and a new sword strapped to his waist. She hoped they wouldn't get into any battles, but at least he was prepared if they did.

Her chest hurt so bad she could hardly breathe. She didn't want to have to do the good-byes. She searched the yard and woods, still not seeing Lotari anywhere. Perhaps he felt the same way.

"Ready to go, Alyra?" asked a voice from behind her. She turned to see Issah walking up from behind Marya's cottage.

"I guess."

He stopped in front of her, and cupped her face in his hands. "When you are part of the Alburnium kingdom, you're part of a huge family. You never say good-bye forever. It's more of a, 'I'll see you again, some future day.'"

"Will I see you again along the road?"

"Absolutely. I'll be there anytime you need me."

She was about to ask why she hadn't seen him since he'd brought Jerin, when his last words registered. He had always been there when she really needed him. She'd been safe here. And he stood before her now, offering encouragement. She smiled and nodded.

"Issah, do you think …?"

"He's on his way."

She'd never get used to his knowing her deepest thoughts.

Jerin's eyes widened when he saw Issah. Smoothing his shirt nervously, he gave a low bow. "Good day, Sire."

Alyra wondered at his strange behavior. Why the formality with Issah? Then, she'd never really understood Jerin. Turning to the woods, she watched the trees for Lotari.

Issah returned the bow. "I was hoping for a few words with you, son. Before you set off."

Jerin's face brightened into a smile. "Of course."

"Good. Follow me." He led Jerin toward the garden.

Marya stepped from the cottage with a large shoulder bag full of food. She nodded to Issah as he passed, then broke into a wide grin and waved. Alyra spun in the direction she was looking and spotted Lotari walking along the road from town, head down. Relief washed over her as she bound toward him, catching his left arm when she reached his side. The white bow was slung over his shoulder, along with a quiver of arrows. A knife and travel bag hung around his waist.

"I'm so glad you came. I was afraid I'd have to leave without seeing you."

He didn't look at her, but a small smile spread across his downcast face. "Well, it appears I'll be accompanying you."

She couldn't contain her happiness. She threw her arms around him. "I'm so glad, Lot. I so wanted you to come, too."

He patted her back but said nothing. Head still hung low, he stared at the white rocks, eyes distant.

"You don't seem too happy about this, Lot. Are you sure?"

"Yes. I've made my decision. I'll not change it."

Jerin returned with Issah, his smile gone and replaced with a stony scowl. He glared at the centaur. Alyra let her arms drop, but stayed at his side until they came to a stop next to Marya.

Lotari didn't acknowledge the boy either.

Marya held up the sack of provisions. "This should be enough to last a few days."

"Lot is great at finding food." Alyra wanted Jerin to realize what an asset the centaur would be.

"Then he can carry the provisions."Jerin motioned toward the centaur.

Lotari finally looked him over from head to foot, then stared at the bag as if it had a stench. Alyra noticed the swollen bruise running along the right side of his face.

"I am no one's pack animal. Carry it yourself."

Jerin's eyes widened at the bruises for a moment before returning to their former scowl.

"I'll carry it." Alyra hoped to keep peace between them.

Jerin, cheeks flushed, and he hung the bag over his own shoulder. "If he's too good to help carry some of the load, he can fend for himself."

"Do not concern yourself over my welfare, boy. I know how to find what I need without carrying a burden mile after mile."

Marya shook her head and gave Alyra a look of pity.

Issah stepped between the warrior and the centaur. "Well, that's settled. I'd like a word with all of you before you begin." They gathered close to him, yet kept an arm's length from each other.

"Each of you possesses something the others need, which is why I have set the three of you together. Your journey will go quicker, *and* more pleasant, once you all learn to respect and care for one another." He went to each one, starting with Jerin, and clasped their faces in his hands as he whispered a blessing over them.

"Help will be there when needed. Listen to your hearts and trust the path." He bowed once more before heading west on the path. To their amazement, a group of Logorians stepped out of the woods and joined him.

Marya hugged each of them holding Lotari a bit longer and then standing on the tips of her toes to plant several kisses on his bruised cheek. His earth-encrusted fingers dug into the back of her shawl. Alyra wondered if he wouldn't break into tears over her shower of loving affection right there in front of everyone.

"I love you all, my dears. Until we meet again." Marya blew kisses at them. Alyra quickly turned away, her chest constricting.

Lotari trotted several paces in the lead.

Jerin's gaze kept flicking to Alyra for awhile before he finally asked, "Did you know about this?"

She shrugged, measuring the best way to answer. "Yes, and no." She spoke in a quiet voice, despite knowing Lot would still hear them with his keen ears. "I overheard Issah's conversation with him last night, after I left you. Nothing had been decided. Issah asked him to come. I don't understand his reasons." She stared pointedly at the large boy. "But I'm glad. He's good, Jerin. He'll be a big help. You'll see if you give him a chance."

Jerin's angry glare at the centaur's back and the slight shaking of his head told her he didn't believe her. Perhaps Marya was right, he would have to learn by experience. Hopefully, he would learn soon.

For the remainder of the day, they walked in silence, single file. Lotari stayed in the lead, eventually keeping to a gait they could keep up with. Alyra followed, lost in her thoughts, a mixture of longing, hope, and fear. Jerin brooded at the rear. The path lay wide open with pastureland on each side. Every once in awhile, they spotted a herd of sheep or cattle and even came across a couple of houses. The scenery was beautiful and made her feel peaceful as if there were no danger, no evil Dark Lord, and no war going on. At least there were some places untouched by his destructive hand.

Was all of this part of King Shaydon's lands? She quickened her pace to catch up with Lotari. "Do the towns and homes on the white path serve Shaydon's Kingdom?"

Lotari brows creased as he continued to focus on the road ahead. "The Dark One's servants cannot stand to touch the white rocks that cover the King's Highway. How many times must I repeat this?" He finally looked down at her with a smirk. "You did read the book on kingdom peoples I gave you, correct?"

She ducked her head, now walking beside him. She could hear Jerin's heavy footsteps right behind and she knew he'd quickened his pace as well.

"If you had, then you'd know that those who take up residence along the Highway have a responsibility to care for and help travelers. Such as Marya and the peoples of Many Waters did. Those who help to establish Kingdom cities are called Planters."

"So that means all the towns we pass will be safe, right?"

"Not necessarily." Thankfully, Lotari didn't seem to be in the mood to press her about the book.

"But you said—"

"What you must understand is that many settlements begin devoted to the Kingdom's way. Unfortunately over time, newcomers will move in, and sometimes Kingdom ways get pushed aside. If a town isn't careful, they forget what they originally stood for. Alburnium ways are strange to those who've never visited Aloblase and experienced it firsthand."

"Mayor Tember said Many Rivers is nothing compared to living in Aloblase." Jerin's steps drew closer. "The city and people he described sounded like a dream, Aly.

"I can't imagine anyone from Yarholm freely giving shoes and traveling clothes to a complete stranger. They'd sell and might even offer a decent deal on a good day, but never give away all they had."

She laughed. "The townsfolk were amazing. I hope I can go back someday."

A pained expression pinched Lotari's forehead.

Jerin chuckled. "They were so happy and content. I could settle down in a town like that, too."

"Could you?" Lotari's brows rose in question. "Their life is not as easy you'd think. To live in total abandon of yourself. To give freely to others. To stand firm against adversity."

Jerin scowled as irritation flashed across his face.

Alyra, trying to understand and trying to keep a quarrel from erupting, asked, "So some of the towns we pass will be Kingdom towns and some won't. How will we know which are safe?"

Lotari sighed deeply. "Basically, if the path goes right into the heart of the town and you see much activity at the meeting hall, then you've found a Kingdom town, no doubt. But if the path skirts around the town, but not directly though, then we should keep our guard up. Most likely, over time, the people have slowly moved away from the path and its influence. You'll know the kind of area we are in by the condition of the King's Highway... It's the same with a town."

"You mean whether the people serve King Shaydon or the Dark Lord?"

Lotari nodded.

Jerin now walked on the opposite side of Alyra. "Or neither. Yarholm wouldn't necessarily be considered a Kingdom town, but we certainly didn't serve the Dark Lord."

"Doesn't seem you were against him." Lotari finally looking at the boy for the first time since they had left the healing house.

Jerin stopped. "What's that supposed to mean?"

Touching Lotari's arm, Alyra silently pleaded with the centaur not to get into an argument, but Jerin added fuel by saying, "If we weren't so busy fighting off you interfering creatures all the time and cleaning up the messes you left behind, perhaps we'd have more opportunity to work for the Kingdom."

"You dare lump me together with *your* problems?" Lotari stepped closer to Jerin, despite Alyra's attempt to keep them apart.

Jabbing his thumb into Lotari's chest, he yelled, "All of you creatures are the same in my book."

"Haven't ventured far from your horse and plow, have you farmer boy?"

Alyra got sandwiched between them. Their sweat filled her nostrils and she decided she'd had enough of the stubborn, prideful boys. She elbowed Lotari then Jerin, catching both in the gut.

"Enough!" She jumped out of their way. "I've heard enough from both of you! Never have I seen such arrogant nonsense in all my years serving Lord Darnel! Wouldn't he be pleased to see you two right now."

She straightened her pack and then jerked the food sack from Jerin's shoulder. He and the centaur simply stood frozen with stupefied expressions on their faces.

"We're supposed to be trying to get along! That's what Issah said before we left. At least, *that's what I heard*!"

They cringed as her voice rose to an earsplitting level.

"I'm tired and I'm hungry." She softened her tone. "I'm going to set up camp." Alyra pointed toward a sprawling oak, which looked like a nice sheltered area alongside the path. "You two better work out whatever problems you have with each other. And don't even think about coming over until it's all settled, or I'll... I'll...."

Lotari's mouth turned up in a smirk. "What, dear?"

"I don't know, but I'll think of something. I always do."

# Chapter 25

Alyra stormed over to the oak, throwing her gear down in a huff. Low-hanging limbs spread out like welcoming arms, creating a convenient sitting area. Dried sticks and twigs littered the ground and made for a good fire. From her pack she took out the small pot and from the food sack she picked a few vegetables for a simple soup.

Angry shouts carried on the wind from time to time. Jerin said centaurs were about as trustworthy as trolls. Lotari responded that Jerin had never met his clan and had no right to judge them. Jerin said he didn't need to meet them, he could tell by Lotari's face how they were. Lotari grew quiet for a moment.

"Well, you're everything Wyndham hates in a human. Arrogant, narrow-minded, and self-centered!"

Alyra fed more wood into the fire. *Please let them work this out. Oh please!*

Darkness crept over the land as their arguments raged on. After filling up on the soup, she set the remainder aside and then pulled out her book of the King's letters. Marya had read from her copy each morning while Alyra washed dishes. She would miss their discussions over the daily readings. Lotari would sometimes join them, as well, and she had found his knowledge of the book astounding. By the firelight, Alyra opened the small black book but couldn't focus on the words.

She glanced up, realizing the shouting had stopped.

Jerin's voice had grown calm. "What happened when you told them you were leaving?"

They had moved closer to the camp, yet remained on the path, two silhouettes against the violet and orange sky.

"This." Lotari pointed at his face. "When Wyndham realized I would not relent, he banished me from the clan. Then he threatened anyone who tried to speak to me or offer aid, saying they'd find themselves in the same situation. So I went to town for the supplies I'd need."

She watched them over the top of the book. Her heart broke for the centaur and she determined that from now on, she'd be his family.

Jerin shook his head, keeping his eyes fixed on the ground. "You can never go back? Why? Why did you do that?"

"Issah requested. I knew the cost, and so did he." Lotari stomped his hoof. "I don't care, really." Then he shook his head, with hands held up. "Not true. I do care. I'll miss my family… but… I've always wanted to travel and see the Kingdom. Perhaps find other centaurs. Maybe…." He faltered a moment, tail swishing. "Maybe I can do something more useful for King Shaydon, something to help stop that black-hearted Dark Lord."

Jerin nodded. "Well, we agree on that."

For a few moments, they both grew quiet as they stared toward the setting sun.

"Are you and the prince good friends?" Jerin sounded wistful.

Alyra sat up. *Prince*? Who was he talking about?

"Yes, he and Marya are very dear to me." Lotari's shadowed face turned toward where she'd made camp.

The book shot up so he wouldn't think she was listening, though what else would she be doing? At least she didn't have to be so obvious.

Lotari added, nodding his head in her direction. "So is she. I want to make sure that child safely reaches Aloblase. I don't want that thief to get his hands on her again. I don't believe he'll be so merciful to her now she's remembering the truth."

His words caused a lump in her chest.

"Besides, I've always wanted to experience the city myself. So are you hungry?" Their steps crunched over the dried grass as they neared her little camp. "Looks like she cooked something for us."

Alyra extended her arms, palms out. "Wait! Are you two finished with your dumb arguments?"

The two stared at each other for a few long moments. Finally Jerin nodded. "I'm sorry, centaur. I'll respect Prince Issah's decision and be more respectful."

Lotari gave a curt nod. "I apologize as well, human. I will avoid harsh words with you in the future."

Jerin's statement about Issah hit her like a rock smacked on the side of her head. "*Prince* ... Issah? *Prince*? As in ruler of—"

"Alburnium." Lot finished.

Jerin chewed his top lip, keeping his grin in check.

"You mean—" She stared at Jerin incredulously. "I told the ruler of this land to 'get lost' the first time I meet him?"

He sat back on his haunches, brows knit in concentration as if trying to remember. "The traveler at the bitter water pond, Oh yeah, I forgot about him."

"His name was Issah. He told Lot to come after me when I ran into the woods."

"Then yes, sounds like you told the Prince of Alburnium to... uh... *get lost.*" He took a bowl and handed one to the centaur before serving them both some soup. "So, what do we have here?" He stirred the contents. "Think this is safe? She could have slipped in a little something to pay us back for our behavior."

Alyra stared mutely at them.

Lotari laughed so hard, he neighed. "I'm positive we venture at our own risk."

"You would both deserve it if I did." She rolled over, turning her back to them. "Rotten boys. Just make sure you clean out my pot when you're done."

Relief rushed through her, along with disbelief over learning Issah's true identity. At least he didn't have her beheaded or something for all her rudeness. And at least Lot and Jerin were finally talking politely to each other. Perhaps they were not exactly friends, but tonight was a start. She snuggled beneath her blanket, glad they were near her again. Glad Issah was a kindhearted ruler and nothing at all like Darnel. She'd never think of them as being alike ever again.

Lotari played his pipes for a while, and the soft music sent a peaceful calmness over the camp.

\* \* \* \*

"Where did he go now?" Jerin demanded as they packed camp the next morning. "We're stuck cleaning up while he's off frolicking through the woods."

214

Alyra shrugged as she kicked dirt over the hot coals of their fire. "We only need to gather our stuff. He's taken his. Maybe he decided to go hunt. Stop worrying."

Jerin stomped out the remaining flames with his large boot. "Not worried. Annoyed. They're so unpredictable. I mean he seems nice enough." He slung the provision bag over his shoulder. "I'm trying to give him a chance, but if he can't prove to be trustworthy, then...."

"Let's get going." Alyra also wondered where Lotari had gone, but trying to figure centaur ways was senseless.

Marya often said they were wild creatures and would come and go as they pleased. Jerin would eventually get used to Lotari's wanderings. Just like, hopefully, she'd get used to Jerin's snoring.

"Waiting around for him will only hold us up."

"You really think we'll lose him? The woods are his home and we'll be on the path. Besides, he has a keen sense of hearing and smell. And it's been how long since you had a bath? He'll catch up."

He glowered at her. "Am I the only one who's bothered by this?"

"Guess so." She shouldered her pack and started along the pathway. "When I was traveling by myself, Lotari always knew right where to find me. He'd pop into camp while I was sleeping, leave food, tend my fire, then disappear without so much as a 'howdy.'"

Jerin followed, lips pressed in a tight line and a scowl on his face. "How hard could that be? You sleep like a log. Especially when it's your watch."

"Really? You're never going to let that go, are you?"

He simply glared his silent answer.

"He'll show up soon. Let's keep going."

They walked along in silence for a short while before Jerin took up his ranting again. "Fine. I don't like it, but fine. What if we have problems? What if..."

"I have complete confidence you can handle any problems that come our way." She soothed with an accommodating smile.

He smirked, not taking the bait. "He's a wild creature. I want to know we can trust him."

"Do you think Issah would have sent him along if he wasn't trustworthy?" *Prince* Issah. She still couldn't get over that realization.

Jerin grew quiet as if considering her words. He said no more as they headed toward the rising sun. The woods were filled with the songs of birds. The grass dampened their leggings and a slight chill nipped at their skin. Taking in a deep breath, she relished the earthy scent of the trees and wildflowers growing along the sunny patches.

"You've had a couple of chances to talk with Prince Issah, haven't you?" Jerin broke her peaceful thoughts.

"Yeah." She remembered walking to Marya's house with him.

He'd asked her to trust him, to be his friend. *The ruler of Alburnium*. He wanted to be her friend. She couldn't comprehend such an oddity.

Jerin didn't respond right away, and she wondered what was on his mind.

"The first time I really saw him, when he came to our aid in that last battle, I thought he was so awesome. He looked so… powerful… so… dangerous. The enemy seemed to lose their nerve the moment he stepped out onto the field.

"But then later, when I was passed out, I heard him calling me. It was so dark, and I'd been scared. Everything hurt. I remember his voice. I'd thought he didn't seem so dangerous after all. I felt such peace when he called me. I tried hard to find my way to that voice."

Alyra waited to see what his point was. He seemed to be struggling with something.

"It's strange you know?" Jerin said with a soft laugh. "I keep thinking about how you said he wrestled in the water with the centaur. And that feast where he danced with you. Or how he found us when we'd drank from the bad water. I didn't even realize, until you reminded me last night." His brows furrowed as his face reflected the turmoil within. "I guess I find it… I don't know…. How could the ruler of this kingdom take time to wrestle with a centaur? To stop for a late night meal or offer to share some fish with us?" He kicked at a rock on the path and when it didn't move, he cringed with pain.

Alyra's breath caught. "I was just thinking the same thing. Darnel would never ask anyone to be his friend. You either followed him or he discarded you. Fed you to the dragon."

Jerin shuddered. "Life there must have been frightening there."

216

"Darnel had his kind moments. When I wasn't fighting him or being contrary. If I wouldn't have been so repulsed over how he treated his subjects, we probably would have gotten along wonderfully." She breathed out a deep sigh. "You know what Jerin? Never in all my time in Racah did Darnel ever say the words Issah has said several times."

"What?"

"That he loves me. I'm not even sure what that means but it felt nice to hear all the same."

"You don't know what it means to love someone?"

She shrugged, feeling embarrassed and stupid. "I suppose it means you care. I just wonder... the word *love*. I don't remember ever hearing anyone say that word. So how can I know what it feels like?" She watched his brows rise in question. "It's hard to explain, so never mind."

She could feel Jerin staring at her, but she refused to meet his probing gaze. Instead, she focused on the trees and the way the morning sunlight filtered through their shimmering orange and yellow leaves.

After a few minutes, he finally responded. "I bet you understand more than you realize." He grew silent again for a while, and absently grabbed at a low hanging branch, snapping the leaves off. "You're so fortunate."

She did look at him then, confused at his remark. The sound of hooves clattered up behind them.

"I hate admitting this." His chuckle had a nervous edge. "I was kind of jealous over your stories of how well you and the centaur got along with Prince Issah. I'm probably being stupid. It's just that the only time he ever talked to me face to face was right before we left. And that was only to tell me he wanted the centaur to come."

Jerin continued to stare out ahead of them as he ripped the leaves into shreds. Alyra glanced over her shoulder and noticed Lotari had finally caught up. The centaur's eyes locked on the boy's back. She stayed quiet, not wanting to interrupt Jerin's train of thought and miss what he struggled to say.

"Maybe I'm being a bonehead after all." He cut a wry look at her. "But, I'm taking this trip, you know? I'm going to Aloblase like General Marcel told me to. What I wanted was to go back home and help clean out my town so we could live peacefully again. But no, they said, 'You go with the girl and see King Shaydon. He will determine if you can fight with us.'" He shrugged and kicked again at one of the sparkling rocks. It stayed firmly in place, and he winced at the pain in his foot. Anger edged his voice. "I'm aware how dumb this sounds to say I feel jealous. I know it, yet I've given up a lot, too. I've done what they told me to do, but..." He shook his head; a pained expression tightened his face.

"But what?"

"Why does he seem so much friendlier with you? And the centaur? What more does he want from me?"

Lotari clomped closer behind them. "Your heart, human. And not under compulsion or because you think it's what's right. He wants it willingly and completely."

\* \* \* \*

For the next week, they traveled at a steady pace. Lotari continued to come and go, much to Jerin's irritation. Yet, by time they stopped for the night, the centaur returned with a catch from his hunts. During the day, Alyra kept her eyes open for wild fruits and vegetables they'd collect along the way. Water remained plentiful, much to their relief.

The green, vibrant woods thinned into wide plains with few homesteads. When they did eventually come upon a home directly on the path, Jerin wanted to stop and see if they'd help with supplies.

"You still have those coins?"

Alyra nodded. "Why?"

"Just in case they aren't as free-giving as Many Rivers. That can't possibly be the norm."

"Marya said it was. If the town was inhibited by true kingdom folks."

They stopped before the gate leading to a sprawling log dwelling. A woman stood in the front yard, hurling feed to a flock of chickens. When she spotted them, she set her bucket down and waved.

"Welcome travelers. Can I interest you in joining us for a meal?"

Jerin's eyes widened. "That would be wonderful, Ma'am." He introduced them, saying they'd not met anyone along the path since

218

leaving Many Rivers.

She nodded, explaining that not many cared to make settlements out in the open as they were. "A bit more risky, but we love the wide-open lands and have a knack with livestock. Matter-of-fact, my husband's out at the smoke house now preparing meats for the winter months. We can stock you up on some jerky for your journey."

"Much obliged, Ma'am," Jerin's relief soothed his stiff stance. "I don't mind doing a few chores to pay—"

"Tut! None of that now. You should know better if you've traveled far on this road."

He ducked his head. "I'm still getting used to people's generosity. I do appreciate your kindness."

She reached to open the gate, but stopped, her eyes widening as she focused on something behind them.

Alyra spun around to find Lotari trotting along the path.

A fearful whimper escaped the woman as she waved them to hurry into the yard. "How can that beast touch the white stones? Oh, get inside quick." She yelled toward the house, "Vernie! Quick, get your bow. There's a beast heading our way!"

Jerin stared at her dumbfounded, until he noticed Lotari's approach.

"No," Alyra gasped. "He's with us."

She glared at them. "What trickery is this? I've never seen..."

A man dressed in leather leggings and vest rushed from behind the house, bow aimed toward the centaur. Seeing the threat, Lot had his own bow loaded faster than Alyra could blink her eyes.

Jerin jumped between the man and centaur's line of fire. "Stop, there's been a mistake. He truly is with us."

Alyra ran out of the yard and down the path toward her friend, urging him to put down his weapon. He shook his head, arm muscles tight and ready to release the bow if necessary.

She stood in front of him, hoping the man wouldn't shoot anyway.

"Sir," Jerin tried again. "Please, the centaur is from Many Rivers. He is traveling to Aloblase with us." He then faced Lot and commanded, "Stand down, Lotari. Now. Prove you mean this family no harm."

To her surprise, Lot actually lowered his bow, pointing the arrow toward the ground. The expression on his face tore her heart. Beaded sweat covered his forehead, plastering his wildly brown curls around his temples. His gray eyes clouded with despair as he shook his head. The bow slipped from his hand and clattered against the stones.

"I'm so sorry, Alyra. I knew this would happen." He reared, turning from the path and bolted away.

"No, Lot, this isn't your fault," Alyra called after him. But he soon disappeared when the land dipped. She figured he'd not stop until finding the shelter of trees again. "Lotari!" She tried again.

Jerin came to her side, picking up the abandoned bow and arrow. He took her hand and pulled her along the path, past the log house. The man and woman were gone now, probably hiding in the safety of their home. Jerin said nothing as they walked, and for a long time, didn't release her hand as if worried she would bolt as well.

Of course, she couldn't. Fear over what she might encounter if she left the Highway's protection kept her glued to the stony path, even if her heart pulled her to chase after Lotari. Wasn't this the one thing he feared the most? That people wouldn't help them because of him?

*He was right, after all. Wasn't he?*

# Chapter 26

"I don't understand. We should be farther along by now." Jerin flicked his map against the breeze bending the parchment. "I was so careful in my research." He finally resorted to spreading the parchment across a fallen log. His thick finger followed the line he'd drawn of the White Road as he muttered about how they should be out of the plains by now.

"We're supposed to pass through another forest before we come to a town called Jolly Orchard. From there, we'll be near the foot of the mountains." Shading his eyes, he searched the horizon. Scrubby hills surrounded them, dotted with clumps of low-growing sprawling trees. Aside from a few edible root-type plants, they were hard put for any kind of vegetation to complement their sparse meals. "I see no sign of forest or mountain in the blasted land. Perhaps we got off on the wrong path?"

"Impossible. You heard what Carah said. Others might meet this one, but this one will never divide or split in different directions. They all head straight for Aloblase."

Wistfulness crossed his blue eyes. "I remember."

Alyra dropped her pack beside the base of an elm, then climbed up into the branches.

"What are you doing, monkey?"

"Getting a better view, slug." She grinned down at him. Reaching as high as she dared, she saw only more hills in the hazy distance. "Hey, if we hurry, there's a stream we can make camp at. At least we'll have fresh water and hopefully find something for dinner there."

Jerin helped her climb back down. "No mountains? Forest? Anything?"

"Nope. Too hazy to see very far."

He shoved the map back into his shoulder bag. "So much for all that planning."

Once they reached the river, Alyra wanted a bath. At first Jerin argued with her, but she promised to stay close to the bridge. He finally gave in, and walked a ways upstream where he could also cool off.

She wondered if Lot would be back anytime soon. He'd taken to staying away most of the day, and meeting up with them by sunset. Jerin hated how the centaur disappeared for such long stretches of time. Since they were able to get help easier without the centaur's disturbing presence, he didn't complain much.

Jerin seldom accepted people's invitation to stick around for meals or to stay the night. Sometimes, he would remain long enough to help an elderly couple chop wood. If someone was sick, Alyra tended their ailments to the best of her abilities. She missed Lot's knowledge on healing. She missed having him around to talk to period and wished he'd stop being so distant and sullen.

After bathing, she changed into her spare outfit while the other dried. Sitting next to the stream, she brushed the tangles out of her hair. In the clear water, three large trout swam lazily along the bottom. Her stomach rumbled at the thought of grilled fish for dinner instead of the bread and cheese left over from the last homestead they'd stopped at. The tinderbox in her pack held hooks and string. If she could fashion herself a rod, like she'd seen Jerin do before, then maybe, just maybe, she could contribute something besides greens for a change. She took her dagger and cut off a long, slender limb from the tree, then searched for bait. In Racah when Tarek fished, he'd catch bugs or dig up worms to use as bait. She searched the tall grasses until she found a small grasshopper. As the hook slid through the green body, she feared losing every meal she'd eaten in the past day.

The twitching insect stayed afloat at first, struggling to get free. She looked up at the trees, the darkening sky, anything to avoid watching the bug. A silver streak broke the surface, and the stick jerked in her hands. She gasped and pulled, unsure what to do next. Below the water, a fish swam in zigzagging circles, yanking and pulling against the string.

"I got a fish!" She yelled to no one. "Oh, now what do I do?"

She lifted the pole high over her head. A trout flew up, flopping at the end of the bent limb, nearly smacking her face. Carefully, she took hold of the wet line and swung the fish toward the shore where she let the stick and everything fall to the ground.

"I caught a fish!" She whooped, dancing a victory dance. "Ya-huh, I did it! Ya-huh! All by myself! Ya-huh!" She sang and danced as the fish flopped back toward the stream. She pounced on the pole and pulled her catch farther from the water.

"Okay, now how do I get the hook out?" She knelt in the mossy grass, willing herself to grab hold of the slick silver body.

Where were those pesky boys now when she needed them? She peered through the trees and found that the camp remained deserted. Taking a deep breath, she shook out her hands. *Just grab it and pull out the hook. Just do it. Go ahead, do it now! How hard can this be?*

With one quick motion, she grasped the fish. "Ewww!" Wet... slimy... cold. "Ew, Ew, Ew!" With her free hand, she yanked out the hook, the grasshopper still attached. "Oh, oh, ewww! Yuck! Disgusting." With a flick, she tossed the fish away from her. It flopped around a couple more times before growing still. She tried to shake the slimy feeling from her hands. Never had she felt so elated and so disgusted at the same time.

"What's all the yelling for?" Jerin's shaggy blonde hair was slicked to his head, and pieces of grass and pebbles stuck to his cheek. He'd probably fell asleep after taking a swim.

Waving her arms with a flourish, she nearly squealed. "I caught a fish. Look. By myself."

A wry grin split his face. "If you can catch two more around that size, there might be enough to make me a decent meal."

"Why do you have to ruin my moment? Why?" Her hands perched on her hips.

Laughter shook him so hard he bent over, clutching his stomach. When he stopped long enough to breaths, he gasped, "I'm sorry... I don't mean..." A fresh peal of laughter knocked him onto the ground.

"Well, there's enough for *me*, thank you. Catch your own. Oh, and you laugh like a girl."

He stopped, sitting up, eyes narrowed. His serious face didn't last very long. In a matter of seconds, he was chuckling again. "That's fine. You can gut and skin *your* fish."

Now her grin went slack like a wet noodle.

Still laughing, Jerin went for his pack, then returned and fashioned his own fishing pole. They sat on the bank together, catching several for their evening meal. Jerin seemed in a much better mood, despite his map failure. They joked, talked about life in Many Rivers, and wondered what Aloblase would be like. After he set the fish over the fire, he gave her a few lessons on shooting with his slingshot. She had a natural ability to hit what she aimed for.

"I like this better than a sword or dagger."

He nodded. "Good. Keep it handy. I'll make myself another one."

Two short whistles pierced the air, signaling Lotari's return. Jerin responded with one long whistle to let him know all was well. Three short whistles signaled trouble.

Lot trotted right down the bank, tossing a dead rabbit and his gear beside Alyra. Without a word of greeting, he trotted into the river and laid down, horse legs folding so the waves washed over his sweat drenched body. As he splashed water over his head, he sighed, "That does feel nice. This day is quite humid." He dunked his head and came up brushing his long, tangled hair out of his face. "Good news. We are nearly to the woods you've been looking for, human."

"Really?" Jerin grew excited as he pulled the crumpled map from his bag. "How far would you say we are?"

"Oh, another day or so of two-legged walking. I would have reached the woods by tomorrow's nightfall if I'd kept going."

Jerin growled, "You need to stop traveling so far away, centaur. What if something happens?"

Lotari smirked, shaking the excess water from his head. "The other good news is I can definitely see the mountains now."

"Really?" Alyra stuffed the slingshot into her pocket. "Do they look high?"

"No, I would say they were only about this big." He held his thumb and finger a few inches apart.

"Very funny, you mule."

Jerin rolled his eyes, then returned to his map.

Lot grinned a moment, then grew serious again. "What concerns me is how difficult acquiring game has become. There's an evil feel to this land."

"Did you see anything? Soldiers?" Jerin stood on the bank.

"It's not what I see, it's what I hear and what I feel." He shook his head at Alyra's perplexed expression and moved deeper into the water. "I wouldn't expect such young humans to understand."

"I still think you should stay closer to the White Road. It'll protect you as well. Then we'll have nothing to worry about."

Lotari's eyes narrowed on the man. "What, you worry? About me? Careful, human, you'll start sounding like you might actually care about a … beast."

Alyra shot Lot a warning look, shaking her head in a silent warning against starting an argument now when they were enjoying a nice evening.

He turned away, sniffing the air. "Is that fish?"

"Yes." Alyra bounced on the balls of her feet. "I caught the first one. All by myself."

Lotari walked up the bank and shook himself free of water, making sure they were thoroughly drenched. Jerin shook out his map, glaring at the centaur, but saying nothing.

"Thanks, Lot. I just took a bath and was nearly dry."

"Well, there's tomorrow's shower." He lifted one of the cleaned fish as if it was no more than an old log.

"You caught these?"

She nodded proudly.

"Well done, girl! I suppose you talked the warrior into gutting them for you?"

Jerin snorted, nodding.

He examined her pole and hook. "You used this?"

"Yes, of course."

"And this contraption worked? How extraordinary."

Folding his map, Jerin studied the centaur for a moment, as if having an inner debate. Curiosity must have gotten the better of him. "Um…what would you use to catch fish?"

Lotari walked back into the water and crouched over the surface, his four legs spread out. Standing as still as a stone statue, his eyes searched the depths. Alyra and Jerin glanced at each other, perplexed, then back to Lotari. With one quick swing he swiped his hand and hurled a fish up onto the shore, followed by another. Alyra jumped out of the way before they hit her. Jerin's mouth gaped.

Lotari looked at them with a smirk.

"Have you always been such a show-off, centaur?"

\* \* \* \*

"I hate this blasted hot land." Jerin put the leather he'd been fashioning into a new slingshot into his pack. "The sooner we're out of this place, the better. Let's get a move on. I'm sure the centaur will catch up when he's good and ready to grace us with his company."

Alyra said nothing. She also worried about Lot's wandering and wished he'd listen to Jerin's advice. At least they'd reached the cover of trees, though sparse, once again.

As they traveled, she practiced flinging small rocks with Jerin's sling. More often than not, the stones hit fairly close to the limbs she intended. Jerin walked ahead, lost in his thoughts. Occasionally, he'd grunt that she'd made a good hit, or advise her to release the cord sooner.

She became so wrapped up in her shooting game she ran into Jerin's back, her face smashing against his metal-studded shield.

"Hey, what did you stop for?" she rubbed her nose.

He pointed down.

"The rocks are gone!" She gasped. Had they somehow managed to get off track again? No, the King's Highway simply disappeared.

A dirt road, wide enough for two carts, crossed over where the path should have been. Jerin stepped out onto the road and looked along the northerly direction, then turned to face the south. Alyra started to follow, but he held up a hand to stop her.

"Stay there while I figure this out. If anything happens, run back the way we came and start whistling for Lotari."

Surprised he'd used the centaur's actual name she returned to the cover of the trees, heart pounding like a woodpecker's beak against a tree. This made no sense. How could the White Road simply vanish?

Jerin continued to search the ground, ending up on the opposite side where he called out, "It continues over here." He followed the rocks into the woods. "The path is so overgrown I don't know if we can get through." Shoulders slumped, he returned to the road and broke the dirt loose with the tip of his sword. "Look!" His eyes widened. "This has to be the work of the enemy."

226

Alyra went to stand next to him. Glistening white rocks peeked beneath two inches of soil.

"I wouldn't be surprised if they haven't somehow caused the overgrowth, as well," he said. "Keep that sling ready and stay in the trees, understand?"

She nodded. "Maybe we should go ahead and whistle for Lotari."

He took out the map again, brows furrowed in concentration as his finger traced the gold line over the paper. "This might be one of the market roads leading into the town of Denovo." He studied the northbound side for a long time. "Maybe…"

"If we get off the path," Alyra said, "we might run into Darnel's soldiers."

"But we can't continue along the White Road, it's too overgrown. Those vines have some ugly thorns. Even if we tried, who knows how long we'll hack our way through." He focused on the map. "We could disguise you."

A tingling crept up her spine, a feeling of apprehension. She wrapped her arms around herself to ward off the sudden chill trembling though her body. "I don't know, Jerin."

His somber gaze focused on the road. "I promised not to do anything that we can't both agree—"

The sound of hooves clattering over the hard packed earth caused them both to freeze. Too many to be Lotari and these came from the south. Jerin pushed her toward the White Road and reminded her to run if it turned out to be soldiers. Jerin hid himself behind a wide oak, his sword drawn and shield held before him.

In a matter of minutes, a brightly painted carriage came into view, pulled by two brown speckled mares and driven by an older man and woman. Alyra remained couched behind the bush, but peered out over the limbs to see the top was loaded with crates and camping gear. The green curtains covering the window opened slightly as a single eye peeked out, then quickly disappeared.

Jerin stepped out from behind the tree, sheathing his sword, but keeping his hand on the hilt.

"Hold up." The man tugged the reins. "Afternoon, son," He gave a friendly nod.

Jerin returned the greeting and walked up to the wagon. The

man bent forward as Jerin opened his map. Alyra strained to listen, but only caught a few words.

Finally, Jerin pointed in her direction motioning for her to come on over. When she did, he introduced her to Glen and Edna.

"They are heading to Denovo, too. They trade goods there."

Alyra eyed the boxes, wondering what they traded.

"I was telling them about how we've come along the white path, but have hit a snag."

Glen croaked in a raspy voice, "That's the exact reason we don't bother. Asides, our wagon won't fit. If you take the white road, you can only take what you can carry. Just silly, if you ask me."

Edna nodded as she waved a blue-feathered fan at her face. "We've worked mighty hard to let all this go." She gestured toward the loaded wagon. "Asides, you probably come to the end, from the looks of it."

Alyra was dumbfounded. General Marcel promised the White Road went all the way into Aloblase. He and Carah, along with many others had warned her to not get off the path. Now here they stood on a dirt road and what they did see of the highway was blocked.

Glen jumped down from his seat and stood beside them. "If you two would like a lift, I'm more than happy to let you sit in the back. The inside is a bit... um, cluttered right now."

Alyra searched over her shoulder into the woods, wondering when Lotari would catch up. She wished he'd listen to Jerin and stick closer. Her stomach twisted with nervousness. Something about Glen bothered her, yet she couldn't put her finger on it. They seemed like a nice couple, despite their aversion to the White Road. And maybe that was the problem. Their disdain toward her and Jerin trying to stay on the path. Everyone else had respected the White Road.

"No thank you, sir. We have another companion traveling with us."

"They're welcome to ride, too."

Jerin snickered.

Alyra shot him an angry look.

"Or if there's anything else you might need."

Jerin spoke up then. "We could use some water. I'm not sure

how far we have to Jolly Orchard. Especially now we have to cut our way through brambles."

"Sure, come on back here, younguns." Glen led them to a large barrel strapped to the side of the wagon. Edna told him to give them the biscuits from this morning as well.

"I've not heard of a town by that name." He called to the front where his wife remained. "What about you, Edna? Ever hear of Jolly Orchard?"

"Nope. Prolly abandoned like that bumpy footpath."

About the time he finished filling Alyra's canteen, Lotari trotted out onto the road and froze, eyes wide when he caught sight of the carriage.

Edna screamed. Glen grabbed a crossbow from the wagon. The jagged arrow point aimed directly at the centaur, as the old man moved between the wagon and Lotari.

Lotari backed away, arms up in surrender. "Put the weapon down, sir. I mean no harm."

Alyra darted around Glen and stood in front of Lotari. "He's with us. He's the other companion I told you about."

Edna gasped. Glen's face took on a look of disgusted shock. "That *thing* is with you?"

Jerin remained behind the man, his hand resting on the hilt of this sword, yet he made no move to defend their friend.

Alyra glared at Jerin, angry at his refusal to stand up for Lotari. "Yes'" Her chin jutted out in defiance. "Prince Issah sent him with us. He's our friend, and I'll ask you to speak more kindly to him."

"Will not," spat Glen. "To think I just wasted my water on… how can you hold your head up and act all proud at being associated with such a beast?" He turned to Jerin, who refused to meet his eyes, or anyone else's for that matter. "Spawn of the Dark Lord. Bred to serve him and nothing more! Don't know who you met on that trail, but it wasn't the Prince. He rules in Aloblase. Not associatin' with the likes of such freaks of nature."

Was Marya, and everyone in Many Rivers, Lotari and his clan, all disillusioned? Jerin stood, appearing as dumbfounded as she felt. His lips set in a tight line as he looked from Glen, to her, then over to Lotari.

That's when she heard a gentle whisper coming from within.

229

*You're heart knows the truth.* She knew that voice. *Issah.*

Glen spoke to Jerin. "You seem right nice, boy. You've just been misled. Come on with us, son. Anyone who didn't know better could have made the same mistake."

The strange man she'd met along the White Road had shown nothing more than kindness. Truth: he knew her, really knew her and he didn't hold that information against her. Another truth: to deny Issah was someone of great authority and wisdom, Prince or not, was no longer an option.

Lotari's hand rested on her shoulder. Her heart stirred with a saddened hurting. Like the ache she'd felt watching Marya kiss away Lot's bruises before they left her cottage. Glen continued spewing foul names at the centaur. He pulled at Jerin's sleeve trying to convince the boy to come along with him and get away from the beast.

Poor Jerin! She silently pleaded for him to come with them, to also remember the truth.

When he made no move in either direction, she said, "Sir, we appreciate the water, but we'll continue on our own, thank you." She wanted no more to do with the hateful couple.

Glenn's eyes narrowed as he made a gesture to his wife. "Think so, eh? I can get a nice price for 'em in the city. Now Edna!"

The woman banged her fist on the carriage. A rumbling noise came from inside before the side door burst open and out poured six small, grotesque looking men. They reminded her of DezPierre the Okbold, except instead of being tree*ish*, these creatures looked like they were made of mud and rocks.

Jerin gasped. "Brownies. Run!"

# Chapter 27

The Brownies swarmed from the carriage. Three held long ropes, the other three were armed with dart shooters.

Lotari grabbed Alyra's arm and shoved her toward the woods. "Get back on the path, now!"

"Stand still centaur!" Glen ordered, aiming his crossbow. "You're more valuable alive, but dead works for me as well, creature."

Alyra was about to jump between them when the butt of Jerin's dagger slammed into the side of the man's head. His sword came out and sliced the nearest Brownie in half at the waist. Lotari had his bow out and loaded, taking down another small creature, but not before several darts landed across his chest and stomach. The centaur staggered backward.

Lotari's grey eyes met Alyra's. "They're laced with sleeping potion." He loaded another arrow, but his dart studded arms shook so hard, he missed.

"Jerin!" Alyra rushed to Lotari's side. "Help me."

She tried to yank as many out as quickly as possible. His horse legs trembled so violently, she feared he'd collapse right there on the road.

Jerin ducked behind his shield as several darts rained down on him. The poisoned missiles plunked off the metal.

"Get him back on the path, Alyra."

She pulled with all her might. Lotari stumbled.

"Lean on me, Lot. Don't stop. We have to get back to safety."

Edna stood on the driver's bench, reaching over the top of the carriage where she pulled out a spear. "Don't let 'em get away, boys!" She drew her arm back, pointing the metal tip directly at Alyra and Lotari.

Jerin kicked a Brownie so hard he tumbled away like a

windblown hat. Alyra remembered how he'd sent the Okbolds scattering through the Yarholm bar room. As the spear left Edna's hand, Jerin moved in front of Lotari. The head veered off the engraved tree on his shield, but sliced across Lot's horse rump, leaving a long gouge. Spurred by the pain, Lot reared and galloped into the wood. Alyra heard his hooves clattering over the rocks before the drug finally took effect, and he toppled over.

The remaining Brownies swarmed. Jerin's sword flew, but they ducked. Alyra ran for the white path. Two pursued her. When she hit the white rocks, a sizzling noise sounded from behind. She spun to find one of the creatures exploding into flames. *The rocks!*

Collecting a handful, she pulled out Jerin's slingshot and slipped a stone into the pocket. The sling swept circles around her head before she released, sending the projectile flying. The first missed. The Brownie growled, yellow teeth bared. It followed them, keeping a few feet away from the path.

She loaded a second stone. The Brownie jumped into a tree and began climbing, its sharp claws digging into the bark. If she missed, those knife-like hands might be digging into her throat next. The creature perched on a low branch and readied to hop down on her. She let the stone fly at the same moment it leapt. The stone connected. The beast flipped and landed directly in the middle of the path. Smoke and sparks shot up as a flame consumed the small body.

Lotari yelled out. Alyra turned to find her friend laid out on the path. Another Brownie stood on his chest, clawed hands extended.

Alyra grasped another stone in her hand. A warm glow flowed from its depths. *She really could make them light up*. She threw the pulsating rock with all her strength. Upon impact the Brownie exploded into powdery dust, like the wolves had. For a moment, Lot's eyes rounded into apricot sized circles before he passed out.

From the road, the carriage set into motion again. Horse hooves clomped over the dirt. At the same moment, Jerin appeared from the surrounding trees.

"They're leaving with the two monsters they have left. Can't believe we ran into head hunters, of all people."

"Head hunters?"

He ducked his face, looking uncomfortable. "There are some people who hunt down creatures and trade them. Not sure what happens to the creatures. Probably sold to the Dark Ruler, I'd guess."

Alyra sank beside Lotari, pulling the remaining darts from his hide. "He's bleeding, bad. Will you help me?"

Jerin lifted Lot's man half, propping him up. Alyra was about to give him some of her water, then stopped. "No telling where they filled their water barrel. This might be bad."

Dragging the unconscious centaur to the nearest tree, he rested Lotari's back against the trunk, Jerin took her canteen and his, poured them out, then jogged off down the White Road for the last stream they'd passed. Over his shoulder he shouted, "Check Lot's water bag."

She did, finding enough to give him a drink and pour the rest into a pot to make a healing tea. By time Jerin returned, she was checking the cut on his horse back.

"It's just a flesh wound. Are we safe here? Can you build us a fire?"

He nodded and set to work.

While Jerin prepared them a simple meal and boiled some tea, Alyra stitched the cut along the centaur's horse rump. The darts rendered his muscles useless. He was awake, but unable to move. Jerin continued to coax him to drink the water and then the tea once it was ready.

By time he finished the cup, Lotari was able speak again. "That's going to leave a terrible scar."

Jerin patted his shoulder. "The mares will love it. Makes you look tough."

Lotari narrowed his storm-cloud eyes on the man. "You blocked the spear. You fought off those Brownies. You could have just gone along with them. I'm sure they'll make Denovo long before we do."

"Right. Traveling with a horde of Brownies. Do you have any idea how bad they smell? Like moldy pond scum." He shuddered, then turned away and busied himself with dishing out bowls of stew.

Alyra took the jar of Marya's ointment from her bag. "Let me put this on the dart wounds, Lot. You'll heal faster. The cream should draw out the poison."

He shrugged, his focus remaining on the flames. "They'll go away soon." His voice broke with his pent in emotions. "Centaurs are strong creatures and heal quickly." He squeezed his trembling fingers together. "See?"

Alyra sat on her knees in front of him and took his hands. Tiny spots dotted his skin where the darts had lodged. She dipped the edge of a cloth in the jar and worked the cream into his rough hands and up along his furry arms.

"That old man is a troll brain." She laughed scornfully. "Can you imagine what he'd say if he'd learned the truth about me? I was Darnel's apprentice. What a fool." A lump formed in her throat, clogging her words. Dabbing at the cuts on his chest and neck, she took several deep breaths until her heart began to settle back into a normal rhythm.

"Still, hateful words hurt, don't they? I remember how they talked about me in Racah. If that couple had known you even a little, they would have realized you didn't deserve to be called all those names. Not like I deserved it. I mean…" She stopped, noticing that his beard was wet with the tears streaming down his face. His head shook, as his mouth opened but couldn't form the words.

Her fist tightened around the rag. "I'm so angry at them! And I'm sorry he said all that to you. You've been so kind to me. And so has Jerin. I wouldn't have made it this far without you two, and I've done nothing but act ungrateful." She wiped the dampness from his face with the rag and added more ointment to the cuts on his cheek. "And I feel all kinds of things I don't understand. I wish I could do something to take all your hurt away."

For the first time that day he smiled, and said in a choked whisper, "See? You do know how to love."

She blinked at the realization. "You mean, when Issah said he loved me, he feels what I'm feeling now?"

"And even more, sweet child." His trembling arms wrapped around her. "Issah loves you more dearly than you'll ever be able to fathom. And because of our love for our King, we are able to freely love each other." He held her out at arm's length, where he could look directly into her eyes. "I love you, too. You have become my dearest friend."

For the first time, she allowed those words to sink into her very soul. They soothed her fiery emotions like a cool mist. How did he do it? No matter how bad she felt about herself, Lotari had a way of seeing things in a positive light. She hugged him tighter, grateful he was her friend. When she started to release him, a heavy weight hit her as another set of arms embraced them both.

Jerin blurted, "I'm so blasted sorry. I should have told that slug to shut his mouth right from the start."

"Not you, too. Both of you stop beating yourselves up." Lotari chuckled at the large boy's unexpected burst of emotions. Even Alyra stared at him dumbfounded. Lotari patted his broad back. "I expected this reaction. Those taken over by the Dark Lord roam around causing trouble while those of us who actually serve the king hide in the woods."

Jerin sat back on his haunches, one big hand resting on Alyra's shoulder and the other on Lotari who looked from one to the other as he said, "It has been a major dispute between Wyndham and myself for a long time. If people only see the bad, how are they ever going to know there is good?"

The man and the centaur looked at each other for a few moments as if they were finally really seeing the other.

Jerin shook his head. "When Glenn spoke out loud things I'd been taught all my life, I realized how wrong it sounded. And deep down from somewhere inside, I kept hearing, 'It's not love's way, and you know that.' Sounded like something Marya would say. And I know she learned everything from Issah. The real Prince who doesn't sit on some lofty throne."

"Yes," Lotari dried his face with the back of his hand. "He was definitely speaking. He reminded me that it only mattered what he thought of me, not anyone else. That's what kept me from…well, never mind what I was thinking of doing."

Alyra gasped, "I thought I heard him too. I was beginning to wonder if what that man said was true, and then I heard, 'Your heart knows the truth'."

"And you did," Jerin squeezed her shoulder. "And the truth is that I also love you. Aly. You'll always be able to count on me as a devoted friend."

She slipped her arm around the tall boy and hugged him, glad that Issah had set her on this journey with them both. Glad to finally understand what she'd longed for in the dark lands.

Then Jerin looked at Lotari. "Please accept my apology and honor me by considering me as your dear friend, as well. I was wrong about you."

Lotari' face brightened up like the morning sun. "Look at us, all hugging each other. Wouldn't Marya be so proud?"

# Chapter 28

Darnel stood in the center of the black marble room before a red painted circle. He turned to the child standing across from him. Brown hair cascaded down her back, tiny ringlets tickling her pinched brows and covering her golden-brown eyes.

"But you said." Her tiny voice trembled. "You said never glow. You said glowing is bad. You said so."

"Yes, daughter, I know. But just this once. Do this for Poppy like a good little girl. And I'll never ask again."

"Cause my light is bad?"

"Yes, and your light frightens people. Your affliction is our little secret." Darnel began walking around the circle, chanting in a language she didn't understand. Fiery smoke billowed from the center.

The child stepped back. "Poppy, I don't want to do this."

He towered over her, face enraged as the flames flickered off his silvery eyes. "You will! If you don't, he'll destroy me. Then you'll be left alone. I won't be here to protect you anymore. That is, if, he doesn't come for you next."

Tears tumbled down her cheeks. She bit her lip to hold in the whimper. Poppy got angry when she showed weakness. When she didn't obey.

"You will wait until I tell you. Not a moment before and not a moment after. Understand? Everything depends on you not messing this up. Do. You. Understand?"

She nodded, holding her breath. *Don't shine yet, don't. Wait. Wait until he says, then you can glow.*

The chanting continued, his voice deepening, the floor trembling, a metallic smoke filled the room. Flames shot high toward the ceiling. Within the cloud, a form began to emerge. Darkness sucked the air from the room. Sweat tightened the curls plastered around her face.

*Don't glow. Wait until Poppy gets what he wants.*

The monster formed from what seemed to be molten metal, red-hot and orange in color. The eyes and mouth were black, endless slits. "Whooo, calls me?"

Darnel silently pulled out a sword made from blue steel, the color of frozen water from deep pools. He swung the blade, slicing down and clipping off a chunk of the fiery monster. An earsplitting screech poured from the beast. Black sparkling powder fell over the floor and at her feet.

"Now," Darnel screamed as the fire exploded knocking him backward. The sword spun across the marble floor.

The child tried to ignite her light, but fear clamped down on her heart.

"Now you insolent bug! Do it!"

The beast began spinning like a dirt-devil, turning in her direction. Screaming, a burst of light filled the dark room.

\* \* \* \*

Alyra bolted up, gasping for air and swatting at her wool covering. The camp fire burned bright. She backed away.

"Easy, now." A hand grasped her ankle as Lotari came into focus. His gray eyes were so wide, the whites showed. "You're safe, sweetheart. You're safe. Take a deep breath and calm down."

She sucked in a lungful of air. Her heart pounded so hard she feared her ribs might crack.

"Alyra, look at me. Were you having a nightmare? You were... glowing, dear. Really glowing." He looked both amazed and horrified.

She started to draw her legs up to her chest, but he held her ankle tighter, motioning for her to come closer. As she scooted over beside him, his arm went around her shoulders. He sat up now, his horse legs stretched out before him. Perhaps he was starting to get movement back finally.

"I'm sorry." She clutched her medallion. "Did I scare you? I'm really sorry."

"It was... beautiful. What can you possibly apologize for?" He set the kettle closer to the fire and crumbled some herbs into a cup. "You were crying. I don't suppose you were dreaming of Aloblase this time, were you?"

She shook her head, trying to unscramble her thoughts. She'd forgotten about when Darnel has summoned the pit demon. He'd wanted the dust. The dust would embolden a creature with incredible strength, but it also blackened their heart so much, they became even more cruel and demented than Bezoar himself. She was sure the wolves had been fed the powder. She'd seen firsthand what happened to a turned creature.

She described the dream to Lotari. The tea settled her trembling and racing heart. "I was so angry after what he'd done. When I saw what the powder did, I told him I hated him and would never call him…. Well, I no longer helped him so willingly."

"Perhaps this is why he stole your memories? Maybe he hoped if you forgot everything, he could try again to win you over."

Recalling the day she'd escaped from Racah, the page and Darnel stood at her bedchamber door discussing how frightening she was. Darnel had sent her into the dark dreams, and she'd made them go away. Had she been glowing all along unaware? He knew and maybe that's why he kept her so close to his side.

Alyra finished the warm tea. "I remember now. How he'd say my glowing was a deformity we needed to hide. He said my light scared people and if they found out, they'd want him to destroy me. He always acted like he was protecting me."

Lotari rubbed his horse legs, trying to get the movement back. He looked much better now. The tea and ointment must have begun working.

His hand rested on her shoulder until she met his stormy eyes. "I'd wager he knew your light would drive that specter back into its fiery pit. He feared your light. He feared you, Alyra. Once you learn to control your luminance, you'll be a formidable adversary to him. Not a deformity, understand? Ability. Gift. Something that can help people, not repulse them."

Alyra drifted back off into a more peaceful sleep, lulled by Lotari's pipes and the soothing melody that calmed her nervous heart. By the next morning, he was on his hooves, walking around, though a slight trembling continued to plague his extremities.

As soon they ate breakfast, they crossed the road to face the bramble barrier.

"I will not leave this path," Lotari hissed between clenched teeth. A slight trembling still plagued his extremities as he tore away more long strands of vines, taking no notice of how they scratched his arms and twitching legs.

Alyra handed him her dagger, "Maybe this will help." She grasped a handful of the vines, ignoring the stinging thorns and held them steady while he cut through.

"Excuse me." Jerin pushed past, shield thrust forward and sword hacking away the tangled briars.

The woods hemmed them in. They gasped for air and constantly wiped sweat out of their eyes. Before long, the sweat ran down their backs like trailing snakes. Despite their exhaustion, no one wanted to stop until the forest backed off the rocky trail and they breathed fresh air again.

Jerin did insist they rest for a mid-day break while he checked his map. They chewed on jerky and nibbled dry bread Lot kept them stocked with. He insisted the nutritional value in them would keep them going even when meat and vegetables were scarce.

"I'm impressed at this map, Jerin," Lot peered over the boy's shoulder. Jerin handed him the parchment, and stood so they could look together.

"We have to be close to Jolly Orchard. Still, I'm concerned about what we'll find in Denovo. See?" Jerin pointed his thick finger at the line passing by the city.

"That is strange. Denovo has always been a major trade center for the kingdom." Lot sighed, shaking his head. "Perhaps, since the demise of The Halls of Knowledge, the town has grown wild."

Jerin rubbed the back of his neck, his face pinched with worry.

Lotari handed back the map. "Let us continue and hope for the best. Though, I have no hopes of anything good being found in this wretched land."

\* \* \* \*

The town of Jolly Orchard appeared out of nowhere. Nestled in the deep woods, one moment Alyra followed Lot who followed Jerin, when the trees opened up and they stood before a tall, glittering white wall. The stone path went directly up to the main gate carved out of polished oak. Like Many Rivers' meeting hall, the entrance doors had intricate carvings surrounding the tree emblem, but among the vines and figures were the words in script letters, Jolly Orchard.

"Strange." Lot scratched his beard as they passed through the wrought iron gates. "The whole city is a Meeting Hall. So wide open. I like this."

His gray eyes took in the various fruit trees and homes constructed within the boughs of sprawling oaks. Instead of stand-alone buildings they'd seen in the other towns, the homesteads were all made from natural materials, or in some instances, built right within the trees themselves.

They were taken to a mound of earth and led through a twisting entrance. Alyra nervously rested her hand on Lot's back. His coat bristled at first from the enclosed space, but in a matter of a couple of minutes, they were in a large underground room lit from windows built in the ceiling.

A chubby faun sat beside a roaring fireplace. He stood and welcomed them to the town, promising to provide anything they needed. Then he invited them to stay the evening.

"We have dwellings you humans will be quite comfortable in." He puffed a long, twisted pipe. "Shall I call for baths to be drawn? You all look like you've been through some ordeal."

"Thank you, sir." Jerin seemed edgy, yet in awe over all the creatures. "We've encountered a few snags."

"I am sorry, young man. Let's get all of you comfortable and we'll hear your tale during the evening meal." He turned to Lotari. "Good centaur, you will find a mineral pool located in the west groves where you can bathe and care for your injuries. I will ask a couple of my cousins to accompany you. We wish more noble centaurs like yourself lived here, but alas, your clans are few and far between.

"Matter of fact," the faun added, between puffs on his pipe. "The last horseman I encountered was several seasons ago. A white stag with piercing red eyes. Went by the name Talos. He came from Wilderland. Was on his way to Aloblase to seek help from the King. I assume you are on the same sort of mission?"

While Lotari stayed and talked awhile with the mayor, Jerin and Alyra were led off to their rooms. By the time they were cleaned up with fresh clothing and a short rest, a large feast was being prepared for them in the central meadow. She was reminded of the banquet she and Lotari had shared with the Prince. She wished more than anything to speak with Issah again.

The one thing that really caught Alyra's interest was the variety of the inhabitants in this town. Many Rivers mainly had only men and dwarves working together, but she met fauns and sprites who loved to sing no matter what task they were doing. There was a group of Okbolds like DezPierre, who worked at setting up the many tables, but they were all happy and cheerful.

Her surprise was mirrored on Jerin's face.

The townspeople gathered around Lotari, so pleased to see a centaur outside of their woods and traveling with humans that they treated him like a champion.

"Oh," Jerin shook his head in dismay. "There will be no living with him now."

Alyra laughed, knowing he joked.

In the middle of the meadow, a tall, white-barked tree grew, like the one she'd seen in Many Rivers. White star-shaped flowers and red fruit filled the branches where someone had hung several lanterns. Alyra considered loading up on some of the fruit to make more tea, but remembered how Beave and Marya said to only pick the fruit when needed. Right now, they had enough.

A group of human and creature children ran past, playing blind-man's tag. She found Lotari watching, laughing as the children ran behind a blindfolded man, pulling at his shirt and darting away. He spun around but didn't try to catch anyone yet.

Standing straight, and still, the blindfolded man shouted, "I think I'll get Gloria!"

A fair-haired faun-child clasped her hands over her mouth to stifle a giggle as she backed to the edge of the group. The blindfolded man seemed to know instinctively where the girl would go next. She trotted around the other children, trying to keep one step ahead of her pursuer.

"You'll never get away from me," the man challenged which caused the girl to erupt in a fit of giggles.

He took that opportunity and grabbed her up lifting her high into the air and twirling her in a wide circle. Her hooves kicked with glee.

Alyra remembered playing a similar game long, long ago. A group of children screeched with laughter, as they darted past tall colonnades and over sparkling streets. Flowers poured over curved arches, and beauty was all around. Alyra ran through those streets. Fair beings laughed and pointed to a hiding place high up in a sprawling aspen. The man pursuing her stopped below the tree looking around and acting like he was searching for her. The other children shrieked with laughter, but didn't give her away.

The man grinned at them and said in a serious tone, "You think I've lost her? Never!" He looked up. Issah! His merry brown eyes shined. "I'll never lose my beloved girl." He held up his arms to receive her. "Come Alyra, your parents are waiting."

She hopped from the branches into his waiting arms, wrapping her own tightly around his neck as she pressed her cheek against his.

"I'll always be there when you seek me, my child." Spinning he repeated, "Always, always, always!"

Alyra blinked, her vision blurred as Gloria pulled the man's blindfold off his head. "You found me again, Issah."

With a hearty laugh, he set the girl on his shoulders and called to the others, "Who's hungry? I'm ready to eat, how about you?" The children cheered and bounded after him as he led them toward the tables.

Lotari draped his arm around her shoulders. "You cry, again? Is something wrong, Alyra?"

She shook her head. "Happy tears this time. I remember him, Lot. I remember playing that game with him in Aloblase."

Lotari planted a kiss on the top of her head. "I like hearing that your good memories are back. Let's go eat. I'm starved for fresh cooked food."

Alyra wiped her eyes dry. They headed for the dinner tables piled with hams, roasted bird, and bowls full of ripe pears, apples, oranges, and peaches. While they ate, she kept trying to remember more, but only the one instance was all that came to mind.

Issah sat with Jerin and a group of young men. She thought about approaching the prince, but from the enraptured look on her big friend's face, she decided to wait.

Once the meal was cleared, the tables were moved away for the celebration. Alyra asked one of the fauns what they were celebrating.

"We need a reason? Isn't life, itself, reason enough to celebrate?" He held up a fiddle and began playing with the others.

"Yes, life, itself, is a very good reason to celebrate." She said more to herself since he'd danced away from her. "Especially now."

She clapped with the music, watching the dancers twirl in wide circles. They reminded her of watching colorful fall leaves spin to the ground.

"I need a dance partner." A familiar voice intruded on her thoughts. She turned to find Issah grinning at her.

"I'm sure you can find better dance partners than I."

"Perhaps. But you're who I desire to dance with." He held out his hand, which she took more easily than the last time.

They wove around the other dancers beneath glowing lanterns hanging in the tree boughs. Her breath caught as they moved to the rhythm of the fast beat, and she marveled at the joy coursing through her body. "This is great!"

He laughed and she felt that fondness... or love, as Lotari had called it, well up from deep inside her. She wanted to tell him but didn't know how. The word felt so awkward, so foreign to actually say.

The music ended, but he didn't release her. "I know you've been through some rough spots since you left Marya's. Are you all doing better now?"

She couldn't help but grin at his uncanny ability to know things. "Yes, lots better."

"I'm so proud of how you stood up for Lotari. You are a brave and loyal friend."

She blushed. "I started to doubt. I wasn't sure what was true. That man said you..."

"And yet, you followed your heart and found the truth in there where it's been all along."

"Something told me to do that." She eyed him suspiciously.

Issah stood before her, still holding her hands in his. "I'll be there for you whenever you need me, Alyra. I love you very much."

He began to release her when she held tighter. "I understand now. Love. Or, I think I understand better." He smiled at her and she went on, "And I remember you. Today, when you were playing games with the children and that girl... I—"

"Remembered us playing the same games?" He finished.

Tears welled up, blinding her vision. Her voice cracked when she blurted, "What happened to me? How did I lose you?"

He pressed her hands tightly to his chest. "You never lost me, Alyra. You merely looked the other way for a while. But I was there even then. I never forgot you and now here you are. Soon enough, you'll remember everything when you are ready."

His arms encircled her and didn't let go until her tears subsided. The music had resumed and they swayed gently to the sounds, until the lightness of the music lifted her spirits again.

After awhile he stepped back from her, his eyes intent and a slight smile on his face. "There is another here who desires to speak with me tonight. Don't forget what I've said." He walked over to a group of dwarves playing cards with Lotari and Jerin. Issah touched Jerin's shoulder. "Follow me, son."

Jerin's eyes widened as the cards fell from his big hands. Immediately, he was on his feet and following Issah who led him deep into the orchard.

# Chapter 29

Tall, jagged mountains rose up into the crisp blue sky, their granite tops shrouded in misty clouds. A sparkling band of water cascaded down into a rocky valley, splattered with red, yellow and purple wildflowers. The river course twisted down along the lower hills until it fed into a large blue pristine lake. The travelers headed for the town Denovo, nestled in the foothills of the Semitamon Mountains.

"Well," Jerin shifted his pack onto his other shoulder. "Such a beautiful sight. Much more interesting and pleasant than the dank woods we've been traveling through."

Lotari took a deep breath, his round, brown eyes glazed over dreamily. "I could call this home and be happy for the remainder of the century. Look at the foliage." He pointed to one particular yellow flower. "The petals will make a wonderful tea for when a person is feeling down. And over here-" He trotted to a dusty-green bush covered with spiked leaves. "-this reduces fever."

Alyra cocked an eyebrow. "Lot, how old *are* you, anyway?"

"Oh, I'm still a colt compared to most in the clan. Why, I'm merely approaching my second hundred years. Look!" He raced down the path and gathered another handful of flowers.

She turned her attention to the breath-taking mountains and wondered if the White Road would lead them over or around tall peaks. Their purple heights caused her head to swim when she craned her neck to see the cloud-enshrouded top.

Jerin sighed. "They said we can see Aloblase once we're on the other side."

"They look awfully tall and steep." Alyra gulped down the growing anxiety clogging her throat.

He shrugged. "One thing at a time. Let's get to Denovo. Then we'll worry about the mountains." Jerin kept bumping into the centaur who repeatedly stopped in his way to gather plants.

"This one will cure a headache." Lotari cast a wry grin at Jerin. "I could use a lot of this."

Jerin gave his chestnut tail a sharp tug. Lotari bolted off. He stopped, shooting him an annoyed glare, which quickly turned into an impish grin.

That night, they camped along the lake shore beneath a band of spruce. A full moon reflected off the lake's shimmering surface. Six weeks had passed since they'd left Marya's.

As usual, Lotari prepared the meal while Jerin stoked the flames. Alyra helped him chop the last of the vegetables from the provisions they'd received in Jolly Orchard.

Once the fire blazed, Jerin sat back with his newly acquired book of *The King's Letters*. He'd never shared what Issah spoke to him about, but something had changed in the large man. Jerin had a quiet confidence now, where he didn't seem so intent on proving himself anymore. Often he'd asked questions of Lotari about passages from the book. Even more amazing to her was the fact he listened with rapt attention to every word the centaur said. Finally, they had become friends.

Two days later, they made their way into Denovo. Three major roads joined at the entrance. Cobblestone streets wove past grayed stucco and wooden buildings. The township flowed upward, following the slope of the foothills at the base of the Semitamon Mountains. The main road, which led right through the middle of the district, was lined with all sorts of vendors and people milling around.

"Where is the meeting hall?" Alyra asked as they continued on the King's Highway toward the settlement's entrance.

"Good question," Lotari's eyes scanned the city. "It should be the most prominent building in a township."

Jerin halted where the path veered away from the city.

Alyra followed the White Road with her eyes as it wound up into the mountain cliffs until it disappeared amidst the crags and trees.

"Now what do we do?" Weariness cramped Alyra's muscles. Jerin refused to stop for their normal break saying they'd rest when they reached Denovo. She stared upward into the misty peaks. "It's so steep, I can't even see where the path goes."

"Climb." Lotari replied.

"Easy for you," Jerin quipped. "In case you hadn't noticed, two of us aren't built like a mountain goat."

Lotari grinned. "Oh, I've noticed. Only I try not to hold it against you."

Alyra shot the centaur a that's-not-funny look.

Jerin watched the bustling city for a long moment. His shoulders sagged almost as much as hers.

Finally, he suggested, "Let's go to the inn and get something to eat. I think we should rent a place to stay for the night and replenish our stock tomorrow. We'll need warmer clothes in the mountains." He grinned at Lotari. "Well, Alyra and I will anyway."

Lotari, put his hands on his waist. "You assume they'll rent me a room? If you think I'm going to stay in the barn while you two toast your ghastly little toes next to a warm fire, you are delusional. And for your information, just because I have a little more fur than you, my warrior friend, doesn't mean I don't feel the cold as well."

Alyra rolled her eyes and with a loud sigh. "Both of you boneheads are missing the most obvious problem."

"What's that?" they asked in unison.

"The white path doesn't seem to go into the town."

Jerin shrugged. "It doesn't matter. We must stop here before going up into those mountains. There are no other towns between the mountains and Aloblase."

"I'm starving. And exhausted." Alyra looked to Lotari who silently stared at the glistening rocks. "We're nearly out of food, Lot."

His brows furrowed with worry as he shook his head. "We'll be taking a risk. This seems all wrong to me. There must be a safe place to get provisions... I know it. Did Issah say anything to either of you about this town?"

Jerin and Alyra both shrugged, before she said, "You were there when he left us that morning."

Nodding, Jerin added, "He mentioned something about an increase in our numbers and to take care with alliances. 'Don't let perspective blind you. Wisdom looks at things from all sides.'" Jerin swept his arm toward the town, "I have no idea what that means.

248

What I do know is we'll have a better chance of meeting people in there than out here. And in the meantime, we can purchase supplies."

"And sleep in a real bed." Alyra was tired of the hard ground.

Lotari looked from the gates, to the mountains, then to them. He horse legs shuffled as they often did he grew agitated. "He also told us to stay on the path."

"But that's what he always says," Jerin shot back. He took a deep breath and said matter-of-factly, "Let's not be narrow-minded about this. When I researched Denovo, all the books claimed this was a kingdom town. The path still goes beside it. Remember how we thought the rocks disappeared when the dirt road covered it? Perhaps the White Road still goes through the town, but it's harder to see.

"Look, I say we remain low key while we're here. I'll do all the legwork. We'll get a room tonight. Lotari, you can manage one day indoors. In the morning, I'll get our supplies. Find out some information. You'll stay out of site with Alyra and keep her safe. Who knows, maybe we'll meet up with someone who can show us an easier way past the mountains."

"What *easier* way?" Lotari snapped. "There's the path, we should remain on it. Simple! That's what we were told, and that's what we must do!"

"Okay!" Jerin yelled. "Enough all ready. I hear you."

Alyra stepped between them and put a hand on each of their arms. "Everyone take a deep breath and calm down. We're tired. We're hungry. And we have to get more supplies and warmer clothes for the trip over."

The men both nodded in agreement.

"Lotari, pull the cloak out of my pack, will you? I'll cover my head, see?" She showed him how well the hooded cape hid her. "Jerin, you do the talking."

Despite any doubts he might have had with the plan Lotari nodded anyway. "Very well. But give me your dagger. If we come into trouble, which won't surprise me in the least, I can fight easier with this than my arrows." He tucked the knife inside his hip pack.

They entered the first inn they came upon and found all manner of creatures from big, burly men to small Okbolds mingling inside. She even spotted two fauns who were part of the musicians playing over the clamor of voices.

Deer and bear heads decorated the dark paneled walls. Shouts and growling laughter came from the pub, off to the left of the entrance way. To the right, soft music filtered in from an open door leading out to a patio. Alyra peered through her hood to see people gathered around dining tables under vine-covered arbors and surrounded by flowers and fountains. What wonderful place to sit back and relax, but the growing tension in her stomach made her doubtful she'd be able to loosen up until they were on the other side of the Semintamons. Lotari's hand rested on her shoulder. She squeezed one of his fingers, glad he was close. His twitching ears told her he was unsettled as well.

Jerin went up to the desk, which sat between the bar and dining area.

"We'd like two rooms please. Lower level if possible."

The attendant, a squat, squint-eyed man nodded his balding head toward Lotari. "What 'bout 'im, ay? Has 'e left 'is ranks, or somet'in'?"

Jerin's brows furrowed. "Pardon me? I didn't get that."

The man's eyes narrowed even more. "Eh, yourn beasty, thar. Es 'e yours?"

Jerin turned to Alyra silently asking for help. She tried to piece together the fractured speech and came up with, "I think he's asking if Lotari is our...beast? Or if he's left his rank? It seems he thinks Lotari is part of a military unit. Are soldiers here in town?"

"Eh, ya thar is, Missy. T'ey comes an' t'ey go. Nasties wit' t'em, too. Ain't ever meet a woolly one, liken 'im, on 'is lonesome, ay?"

"Oh, I see," Alyra explained to Jerin, "soldiers have been coming and going. Sir, do they wear black helmets?"

Dread filled her chest. Lot's nails dug into her shoulder.

"Ay, tey do."

"Wonderful." Sweat beaded up along her forehead and neck. *Please don't let Bezoar be here!* "They have, uh-" She glanced tentatively at Lotari. "-nasties. I'm guessing they are some of the beasts. Probably trolls, dwarfs, and evidently centaurs. He thinks you've left your unit, Lot."

"Well, I most certainly have not!" His chest swelled as he

bristled with anger.

Alyra grasped the centaur's hand, still digging into her flesh. She patted his arm to silence him.

Jerin turned back to the assistant. "Can we get those rooms? He is traveling with us and will share a room with me."

The man scratched his whiskered chin. "Well, I'll be. Two will do. Only has upper floor. Take et or leave et."

Lotari's face paled.

Alyra whispered, "You can do this. Just one night, Lot. That's all."

Jerin held out his hand for the keys.

The innkeeper dropped them into his palm with a chuckle. "Jus' wen you t'ink you see all…you see ever more, eh?"

"We'd appreciate if you'll send up three dinners?"

"Ay." He leaned over the desk closer to Jerin, "I say keep yer pet out a sight, ay? T'ay keen on 'em, know wat I mean?"

Jerin's hand rested on his sword hilt. "I hear you, thanks. I trust you to keep quiet about us, as well."

"Aye. I nevah speaks on who stays 'ere. Nevah."

With a nod, Jerin pushed Lotari him toward the stairs.

The centaur glared at the man. "Did he just call me your pet?"

"Move, Lot." Alyra and Jerin both shoved him ahead of them. When they reached the upstairs landing, Lotari spun around, bumping the walls of the narrow hallway. "I don't understand. But I see it on your face. Why did that…that human speak of me in such a manner? What did he mean?"

Jerin held up both his hands to stop him. Opening the second door along the hall, he motioned everyone inside.

Setting the lock, he heaved a long sigh. "We all know they use centaurs. That couple wanted you for a bounty. Most don't freely enlist to fight for the Dark Lord." He looked away from Lotari's questioning stare. "Centaurs are more efficient than a horse. They can carry a rider and are fierce fighters."

Lotari narrowed his eyes on Jerin. "You fought my kind in battle, haven't you?"

Jerin nodded.

"And that is the reason you hated me at first. But, you've kept what you've seen to yourself. Why?"

Jerin's hands trembled, as a deep intake of breath puffed out his chest. He moved away from the door and went to the window, his blue eyes focused on something far away, something that caused his face to blanch with pain.

"I watched as one of them ripped off my friend's head with its bare hands. It then reached down into his body, pulled out his heart, and ate it."

Alyra thought she was going to be sick. No wonder Jerin kept such a tale to himself.

Burying her face in her hands, she knew what caused such a demented madness in a creature. She'd been the one to help Darnel obtain the power to create his monsters. She clutched her stomach, fighting back the wave of nausea washing over her.

Lotari's fist clenched into tight balls. His tan coloring paled. Alyra wondered if he felt as sick as she did.

Jerin turned to Lotari. "Something was wrong with that beast. Its eyes... they were the color of the wolves we encountered." He glanced at Alyra. "And its hands were twisted. Like," He shook his head, struggling for words. "I don't know. I just... know... after seeing you, and some of your clan, I know the dark one had... altered the creatures we met. But, when I first met you, every time I saw you, I'd see my friend's death all over again and again."

# Chapter 30

Lotari's voice grew grave as his shoulders slumped. "I had no idea. No wonder you hated me. No wonder people are so intolerant of me. How could they know the difference?" He clomped over to the window and collapsed, as if his legs had given out. His forehead rested against the pane. "I understand so much now."

Jerin pulled a chair next to him and sat. "You're right, Lotari. If they aren't running wild, then they are being harnessed and used for the Dark Lord's purposes."

Alyra dropped her pack on the floor and went over to her big friend. He seemed so crestfallen, her heart broke. She'd told Lot of the dream about the black powder and wondered if he'd made the connection yet. Guilt and repulsion weighed so heavy on her conscious, she couldn't find words to speak.

His focus remained outside the window instead of on them. "I knew there were herds of centaurs running wild and causing trouble. Several of us had wanted to try talking sense into them, but Wyndham refused to let us." He rubbed his hands over his face. "Wyndham is merely an excuse though. If enough of us had banded together and decided to go, he couldn't have stopped us. Deep down, I always knew that, too."

Jerin crouched, elbows on his knees. "Perhaps Wyndham knew the Dark Lord sought out centaurs as slaves and was concerned you'd be caught if he allowed you to go."

Lotari blinked, considering his statement. Then he turned to Alyra. "The boy is a paradox. One minute he talks foolishness, and the very next he speaks with the wisdom of a philosopher. You humans never cease to amaze me."

Jerin chuckled as he grasped the centaur's head in his big hands.

"You mule." He jibed. "But I suppose, if I had a pet, you'd make a right decent one."

Lotari' eyes flew open in shock. He threw his arms around the man's waist and knocked him down to the ground.

"Hey you two!" Alyra jumped out of the way. "There's not enough room for your horse playing."

Both burst into a fit of laughter. Jerin twisted as he tried to wrestle the strong centaur's hands loose from pinning him down.

"You'll break something," she tried again.

Jerin managed to get back to his feet. "Ah ha! Got you now, you mare."

She grabbed her backpack and the other set of keys from the table and left them to their tussle. Her room was right next to theirs. As she settled in, a crash sounded through the wall followed by more boisterous guffawing.

After bathing and putting on a clean set of clothes, Alyra washed her traveling outfit, and then went over to the boys' room to eat. Jerin joined her at the small table. Lotari remained in the corner, staring out the window.

Alyra asked if he'd eaten.

"A little. I guess he's still fuming over being called our pet. Plus the fact I finally wrestled him down to the floor." He winked over his cup. "No small task, but one I'm obviously up to."

Lotari gave a disgruntled snort. "Well, you've managed to guess wrong again, farmer boy. I allowed you to win. I do so hate seeing you sulk all the time."

She was glad to see him in a better mood, though Lot still seemed distracted by something.

After clearing the dishes and setting them outside, Jerin broached the subject none of them wished to discuss. "We'll have to be extra careful with the soldiers in town. They might be here scouting the area, Alyra."

She remembered the bag of fruit in Darnel's kitchen coming from Denovo. Evidently, the town had been trading with Racah for some time. Why hadn't she made that connection before? She sighed, rubbing her aching forehead. Perhaps Jerin's statement was on mark. Perhaps they were here for trading and nothing more. Her gut churned knowing the soldiers most likely had been warned to keep an eye out for her. No matter what their reason for being in town was.

Jerin added wood to the fireplace. "I'll go in the morning and purchase what we need. Then we are leaving this blasted place as soon as possible."

Alyra slumped in the chair next to where the centaur lay. "If Bezoar is here, I'm done for."

Lotari reached out and tugged at her sleeve. "Not so, child. He has no more power over you than what you allow him to have."

"You've never seen him, Lot. He swore he'd slit my throat if he caught me again. Jerin knows. He saw him." Fear gripped her chest, making breathing difficult.

"Twice." He stared at the roaring flames as an obvious shudder ran from his shoulders and down his arms. "The troop we came up against before I was brought to Many Rivers was led by him. He's evil for sure."

"Evil, yes. Powerful?" Lotari cupped her chin with his finger and thumb so her eyes met his. "Not unless you allow it. Understand?"

She didn't but said nothing. Lotari, like Issah, had a strange way of talking. He stared intently at her for a few seconds, as if knowing she didn't truly comprehend his words. His hand fell away, as he obviously decided to let the matter drop.

Lotari stood and clomped over to one of the small beds. He chuckled, shaking his head as he grabbed a blanket and returned to his corner, next to the window. "I am going to miss the crickets singing to me tonight." Once he settled himself, he added, "I do not understand your complaints over not having such nightly accommodations. It is stifling in here. There are no comfortable grasses to rest on, and this place has a stench." He arched an eyebrow at Jerin.

"Hey friend, don't look at me, I had my bath."

Alyra went to her room. Jerin followed and built up her fire after checking to make sure everything was safe and locked down. When he left, she climbed beneath the warm blankets which hugged her into a cushy softness. Lotari could have his damp grass, if it pleased him, but she'd really missed sleeping in a comfortable bed.

* * * *

The next morning, Jerin left for town after they'd eaten some sweet bread brought to them in a basket by the innkeeper. Alyra sat on her bed and busied herself by organizing her knapsack. The task kept her mind off what was going on in town. They were supposed to be ready to leave as soon as Jerin returned. She looked at her medallion again, light dancing off the carved flames. *A light would come out of darkness* the prophecy had said. Flames produced light. The coin turned in her hand to the side with the tree.

A memory of a house built around an enormous tree popped into her head. Rich wood railings rubbed against her hand as she jogged up the winding stairs and came into a brightly lit bedroom. A woman with long curly hair, the same reddish brown as her own, greeted her with open arms.

The dream-woman wore a medallion also with a flame emblem. Closing her eyes, Alyra pictured her again. She had a warm smile, and long, reddish-brown hair like hers. The woman must her mother.

"Okay, honey." Her mother grasped her hands. "Concentrate and do like me." A bright glow surrounded them, and its source came from her chest.

A crash came from next door, followed by a muffled yell. Alyra jumped and looked around the small dingy room. She shook her head, wondering if the memory had been real. Had her mother really been able to glow, like Lotari had said she'd done?

Lotari swore as something else banged loudly. He had begun to find the close quarters claustrophobic. She wondered if he'd ever been indoors before. Closing the flap on her backpack, she decided to go over and sit with him. Maybe they could distract each other.

When she entered his room, he was trying to put a lamp back together. His face had a deep red hue, and his eyes were wide and wild looking.

"Let me get that." She moved the lantern to a dresser far away from him. "I bet you're ready to get out of here."

He nodded and returned to the window. "I found the Meeting Hall," he said as she came to stand next to him. "Just up this street and around that corner."

"Good to know the town actually has one. There's hope, right?"

"That's where we should seek aid for help in getting over the mountain."

"What makes you think they'll help?" She peered through the dirt-smudged glass in the direction he'd indicated. Peeking over the top of the shops, sparkling white turrets stood out against the gray starkness of the township.

"They are supposed to." Then he sighed. "However, I'm finding there's much I don't understand about the world outside my forest.

"Do you regret leaving?"

"No." He smiled down at her. "I suppose I'm experiencing a pride dilemma over finding I don't know as much as I thought. So hard for a perpetual know-it-all."

"Aw, Lot, you're the smartest person I've ever met."

"Considering you've not met many people on your travels, my dear child, your sentiment doesn't help much." A smile played across his lips

"Smart-alack. Fine, if you're going to be that way…" She turned to go.

He laughed. "Such a feisty girl. Don't leave yet, I have an idea."

She stopped at the door and waited for his *idea*.

"I believe we should visit the Meeting Hall while Jerin acquires our provisions. Perhaps they will know the path's conditions and what to expect as we travel over the mountain."

"He told us to stay here."

"I've told him many things as well, but he listens to only half of them." He shrugged. "If you think it's a bad idea—"

"No, no. I like the idea. Especially the part where we can get out of these smelly rooms. We'll leave Jerin a note to tell him where we've gone. But what about the soldiers?"

"I've taken that into consideration. I realize a disguise won't keep you completely hidden from them, but perhaps you'll be less conspicuous long enough to reach the Meeting Hall. You're already dressed like the townswomen. They wear bright colors and scarves. We'll cover your head in the same manner and you can go along like you are shopping. If any soldiers come near, duck into a shop until they pass."

"You really think this will work?" She returned to the window and watched the people below. The women did wear bright clothing. She'd put on the yellow outfit that the Logorian, Meghan, had made for her. The long sleeves and warmer material would hopefully protect her against the falling temperatures. The Logorians had most likely known she'd need such clothing.

257

"So, what do you think about my plan?"

"Let's do it."

"That's my girl." He patted her cheek. "First we'll need to take care of a couple of things."

He had her sit in a chair while he braided up her long, brown curls and tied a torn piece of his blanket around her head as a scarf. She scribbled a note to Jerin telling him where they went.

"What about you? Will you be safe?"

"Absolutely," he said. "I do not belong to their unit. They have no claim on me."

"I'm just thinking about what the attendant said."

"Oh yes, the one who mistakenly thought I was your pet."

"You are not going to let that go, are you?"

He handed her the basket their breakfast rolls had come in. "I'll be right behind you. If anything does happen, you run for the meeting hall and wait for Jerin. I can take care of myself, understand?"

Alyra nodded. Lotari stood before her, placed his hands on the sides of her face, and pressed his forehead against hers. "Blessing and protection upon you," he whispered.

"And upon you."

"Stay alert, Alyra, and don't forget what I told you."

"I won't. Meet you at the hall." She said before slipping out.

No one gave her a second glance as she went downstairs and exited the inn. Outside, she found a group of women walking beside the shops and followed close behind them. When they stopped to examine a fruit cart, she stopped as well. They were so busy chattering to each other, they didn't even notice.

The pounding in Alyra's chest eased as she began to relax and actually enjoy the sights around her. The shop windows contained a beautiful assortment of trinkets and goods she'd never seen before. She stopped before a bookstore, face pressed against the glass as she gaped at the enormous selection of tomes contained inside. Oh, how she missed the library in Many Rivers!

The scent of roasting sausages, breads, and sweets filled her nostrils. One particular store sold small colorful candies, and she wanted one so bad she almost regretted giving Jerin all her coins. Then she remembered the plan to get to the Meeting Hall and quickened her steps.

A glance over her shoulder told her Lotari still followed. He'd taken up with a dwarf and the two fauns who she'd seen playing music at the bar the night before. When she turned back toward the Meeting Hall, she spotted two soldiers clad in black standing across the street. She did a double take, noticing a bit of golden hair peeking from beneath the helmet of one. No, she had to accept Tarek was probably gone. And if he was still with the Racan soldiers, she certainly didn't want to be caught in the middle of town by him. Up the road away, Jerin walked toward her, his eyes focused on the soldiers.

She quickly faced a window full of various candles and watched their reflection in the glass. Both soldiers had Tarek's build. Would Bezoar give him another chance? Had he somehow managed to survive the waterfall?

She gritted her teeth, biting back those hopeful thoughts. Tarek was gone to her. Either way, he had made his choice. And she had made hers.

The soldiers hurried out of her field of vision. She went on down the street. Jerin nearly walked past her, too, but she reached out and caught his arm.

"Hey, I'm not interested!" he yelled before recognizing her. "What are...?"

"We're heading toward the Meeting Hall," she pulled him off the walkway, ducking into the candy store's doorway. "It was Lotari's idea."

He jerked free. "Well, it was a bad idea!"

She noticed his empty arms. "I thought you were shopping for us."

"I did. The goods are back at the Hall. I've already been there and was coming to tell you what I found out." He kept his gaze glued on the soldiers. Suddenly, his eyes widened. "Oh, no."

Alyra turned to find the Racan men standing on either side of the angry centaur, swords drawn and pointed at his chest. The dwarf and fauns had run off in different directions, leaving him alone.

Jerin grabbed Alyra by the shoulders and commanded, "You get to the hall. Run! I'll get Lotari. You stay there until I get back."

She hesitated, not wanting to leave him.

"No, Aly. Please do as I say this time. There is a group of people who are willing to help us. Go up the stairs and to the right. They are in a room with a black door on the second floor. Tell them what's happened."

He gave her a shove toward the white building and as she started off, he disappeared into the crowd.

# Chapter 31

Alyra raced for the Meeting Hall, its white exterior gleaming in the morning light. A glance behind her showed more soldiers closing in on Lotari. Ropes bound his neck and three of the black-clad men struggled to get his arms tied. The fourth lashed a whip at his back, but the centaur didn't stop struggling until one of them poked a spear against his face.

One fighter remained at the edge of the group, searching up and down the street until his gaze locked in on where she stood on the steps. He quickly looked away, ducking his head.

Jerin was nowhere to be seen.

Her foot caught on a loose flagstone. Tumbling forward, she righted herself before smacking her face. Ignoring the dull pounding in her knees, she hobbled up to the arched doors. Carved into the gleaming wood, like all the other Meeting Halls she'd encountered was a tree with the star shaped leaves.

She pushed through the two massive oak doors. The white building towered three stories above her, and she figured there must all kinds of activity going on. Yet, when she entered, the inside was nearly empty.

Straight ahead rose a spiraling staircase. To the right, a room where she found neat rows of cushioned benches surrounding an ornate stage. A few people sat quietly, listening to solemn music played by a solitary flutist. In the opposite wing were several other smaller room, all deserted as well. She searched for vendors, children, or any other people, beside the somber group in the music area, but found no one.

"Excuse me," she whispered, hating to interrupt. "I—"

An elderly woman sitting on a back seat put a finger to her mouth and hushed Alyra.

"—need help."

Nobody else turned her way or made any indication they cared whatsoever. A clicking on the spiral metal stairs caught her attention. Alyra hurried toward the sound, nearly colliding into a pale, black-haired girl with delicate features like one of the Logorians. Yet she was small, as if she'd only seen ten summers, though her deep, cobalt-blue eyes looked like they'd seen a hundred or more.

"Excuse me, I need some help. My friend is in trouble." Alyra couldn't help but gape at the girl, though she was unable to put her finger on why.

"Trouble?" Her voice had a strange lilt.

"Yes, he's a centaur. We were heading this way and ran into a couple of black soldiers."

"Centaur?" Her delicate hand went to her mouth. "You are Jerin's friend, no?"

"Yes." Alyra gasped with relief that the girl knew of her. "Are you one of the people he said were willing to help us?"

"Yes." She made such jerky nodding movements, her whole body bounced along with her head. "My name is Katrina. You come with me, yes? The others are very eager to meet you, too." She grabbed Alyra's hand.

"Will someone be able to help Jerin with our friend? He went after the soldiers, but I don't think he can fight them all by himself."

"He must not fight the soldiers!" Katrina dragged her up the steps and down a long corridor that ended at the black door. "Jerin says you have trouble with soldiers. They look for you, yes?"

"You could say that." Alyra wondered just how much Jerin had revealed about their situation. She decided to proceed with great care until he returned.

Katrina knocked at the door three times, waited a moment, and knocked two more times. The bolt turned and they entered. Five others sat around the spacious room. Two men and a woman stood at a long table looking over a map, while two girls, not much older than herself, were on a brocade couch knitting.

"Is this Alyra?" The woman at the table asked.

She had the same golden hair as the two younger girls, and Alyra supposed she might be their mother. One of the men looked similar to the woman, as well, and the second man had darker features with brown hair and a long, grizzly beard. Yet Katrina's features favored none of the other people. She wondered whom the young, black haired girl with the dusk colored eyes might belong to.

"Yes, yes." Katrina spoke with excitement. "I think there is trouble, no? With the centaur, right?" She gave Alyra a questioning look.

"Yes, he's a centaur." She waited to see if any of them might make a remark or derisive gesture.

If they had a problem with Lotari, none showed it. Jerin must have already filled them in. She quickly explained what happened in the street.

The woman nodded to the men, and the one who favored her immediately grabbed his coat and dashed out of the door saying, "I'm on it. Back in a bit."

"Don't worry, dearie. They have most likely taken him to the stables with the others." She extended her hand. "I'm Christina. This is my husband, Harp." She pointed to the tall, bearded man. He had a friendly face, and looked like one who stayed outdoors most of the time. "The one who just left is my brother, Frank. I see you've met Katrina. She joined up with us a month or so ago when she heard we were looking for a way to Aloblase. Says she's been waiting for someone to travel there with."

Alyra considered Katrina, wondering if she might be the one Issah had spoken of. She turned to the others, perhaps they were to join with the whole group.

Christina continued, "I'll let her tell you her story later. Anyway, over here are my two girls, Ella and Sue. They are making scarves and hats for our trip through the mountain. The nights are starting get quite chilly."

Trepidation churned Alyra's stomach. She tried to shake the feeling off by telling herself these people were willing to help.

"Why don't you come over here by the map and let us explain our plan. That way, when Jerin returns you can make a knowledgeable decision."

Alyra stepped closer to the table. Christina ordered Katrina to heat a pot of tea. Harp pointed to a spot on the map, explaining the various trials leading throughout the mountains.

"The White Road, heads straight up and then down." His weathered hand rose, then plunged downward to make his point.

"This path we tried back in the fall, but it just wound round and round the mountains. And this one..." he pointed to another black line heading due north. "It takes you completely around the tallest peaks and back, but you'd be traveling for months."

Katrina brought them a tray laden with cups of tea. She served Christina first. Adding sugar and cream to the second up, she handed it to Harp.

"Cream?" She asked Alyra. "Sugar?"

"No thanks. I'm not thirsty."

Katrina moved on to the girls. Finally, she returned to a chair in the corner and sipped her own cup. Was Katrina their friend or servant?

Alyra asked, "Have you ever tried the white path?"

"Eh? No, of course not." Harp laughed. "Why one look and you know what they say is true. It's a tough climb. The King's Highway isn't really supposed to be an easy trek, right?"

She shrugged. Sure they'd found some hard spots, but had managed to chop through the overgrown part. Hard at times, perhaps, but not impossible.

"So how many times have you tried to cross the mountains?"

Christina rolled her eyes. "Six. But don't let that get you down. I think this time we are definitely on to something..."

"Six?"

"Well, you don't know until you try, right?" She defended. "You all are more than welcome to climb over those steep peaks if you'd prefer. We know there's a better way."

Alyra couldn't believe her ears. She chewed on her bottom lip, keeping her silence and hoping Jerin returned soon with Lotari.

Harp pointed at the map again. "This trip will be the one, I say. We've found a series of tunnels."

"Tunnels?" Shivers tickled down her back as she wondered if they were like the ones Lord Darnel built below Racah?

"Yep, right smack through Semitamon's belly. Carved hundreds of years ago, I figure. If my calculations are correct, it'll take us two day's travel to reach the entrance and perhaps a day, maybe a bit more, to get to the other side."

Katrina spoke up from her corner chair. "The tunnels are said to have been built by the ancient Wisdom Keepers. They are all gone now."

Alyra studied the strange girl for a long moment before finally asking, "Where will the tunnels come out?" She wished Jerin would hurry back. The minutes passed like waiting for bread to rise when you're starving.

Harp's beard puffed around his grin."The other side, of course. Then one just rejoins the white path and off they go." He pointed again and leaned down close to the old, yellowed parchment. "See? It's not too far at all to where the King's Highway comes down from the eastern peaks."

Alyra plastered on her fake intrigued face. She remained silent, not wishing to express her real feelings and get them in more trouble.

"I have a good feeling," Harp went on. "And just think if we find an easier way, people will be thrilled. We'll make a bundle of coins letting them in on our secret passage."

Christina patted her husband on the back. "He's so smart, isn't he?"

Katrina returned with another steaming pot and refilled everyone's tea. Alyra decided to accept a cup, wanting to wash the bad taste forming in her mouth.

The girl's blue eyes bore into her, as if trying to read Alyra's inner thoughts. Slowly, her gaze moved down and settled on the medallion hanging outside her shirt. Alyra quickly tucked the disk back inside.

*Hurry up, Jerin!* She really wanted to get out of there.

"So," Christina said, "Now that you've heard our plan, what do you think?"

"Um, well…I'll need to talk to Jerin and Lotari." She knew the centaur would never agree to such a plan.

"Of course," answered Harp. "Such dedication to your friends is something to be admired."

Fortunately, she didn't have to wait much longer. By the time she finished her tea, the men returned. Jerin sat at the table while Frank hung his coat on the peg.

Jerin turned to Alyra. "They've chained Lotari up in the stables." When she started to speak, he raised his hands to stop her. "Frank knows the stable keeper. Luckily, the keeper hates the soldiers and knows Lotari doesn't belong to them. He's promised to help, but we have to wait until tonight. And we'll have to get past the livestock guard. The keeper seems to think he'll be easily swayed into turning the other way when we go to release Lotari."

Frank added, "We need to be prepared to go. Soon as the Racan soldiers find out, they'll come after us. Centaurs are quite valuable to them."

Alyra hoped he'd stay calm until they came for him. But if they had to leave tonight, would they be forced to go with these strange people? She looked at Jerin questioningly. The others had moved away to give them privacy. Jerin motioned her to follow him outside into the hall.

As soon as the door closed behind them she ranted in a harsh whisper, "What's their deal and how did you meet them? You and I both know Lotari isn't going to agree with us leaving the path to travel with these…these…well they're just strange. Harp plans to charge people to take the tunnels. If his plan even works. Lotari will have a hoof-stomping fit."

Jerin stood silently looking down at the sparse group below.

"Issah couldn't have meant for us to join with this family." Then she added, "This place is really dead."

He nodded and started walking toward the stairs. "Yes, I know. Frank said the main crowds only meet once a week. His family lives here in return for keeping the building clean."

Alyra followed him toward the rear of the building. They came out beneath a portico. In the center of the courtyard grew one of the white trees. A pile of the star shaped leaves lay on the ground, all brown and twisted. The pale branches held only a few of the blood red fruit, but they didn't shine brightly as they should. A brisk breeze scattered the dead foliage across the yard. The few remaining leaves fluttered as if hanging by a thin string.

Jerin sighed and rubbed his head, looking completely worn down. "I don't particularly like this family either. But there's something about Katrina that I just can't put my finger on yet." He grew silent for a few minutes.

Alyra was about to tell him she didn't want anything to do with any of them when he said, "But the thing is, we are in a bit of a mess, especially now Lotari's been taken prisoner... on top of

266

everything else."

"What else?"

"This city is swarming with soldiers." Jerin sat on the stone wall and indicated she should join him. Her head swirled, causing her to feel sick. He leaned close. "After we'd done all we could for Lotari, I walked outside of town with Frank. We found a group of soldiers outside the gates, close to the white path. I heard Lotari state that he belonged to Shaydon's kingdom. I'm sure the soldiers are being extra diligent now."

Alyra felt as if the floor dropped out from beneath her. "What are we going to do? They must know I'm here then. What will...?"

"What can we do?" He snapped, cutting her off. "I think we should go with these people now. Neither of us will be able to break Lotari out by ourselves. The keeper would only speak with Frank. I had to leave so he could talk to the man privately. Besides, we're safer in a group. If this tunnel really exist, we'll go on through with them, and then be on our way."

Alyra leaned against one of the columns. Seemed they had no choice.

Jerin went on, "Frank is willing to help us get Lotari out. He didn't have to, you know. To be honest, I'm grateful for their help"

Her shoulders slumped. Jerin was right.

"What have you told them about me?"

"Only that we'd had a couple of run-ins with the solders and needed to get out of town without them seeing us. They seemed satisfied with that."

"Let's not let them know any more, okay?"

He nodded. "So are we agreed?"

She didn't answer right away. "Lotari won't go for it."

He took a deep breath. "I promised not to do anything you didn't agree to first. If you say no, then I'll do my best to find another way. Under the circumstances, he needs to go along with what we decide."

She couldn't think of another solution, so in the end, she agreed. They headed back inside to tell the others who were quite glad to include them. Everyone moved into action, Harp planning on what to carry along and discussing with Frank how they'd get the centaur released. Jerin and Katrina returned to the inn to get their gear.

While the men went out to get supplies and a horse secured from the stable keeper, Alyra busied herself helping Christina pack food and blankets for the trip. One of the girls who still sat on the couch knitting suggested they use the centaur to carry their load.

"He's not a pack animal." Alyra replied.

"Well," said Ella, "he sounds prideful."

"Or lazy," added her sister, Sue.

"No he's not," Alyra shot back, defensively. "He hunts, cooks, and scouts the area to be sure we're safe. He's not lazy at all. He's very wise and loyal to his friends." Unfortunately, she wasn't feeling too loyal herself at the moment.

# Chapter 32

With a waning moon providing a dim silvery light, Alyra followed seven cloaked travelers through the dark streets of Denovo. All carried a hefty pack of provisions strapped to their back. When the group reached the stables, Frank tapped twice on the keeper's door. From within the weathered, gray-boarded shack came the sound of muffled grumbling, something scraping the floor and then metal rattling against metal. A rectangular beam of light fell across the yard. One eye peeked from the opening, and a ring of keys flew out the doorway into Frank's waiting hand.

The keeper hissed, "Yorn mount all ready behind me house where they won' takes notice. The beastie is in da last corner stall. Toward'n the rear side. Toss me keys inta the woodpile when ya leave." The door closed and they were left in darkness again.

The women waited outside behind the stables. Alyra insisted on being the one to get Lotari. Jerin approved, hoping she'd have a better chance than he of convincing the centaur to agree to their plan. Harp waited near the entrance with Jerin.

Frank entered the spacious building with her, putting a finger to his mouth as he pointed to the first stall. Inside slept a very large centaur, much taller than even Wyndham. He was glistening black, like a stallion, with black wavy hair flowing down his back and a curly beard covering his chin. He laid in his stall snoring loudly, a bow across his shoulder and a jagged-bladed sword secured around his waist. She shivered clutching her medallion and sending up a silent plea that the fierce-looking centaur wouldn't wake.

Frank handed Alyra the keys. "I'll get the horse. You find your friend."

She made her way toward the back walking slowly and trying her best not to make too much noise. Still, her boots on the straw sounded like firecrackers in her ears. Each of the stalls slept at least

269

two adults. One held four young males, their coloring varying from chestnut red, white speckled, and earthy brown. The nearest horseman was a palomino with tan curly hair and slight fuzz on his chin. He wore a leather necklace of small shells and stones and had a couple of feathers dangling from behind his ear. Her heart ached for the youths, wondering what they'd possibly use such young centaurs for. They couldn't be old enough to fight.

Remembering she needed to hurry, she went on to the last stall. The sound of chains rattling confirmed it must be the right one. Carefully, she opened the gate and slid in. Lotari rested in a corner, pulling at the shackles attached to his wrists. She hurried over and threw her arms around his neck.

"Are you okay?" She whispered against his ear. "Did they hurt you?"

"Oh, my pride more than anything else." He whispered back. "Did you see all of them? Did you see the little ones?" His voice cracked as his arms hugged her so tight, the iron shackles dug into her shoulder blades. She nodded, as he continued, "They should be running though the woods with the hinds and cougars." He trembled with rage. "I've never been caged like this."

Hoping to quiet him, she hugged tighter. "Listen to me. We have to get out of town right now. You'll need to trust me and Jerin, please? Promise you'll come along and not kick up a fuss. Can you do that?"

His breath felt like flames on her neck as he said, "This is going to take us off the white path, isn't it?"

She straightened and stared at his red-rimmed gray eyes, holding her own gaze firm. "Only until we get through the mountain." Her hand clamped over his open mouth. "Please Lot, we don't know what else to do." She silently begged him to agree. His shoulders sagged as he nodded in resolution. She took the key and unlocked the shackles from his wrist. A few welts covered his arms and back, but her ointment would fix those. At least he wasn't bleeding.

"Climb on and let us go. I won't protest." He whispered in a resigned voice. "I have much to tell you when we are safe."

He helped her onto his back and then headed out making less noise than she did. He paused next to the stall with the young centaurs and shook his head. The palomino seemed to have shifted and now slept leaning against the sagging boards. Alyra nudged him to hurry. They'd already tempted fate beyond measure. He trotted outside and around to the back toward a cluster of trees where the others waited.

Jerin grasped his hand in a shake then hugged him quickly before turning to the family and introducing them. They each bowed a greeting. Alyra slid off, took her pack and gave Lotari back his weapons and travel bag.

Harp pointed toward a trail disappearing into woods. "We're going to follow a footpath up to a series of caves. That's where we'll find the tunnel that leads though the mountain."

"Tunnel?" Lotari gasped.

Alyra placed a hand on his arm to remind him of his promise to her. His lips turned white in his attempt to clamp them shut.

The group headed into the forest at a casual yet intent pace. Frank suggested they travel as if they were in no hurry in order to attract less attention. Since Denovo was a trade town, people traveling in and out at different times of the day and night was a common occurrence.

The colorful buildings had nearly disappeared behind the cover of spruce when the sound of hooves pounding over the earth sent panic through the whole group. The sisters started to run in different directions, but their parents stopped them short. Jerin pulled out his sword and Frank withdrew a crossbow from the horse's pack. Harp stood in front of the girls with a long dagger. Lotari strung his bow and blocked Alyra and Katrina.

The pursuer bound into their midst, sliding to a stop at the sight of all their weapons. The young palomino centaur held up his hands in surrender. "I'm alone. Don't shoot me, please."

Frank and Lotari both lowered their arrows.

"Take me with you." The youth eased nearer to Lotari, his green eyes wide and pleading. "The others were all afraid to trust you. But I thought if I went to see the King myself and if what you say is true...well? Then I can come back. I'll tell them what I've seen. They'll have to believe. Right?"

Everyone stood with open-mouthed disbelief at the centaur. Jerin looked from the palomino to Lotari then back to the palomino.

When no one answered, his voice rose in desperation. "Please. Even my groomsman whispered to me that Aloblase was real. But he's kind of crazy. Think they've beat him too much. And he wanted me to share my dinner with him. The other soldiers won't feed him cause he's such a failure." The centaur shook his head, stomping his hooves. "Look, I don't know how to get there myself. And...and...if they catch me..." he buried his face in his hands. "Oh, they make traitors drink the black liquid. And if they find out that I slipped sleeping tonic into Erbon's dinner.... I'm in so much trouble right now."

"Who's Erbon?" Jerin kept his sword pointed at the beast's chest.

"Our Captain, the black stag, he was supposed to watch out in case someone came to rescue him." He gestured toward Lotari. "But I knew if you managed to escape, then I'd have hope of escaping as well. So, before I took him his evening meal, I added a few drops of juice the soldiers use to keep prisoners quiet." His white teeth flashed in a childlike grin.

Alyra stared at the young centaur in amazement. Deep down she'd thought that had all been too easy. She and Katrina both stepped in front of Lotari and said in unison, "Yes, you can come." They looked at each other strangely then smiled.

Harp sounded a bit more reluctant. "I don't know. We already have one of these ruddy beast, but now two?"

"Maybe he's not too prideful to help carry our stuff." The sisters pled with their father.

"Absolutely." The palomino sounded eager. "I'll carry your gear. I can hunt. I'll do whatever you tell me to do. Just say I can come."

Lotari's mouth dropped with what must have been astonishment at the youngster's complete lack of self-respect. "You certainly talk a lot, even for a colt."

Alyra stepped closer. "Of course you can come with us. What's your name?"

"They call me Stitch."

Lotari snorted from behind her and muttered, "That's no name for a centaur."

Alyra smiled. "Well, King Shaydon will probably know your

272

real. But we must hurry and get going before the soldiers realize two of you are gone."

"I can come? Really, I can come?" He began a cantering dance around Alyra and Katrina.

Katrina giggled and grabbed his arm to make him stop. "Yes, yes, silly one. Now we go."

The others put away their weapons. Frank yanked the horse's reins to move it along. "Let's hurry before something else happens. Everyone needs to be extremely quiet." He shot the excited newcomer a warning glare. "At least until we get to the foot of the mountains and out of this township."

\* \* \* \*

Shadowy pines towered against the black night sky like swaying specters. The travelers scrambled up the rocky slope constantly looking over their shoulder for a sign of pursuit. Katrina stumbled, sending a cascade of dirt and stones down upon Alyra and Jerin. Stitch bound to her side, helping her back to her feet. The centaurs were the only ones not having a problem with the climb, so when one of the others got stuck or fell, they were there to help them along. Alyra didn't know if she should be grateful or envious of them.

Frank and Harp insisted they travel all through the night to put as much space between them and Denovo as possible. The dark soldiers would come after them once they found their centaurs gone.

Lotari protested. "I do not belong to them, sir. Nor will I ever serve them as long as breath moves through my lungs."

Stitch said nothing, but Alyra caught the shudder that shook him, and knew she was responsible for helping to get the black powder they'd force him to drink if he were recaptured. Her heart felt as though it'd been punctured with a large thorn. He'd also been marked with the moon and stars brand on his shoulder as if he were no more than a head of cattle. She rubbed her shoulder as he turned toward her, a quizzical expression on his face.

When the sun peeked over the mountaintops, Christina and her daughters insisted they stop to eat and rest. Harp reluctantly agreed, even though Alyra didn't think he had much of a say in the matter. Everyone slumped onto the rocky ground in exhaustion unable to move another step. Katrina and the sisters were too tired to even eat.

Jerin sat upon a rock and drank deeply from his water. He'd remained silent since they'd taken on Stitch, spending most of his time at the rear of the group. He bit into one of the sandwiches Christina had packed them watching the area below.

A throbbing ache pulsated in Alyra's legs, though she'd become adept at walking, the constant climb aggravated muscles she didn't even know existed. She sat next to Jerin to help watch for possible enemy advancement. By now, they should be waking to find their prisoner missing.

After a blink of a rest, Frank and Harp insisted everyone continue. The sisters constantly complained about being tired and sore. They wanted to ride the horse, but Harp told them to hush. The horse was to carry their gear and could hold no more. Stitch, either weary of listening to them, or out of sheer kindness, allowed them to take turns riding. Lotari, seeing the other sister eyed him expectantly, darted off into the woods saying that he should scout the area. Finally, by the late afternoon, Christina demanded they be allowed to stop again.

"We can't keep on like this." She explained. "Let us get some sleep, and we'll start again tonight."

Frank started to argue, but her look stopped him. "Only a short rest, sister. The soldiers might be on their way as we speak." He led the horse to a grassy area and tied it to a tree.

Harp muttered to himself about bringing trouble by including strangers, and how no one would listen to him. Now they had those ruddy beasts to contend with as well.

"Enough!" Frank snapped. "We're close, I say. We'll need to get a move on, and soon, if we're to beat their horses."

They found a sheltered spot next to a small waterfall. The sound of rushing water seemed to help calm anxious nerves. They decided against a fire, so Christina prepared a simple meal of bread and cheese. Lotari's withers twitched with apprehension and Alyra knew he was unhappy over the situation they found themselves in, but nothing could be done about it now. He ate quietly before leaving to explore the woods.

The palomino stayed close to the camp and did everything he was asked. The sisters took full advantage of his assistance. They sent him off to gather leaves and pine needles to make their sleeping area comfortable.

The more Stitch ran around like a lowly servant, the angrier Alyra became. So she followed him down to the stream where he worked on filling everyone's canteen in hopes of having a little talk to him.

"You don't have to do that, Stitch. Harp asked the sisters to take care of the canteens, not you."

He gave her a toothy grin. "I don't mind, Miss. I'm used to helping. We're too young to fight, so we serve the elders between training sessions." He waded out until the water reached his hocks.

"But you deserve to be treated with respect, just like everyone else."

"I'm very grateful to be away from Racan soldiers. I'll do whatever they ask for letting me stay."

Alyra put her hands on her hips with a loud huff. "You don't owe anyone anything. You have just as much right to go see King Shaydon as the rest of us. Okay?"

He sighed, while popping a cork on one of the water bags. "Ah, I can't wait to meet this King. I certainly hope he is nicer than the Dark Lord. That one, Miss, gives me the willies, for sure."

"You've met Darnel?"

He turned to her, brow cocked. "He came out to the training grounds and gave our unit a special visit. Said we'd been given a great honor." He snorted, shaking his head. "Anyway, he prattled on about how we were being sent on this *secret, important* mission to reclaim some treasure he referred to as his *precious light*." Stitch tossed the filled bottle onto the shore and began to fill another. "He said this treasure would enable him to extend his kingdom all across the land. What's wrong, Miss?"

Alyra realized she'd been standing there with eyes wide and mouth gaping. Stitch wasn't talking about her, was he? Darnel never consider her a treasure, did he? Yet, what other explanation was there for his unrelenting pursuit of her?

Her breaths snagged in her throat. She swayed as her vision swam. Before she knew what was happening, Stitch grabbed her arms and led her to sit on a rock.

"Breathe, Miss. Try to breathe."

She sucked in a lungful of air, but felt as if she'd been punched

275

in the stomach. Deep down, she'd known Darnel kept her alive, kept her close for some reason. Had he planned to use her against King Shaydon, and Prince Issah, like he used her to hold back the pit demon? Was she in some kind of tug-o-war she had no idea about?

Stitch brought her a canteen and ordered her to drink. She took a couple of gulps, and slowly regained composure.

"Thanks," she gasped. "I'll be fine. I am fine. I ... I guess I'm really tired."

His eyes narrowed, boring into her. She returned the water container and offered to help him finish filling the rest, hoping that would take his mind off her recent episode. He grasped her wrist instead of the bag and pulled her closer.

Alyra squirmed, trying to break free of his iron grip.

"Hey, don't—!" She kicked at him.

His lips tightened into a thin line as he pushed her onto the sandy shore, his horse body pinning her down. She tried to scream but his hand clamped over her mouth.

Before she could stop him, he yanked her shirt off her shoulder revealing the black crescent moon tattoo.

"You have the servant's mark." He gasped, looking around wildly. "Troll's breath! Can it be? Are you his precious light?"

# Chapter 33

Alyra swung her free arm pounding his chest.

"You must stop, or I can't let you go. Don't call the others. It will be bad if you do." Stitch didn't even flinch as he grasped that hand as well.

She glared at him, knowing they'd been duped. Did Bezoar know she was traveling with Jerin and Lotari and sent this scoundrel after them? Or was Stitch working on his own, hoping to gain status for himself?

How had she been so stupid to insist he come along? When would she remember to never ever trust anyone?

"Be good now and don't scream." He slowly moved his hand from her mouth.

"Let me go!"

His finger touched the chain at her neck, and he pulled out the medallions. "You have two. You must be the one who set the dragon free, and the messenger.... Which is yours? "

She remained silent, waiting for him to loosen his hold.

He held up the trumpet medallion. "This one must be his. Why do you have it? Didn't he escape?"

She shook her head no. The centaur's weight threatened to smother her.

"The dragon? She got him? But not you?"

Her whole body trembled. Would Stitch take her back? Tears filled her eyes.

"King Darnel is furious over losing his dragon. Furious." A small smiled played at Stitch's thin lips. "Hard to protect his mountain now without her."

Alyra gasped for air.

Stitch slightly shifted his weight off her, while keeping hold of her wrist. "And he's desperate to find his treasure." He began to laugh, "How ironic, my groomsman has been in such trouble for not capturing you. Demoted to caring for the livestock. And I'm the one to find you now."

She froze, wondering if he spoke of... no, impossible. Tarek couldn't have survived the waterfall at Many Rivers. "Tarek?"

His eyes narrowed on her. "I see you know my groomsmen, as well. I'm right. I know I'm right."

Alyra thrashed her arms and legs, hoping to dislodge herself from him.

His laughter stopped as he leaned closer, putting a finger over her mouth. "We keep this to ourselves, Miss. Any of them know?"

She shook her head until he moved his hand from her lips. "My friends know where I come from. I'm no treasure. I'm not a precious light. Can't be me."

"Oh, it's you all right, Miss. We were stationed in Denovo to wait for you. King Darnel said there were two cities you might pass through, though lucky for you, he figured you'd take the easier southern route. His larger troop awaits you there with the Baykok Captain."

A toothy grin split his face. "But you slip on through. *Again.* And you take Stitch with you. I have you, and I'm free." He chuckled as he backed off her, extending his hand to help her up. "I can make sure they won't get you now!"

She got to her feet without his aid. Did she hear him correctly?

He returned to the river and continued filling canteens. "Lotari and the warrior boy, they are your friends?"

She nodded.

"The family, we don't tell them. Not even Katrina. She has a good heart, but the less said the better for now. Those others, they are bad, Miss. I feel their badness, and I hear their bad words. Don't let them know. Understand? Especially those little *Prissy Missies.*"

Tarek had survived and was paying for his incompetence. While they filled the canteens, Stitch explained how Bezoar wouldn't kill Tarek, but made him suffer for allowing her to escape. Stitch figured they would use him as bait if the opportunity arouse. She realized the golden-haired soldier in town must have been Tarek, and he'd seen her too but had decided to not acknowledge her. How much more trouble would he suffer for allowing the centaurs to escape?

Worry over his fate kept her from finding sound sleep. She'd finally dozed off when awakened by a hoof nudging her shoulder. Lotari had returned and everyone rushed about gathering their gear.

"Get up and gather your things. Quick now." He ordered.

Alyra rubbed sleep from her eyes. "What's going on?"

Jerin set her backpack next to her. "Soldiers. According to Lotari, they aren't too far behind."

The centaur's face held no expression of *I-told-you-so,* but rather his brows furrowed with deep concern and perhaps fear.

Stitch scrambled around, trying to help pack the equipment despite his trembling hands. Alyra rolled up her mat and shoved it inside her bag, wondering if she should tell Lotari what had transpired earlier between her and Stitch. The urgency for speed determined she wait.

Jerin's voice reeked of sarcasm when he asked Lotari, "You going to tell me now this was a bad idea?"

The older centaur's eyes leveled on Jerin. "My opinion wasn't sought before this decision was made. I don't know why it should matter now."

*Ouch, that hurt!* Alyra winced, knowing she was as much to blame as Jerin. The man's mouth snapped shut as he lowered his head.

Lotari's face softened. He laid a hand on Jerin's shoulder. "Of course, how could I expect you to do that for me, when I didn't respect you in the same manner? I should have waited."

Clasping the centaur's arm, Jerin nodded. "We'll make the best of this."

"Absolutely. Hope has not abandoned us." Lotari smiled at her and winked.

After several hours of climbing, the land leveled out. The night chill went through her cloak and touched her bones. Hoping to generate some warmth, the group walked close together. No one spoke, not even the sisters dared to whine, for fear their voices would be heard by the pursuing militia. Harp ran ahead of the others.

Tall cliffs towered over them like black walls against the starry sky. The ground had a more manicured appearance, though completely overgrown. The rocks formed a series of stairs and barren fountains leading up to three large entrance ways in the face of the cliff.

"This is it," Harp exclaimed as quiet as possible. "This is where I found the tunnels." He pulled out a map and asked for someone to light one of the torches. Frank tried, but couldn't coax a flame.

"Well, never mind, I got it memorized." He stepped back and pointed toward the cliffs just ahead. "There are three entrances to the right. But we don't want them. We're gonna look for the hidden one over to the left here. We'll have to search around. It'll be big enough for the horse to go through. If you find it, give a wave."

Everyone spread out and began searching along the cliff face, behind bushes, and sometimes touching the stones in case there was a secret door. Alyra looked for something else. In the dark lands, tunnels were never obvious, but rather hidden behind brush or tree. Most were up off the ground, so nobody would accidentally wander into them.

Remembering these facts, Alyra remained standing in one spot, searching the rocky crevices. At about twenty feet up, she found an old twisted tree, its bark white like a ghost clinging to the side of the rock. Its roots dangled like long fingers gripping the dirt. Her eyes scanned for some kind of trail and found the rocks cut in a particular sort of zigzagging stairs.

"We don't have time to stand around, Miss." Stitch came up beside her. "They'll be here soon. I can smell them nearing."

She pointed. "Up there, I think. Right under that dead tree."

"I'll go check." He trotted up the side.

Jerin spotted him and joined Alyra. Slowly, the others did as well.

Frank asked, "What's that fool doing now?"

"We might have found your entrance." Alyra stared at the man.

When Stitch disappeared under the tree, she held her breath. The earth had begun to thump with the approaching soldiers from below. They all spun around and saw the glow of their torches in the distance. *Hurry, Stitch.*

A few moments later, he appeared over the ledge and waved them up. Stitch's gaze traveled down the side of the mountain, and he motioned more frantically for them to hurry. In single file, they walked up the stone steps. Even the horse had no problem with the incline. Frank and Harp tried to light the torches again. When everyone reached the landing, they waited while the men including Lotari and Stitch tried working the fire-starter Frank had purchased in town.

Lotari grumbled how those contraptions never worked properly and only the old fashioned way was the tried and true. He pulled out his flint to start a small fire with dead wood from the tree.

"This can take forever," Christina's voice sounded panicky. "They are nearly right on us. Everybody get inside and we'll try to get the torches lit in there."

Ellen and Sue both cried, "I am not going in without a fire."

Alyra, heart racing with fear of the darkness, agreed. Panthers or bears may have set up residence inside. "We need the light."

At that moment, the hillside alighted with a glow. Alyra thought Lotari had finally managed to get a spark but the radiance was too bright for a small flame. Everyone else gasped and stepped away. Frank backed up so fast he nearly fell off the side of the cliff. Jerin managed to grab his arm before he tumbled over the edge.

Lotari gaped at her in utter amazement. He turned toward the approaching army below. Before she could register what was happening, Lotari grabbed her arms and shoved her through the opening. "Inside, now! Hurry."

Everyone poured in after them, keeping their distance from her.

"What's wrong?" she asked.

Lotari thrust her toward Jerin, who looked as astonished as the others. Grabbing a rope off the horse's saddle, Lotari motioned for Stitch to follow him outside.

A large smile split Jerin's face. "You're all lit up, Aly. I've never... it's so...."

"Beautiful," Katrina finished. "I read about the Illuminate ones before, yes!"

Stitch and Lotari darted back inside the tunnel each holding an end of rope.

"When I say three, pull hard," Lotari instructed.

The men must have caught on to what they were doing because they all grabbed an end and pulled with them. A loud crack sounded from outside, followed by a shower of dirt, rocks and roots. The tree broke loose, causing the roof to crumble and crash down over the opening. Everyone ran deeper inside and stopped in a large room.

The glow from Alyra shone off the soaring granite walls and marble pillars.

The light pulsated with her rapid heartbeats. She tried not to panic over what was happening to her. Only Katrina stayed by her side, her small white hand grasped Alyra's. Christina huddled against the farthest wall with her daughters. The sisters both whimpered as one of them said, "She's scary, Mother! It must be some kind of dark magic!"

Lotari trotted into the grand room rubbing dirt from his curly hair. The men followed close behind. "Not dark magic. It's a gift from King Shaydon, whom I'm starting to believe you have no concept of whatsoever." He took a long drink from his water bag before offering a sip to Stitch who was also covered in dirt.

Alyra gawked at her glowing hands. Gingerly she touched her chest where the brightest part came from. "I'm like some kind of human lantern!" Even her hair emanated light.

Katrina smiled shyly. "You, dear one, are an Illuminate. Once your kind helped the people of Alburnium, but the dark one has extinguished many of the lighted ones, or driven the remaining into hiding."

She gasped. "Why didn't someone tell me all this before? Have you known, Lotari?"

"Not near as much as our new knowledgeable friend here." He stared at Katrina as if realizing something, yet he said nothing more.

Stitch leaned in close to her ear and whispered so only they heard. "I told you that you were the 'precious light' he's been looking for."

Alyra's knees buckled, and she collapsed onto the cold, stone floor. Katrina and Stitch grabbed her arms to steady her.

Jerin looked from Lotari to Alyra and then back to Lotari again. "Does this mean…?"

Stitch hissed, "Not here, ay?"

Lotari nodded and addressed the family who were still huddled at a fair distance from them. "We are fortunate to have an Illuminate in our midst. She is new and lacking understanding of her abilities. But she will be able to help us get through this black pit."

His words comforted her and the light went out.

Frank's voice echoed across the room, "We were fortunate, you mean?"

One of the sisters screeched.

The darkness felt like drowning in inky soup. Her heart began to race again and the glow returned, yet dimmer than before. She barely made out Frank and Harp working on the torches. Lotari pulled her to her feet and spoke against her ear.

"Relax, Alyra. Right now, fear controls your ability to shine. Think about how we need to get through. Focus on the need to see. Can you try?"

Her glow wasn't much brighter than a candle flame. She closed her eyes and tried to concentrate on needing light. She didn't like her predicament at all! No wonder Issah had put off explaining.

Her eyes flew open, and she looked into Lotari's worried face. "Will Shaydon use me against Darnel? That's what Master's afraid of. Right? That's why he's still after me?"

Lotari shook his head. "You are a child of the King, not a pawn. I swear. I can't explain here. Not right now. Please believe me."

She searched the expectant faces surrounding her. They needed light, and she had to get out of the tunnel. One thing was certain, if Darnel had her, then he was assured his Kingdom would grow stronger. She wasn't sure about King Shaydon. She'd grown to love Issah. No one had shown her the kindness and love he had, though Lotari came close. The centaur was asking her to believe in him. She glanced at Jerin, who seemed as bewildered as she was. They needed light. They needed to get out. They needed to keep out of reach of the soldiers. Not only for her sake but everyone else as well.

The chamber filled with brightness again, and despite any reservations they might have, a sigh of relief went around the group.

"Very good, sweet girl." Lotari grinned at her.

Katrina grinned. "We go now. Yes? This big mistake. No? But we keep going on and find a way through. Yes? Find the White Road. Right?"

Lotari laid his hand on her shoulder. "Yes, we'll get back to the path. Yes, let's go."

With Jerin on her right and Katrina on her left, they hurried through the widest tunnel passing several rooms and side passageways. A few had been blocked off. Familiar symbols were carved into the stone over the openings. Chills coursed up Alyra's spine.

The effort it took to continue glowing began to wear on her. If her thoughts drifted, she started to dim, and the sisters would scream. Alyra wondered if this ability always took so much energy to keep going. Her fingers gripped tight onto Katrina and Jerin's arms. So tight, Jerin stared down at her with concern.

"Are you all right?" He motioned Lotari over.

"I'm getting really tired. This is hard."

Lotari stopped the others and told the men they needed a break. Jerin helped her sit while Lotari took Frank's fire-starter and tried again to light one of the torches. He finally resorted to taking out his flint and tinderbox and getting a small fire going that way. Once they had a flame, Alyra heaved a sigh of relief, and her brightness dimmed. Yet, as she looked at her hands, she knew her fear was keeping her lit up to a small degree. Had she always done this? What made it happen this time? She hoped Shaydon would explain everything. She refused to acknowledge the nagging voice saying, *If. If you make it.*

With the torches lit, the group began to look around. They'd stopped in a corridor of sorts where four passages met.

Frank said, "How are we supposed to know which is the right tunnel, Harp?"

He shook his head. "Dunno. I just thought only one led straight through. It's like a whole underground network here."

Frank fumed. His face set in a scowl as he yelled, "We could be wandering in here for days and not know. Didn't you check to see who made these tunnels?"

"What difference does it make? The map just showed a passageway from our side of the mountain to the other. We're going the right way."

Jerin settled next to Alyra and asked if she felt better now. When she told him she was fine, he said, "I'm also worried about who made these tunnels."

"You should be." She whispered so only he heard. "Those marking are Racan symbols."

# Chapter 34

Jerin rubbed the back of his neck. "How do you know?"

Alyra remembered the countless hours spent with Darnel's scribe as he made her copy the strange letters over and over. He'd never allow her to read the books, instead writing short snippets, or lists of rules for her until she had a good command of the dark language. "I was taught the language in Racah."

At least her parents taught her the common language before she ended up with Darnel. Anytime she did find a book, she'd sneak it to her room or her secret passage to read.

Jerin closed his eyes with a groan. "I've really blown it."

She gave his shoulder a squeeze. "We decided together. Don't start blaming yourself."

The argument between Frank and Harp began to escalate. Christina tried to break them up by suggesting they eat something and take a rest.

Frank removed the horse's saddle and set a feed sack over the mare's snout. "I think we should split up and explore where these tunnels go."

Lotari groaned. He motioned for Katrina and Stitch to come over and took some jerky from his bag to share with them. They sat in their own little circle while the family argued over what to do. Lotari looked at each of them. "If they split up, I suggest we stay with this passage. I feel a breeze that's not stale or smells of death."

Alyra pointed at the markings on the widest arch. "That says this main tunnel leads to the exit. I agree with you."

"You can read the symbols?" He asked.

Stitch smiled when she nodded. "Me, too."

Lotari looked over his shoulder as the family continued bickering. "I think we should tell them. I'd hate for them to split up and get lost."

Stitch rolled his eyes, "Who cares? Let them do their thing. They have bad hearts anyway."

Lotari's brows shot up. "Doesn't matter, son. We are no better if we sink to their level and treat others in a way we would not wish to be treated ourselves. They have allowed you to travel with them. They have even shared their food with you. Do you really wish to sit there and tell me you do not care what happens to them?"

Stitch's cheeks reddened, and he ducked his head. "Not when you put it that way, Lotari. I'm sorry."

The older centaur smiled, as if relieved there was hope in the youth turning out decent despite his training.

Lotari offered them some jerky and told them Stitch could read the symbols. "We're definitely on the right track."

Christina turned to her husband and brothers. "If you boys want something to worry over, then start figuring out how we'll get out of here if those soldiers have managed to beat us to the other side."

\* \* \* \*

The passage filled with the sweet tune of Lotari's pipes. Alyra, exhausted from being a human lamp, drifted off into a strange sleep and dreamed of a gathering. She stood across the familiar mound of dirt, yet now found two men who talked in quiet voices. Her chest ached, not from a physical pain, but from crying herself dry. For some reason, her heart felt like crumpled parchment paper.

"This is the only one?" asked one of the men. He was round in face and belly, wearing a dark cloak and knee-length polished black boots. "I thought my sister had more children. Where are they?"

The taller man, who had curly brown hair much like hers, along with her golden-brown eyes, continued to stare sorrowfully at the knoll. "Our son attends school at the Academy. Prince Issah is bringing him tonight when he comes for Alyra."

Somehow, she knew the men were related to her. The sad looking one she called Da. The other darkly dressed gentleman was Uncle Macken. Beneath the dirt lay her mother, who she called, Mo.

"Tonight, huh?" Macken tugged uncomfortably at his gold-trimmed vest. "This wee one will attend Academy so soon? Why, she is but four or…."

"This will be her sixth summer." Da stated, his voice deadpan.

"She is going early. Under the circumstances, we feel she'll be safer there."

Uncle Macken's shaggy brows rose in question. "You don't suspect foul play, do you brother-in-law?"

"I don't know what to think. I'm not even sure why Mo agreed to go on that quest." Da sighed deeply. "Her party came upon an ambush." Da's gaze fell on her and he said more carefully, "I'm not sure what the enemy was doing there."

"Did any return?"

Da shook his head. "The people wanted to start a new community in the south. I discouraged her from going until she'd heard from Issah, but they were in great haste, so she went anyway. You know, besides illuminating, part of her gifting was the ability to lay new paths."

"My, my, my," exclaimed Uncle, puffing his round cheeks. "Such a shock and such a shame." He stared intently across the raw dirt, as if sizing Alyra up. "Is this child … ah … like her Mo?"

Da nodded. A tear escaped down his cheeks as he continued to focus on the newly turned earth.

The uncle spoke a bit louder as if wanting her to hear, "Ah, then she will be expected to take on her Mo's responsibilities. Poor child will be risking her life as well, trudging through dark, lonely places, and now, she has nobody to guide her."

Alyra's throat constricted as if a noose tightened around her neck.

Da's head came up, and he peered hard at the uncle, eyes narrowed at the man like they'd narrow at her when she was up to trouble. "She will be trained at the Academy like the rest of us … and like yourself." He jerked his index finger at Macken. "Before you decided to leave, that is."

"Well, lot of good her dedication did her." Uncle swept his hand toward the grave. "As for myself, I decided I wanted something different from what I could get here."

"Did you find it, Macken?"

Uncle shrugged. "Eh, I find profit at times." He was staring at Alyra again in the same mesmerized way her brother stared at a plate of dessert set on the table.

"Profitable." Da spat the word as if it tasted bad. "Yes, I see how such things can be alluring to a man like yourself." Her father wiped his face on his sleeve and turned to Uncle. "Good to see you again, Macken. I'm surprised you heard so quickly of your sister's death. I do, however, appreciate you paying last respects." Da strolled over to Alyra and extended his hand. "Time to go, Pumpkin."

She stepped closer to the grave. "Da, please, let's not leave her here."

He picked her up. "She is not here anymore. Our Mo has gone to Everlasting beyond Shaydon's throne. We will see her again one day."

Alyra's arms became like steel pipes as she pushed against his chest. He held her firm. Kicking her legs, she yelled, "I want her now! Please, Da. Take me to Mo."

"Wake up, Alyra!" Jerin ordered, shaking her hard. "Wake up, what's wrong? Why are you crying?"

"I want… my Mo… she's…." Alyra sat up finding she was inside the cave and not next to her mother's grave.

Her fingers dug into Jerin's burly arms, as her memories flooded back into her conscious. Uncle Macken had found her before he left in his fine carriage parked out on the street.

Uncle crouched next to her. "I know of a land where they'll never expect you to trek around desolate dark places, like your Mo."

He went on to tell her how the prince would teach her to use her light. Then he told her all kinds of scary things she'd be required to do.

Alyra had sat in the garden, making holes in the turned earth with her finger. She dropped a dead beetle she'd found, into the hole before gently piling the loose dirt into a tiny mound. Had the bug gone to the lands beyond Shaydon's throne? The place just beyond the rainbow colored curtains?

"Do you think this beetle is with my Mo now?" She asked, patting down the dark earth.

Uncle Macken glanced toward the house beads of sweat wove streams down his fleshy face. His gloved hands trembled on her shoulder. "What if I took you to your Mo?"

Her head snapped up expectantly. "Can you?"

He shrugged. "That might be exactly what will happen. I know of someone who has sent many to the land beyond Shaydon's throne."

"There is someone who can do that?" No one was allowed to go near the curtains.

Uncle Macken nodded. "Do you really want to go with the prince? You'll be sent to that boring Academy."

"I want my Mo," she'd said.

"Then come with me, little one." He held out his hand.

She'd stood, brushed the dirt from her skirts and walked away with him. No questions, no fuss. They traveled a long, long way, and then one day he simply left her with a kind looking old lady who owned a fat, yellow cat.

Rough hands shook her. "Come on, child, snap out of this." She blinked to find Lotari sitting beside her, his face etched with alarm. "Come back, Alyra!"

"She must still be dreaming," Jerin said, as the fogginess in her head cleared. and she was back in the dank passageway.

Her white-tipped fingers still dug into Jerin's arm. She released him. How could she simply have left? Walked away with her lunatic uncle who'd sold her to the witch for a bag of gold? She covered her face with her hands and wept. *Oh Shaydon help me, I remember everything now!*

"Get her a drink of water," Lotari ordered. Cold wetness flowed over her lips. "Calm down. Try to breathe. You're safe, sweet girl."

"I left!" she gasped, choking on the drink. "I knew Issah was coming for me. I chose to leave. I didn't even fight." Shame flooded her. Would Issah want her back if he knew she'd left on her own? "It was all my fault."

"That's in the past, Alyra. You must get hold of yourself. Hush, you hear me?" Lotari's hushed voice became more insistent. "Jerin, you stay there while Stitch gathers our things. Let your size be of use and block their view of us."

"Hey," he replied defensively.

Try as she might, she couldn't stop shaking. Her vision became so blurred she didn't even see Katrina approach. "Here, you eat. Yes? They are wondering what is wrong. I go distract them. Yes?"

"Good girl," Lotari said. "I'm working on calming her. Tell them to pack up and get ready to leave. I'll carry her if I have to."

Jerin offered her more water. "Come on, Aly. Whatever happened doesn't matter now. okay?"

"Is the kid having a fit, or something?" As usual, Harp sounded gruff.

"No, she had a nightmare. She's fine. You know how kids are." Jerin chuckled. "Is everyone about ready to leave?"

Alyra took in a deep shuddering breath, knowing she needed to shake this off and go on. The canteen quivered as she drank gulps of water trying to steady herself. She splashed some of the cold liquid on her face. Jerin handed her a cloth.

Lotari pushed back her tangled hair. "There you go, good girl, just take a couple more drinks and eat something."

Her hands would not stop trembling as she bit off a piece of bread. Lotari stayed right next to her. Jerin rolled his blanket and then hers, but continued to block their view of her. She watched Katrina smiling as she served the others hot tea and some of the loaf.

She looked up at Lotari and whispered, "My Mo died. But I had a Da and a brother." She set the bread aside, not having the stomach to eat. "Only I don't remember him at all."

Lotari squeezed her tighter. "I'm sorry, Alyra . Hopefully, when you reach Aloblase, you will be reunited with those who remain."

Knowing they had to get a move on, she forced her emotions down. Taking her blanket from Jerin, she quickly repacked her bag.

Following her friends, Alyra walked blindly, lost in her troubling thoughts. Issah had said that many had been sent to tell her of the Kingdom. The dragon, upon Darnel's orders, had killed them. *All those lives.... All her fault.*

"Is that light up ahead?" asked Frank.

Lotari, who'd stayed at her side, draped an arm across her shoulder and slowed their pace until the others were a good distance between them. "Alyra, I see you are pondering many thoughts. I implore you to put them aside. Now is the time to keep your wits. Do you understand?"

She nodded, dread replacing the worry buzzing though her mind.

Lotari went on, "According to their map, the White Road lays to the south. We must head straight in that direction. If misfortune befalls us, and we are separated, I want you to remember the path will keep you safe. Is that clear?" His arm tightened around her neck to emphasize his point.

Her heart threatened to burst from her chest. Tilting her face up to his, she whispered. "Lotari, why are you talking like something bad is going to happen?"

He stopped. The others, intent on the growing light, didn't even notice. "What instructions have you been given since the very beginning of your journey?"

She sighed. "Stay on the path."

"What has resulted when you deviated from that advice?"

Shoulders sagged. "Something bad happened, except for when I met you. That was good."

"That was no chance meeting. I was sent to help you return to the highway before harm befell you.

"Understand, dear one, each time you step off the White Road, the risk of running into peril increases. There is no protection from the enemy away from the path."

"How are we to find our way back?"

"We must listen for Issah. Run south. No matter what they choose, we will hasten in that direction." He planted a kiss on top of her head, then pulled her hood up to cover her hair. "Keep your head down stay close to us. Jerin and I will keep you safe."

She gripped her medallions, hoping Issah was near, that he knew where they'd gone. Then a flash memory popped into her mind. Music playing, her hand in Issah's as he spun her beneath the lighted trees. "I'll be there for you whenever you need me, Alyra. I love you very much," he'd said as they danced in Jolly Orchard.

The tunnel opened upon a large portico where some of the roof had fallen from crumbled columns. She blinked against the brightness as the group moved out into the welcomed sunshine. They'd emerged at the bottom of a small amphitheater. Wide steps gracefully wove up the hillside. Broken statues of the earth's various creatures lined the walkways above. Motionless horses ran wildly through a dried, crumbling fountain. One steed's head had been knocked completely off.

Katrina's face contorted as she stifled a gasping cry. "Oh, it's worse than I thought."

Yet, not all shared Katrina's remorse. Harp spun around, with his arms out wide, and swooped up his wife with a loud whoop. "Didn't I tell you? Right through the mountain we went." Christina hugged her husband as the daughters laughed and danced around their parents. Frank was slapping his brother-in-law's back and hugging his sister as well.

"Hush you fool," hissed Lotari, glaring at the joyous family. "We are by no means out of danger. Let's make haste and find the path before soldiers show up."

Their grins faded and were replaced with angry narrowed stares. Harp slowly moved toward the horse and reached within the gear. "Fool, eh?" He withdrew a long sword. "I've about had enough from all of you."

Jerin's hand grasped his hilt, but Frank stopped him, pointing his crossbow menacingly. "Everyone just hold on." Frank stepped closer to his brother.

Stitch was beside Lotari, a dagger clutched in his fist. Katrina stood between the two groups, looking from one to the other, her damp eyes wide in astonishment. "Harp, they wish for no trouble."

"Well they've been nothing but trouble. Now you get over there by Ma and the girls and hush."

She didn't move.

Alyra began to step forward, but Jerin blocked her with his extended arm. Something in the woods surrounding the top of the theater flashed within the darkness. She glanced at Jerin to see if he noticed, but his eyes stayed glued on the family.

"Sir," Lotari began. "All we desire is to return to the King's Highway. Why don't you go your way, and we'll go ours. There's no need for anyone to get hurt." His fierce eyes flashed a warning to the men.

Harp held up the sword threateningly. "You'll stay till we reach the bottom of the mountain. Eventually we'll run into the white path again. You can go then."

"We'll not be safe from soldiers until we're on the path." Lotari shook his head, taking a step backward.

"That's why you are all coming with us. I know they are after you. An' not only the centaurs, but the glow-bug girl as well."

Alyra gasped, which caused Harp to chuckle. "Yeah, see? I knew something was up. Told you, Frank, when I heard they was avoiding the soldiers. Now, we have us a bargaining chip if we run into trouble. We'll offer up the girl and the centaurs if they'll let us go on our way."

# Chapter 35

While Alyra's friends faced the family, she peered from beneath her hood at the trees bordering the amphitheater, sure she'd seen a flash of metal within.

"You may get off one shot," Stitch stomped his hooves, "but I'll have your head ripped from your body before you can reach for the second." He glared at each family member, stopping on Harp.

Jerin's face paled as he stared at the palomino centaur. "I'd listen Frank. I've seen his kind in battle and ripping heads off is nothing to them. They aren't easy to kill either. You don't have enough weapons or time to take them both down, I promise you that."

The two men glanced at each other with uncertainty. A prickling sensation ran down Alyra's neck. Up above, the woods seemed to be alive. Studying the foliage, Alyra squinted, catching a glimpse of movement. She grabbed Jerin's arm and whispered. "Do you see anything up there?"

He shaded his eyes with his big hand. "No." His sharp intake of breath told he had. "Head's up, we've got company, people." The sword slid from his scabbard as he pushed Alyra away from the others.

"They'll not bargain Harp," she said. "It's not their way."

The marble wall above the entrance exploded at the impact of an arrow hitting it. Soon the air whizzed with the sound of more feathered shafts flying past. Jerin held up his shield, keeping Alyra sheltered behind his body.

"If you want to try, you go ahead. But I'd advise you to run now as fast as you can." Alyra tugged at Jerin's arm as she asked Katrina, "You coming?"

The girl nodded and hurried after them with the centaurs following close behind. They ran southward, along the wall and up the stone-hued steps, not stopping until they found a small enclosure amongst the rocks alongside the stage area.

*Go up, child.*

Alyra turned to Lotari and asked, "I thought you said we needed to head south?"

"What?"

"Why are you telling me we need to go up now?"

His brows furrowed in confusion. "I didn't tell you… Wait," his long ears twitched as he sniffed the air. "Who told you to climb?"

"What?"

They looked at each other, perplexed.

*Alyra, start climbing up the mountain.*

She caught sight of the family disappearing back into the tunnel. Soldiers poured from the tree cover, some running after Harp's clan while another group gestured in their direction. "Lotari did you hear it that time?"

He grasped her shoulders. "Are you frightened? Do you recognize the voice?" He also kept his focus on the soldier's movements.

In her mind, she pictured Issah grinning down at her while they'd danced. "No, I'm not. It's Issah. I know it."

A heat radiated from her chest, like that day he'd tended her burns, and the moment she'd laid her hand in his when he wanted to show her the feast. Even the times he'd danced with her beneath the flickering lanterns. *Yes, she knew.*

From their position, a trail wound along the base of dense spruce growing up the incline. They would need to hurry upward through the piney forest and not waste time trying to get around.

"The trees might keep us somewhat safe." She said.

"Let us hope." Lotari addressed Jerin and Stitch. "We need to climb. Jerin will you cover the rear while we get the girls up the cliff? Soon as I reach the next ledge, we'll cover you. Do you both still have your slingshots?"

Jerin held up his. Alyra fished in her pocket for hers. Wrapping the strap around her wrist, she helped Jerin collect as many rocks as possible.

Lotari turned toward Stitch. "You help Katrina. Protect her, do you hear me?" He grasped the youth's burly arm. "I don't care how scared you are. Do not abandon her."

Stitch, ashen-faced, nodded and took hold of the dark-haired girl. "I'll be right behind you, Kat. You can ride my back when we get onto more level ground."

Lotari waited a second as shouts from the troops filled the air. They'd been spotted for sure. He nudged Alyra and ordered her to climb fast.

"Issah, if you're anywhere near-" She said between gasps, "- please help us."

Arrows bounced off the stony edifice.

Lotari shouted from behind, "He's close. We need to do what he says."

They scrambled between spiked-branched spruces, the needles scratching at their clothing and faces. Once they reached the first rocky shelf where Stitch and Katrina waited, Lotari loaded his bow and aimed at the soldiers following as Jerin made his way through the pines. The soldiers struggled in their own climb, unable to shoot through the thick trees. Lotari managed to take down two, and Stitch three. Alyra sent several rocks on the men, but only managed to give one a possible headache.

Below, the horsemen followed the path and Alyra wondered if they'd be able to find a way to cut them off. She hoped not. When Jerin's head appeared, Lotari helped him onto the narrow ridge.

"For once, we two-leggers have the advantage, eh boys?" Jerin grinned at Lotari and Stitch.

"We'll manage fine." Lot retorted, biting back his own smile. "Keep going, Stitch."

As the first two headed into the next climb, Jerin continued gathering more stones that he loaded into the empty food sack. Lotari pushed Alyra to get moving. The narrow ledge created natural steps and she found the rise easy. Lotari stayed just behind. She tried not to look down or worry what pursued them. Instead, she focused on scampering up the rocks as quickly as possible.

When they reached the top of the next plateau, the land leveled out for a good distance before slamming into another walled outcropping.

"We're trapped," Stitch gasped.

Sure enough, the tall cliffs circled the meadow, enclosing them in a basin.

"We're going to have to fight," Jerin limped toward them, his breathing labored. A bruise darkened his cheek.

Lotari searched the area. Shouts sounded from below. Alyra's heart sank when the pounding of hooves joined the soldier's yells. Soon the basin would be full of enemy fighters.

"See that crevice?" Lot pointed toward the rocky walls. "We'll make for there. Get on my back, Alyra."

Stitch pulled Katrina on and raced away as if a panther was on his tail.

"Come boy, I will carry you as well." Lotari held out his hand.

Jerin shook his head and loaded a rock into his sling. "I can take care of myself. Get the girls and yourselves out of here."

He hesitated for a second, nodded, then galloped across the clearing.

Racan horsemen burst into the valley from the tip of the basin's arm. From the trees foot soldiers, trolls, dwarfs, and other beast hefting axes, bows and swords ran forward with their battle cries. Jerin sprinted full speed directly in front of the horde, blue eyes wide circles. Alyra watched over her shoulder as a giant sized warrior bore down on him.

"Run, Jerin!" she screamed.

Lotari slid to a halt. Alyra peeked around his sweat-drenched back to see what caused him to stop running. Stone pillars rose up like jagged teeth lining the cliff's face. Several yards ahead, Stitch was already making his way through the gaps, Katrina clinging to him as she buried her face in his golden hair. Alyra realized the incline wasn't what made Lotari freeze in his tracks.

Lined along the top of the precipice stood rows of gold-clad warriors. *Issah*! The prince stared down as Stitch and Katrina picked their way up the narrow crevice leading to the very place he waited.

*Come on, daughter, hurry*!

Alyra dared another glance behind to find Jerin running with all he had. An arrow stuck from his backpack.

Taking the bow from his shoulder, Lot loaded and aimed for a goblin bearing down on the boy, carrying an ax twice his size. The shaft flew straight hitting the dark emblem on its chest. A second, shot from above, found its mark in another goblin. The Alburnium warrior's battle cry filled the enclosure as they swooped down along the sides, blocking the Racan beast and soldiers in.

"Go, Alyra. Follow Stitch and get up to Issah. He will keep you safe."

"No, I'm not leaving you two." An arrow whizzed over her head.

He pulled her off his back and pushed her away. "Get out of here, you stubborn girl. Go now!"

"No!"

The clang of sword against sword broke off their argument. Jerin fought in hand-to-hand combat with a burly, trollish soldier. Alyra backed away, thinking he reminded her too much of that disgusting governor Darnel wanted her to marry.

Jerin managed a spin and hefted the head off the large beast. Behind the first one come another. Lotari shot and slowed him but didn't stop the monster. Jerin sprinted toward them with renewed vigor.

"Go!" shouted the centaur, his hooves stomping hard on the ground. "Go, so I can help our friend survive this."

*Do as he says, Alyra. Come on up to me.* Alyra glanced up to find Issah motioning for her to climb.

Jerin wasn't too far away now. Issah was definitely close. Reluctantly she climbed up the incline. Some areas she could walk. Others she had to scramble up the rocks. Stitch's hoof prints directed her. There was no sign of the girl or the palomino.

Breathing hard, she paused upon a small ledge to check her friend's progress. Down below, Alburnium warriors fought hand-to-hand, swords glinting in the afternoon sun. Several, wearing gold breastplates, swarmed into the fray.

A loud cheer rose up from the dark army. Terror gripped her. Had they gotten them?

"No, please." She wanted to go back and find her friends.

*Don't stop,* Issah called, *keep going*!

Jerin and Lotari ran for the cliffs arm in arm. She couldn't tell who might be supporting the other. Stinging pain burned her hands as her fingers slipped from the rock, leaving a dark-red smear. Her palms bled from clutching so tight to the jagged stone, and her legs trembled with the effort to climb.

"Keep going," called a voice from above. She looked up into

Issah's face as he reached down toward her. "Come on up, Daughter."

Alyra glanced down once more as Jerin's sword took the head off a dwarf. Arrows flew out from a hidden crevice.

"Take my hand, my child." The Prince urged. "Before it's too late."

She reached up and clasped his wrist as his fingers circled around hers. He pulled her up into his firm embrace. Immediately, more warriors waiting behind him leaped down the rocks while another group stepped forward and sent a rain of arrows on the soldiers. The only escape was back the way they'd come which was now blocked by the Alburnium forces.

Issah wrapped his arms around her, leading her from the gruesome battle scene.

"No, we can't leave them, Issah." Alyra cried.

He continued though through a copse of trees, which cleared to reveal a beautiful lake-filled valley. The bluffs rose like castle turrets around the crystal blue water. Next to the lake sat Stitch and Katrina looking worried and tired. A crackling fire blazed to warm them. Just beyond the small campsite ran a band of white glittering rocks: The King's Highway. She bowed her head and began to sob.

"I'm so sorry, Issah." She remembered the dream and all her turmoil came pouring out. "I didn't listen to what you've told me. Not now and not when I was small. If they are hurt, that will be my fault, too. I should have insisted we stay on the path. I should have waited. I…."

"Hush, child. You're safe. I've got you now." He led her next to the fire, gave her a cup to drink, and then checked her bloody hands. Tenderly, he wiped the dirt from her face, and poured cooling water over her raw palms. "Here, Alyra, squeeze this cloth. It'll stop bleeding in a minute."

"But Issah, you don't understand…"

"Yes I do." He gripped her shoulders firmly as his intense eyes penetrated her very core. "And I know everything that happened. I know ... everything."

*Of course he knew.*

He leaned over and kissed her forehead. "Rest here while I go to the others. They have fought hard and will also need tending." He stood and left her there with the other two.

Katrina came over to her, tears streaming down her face and wrapped her arms around Alrya's shoulders. "I thought the beast men got you, poor dear. Where is big centaur, and our warrior friend, Jerin? They are okay? Yes?"

Alyra's throat burned with scalding tears. "I don't know. Jerin was fighting...." She buried her face in the girl's neck.

"We are back on the white path. Yes? We are safe again."

Alyra sat arm in arm with Katrina while Stitch paced beside the deep blue lake, blond tail swishing. Finally, the Logorian warriors returned. The girls stood and hurried to meet them. A large group came through the woods carrying something she couldn't make out toward a shallow cave. Was it Jerin? Or Lotari? Or one of their own? Could the Logorians even get hurt in battle? She slowly made her way toward them, searching the crowd for her friends.

Jerin emerged from the trees, supported by two tall warriors. They sat him on a rock, outside the group gathered around the cave. Alyra ran to him with Katrina on her heels. The sight of the large gash on his forehead, and the blood splattered on his clothes drew Alyra to an immediate halt. Katrina hurled into her, knocking her a few steps forward. She gasped. His hands and arms were also covered in dark stains. Then she spotted a long cut on his left thigh, which one of the men began to close up.

"You've been hurt." Alyra said.

He turned toward her with his blue eyes full of frightened sadness. "I'm fine. But they got Lotari. They got him really bad."

Alyra spun away from Jerin, shoving through the crowd of warriors. Finally, they began to stand aside, allowing her to pass into the shallow cave where most were gathered. She froze, finding Lotari lying with his head in the Issah's lap. Four arrows stuck from his chest, arms and three from his flank and thigh. Blood seeped from the wounds and she wondered how he still managed to breath.

"Easy there, my friend." Issah stroked Lotari's pallid face with a wet cloth. "We're going to get those arrows out first. Then we'll need to make a decision."

Lotari nodded, his bloody hands clutching at Issah's coat as if fearing he'd be swept away if he let go.

Alyra fell to her knees beside him. "Is he going to make it?" she asked, while stroking his horse leg.

Issah's brows furrowed. "Our friend is quite stout. A centaur is not easily destroyed. We will tend him the best we can here. Then decide what course to take next." He met Alyra's eyes. "Go rest. He's in good hands."

"I'm staying," she declared, knowing it would push his patience. She fully expected him to unleash his anger on her like she deserved. "Please, Issah. I can't leave him like this." If he died, it would be all her fault.

"Sire," Lotari gasped. "Obedience simply isn't her way. You do get used to it… after awhile."

To her surprise, Issah chuckled, his face turning to amusement, not fury.

"He jokes." The prince nodded. "You have been good for him, child. Come sit here while I prepare a drink to ease his pain."

She gently took Issah's place, allowing Lotari's head to rest against her chest. Issah walked away conversing with some of the Logorians. The tears flowed as she said optimistically, "I've seen Issah heal before."

"I'm not one of the children!" Lotari's teeth clenched so tight that his jaw muscles bulged. His grip on her hand became excruciating. "I need to be sent to where my ancestors dwell. I can't go on like this"

Alyra held him, planting soft kisses on his head and rubbing his velvety, long ears. She didn't know where his ancestors were, but she knew it probably wasn't in this land. "You're my best friend, Lot. You have to get through this."

His eyes squeezed shut, as he battled to collect air in his strained lungs. "Speak to the King on my behalf, will you?"

"We're not in Aloblase yet." Was he losing touch with reality?

He sighed. "Haven't you listened to anything I've taught you?"

Jerin limped over toward them and knelt next to Alyra. He laid a hand on the centaur's shoulder. "We will speak to him, my friend. Don't worry. I'm sure your act will be rewarded."

He grinned at Jerin, his red-rimmed eyes full of awe. He extended three fingers. "With one swipe of your sword. You are a mighty warrior. Amazing."

Lotari the centaur lost consciousness.

# Chapter 36

Pink and orange hues splashed across the eastern sky. Alyra dipped her hands into the cool water and watched it turn from clear crystal to cloudy crimson. The smell of sizzling meat and fried eggs wafted toward her, turning her stomach. Katrina and Stitch sat next to the fire where one of the remaining Logorian warriors prepared morning breakfast. How they always managed to have access to fresh food and an excessive assortment of cooking gear never ceased to amaze her.

Jerin had wandered down the shore and in the growing light, she spotted him sitting on a rock at the water's edge, his head propped in his hands.

Last night, before Issah started working on Lotari, Jerin took her hand and placed his other on the centaur's shoulder. Then, just as she'd seen Marya and even General Marcel do, Jerin petitioned King Shaydon for help. He'd broken down in sobs as he recounted their friend's bravery and loyalty not only to them, but to the Kingdom as well. Afterward, the Logorians and Issah began the harrowing work of removing the arrows from the semi-conscious centaur.

Gravel crunched from behind bringing Alyra out of the reverie. One of the warriors, still dressed in armor, approach with a wooden plate heaped with meat and eggs.

"Eat." He commanded. "You must leave soon." He clutched a spear, nearly twice her height in his free hand.

She stood, water droplets falling from her fingers, and faced him. "Where did they take Lotari?"

"Prince Issah will do what is best for the centaur. This should be enough information for you."

"Well, it's not!" Her yell broke the morning silence, sending a flock of birds scattering from a nearby trees. Immediately, she regretted her tone. He was a warrior of the King, after all. She looked down at the plate and said in a more somber voice. "I'm worried about my friend. Will he live?" Her mind tried to piece together what had happened. Issah seemed so sad, and Lotari had grown so still….

The Logorian stood nearly a foot taller than Jerin. His perfectly etched face and diamond colored eyes softened slightly. "The centaur is strong. His spirit can never be destroyed. King Shaydon decides in what form it will continue. *You* must focus on completing your journey. Eat." He shoved the food toward her, which she took despite how her insides crawled.

While Lotari was conscious, he had begged Issah to send him to his ancestors. Hoping to keep her friend's mind off his pain, she'd asked where they lived. He'd told her they ran amongst the stars. He was always talking strangeness like that. She wanted his hooves to remain on the ground, not galloping across some starry sky.

Alyra clutched the plate. "How can I go on when I don't even know what's happened to him?"

The warrior's spear hit the ground with a force that echoed across lake filled valley. "You embarked on this journey with no one."

"But—"

"Look around you!" He pointed toward Katrina and Stitch, then over to Jerin. "You have many friends now, and they must get to Aloblase, as well. They need you, as you need them."

His words cut her. Shame poured out. "I've done nothing but cause problems. What help have I been to anyone?"

His massive chest swelled as he sighed. "None are without blame, daughter of Alburnium. All have the ability to choose. Choose well, and stay on the path! The White Road will protect you from further harm." With that, he strode away to join the small group of remaining warriors.

Stitch slowly made his way over to her. His furry arm draped around her shoulders. "I think we better do what he says. They don't seem like the type who care to debate matters."

Feeling her heart had been beaten into something unrecognizable, she buried her face into the downy fur on his chest. The plate was lifted from her hands, as he guided her over to the rocks next to Katrina.

"We are worried about Lotari, too, Miss. But the big man is right. We have to finish this. We can only hope to find all our answers in Aloblase."

Jerin limped over to the group and took the last breakfast plate. "We'll need our strength."

He glanced at Alyra as he spooned a mouthful of eggs. He too was covered with the centaur's blood. They had both remained at his side, trying to comfort their friend while Issah and the warriors worked on his many wounds. A human would have died before they even got started.

Katrina urged Alyra to try to eat. The aroma smelled wonderful but her stomach rebelled after swallowing a few bites. Stitch began packing their gear while Katrina went to refill everyone's canteens.

Jerin pushed more food around the plate than he actually put into his mouth. When they were completely alone, he scooted closer. "If anyone is to blame, it's me, not you. I'm always looking for a shortcut." He shook his head. "I'll never learn!"

The Logorian cleared his throat to get their attention. Tossing a bulging bag at Jerin's feet, he gestured toward the White Road. "When you find you can trust the path, then you will start learning."

The other warriors approached, carrying various fighting gear. "We wish to equip you with proper weapons before you go on your way."

A chill snaked up Alyra's neck. *Why now?*

She, Jerin and Kat were provided with shields. Stitch took a quiver full of arrows and a new bow, along with a breastplate. Alyra kept her slingshot. She wouldn't accept anything else, not knowing what to do with such items. Katrina picked a spear but used it as a walking stick. Jerin traded his old sword for a Kingdom made one that he found larger, yet lighter.

"Three days should find you at the border of Aloblase. You will be helped on along into the city from there." The Logorians bid them good-bye and in a bright flash, were gone.

Jerin jumped backward, hiding behind his new shield. "I'll never get used to that."

Stitch grinned. "Wow! Awesome! Just like the way Prince Issah disappeared with Lotari last night." His arms waved over his head as he made a whooshing sound like wind. "Dust and leaves blowing everywhere. I could hardly see a thing. Then…."

"Gone." Jerin finished. "Vanished. Right there…then not. Along with half the warriors."

\* \* \* \*

They traveled at a slow pace until midday, heading downward now as the path zigzagged against the mountainside. When they came upon a crevice in the rock, the trail turned into a bridge made from golden rope. For the most part, the trek was pleasant and easy. Alyra could have kicked herself.

Jerin remained quiet as if needing every ounce of concentration and effort to stay on his feet. He often stumbled, but refused help. Alyra offered to break for short rests. Jerin insisted they keep going. Stitch tried to coax him to accept a ride, but Jerin said he was fine walking. Alyra wondered why he remained so quiet and distant. Was he still in pain? When they stopped, she'd make him some healing tea and check his leg. Hopefully he wasn't getting an infection.

They walked on until shadows crept across the mountain slopes, turning them from purple to black against the glittering sky. The path followed a watercourse, so they camped next to a small waterfall, beneath the shelter of trees as tall as a three-story building.

Stitch headed into the surrounding forest to gather more firewood. Katrina worked on a stew of dried meat and potatoes from the provisions bag. Jerin collapsed beneath a tree and fell asleep before he even got a chance to put out his bed roll.

While the herbal tea brewed, Alyra studied the gray cliffs which resembled ramparts and porticoes or windows high above.

"Funny how these rocks look like an abandoned castle. Do you see?" She asked Katrina.

"A city, actually, formed within the mountain peaks. The City of Knowledge." She added at Alyra's amazed expression. "At one time. Yes."

"When?"

"Oh, long years ago. The evil one brought a battle and defeated the Curians. I was merely an infant when it happened. So I only know the stories my foster parents told me."

Alyra poked at their small fire. "Lotari-" The name clogged her throat, "-mentioned them once. He said the Curian people were special instructors?"

"They were the all-knowing ones." Katrina also stared into the fire as if lost in her thoughts. "Some believe a remnant survived but none have located them." She sighed. "Perhaps they never will. No?"

Alyra shrugged. "Who knows, Katrina. Maybe someday."

Stitch nestled down next to her. "Wait a minute, Kat. That battle happened nearly eighty years ago. How could you have been an... oh, oh wait."

Her thin lips turned up in a crooked smile. Alyra noticed they'd become as good of friends as she and ... She shook her head of that thought.

"Yes, my years exceed my appearance."

Alyra sat up, realizing the girl who seemed not much older than fifteen summers was really somewhere in her eighties? *Amazing.*

"My family was killed in the battle. I was taken to a northern village by the town's healer and raised by a kind couple. Once I learned the truth about where I'd come from, I came back here."

Stitch reached over to her, pushing aside the black curtain of hair that always hung against her pale face. Alyra straightened, leaning forward, unsure of what she was seeing. Where a centaur's ears pointed upward, hers drooped down and had dark swirls running along the lobe.

"Kitten..." He gasped. "Oh, I can't believe this. I not only know the evil one's precious light treasure, but now one of the Wisdom Keepers he desires to have, as well."

She gently pushed his hand away and covered her ear. "This is our secret. Yes? I'm aware of Lord Darnel's intent. My hope is to locate the lost remnant before he does."

"Do you really believe they will be found again, Kat?" Jerin was not asleep after all.

"Yes." She grew quiet, stirring the bubbling soup.

Alyra nudged Jerin and offered the cup of tea.

He accepted the drink. "I guess there's little hope of the city being revived until the Dark Lord is gone?"

Katrina shrugged. "Only his influence. Yes? The people's passion for Shaydon needs to be rekindled, and when their passion burns again, nothing will hinder this city from coming back to life."

After they ate, Stitch offered to take first watch. Jerin told him to wake him next. "Save Alyra for last. Maybe if she gets a good night's sleep, she'll actually stay awake for her watch."

She glared at him, but didn't respond, knowing he spoke the truth. He and Lot had eventually given up on letting her guard during the night as she always managed to doze off.

"I think we can reach the bottom of this summit by tomorrow evening." Jerin settled beneath his blanket. "The path will weave down through more cliffs and then across a plateau. Once we make our way past that valley, we'll come upon a bridge which is the entrance into Aloblase."

"The Logorians told you that?" Alyra asked.

He nodded. "They updated my map for me so I'd know how far we should progress each day. If we don't poke around, we'll reach the city in two more days."

Stitch leaped to his hooves. "Whoo-hoo! Almost there, folks."

Alyra smiled, despite her racing heart. She wished more than anything that Lot was there to lull her to sleep with his pipes and soothing music.

The next morning, Jerin seemed more alert, but still weak. All three refused to take another step, insisting he ride upon Stitch until he relented.

Alyra checked his leg, and found it healing nicely. "Jerin, do you feel ill?"

He shook his head. "I'll be fine. I don't need all this fuss, really."

"You're not fine." She helped him to tie his bed roll. "You seem…"

He stared down at his pack. "I'm just…It's…" His eyes closed. "I can't get over how stupid I've been."

"Don't Jerin. We're both to blame. The decision was mutual."

"I know … I … can't shake this off."

She felt completely helpless and wanted to tell him to get over it. However, she struggled with the guilt as well.

"We'll be there soon, right? Then…" *What exactly did they hope would happen?*

Stitch trotted into the camp with everyone's water bags refilled. He patted his horse back. "Hop on, Cowboy. I'll be sure to give you a nice ride."

Jerin stared at the spotted centaur for a moment, before turning to Alyra with skepticism. "He is so completely different than Lotari, isn't he?"

She chuckled. "Yeah, but he has an endearing quality, you know? You can't help but like him."

"Well, he seems friendly in a mischievous sort of way." Jerin secured his sword belt around his waist. "Endearing is a bit of a stretch if you ask me."

Stitch eyed him impishly as he waited for Jerin to slip on his gear and pack.

"Aly? What is it about your ability to befriend any blasted beast that comes your way?"

Her mouth turned up in a sly grin. "I don't know. Why don't you tell me?"

"Ha-ha." Jerin shook his finger in her face. "Very clever, very clever." He climbed on the centaur saying, "Behave yourself!"

This caused Stitch to grin even more.

The sun shown down through the dwindling forest, heating their faces until beads of sweat began to form. Stitch stayed in the lead. Katrina and Alyra fought desperately to not laugh when he would ask Jerin to scratch his back from time to time. At first the boy obliged, until the itchy spot kept moving.

"Must be a flea. Can you get it for me?"

"I'm getting off of here," Jerin readied to jump off despite his hurt leg.

Stitch swore on his sweet mama's honor to behave. Of course, his promise only lasted an hour before he found something else to joke about.

Finally, after mid-day they came to the plateau where tall cliffs fell into the open plain below.

Jerin climbed off the centaur and hurried to the edge of the precipice. His wide grin floundered. Katrina let out a gasp. Alyra joined them, and thought her heart would fall right out of the bottom of her boots. To their horror and astonishment, the plain below was filled with hundreds of black clad soldiers. They were like coffee grounds scattered across a yellowish-green tablecloth.

The girls ducked down and hid behind rocks, hoping they hadn't been seen.

Stitch pointed. "Look, the path goes right through the middle of their camp."

From their vantage point, the White Road went straight out from the foot of the cliffs, and across the basin until reaching another stand of trees. In the hazy distance beyond, mountain spires rose into the sky. What appeared to be several villages surrounded the sharp peaks.

Alyra pointed, "Is that ... Aloblase ... do you think?"

A scowl took over Jerin's face and he threw his shield and pack down. "I can't believe this. All the trouble we gone through to avoid *trouble* and...they are still blocking our way! I can't—" He kicked at the white rocks, and yelled out in pain.

Alyra wondered if he'd ever learn. With an angry yell, he stormed off into the trees, away from the path.

# Chapter 37

Stitch stared at the Racan soldiers camped in the valley, their star and moon flags waving in the breeze, whipping like the flick of a lizard's tail. His eyes widened as he stepped back with a whimper.

Katrina, on the other hand, nestled behind a large stone with the book of King's Letters in her lap. She rummaged in her pack and pulled out a couple of carrots, crunching on one as she flipped the pages.

Alyra liked the strange girl but found her to be a big question mark at times. "What do you think you're doing?"

Katrina blushed, "Oh, how rude I am." She pulled out a few more carrots. "Would you like?" She offered some to Stitch who gladly accepted one.

"No, thank you."

"I also have wafers the Logorian's gave me. You prefer?"

*"No, thank you!"* Alyra stomped her foot, frustrated. "How can you sit and read at a time like this? We are obviously in deep trouble here."

Katrina looked up innocently. "Because this time reminds me of something I read before. Something about trouble. See?"

Alyra had no idea what she meant. She stormed after Jerin, hoping he'd gotten over his temper tantrum. He leaned against a tall pine, yanking needles from a low hanging limb and crushing them up in his big hands.

"So…" Alyra's fist rested on her hips. "Katrina is going to sit and read. Stitch is eating, and you're—what? Collecting scented foliage for spice bags?"

"What do you want me to do?" He growled with exhaustion.

She knew he wasn't feeling well and pity tinged her heart, but they couldn't give up now. "Jerin, we can't just sit here. We have to find a way to get around them. Something."

He sent a pine cone flying into the woods with his sling shot.

"None of my plans work out. Matter of fact, seems my plans only end in disaster. You'd think I learned after nearly losing my own life. But no, I have to keep going until someone else gets hurt, or killed for all we know." He rubbed his eyes, leaving teary smudges along his temples. "I'll not allow anyone else to get hurt because of my..."

"Jerin..."

"Oh, Shaydon help me!" Jerin's damp eyes met hers. "You know, I thought I understood bravery. I'm not afraid of a fight." He got up and stomped around the tree, fist pounding his open palm. "Lotari stood there taking arrow after arrow trying to make sure I reached the hill." Jerin stopped, his voice beginning to break.

"He...an arrow was coming right for me. He...he pushed me aside. Knocked me down to the ground and took it himself." Jerin hid his face in his hands. "I spent most of our journey together looking down on him and calling him names. Thought I was so much better than a creature. He never even hesitated in blocking me from harm. I didn't deserve what he did. I should be the one struggling to live, not him." His chin trembled as he bit back his emotions.

Alyra couldn't help herself. She wrapped her arms around him as tears flowed. "None of us deserve it." She pulled out her medallions and held them up for him to see. "The messenger died trying to help me get free. I don't know if I will ever understand what it means to give up your life for someone else. But I think their love for King Shaydon and for Prince Issah drives them to do so willingly. I certainly don't know if I'll ever love like that."

Jerin wiped his sleeve across his face. He cleared his throat a couple of times. "In the King's letters, he wrote that there is no greater love a person can show another than to lay down their life for them." He took in a shuddering breath. "I hate how I keep...that all I think about is what I want. How will all this work out for me? When can I get what I need?" He began to pace. "I don't want to be like this."

For a long moment, he watched Katrina with her nose still in the book. Stitch, now lying beside her, rested his head next to hers as he read along. Both continued to munch on carrots. "What do you suppose the Prince would tell us to do?"

"Stay on the path. Stay on the path. Stay on the path. Stay…" Alyra chanted.

Jerin snorted a laughed. "Sure wish he was here."

Alyra didn't respond. She wished he were too. He'd call in his warrior armies to chase away those brutes down below. Yet his absence was no oversight. Jerin must have felt the same.

"When Issah saw me after the battle, his only words were, 'Son, why didn't you trust the path I laid for you?' Talk about breaking my heart."

"Wow, I guess so." She wondered if Issah meant for them to stay on the White Road, even with such a large army blocking the way. Her thoughts rolled around like leaves on a wind as she tried to figure it all out. To walk right into their camp would be madness.

Failing to come up with an acceptable plan, she offered to make a meal while they waited. For what, she didn't know.

As the day waned into late afternoon, they all sat around, lost in their own thoughts. Jerin slept on and off. Katrina's nose never came up out of her book. At times she would rub at her eyes, but she never stopped searching. Stitch ate, dozed, peeked over the rocks from time to time, and picked fleas from his coat. Alyra grew increasingly bored of staring into the flames. She cleared her mind the way Lotari had instructed, tried to listen, but came to the conclusion Issah was no longer speaking. Her only reflection was of Lotari reminding her that the path was safe.

"You can trust Issah," he often said. "You can trust the path."

But could they simply stroll though the enemy camp like strolling through a spring time meadow. *How?* "How!"

"Pardon?" Katrina looked up from the book.

"Oh, I'm sorry," Alyra's cheeks burned from speaking her thoughts out loud. "I'm just trying to figure a way out of this. We've tried going around, which ended in disaster. If only we could fly over…or dig under. Anything besides going through."

"Yes, that's the one!" Katrina yelled, leaping to her feet as she flipped to a new page. Her eyes darted across the words. "I find it. At last! Listen to this:

*'He who trust in the King and walks along his pathways, has nothing to fear.*

*He will cover you as a mother bird covers her young with her wings.*

*He will be your shield and rampart.*

*Don't fear the terrors of the night, nor the arrows that fly by day.*

*A thousand my fall at your side, ten thousand at your right hand,'"*

She began to bounce excitedly. "Get this, yes?"

*'They will not come near you!'*

"You see?" She giggled. "Yes? We are safe. The path keeps us safe. We will walk. Yes?" She motioned with her fingers walking across the open book. "We walk right *through*. He promises. Yes? He promises they won't hurt us."

Stitch pointed beyond the army. "Oh, look!" he gasped.

In the distant mist, a light began to burn. Not simply city lights, but instead the whole mountain glowed.

"Trust the path." Jerin's eyes were as round as full moons. "That's what Issah asked me. 'Why didn't you trust the path, son?'"

Stitch threw his arms around Alyra. "We must be brave. His book says so." He stared at the camp below. "Oh, help me to be brave."

Alyra looked from Stitch's nervous face, to Katrina's calm, assured face then to Jerin's resolute face. She knew what they needed to do, but if they looked at her face, would they see the fear she felt inside?

Jerin stood. "Let's get ready to go."

"Now?" Alyra protested. "Shouldn't we wait until morning?"

His eyes focused on the luminous mountain. "No. The darkness might provide a little cover." Jerin readied his sword. "I want Aly and Kat to hold the shields. Stitch, ready your arrows. But don't shoot unless I tell you."

Stitch nodded. "You can still ride, if you need to. I've been trained to fight with a rider on my back."

Maybe the sight of Shaydon's mountain renewed Jerin's strength. All Alyra knew was that his face turned grim with determination. A light she had never seen before shone in his eyes.

He shook his head as he thanked Stitch. "I'm better now."

As they descended, the King's Highway became a narrow, winding footpath, carved in the crevice of the cliff. For the most part the rocks kept them hidden from view to those below until they reached the bottom.

The moon's soft light glowed upon the ocean of swaying grasses. The camp seemed to float right in the middle like a dilapidated old sea-barge.

Alyra's legs trembled like twigs, and her heart raced as if she'd run all the way down the incline. Stitch huddled close to Jerin, who kept giving him odd looks. Katrina clutched her book in one hand, and the shield and spear in the other. Jerin put the girls in front of himself and the centaur. If the enemy were to shoot, he said they were to kneel behind the shields. Jerin had his slingshot readied, and Stitch held his bow loaded.

A few campfires still burned, and dark forms roamed among the shabby tents. The majority slept outside, as only the higher-ranking officers had the privilege of shelter. The White Road flowed from their feet like a beam of light shooting across the dale.

"Everyone quiet." Jerin ordered in a harsh whisper. "Stay together. Either we will be protected, or not. If I'm to die, I'd rather it happen while I'm on the path than off."

The others nodded in agreement. Each may have been full of fear, but none wanted to give up now. In the distance, the mountain glowed even brighter as if beckoning them like a warm flame on a freezing night.

"Let's go, then," whispered Stitch.

They all moved forward quietly except for their heavy breathing and the scuffing of boots on the rocks. Stitch tried to step lightly so his hooves wouldn't make too much of a clatter.

As the camp loomed larger a particular smell, or more of a stench, permeated the air. The girls pinched their noses. Alyra's stomach churned at the familiar odor.

Stitch leaned close to her ear. "I haven't missed that evil stink."

Jerin hushed him with a nudge of his elbow. Alyra glanced around at the sleeping brutes. Most were trolls, which would account for the smell, along with scowling dwarfs and even some Okbolds like DezPierre. Prowling in the darkness were familiar twisted canine-like creatures with spikes running down their backs. An ear-splitting howl rent the night. One of the deranged wolves charged toward them, stopping at the edge of the rocks and barking furiously.

"Keep going," Jerin ordered everyone as his pace quickened. "Don't run, but walk faster."

The camp erupted with commanding shouts and clanging weapons. Soon both sides of the path were lined with all sorts of sinister creatures, yelling, jumping, and waving their spears and swords.

Alyra stopped, finding it impossible to focus on the highway. Jerin nudged her back, but her feet had embedded into the ground.

"Don't let them scare you, Aly. We have to keep going."

The angry soldiers thrust their swords and spears, but never got near the white rocks.

When she didn't move right away, he growled, "Don't make me pick you up and carry you."

The imaginary roots disengaged and her feet started working again. Katrina walked on beside her, not bothered at all by the enemy surrounding them. A calm smile slipped across her peaceful face as she stared dreamily at the lighted mountain ahead.

Stitch, on the other hand, rested a hand on her shoulder, his fingers digging into her collarbone. "I don't have enough arrows for them all."

"You don't need them unless they actually try to come at us." Jerin replied. "Doesn't look like they are too willing to take that chance."

The moment his words met air, a long spear sailed over their heads and landed behind them right between the feet of an Okbold. Stitch aimed his bow. The girls walked faster, holding the shields up to protect their bodies. The wonderfully lightweight guards covered them from the chin down to their knees. Jerin stopped Stitch from actually shooting, but loaded a large rock into his slingshot as well.

Another two spears flew out from different directions. They each landed to the right and to the left side in the dirt. Alyra's breath caught in her throat, blocked by a scream threatening to rise up. The spears teetered a moment, then fell over with a loud clatter.

Next, the soldiers sent a rain of arrows into the sky. All four ducked holding the shields over their heads. There was no sound of contact. No *ping, ping* of deathly tips. When they peered over the armor, the shafts lay all around along the sides of the path, but not on the rocks.

"It's true," Jerin breathed.

They stood again, and continued on, eyes wide as saucers at the weaponry lying next to the trail.

"See?" Katrina grinned.

Stitch whooped. "We're home free!"

Their spirits soared and they strolled a bit straighter and faster. The path had become wide enough for a horse-drawn carriage to easily travel on. As long as they stayed close together, the enemy's spears and swords couldn't touch them.

Stitch laughed at them and stuck out his tongue. Jerin elbowed him again telling him not to get cocky.

"Almost there." Katrina's encouraging words eased Alyra's fears.

The band of trees surrounding the plains grew larger. They only had to reach the end of the valley and then cross the bridge leading into King Shaydon's lands.

Before the thrill of victory settled on Alyra, she caught a movement from the corner of her eye. To her horror, a cloaked figure followed them next to the path. His long, bony hand reached up and pulled back the black hood hiding his pasty face. Bezoar! Remembering his last threat, her throat tightened. Her feet seemed to forget how to work, and she stumbled. Both Jerin and Stitch grabbed hold of her to keep her from falling.

"What, Miss?"

"Bezoar."

"No, not the Captain of the Chief Guard. Oh no! He has that whip, Miss. I hate that whip."

They started to jog.

"Princessss," came his throaty hiss. His dark, sunken eyes gleamed at her. He cracked the whip against the dirt, sending several of the soldiers diving out of the way. His strides matched theirs as he jeered, "Princessss, I've been waiting for you." His cold voice wrapped around her like a serpent, dragging her steps.

Katrina circled her arm in Alyra's. "Try not to listen. He lies. Yes?"

"Is it lies, Princesss that your Prince Issah has not come to save you? Now that he must face me. Is it lies that he has left you to contend with me, all alone. Not lies at all!"

Alyra tried to fill her mind with more pleasant thoughts.

"Shaydon knows all about you. Everything." Bezoar spat the words out one at a time, slowly. "That you are dirty. Disobedient. Rebellious. You...are...a...traitor." This last word he emphasized. Even he knew Darnel had obtained the black powder with her help. A gray wolf, twisted and demented most likely from that very poison, followed Bezoar, growling and snarling.

Alyra buried her head as tears burst from her eyes. Issah said he knew, yet did he really know everything as he claimed? He couldn't possibly.

The Captain didn't let up. "Do you actually expect him to take you back, Princessss? After you abandoned the Kingdom? Aided the Racan King in gaining power? Watched, and yes, even aided in destroying Shaydon's own people? To think you'll be received with open arms is also a lie."

How could she expect anything? She certainly deserved nothing. She'd already had everything, except her Mo. She'd been too young, perhaps, to understand. But, no, she knew Mo had gone to the wonderful lands beyond Shaydon's throne where no one ever got hurt and everyone lived in peace. And Da was right; they would have joined her there again someday. That hadn't been good enough. She'd wanted what she wanted right then and didn't bother to think of the consequences. In truth, she hadn't changed much.

Katrina gave her a reassuring squeeze. "Don't slow down. No! Don't listen. Talk to me, instead. Yes?"

Alyra opened her mouth, but her mind was so cluttered, she couldn't manage to say anything, or think anything else. Now three other chief guards joined their captain.

Stitch whimpered, as his hands trembled so hard, he dropped his bow. Jerin muttered to himself. Katrina's eyes widened and brow furrowed. She clutched her book and whispered passages she had memorized.

"Your Prince is angry because the centaur. He cannot possibly recover." Bezoar laughed nastily. "We wounded him too deeply. Not even a creature will survive such wounds. And it's entirely *your* fault. *You* didn't obey. *You* worried only about *your* comfort. *Your* safety. How selfish. How fitting you are for King Darnel, your master. He misses you. He'll take you back. He's proud of your behavior. He holds no grudges. Come back now, and there will be no punishment."

"He's not my master anymore!" She replied through clenched teeth. "I'll never be his prisoner again!"

She'd rather beg Issah and King Shaydon to allow her to be a slave in Aloblase, then return to that stinking, miserable castle. Trying to calm the pounding in her chest, Alyra breathed deep. Fear and guilt stabbed at her heart and worry clouded her thoughts as she wondered if Bezoar was right about how the King would receive her.

Bubbling laughter rose up inside her very being and not knowing how she knew, she realized there were no slaves in Shaydon's land. Then another thought struck her. Bezoar hadn't been in that battle. Stitch said he'd taken a unit to a southern town. How did he know anything about Lotari? Even the Logorian warriors didn't know of her friend's fate.

Jerin yelled, "Enough!" and hurled a stone at his tormentor. The rock whizzed right past the Baykok causing him to laugh raucously. The soldiers behind the chief guard quickly dodged the white rock, looking quite worried. Jerin covered his ears, not realizing they were speaking into his mind, and not out loud.

Tears flowed from Katrina's dark eyes, yet she kept her chin up and face forward. "I don't care," she kept saying over and over, "I don't care. All is not lost. He said so. I'm not..."

"Princessss," Bezoar continued, the insistence in his voice intensified. "Even if Shaydon does accept you, which is unlikely, you'll be sent out again. You cannot stay in Aloblase forever. He expects service. He expects you to give up all your desires, your wants, and your needs. Give everything up for him and what he wants. You're much too selfish to do that." He seemed to grow taller, and to her horror, he moved across the path halting right in front of them.

The travelers stopped, Katrina had tears flowing down her cheeks. Even Stitch whimpered and cowered behind the girl, his hands covering his face. Jerin still muttered to himself, saying that he hadn't meant for that to happen. He fell to his knees, weeping.

"King Darnel was only trying to keep you safe." Bezoar continued, slowly pulling his sword from its sheath. "You see, stupid girl, you *are* the light child the prophecy speaks of. You will be

asked to return as an adversary. That cannot be allowed to happen!"
He held the sword up over his head. "I'll give you one more chance
to come back home or you'll die like your mother. Last time she and
I spoke, I'd sworn to kill you myself. Just as I killed her."

*He killed Mo? But why?* What threat could she have been?
Anger surged like water from a busted spout. She threw down her
shield and pushed away from the others yelling, "You rank,
disgusting maggot!" Her hand seized a stone from the path and as
her fingers closed around the white rock, a surge of power coursed
through her body.

"Shut up!"

The glowing rock sailed from her hand and hit Bezoar right in
the forehead knocking him back like a feather caught in an updraft.
Alyra realized he wasn't actually on the path, but hovering inches
above.

Pointing, she shouted, "You'll regret the day you ever messed
with me or my family!"

Radiance burst from her outstretched arm like an explosion,
wrapping tendrils of light over the distraught travelers. The howl
from the soldiers was deafening. Bezoar, reeling from the blow to
his head, was hit full force by the glow. He landed backwards on the
white rocks and with a sizzling pop burst into flames. The chief
guards screeched and vanished in a puff of black sulfurous smoke.
Such brilliance shone about her and the others that the dark soldiers
dove in all directions to get away. Alyra turned toward her friends to
see an intricately woven cap of light, like ice crystals on a glass,
covering them as well as her.

Bezoar had been the one who killed her mother. That thought
tightened around her like a noose. Was her death a mere
coincidence? Or had she been victim of some kind of trap? Maybe
that's why Issah had been coming for her after the burial, to take her
somewhere safe? What could a small girl like herself do to cause all
this trouble? Her knees buckled and she wobbled on her feet. Maybe
the prophecy really was about her.

Stitch whooped. "Excuse the pun, Miss, but that was brilliant!
They really fear your light."

Alyra's head swam, the lights spinning then suddenly going out.
All her strength left her, and she collapsed into blackness.

# Chapter 38

Mesmerized, Alyra stood beneath the entrance gate. The city gently sloped up the hillside in a series of twisting streets, made from the same glittering rocks she'd followed throughout her journey. Colorful, grand buildings rose up on each side, adorned with wisteria and sweet scented jasmine pouring down from the balconies and open windows.

Bezoar's words still taunted her. *"How do you expect them to take you back now, Princessss? After you willingly left? After all you've done for the Dark Lord?"* What would the King think of her returning with nothing except two scratched and dented medallions? One of them belonging to his messenger who'd been killed because of her.

Alyra hung her head. Why bother?

Gwynedd stood beside her, arms wrapped around Alyra's trembling shoulders. "Welcome back."

"What if—"

"Come child, King Shaydon is waiting." Gwynedd tugged at her.

Gardens lined the walkways, budding with every kind of plant imaginable. Large tropical flowers and plants grew that smelled so sweet and tangy she wanted to taste them. Morning glories and honeysuckle spread over archways and brushed against her cheek as she passed. The city was filled with various manners of people and creatures.

"Do they all live here?" Alyra asked.

"Most. Mainly those who attend the Academy. Others are visiting, or have an audience with King Shaydon."

"It's even more beautiful than my most vivid dreams."

After the encounter with Bezoar, she'd awakened in a healer's house on the border of Aloblase. Jerin had remained by her side, while Katrina and Stitch continued into the city. A Logorian messenger showed up insisting he also proceed to the city and meet with the King. Once Alyra regained full consciousness, and Jerin knew she'd be all right, he agreed to leave with his own escort, making her promise she'd come as soon as her strength returned. The healer's fruit tea soon had her back on her feet and by the next morning, Gwynedd arrived to bring Alyra to Shaydon's throne room.

They crossed a bridge. Her escort's yellow curls blew in the soft breeze as she stopped and peered into the crystal clear water rushing past. Gwynedd wore a flowing emerald green dress that offset the gold in her almond shaped eyes. A circlet of silver sat on her forehead, adorned with dangling emeralds and other jewels.

"Alyra dear, this is the source of the rivers you often stopped at for a drink or rest. It flows all through the kingdom of Alburnium, bringing nourishment to the lands and people."

Alyra remembered the day she and Jerin had drunk from the Dark Lord's bitter waters. After that fiasco, she'd learned to be more careful.

"Gwynedd, where are my friends?"

"You'll see them again soon."

"What about Lotari? Is he alive?"

Gwynedd stopped between two pillars of green jade. "All your questions will be answered soon, my dear. One thing at a time. Are you ready to go in?"

Alyra looked around, wondering where "in" was. Between the many columns, a variety of trees, shrubs and flowers grew, full of assorted bird songs. The sky was as bright as a midsummer's day. The river flowed from nowhere. She peeked between the pillars and found its source was a rather large pond, or perhaps a lake since the water continued on beyond view.

The dream where she'd chased Issah right up to these pillars came back to her. A memory, not a dream, after all.

Taking her hand, Gwynedd led her along the path that stopped at the water's edge. The lake circled around an island of sorts where two white trees grew, their branches interwove into a canopy. They were the same as she'd seen in the Kingdom towns and carved into the meeting hall doorways. The yellow star-shaped flowers and strange red fruit filled the boughs.

321

"Where is the king?" Alyra asked in a stunned whisper.

Sweet-smelling grass grew between sparkling rocks. An irresistible urge took hold to remove her shoes and allow her toes to feel the soft earth. Her feet slipped from her boots. She gasped, enjoying a most delicious sensation.

With each step, her perspective changed. The plush, green land seemed to stretch out for miles. *Impossible!*

An elephant rumbled past, trumpeting. She squeezed her eyes shut tight, only to open them and see wild horses running over a plain on her left. A screech caused her to look up at an eagle soaring overhead. Then she gasped. The bird soared not against a blue, cloud-dotted sky, but the universe. Stars by the billions, and bright round planets, some with glimmering rings, filled the vastness above. Her neck craned back as a meteor shot past. What kind of wonderment had she stepped into?

A voice boomed, "Why are you here, Alyra?" It came from everywhere all at once. A brilliant light burst from between the trees, burning her eyes and blocking out her surroundings. "What are you seeking, child?"

She ducked her head, allowing the backpack to slip to the ground. She felt exposed. She felt shabby and dirty. She felt completely unworthy to be standing there. Her legs buckled and she fell to her knees.

"I shouldn't be here. I don't deserve to be here." Her shoulders shook with sobs as she said over and over, "I am sorry. I came back as soon as I…realized. I finally woke up to the truth." The day Dean showed up was like a light illuminating all the darkness she'd been trapped inside.

A rushing wind swept past, stinging her skin and whipping her tangled hair. Her arms blocked her face from the tempest. The urge to run pulled at her, but she couldn't move. Did he plan to destroy her? She peeked from between her wrists. A roaring fire streamed around her, consuming her clothing, and the marvelous pack, but surprisingly not harming her flesh. When the flames passed, rain poured down, washing the remaining residue from her body. Water drenched her hair, washed down her face, and over her back.

Then the downpour ceased and everything grew quiet.

Her breath caught in her aching chest. She was afraid all the beauty had been burned away. What would he do next? This was not what she had expected.

A voice called across the waters and pierced her to the core. "Arise, daughter!"

Her whole body trembled. Slowly, she raised her head. The fire had touched nothing. Water, from the rain, glistened over the deep green grass. She began to stand, but realized she was unclothed, and remained crouched, hiding herself, not knowing what to do. When she glanced at her arms and legs, she found her scars were gone. Darnel's moon and stars insignia on her shoulder was gone as well! Her skin glowed pale and pure like a newborn. The only thing remaining were the two medallions hanging around her neck.

She was alive. He hadn't destroyed her. He'd healed her!

A satiny cloth slid across her back. Gwynedd helped her to stand, and secured the midnight blue gown with a golden belt.

Her escort kissed both of her cheeks. "Go, he calls for you."

Alyra started toward the smooth lake. The dazzling light broke apart and danced over the misty surface like dust in a sunbeam. The luminous balls moved faster and faster until all the particles joined once again a short distance from where Alyra stood on the shore. She blinked, shielding her eyes. From within the radiance, a figure of a man stepped out and strolled toward her on the water. As he neared, Alyra couldn't help but smile.

Issah stopped right before her, now appearing in all his finery and majesty. His white satiny coat reached to his knees and was tied at the waist with a red sash. A golden crown rested upon his head and a necklace of diamond stars hung about his neck. His eyes blazed like fire as he stretched forth his hand.

This time, she accepted his gesture without hesitation.

"Well done, Alyra." His grip left her no choice but to follow as he led her across the waters. Cool wetness seeped between her bare toes as if she walked on wet silk. Amazed, she peered down to make sure her feet really tread on water. There were no fish or plants below the wavy surface, but rather a bird's eye-view of forest, towns and valleys of the kingdom. With a startled gasp, she stumbled.

Issah steadied her. "Do you trust me to keep you safe, child?"

"Yes. Yes, I trust you."

They continued on toward the small island rise where the trees intertwined over the ball of light. Behind the trees, a gossamer curtain hung that shone with all the colors in continuous movement. She remembered now how the curtains created the border to Shaydon's everlasting Kingdom. Mo and Dean the messenger dwelt in those lands.

The Prince bowed before a pulsating light. "Father, the Sovereign-Strong! True are your ways, O King!"

Alyra could not make out King Shaydon's features. Yet it wasn't what she beheld, but rather what she experienced. Compassion. A complete understanding of who she was and all she'd done. Such a love emanated from within, she bowed at Issah's feet.

The voice of the King rang out again. "Behold, my daughter returns! She was lost, but now she is found. This is a blessed day! Bring forth the celebration."

Alyra sat up. He wanted to celebrate her return? She'd run away from him. She'd lived in the dark lands as Lord Darnel's servant. She'd been disobedient to Issah and often downright rude as well. And they wanted to celebrate?

Issah pulled her back up to her feet. "My daughter, all is forgiven and will never be brought up again."

Fiery words appeared in the branches of the trees, spelling out the deeds she'd done. Even all the deeds she'd helped Darnel accomplish. They did know. Suddenly, the words dissipated like ash caught in a wind.

"As far away as the east is from the west. Your love for others and your desire for what is right has carried you through many trials. And now you have made it back home. Well done, Alyra." He leaned closer, and whispered into her ear, "You have some who are dear to you. They've eagerly awaited your arrival."

A cheer went up all around her from a crowd of Logorians, creature and people alike lined along the shore. They clapped and cheered, holding their cups in salute.

Still grasping her hand, Issah led her into the throng of the celebration. Her lungs filled with the fragrant smorgasbord of flowers and shrubs growing everywhere. Fountain's spewed frothy water, pouring down rocks and flowing into the streams. White linen tables were laden with every food imaginable. Soft music played in the background. People laughed, danced, and talked. Many came to congratulate her for standing up to Bezoar and not losing heart on the journey.

Katrina, wearing a glimmering gown of gold fabric, found her first, bounding into her arms and hugging her tight. Issah laughed as she dragged Alyra off to find Jerin and Stitch. She couldn't bring herself to ask about Lotari, fearing the worst since none had mentioned him yet.

Jerin, dressed in fine military gear, sat with a group of warriors trading stories. Katrina tapped him on the back. He swept Alyra in a bear hug, spinning around in a circle.

"You're here." Jerin sat her down and excitedly told her about how he would begin his training soon. "See?" He held the warrior's medallion. "It slightly different from some of the others, but I really am a warrior."

Alyra noticed Katrina's medallion had an open book on it. "What does yours mean, Kat?"

"It means I am one of the Wisdom keepers. It means I will one day return to the Halls of Knowledge and teach."

"But—"

"Someday. When the time is right. Yes? For now, I will stay here and study at the Academy."

Jerin put an arm around both girls. "Stitch is waiting for you as well. He's right over there."

The young palomino sat with a group of Logorians playing a violin. She had no idea he could play such a beautiful instrument. His eyes were closed and he appeared lost in the song. He looked happy, content, and so clean and well groomed. She hesitated to interrupt.

Katrina leaned closer. "Stitch finds what he hoped. He found a big welcome from the King. He say Shaydon was everything he hoped and more. Yes?"

"Yes, me, too."

"Go over and speak to him." A sly smile crossed Jerin's face. "Go on."

She headed over to the group and stood just behind Stitch. The bow flew across the strings as he swayed to the harmony. Then as if answering, someone played a sweet melody on the pipes. Tears filled her eyes as she thought it sounded so like Lotari's favorite instrument. Noticing his servant's mark was also gone, she gently reached up and touched Stitch's shoulder as his part ended.

He turned to her with a brilliant toothy smile. "We've been waiting for you forever."

"We who?" She laughed at his exaggeration as he also swept her up in a hug. "I've already seen Kat and Jerin."

"Well, what about him?" He nodded to the one playing the panpipes.

Nearly hidden between the other musicians sat Lotari. Bandages covered his chest, shoulder, and legs where he'd been shot by the many arrows. He looked quite pale, but when he saw her, his eyes brightened and he held out his arms.

She bound into his embrace, hugging his neck, yet trying to be careful with his wounds. "You're alive! You're here. I can't believe it! Lotari, you survived."

"As are you. Sweet girl, I heard all about what you did in that valley. Telling the chief guard of the Dark Lord to shut up." He cupped her face in his hands. "Oh, I would have given my tail to have seen that."

They both laughed as she shook her head. "What happened to you?"

He shrugged, his fingers sliding over the thick bandages. "I'm still deciphering the facts, and in truth, it all seemed like a dream. I believe I died, or came near it. We centaurs are not easily destroyed either. What I do remember is finding myself in Shaydon's presence. I wanted to join my ancestors. The pain was unbearable, and I longed for it to end." He shook his head and stared off toward the crowds. Stitch and the others had left them alone to talk.

"The King asked me if that was my true desire." Lotari gave a wry smile. "I desired the pain to cease. However, I wasn't ready to leave this earth. Then he inquired as to what I wished to do with my life should I be allowed to continue." Tears flowed freely down his cheek. "Remember the young centaurs in the stable? The ones Stitch was with?"

Alyra nodded.

"I want to return to them. I long to do this more than anything, Alyra. They are clueless as to whom they are involved with. They do not even know about King Shaydon. They've only been fed horrible lies. I told Issah that if I could return to my former abilities, I would never hide myself away in the forest again. I've sworn to find those wild centaurs and tell them about this Kingdom. As soon as I regain my strength, I'll be setting out. Stitch is to accompany me on this venture."

Alyra touched his bandages. "So why didn't he just heal you?"

"When he heard my desire, he breathed life back into me. I asked the same thing and Issah said they knew I'd be eager to go. He said there are a few things I must learn first. So my life was spared, but my body has to heal. By the time I heal, it should be time for me to go."

A medallion hung around his neck as well. Upon the disk was an emblem of a needle and thread.

When she held it in her hand, he said, "Stitch has one similar to mine. We are to be menders. We will help restore the broken relationships between the creatures and humans."

Her brows wrinkled, then she laughed. "I get it, like stitching something together. That's what his name means, right? Or did he find out his real name?"

"Oh, he did indeed, but refuses to disclose it. Issah says the name he goes by now suits him well. I, of course, think it's silly."

She giggled. "Lot, can go with you?"

Lotari grasped her own medallion. "I know you also have something special you need to do."

Her heart raced, wondering what her task might be and if she would be up for the challenge when the time came.

# Chapter 39

Over the next few months, Alyra began training at the Academy. She had two classes with Katrina and History of Alburnium with Stitch and Jerin. Stitch, who became antsy during long lectures, often slipped away to roam the beautiful countryside. He convinced Alyra, who sneaked off with him, they'd learn more first hand from the animals and people they met along the way.

Jerin spent most of his time at the arena, training to be a warrior and also bristled over being cooped up in a classroom. "I need all the practice I can get. The General should arrive anytime with his unit, and I want to be ready."

Alyra joked, saying he only wanted to be ready to show off to the maiden warrior, Carah.

Katrina and Lotari loved all their classes and couldn't get enough of the vast books in the library. One never found either of them without a book of some sort in front of their face or tucked under their arms. Lot spent hours studying with her.

On one particular spring day, as Alyra and Katrina left A deeper look at the King's Letters class, they met Issah waiting next to the exit. He still wore the attire of a Prince, but not as stunningly brilliant as the first day she entered his throne room. Alyra hadn't seen him since the celebration, and they ran to greet him. He hugged them both, and asked Katrina how her studies were going.

"Wonderful,. Yes? I have Alburnium Cultures class next."

"I love your eagerness to learn, child." He patted her cheek, then turned to Alyra, "I wondered if you would take a walk with me?"

Lotari had promised to tutor her for a history exam between classes, but she knew he'd understand her lateness, so she agreed.

Spring in Aloblase was even more beautiful and tantalizing to the senses than when she first arrived back at the beginning of winter. Blooms cascaded down from balconies and across the bridges and along the busy streets. Alyra followed Issah through the city and out toward the pasturelands. Lot especially loved strolling though the open lands, so different from his dense woods.

"How are you enjoying your studies, Alyra?" Issah stopped beside a bubbling stream, slipped off his boots and waded out.

"There's so much to learn. My head spins with it all." She also kicked off her shoes and followed, gasping when the coldness sent tickling chills up her legs. The sun shone down bright on the rippling waves and she squinted against the glare.

He chuckled, eyeing her suspiciously. "I'm sure you find your explorations with young Stitch more enjoyable, don't you?"

"No hiding anything from you, is there Issah?" The fact that he still loved her despite all her willfulness still amazed her. "Neither of us has ever seen such beauty. We can't help ourselves."

He found a flat rock and patted the spot beside him for her to sit. "Some learn more by experience than by books. I'm glad you're taking advantage of the various alternatives."

"Issah, when will I start learning about how to light up? Or at least how to control it better."

"Soon. I have someone in mind who will provide your training. In the meantime, I'd appreciate you keeping Dean's medallion a bit longer."

She nodded, clutching the two disks she kept beneath her shirt.

"Now Alyra, what I want to talk about is the meaning behind your medallion." He slid off the rock and walked out of the stream, motioning for her to follow as he headed across a wide field.

She put her shoes back on and hurried to catch up. "It's something to do with the prophecy, right?

Red and purple flowers adorned the tall, wavy grasses. Off in the distance, lay Aloblase and the Academy, nestled against the mountainous peaks.

"There was a word, given long ago, how a child of the mountain city will come forth and lead others toward the destruction of evil's hold on the land. The child's brightness is to light the way into the innermost part of the Dark Ruler's stronghold."

"Am I the one who's supposed to do this?"

Issah stopped to face her. He studied at her for a long while with those brilliant eyes she always felt were so probing. Her breath caught as she waited for his answer.

"Perhaps. Perhaps not."

She stomped her foot in exasperation. "There you go again!" She began to pace, wishing he'd simply tell her right out. "It seems evident that I am. That's what Darnel thought? Right? That's why he kept me alive?"

Issah's brows arched in amusement. "Very good. Yes to two of your questions. Darnel assumed that a child of the Illuminate would be the means to his destruction. So he sought to destroy all of the Light People he could. Until you were brought to him, and he thought you'd be that child since you were the one who had entered his realm. So he kept you and tried to turn you toward his ways.

"Now his assumption isn't true. King Shaydon will bring the traitor Darnel to justice. However, there is someone who can begin the process and end his reign as it now stands."

"Me, right? I'm supposed to be the one? And when I return to Racah, he'll kill me. Bezoar said so."

"Alyra, you have many talents. Lighting up dark places is only a fraction of your abilities. Your talents are only aids to help you complete your purpose. Nevertheless, you have a choice to follow the King's purpose or your own. All my children have a free will. You chose your own destiny."

In Racah, life was dictated by Darnel. People did what he wanted, or suffered his punishment. Issah was telling her the complete opposite. Her love for him grew even more, though she didn't know how that was possible.

"So it's up to me if I'm the one or not?"

"Yes."

"If I want, I can live here in Aloblase forever and ever and never leave. And you won't be disappointed in me?"

He sighed and laid his hands on her shoulders. "My love for you does not depend on what you do."

"If I did decide to go, he'll kill me."

"He will try. Even if you stay here, he will always be searching for you, looking for a way to recapture. You are a danger to him, even more so now, than when he had you in captivity." He must have seen the frightened expression on her face because he added, "I will never send you back into his territory without protection and preparation. Still there will be risks."

"My Mo took a risk, didn't she? Now she's dead."

His face darkened with sadness. "I never told her to go on that expedition. She went of her own accord."

"So what you're saying is, when we choose to do something on our own, we're no longer under your protection?"

The sky darkened. A loud clap of thunder sounded, followed by a flash of lightening. The Prince pulled his cloak over their heads. Then, as if a bucket had tipped over, a heavy rain came. "We should head back. Where were you heading after your class?"

"To meet with Lotari." She hunkered under his coat, wondering how such a storm could happen so suddenly.

"Ah, wonderful." They started walking back toward the city. Alyra pondered all he'd said and had become lost in her own thoughts. Halfway across the field, Issah turned away from the direction she was going. The downpour drenched her hair and clothes as if someone had dumped a container of cold water on her head.

"Issah wait!"

He faced her, still completely dry under his cloak. "Yes?"

"I thought you were going to go with me to see Lotari." Water ran into her eyes.

"Oh, I would love to go visit him," he answered casually. "But I can't right now."

"You didn't tell me."

"You didn't ask me where I was going." He stepped closer to her but not enough to cover her. "Even though I asked you."

She felt bad-selfish and inconsiderate. "Okay, point taken. I'm sorry, Issah. Would you like for me to go with you?"

His face crinkled in a big smile. "Absolutely."

He covered her again with his cloak, not that it made much difference, because soon the sun came back out and he draped it back over his shoulders. She remained soaking wet, even though everything around them quickly began to dry.

"Alyra, I'll love you no matter what, just as I love all my children and friends. You are free to decide where you wish to go. I do, however, hope you will remember that every choice has an outcome. Be sure you are willing to live with the resulting outcome."

331

He hugged her tightly, not seeming to mind her sodden clothes dampening his princely garments.

"Tell my friend, Lotari, that I will come soon to speak with him." Before she could say another word the air began to swirl around her so fast, she couldn't see anything. The next instant, she stood before Lotari who was trying to clean up a spilt drink.

"Is this your new way of making a dramatic appearance?" He mopped up juice from the table with a napkin.

She gawked at the dusty stacks of books surrounding the centaur. Shelves towered up the walls crammed full of even more tattered textbooks and manuals. Beams of light filtered in through tall, narrow windows in the stone walls. Several candles burned around the table where he worked.

"You're all wet," Lotari said.

"I've been with Issah." She managed to reply.

A low chuckle shook his shoulders. "Say no more, I completely understand now."

\* \* \* \*

Wanting to keep the ties made on the King's Highway, the travelers vowed to meet once a week for a meal. Katrina and Alyra shared a roomy apartment near the Academy. Stitch and Lotari lived in the open spaces, seldom in the same place twice. Jerin bunked with the other warriors in training, so everyone agreed to meet at the girls' residence.

Katrina and Lotari looked over a book together, something they both found a common ground. Stitch browsed through her collection of maps, looking for towns he hadn't visited yet. Alyra rested in one of the overstuffed chairs beside the balcony doors where a cool breeze ruffled her hair as she watched her friends. She wished they would always meet like this. Yet, she knew soon Lotari and Stitch planned to leave on their assignment to win back the rebellious centaurs. Jerin practiced everyday to fight with Shaydon's warriors and set out protecting the lands from Darnel. Katrina hoped to eventually return to Denovo and start a school there.

What would she do? Alyra sighed, hating the thought of being separated from her friends. Perhaps she could ask to go with the centaurs or maybe with Kat and help her in Denovo. Issah said she was able to make her own choices.

However, Lot often told her centaurs didn't allow humans near their warrens. And Denovo had turned to Darnel, and she'd never be safe there on her own.

Jerin finally arrived out of breath from running. He stopped in the doorway. "General Marcel is about to have an audience with the King. Issah sent me to fetch all of you. Said you'll want to hear his report."

When they entered the throne room, Jerin caught sight of Carah, and their gazes held as she broke into a big grin. Alyra wondered if he was still breathing.

Looking up at Lotari, she said in a singsong voice, "He's so in love. His wittle heart just pitter patters."

"Not funny," Jerin growled, despite his goofy smile. "True, but not funny."

Lotari patted his back. Katrina chided her for teasing him.

Prince Issah stood before the throne of King Shaydon. The General and his troops gathered upon the crystal waters as if it were dry land.

Issah asked, "What news have you brought?"

The General spoke in a soft, authoritative voice. "Your Highness, we've secured the town of Yarholm once more," Jerin gave a quiet cheer as Marcel went on, "and brought some of the people with us for training. They came willingly and are eager to learn how to become a Kingdom Township."

The Logorians led the group in between the pillars. Which included Rog and Lydia, the Inn Keepers. Then to Ariel's utter surprise, DezPierre entered last, his big eyes wide as maple leaves. She grabbed Jerin's arm and pointed.

"Welcome, guests." Issah bowed in greeting.

They bowed in return, remaining on the shore. She knew their time to approach Shaydon's throne would come later. Jerin waved at those he recognized. They nudged each other and whispered, seemingly just as surprised to see him as he was to see them.

Prince Issah grinned at the exchange. "As you see, one of your sons is already here and in training. You may visit with him during the celebration."

Stitch gave a quiet whoop. "Awesome. I love celebrations!

Issah turned back to the General. "This is a great victory. Well done, all of you."

The General nodded. "Thank you, Sire. After we secured the town, some of our unit moved toward the Racanian Mountains. They discovered that the guardian dragon is no longer patrolling the ranges. We feel if a way can be found past the cliffs, we may gain entrance into the heart of the city and the castle itself. For now, we do not have enough warriors, or a means of finding our way in. We come to humbly request your advice on these matters and submit ourselves to whatever you declare is the best course of action to take. Yours is the greatest wisdom."

Alyra's breath caught. They wanted to try to enter Racah? Now? Her heartbeats quickened.

The General bowed low again, and his unit all knelt on their knees behind him, waiting for the King's answer.

The Prince turned to King Shaydon, a bright light upon the throne as before. After a long silence, Issah said, "We are aware of the need of a strong, unified military force before we embark on the Dark One's stronghold. We will be meeting more with knowledgeable minds to discuss this further. Your unit is invited to remain here awhile and partake in the dialogue?"

Marcel seemed taken aback by the King's statement. Yet he straightened and gave a slight, bewildered nod. "Of course. We'd be honored."

"Very good. Is there anything else, General?"

For a moment, Marcel stood frozen, as if in some sort of stunned trance. Carah moved to his side and whispered something that snapped him out of his thoughts.

"Yes, there is one more matter we seek counsel on." Marcel made a motioning gesture with this hand. "We encountered a small enemy unit which we overtook fairly easy. All perished, except for one who we found unarmed and unwilling to fight. We've brought him back as prisoner. Though he has no inclination to hear about you or your ... uh, as he says, 'fairy tale kingdom.' We simply are unsure of what to do with him."

From the crowd, someone yelled, "If he's not for Aloblase, he is against it and should be destroyed."

They led the ragged prisoner in. Alyra's heart broke as she remembered how tattered and beaten Dean the Messenger was when he'd been dragged into Racah. Surely Prince Issah wouldn't leave this unfortunate soldier to the same fate that Darnel sentenced Dean.

Issah held up his hands for silence. For a long moment, he simply stared at the prisoner. Eventually, the man lifted his face. Alyra heard the centaurs standing on either side of her let out a gasp.

"Isn't that…?" Lotari began.

"Our groomsman." Stitch finished.

Alyra shook her head. "Tarek?"

Whatever was being said between Issah and Tarek, she couldn't hear. Finally, Tarek looked away again as Issah ordered, "Take him to the prisons. General, thank you for sparing his life. Now, let's all enjoy some festivities."

Stitch whooped, racing off for the food tables. Jerin rushed over to greet his townsmen. Katrina gave Alyra a questioning look, but when she didn't respond, the Curian followed Jerin and the others toward the feast. A hand resting on her shoulders broke her troubling thoughts. She glanced up at Lotari, his eyes full of concern.

"See, I told you not to speculate."

Alyra nodded. Taking in a deep breath, she settled her heart on two things. First, she'd ask to be involved in the meetings to plan how to bring about Darnel's downfall. She knew as long as the Dark Ruler reigned, she'd never find peace. Second, she needed to figure out how to get Tarek out of prison. And quick.

# Author's Note

Dear Reader,

Thank you for following Alyra on her journey and hope you enjoyed the adventure. There's more to come. Check out The White Road Chronicles at *www.jackiecastlebooks.com* where you can find information about the next books in this series: *Luminous* and *Radiance*.

Look for *Luminous* to be released in the summer of 2013.

Check out the character bio pages, *Illuminated*'s music playlist, plus more in the coming months. You'll also get weekly updates and background information on book two as it's being written.

Also, if you were touched by the character Issah in this story, check out the page about the real influence behind the Prince of Alburnium.

All authors depend on the grassroots efforts of readers to help get their books noticed. If you enjoyed this story, please visit my webpage, leave comments and hit the follow button. Other ways you can help is to leave reviews, like the author's page and book, share what you're reading on Facebook and Twitter and Goodreads.

Thanks again for reading my story, and I hope your own journey will lead you into the grandest adventures.

Jackie Castle

The White Road Chronicles

## About the Author

Jackie Castle is a freelance writer, storyteller and elementary educator. She lives in Texas with her husband, two teenagers and her dog, Ginger (aka ginger-roonie). She looks for the extraordinary in the ordinary in everything she experiences.

She has published articles and short stories in several magazines, but her main passion is writing novels for children and young adults.

Visit Jackie at...
www.jackiecastle.com
www.jackiecastlebooks.com
www.castlereads.blogspot.com (The Castle Library)

Made in the USA
Charleston, SC
04 February 2013